◆ALTERNATIVES *is a series under the general editorship of Eric S. Rabkin, Martin H. Greenberg, and Joseph D. Olander which has been established to serve the growing critical audience of science fiction, fantastic fiction, and speculative fiction.*

Other titles in this series are:

Astounding Science Fiction: July 1939
Edited by Martin H. Greenberg

The Best Science Fiction of Arthur Conan Doyle
Edited by Charles G. Waugh and Martin H. Greenberg

Bridges to Fantasy
Edited by George E. Slusser, Eric S. Rabkin, and Robert Scholes

Bridges to Science Fiction
Edited by George E. Slusser, George R. Guffey, and Mark Rose

Coordinates: Placing Science Fiction and Fantasy
Edited by George E. Slusser, Eric S. Rabkin, and Robert Scholes

The End of the World
Edited by Eric S. Rabkin, Martin H. Greenberg, and Joseph D. Olander

Fantastic Lives: Autobiographical Essays by Notable Science Fiction Writers
Edited by Martin H. Greenberg

Fantasy and Science Fiction: April 1965
Edited by Edward L. Ferman

No Place Else: Explorations in Utopian and Dystopian Fiction
Edited by Eric S. Rabkin, Martin H. Greenberg, and Joseph D. Olander

Robots, Androids, and Mechanical Oddities: The Science Fiction of Philip K. Dick
Edited by Patricia S. Warrick and Martin H. Greenberg

The Science Fiction of Kris Neville
Edited by Barry N. Malzberg and Martin H. Greenberg

The Science Fiction of Mark Clifton
Edited by Barry N. Malzberg and Martin H. Greenberg

SHADOWS OF THE MAGIC LAMP

Fantasy and Science Fiction in Film

EDITED BY GEORGE SLUSSER
AND ERIC S. RABKIN

SOUTHERN ILLINOIS UNIVERSITY PRESS
CARBONDALE AND EDWARDSVILLE

To the memory of Tomás Rivera,
Chancellor of the University of California at Riverside,
scholar, poet, humanist

Copyright © 1985 by the Board of Trustees,
Southern Illinois University
All rights reserved
Printed in the United States of America
Edited by Daniel M. Finnegan
Production supervised by Kathleen Giencke

Library of Congress Cataloging in Publication Data
Main entry under title:

Shadows of the magic lamp.

Bibliography: p.   ·
Includes index.
  1. Fantastic films—History and criticism—Addresses,
essays, lectures. 2. Science fiction films—History and
criticism—Addresses, essays, lectures. I. Slusser,
George Edgar. II. Rabkin, Eric S.
PN1995.9.F36S5 1985   791.43'09'0915   84-22150
ISBN 0-8093-1150-X

89 88 87 86 85   5 4 3 2 1

Contents

Introduction: Shadows of the Magic Lamp

George Slusser and Eric S. Rabkin

Cinema from its beginning has operated under a paradox. For if film is the most mimetic of artistic media—copying what is there and documenting its reality in the act of presenting it—through these same images film also presents what is not there, visualizes (and hence realizes) other or future worlds, gives us as seen what has not yet been seen. If the lamp of cinema then has always been magic, it may be even more so today. Indeed, as film after film of fabulous intent fills the screens of our theaters, we realize to what extent the not-yet-seen dominates our present cinema and consciousness, and pause to reflect just how many classic films are really horror or science fiction or fantasy films in the broader sense. And in reflecting we realize that a new perspective on cinema history—taking its direction from this present trend toward fantasy—may provide new terms for analysis. In this perspective the traditional dichotomy of reality and illusion gives way to what may be more significant pairings, such as future against past, or the marvels of progress against the mysteries and terrors of the mind, or even cinematic escape against historical time and death. We are impelled then to redraw the map of cinema, and in doing so return the lamp to what may be its origins in speculation and wonder.

This volume constitutes an interesting experiment. Fourteen critics, using very different methods and with widely varying ideas of what fantasy is and where its center in the corpus of world cinema might lie, have written essays addressing the general question of fantasy in film. Historically, their "texts" cover the entire span of Western cinema—from Méliès and Lang to very recent films like *E.T. the Extra-Terrestrial* and *Raiders of the Lost Ark*. In essay after essay however, this diversity seems to organize itself around a persistent point of reference, one that tells us much about the nature and direction of cinema as a whole. At the center of a series of independent speculations on the wide spectrum of fantasy subgenres—horror, the Arthurian romance, Gothic expressionism, the animated film, Robbe-Grillet's ludic fantasies, even the musical—we find one common form increasingly suggested or invoked: science fiction. Possibly linked on the deepest thematic and structural levels with the possibilities of the medium itself, science fiction appears here (openly or tacitly) as the form in relation to which other forms of fantasy film, and all film perhaps, shape and define themselves. It is, for example, against science fiction's pretensions of collective rationalism that we understand the filmic horrors of personal and irrational alienation. Or in an opposite sense it is against science fiction's own nightside—its prediction of grim futures—that we chart the yearning for a nostalgic Arthurian past. As such connections and directions are revealed, we glimpse perhaps the shadow within the shadows of fantasy's magic lamp.

In their interacting resonances then, the following essays reveal how and in what ways speculation on the concerns of fantasy in film seems to gravitate toward science fiction. The first group of essays moves through generic discussions of horror and Arthurian fantasy to a clarifying focus on the genre of science fiction per se. In the second group, discussions of film technology and technique—centered in the animated fantasy and the musical—yield to what prove the broader and more encompassing concerns of special effects in the science fiction film, indeed to consideration of the "videology" of such films and film in general. Two final papers then—one a broad analysis of generic transformation in the cinema of fantasy, the other a precisely focused discussion of film's use of the Frankenstein monster—return to the problem of the relation of science fiction to horror. By considering horror however in the most general epistemological and ontological sense, these essays transpose discussion of this problem to the widest general level.

In his essay on the recent films of the 1980s, "Genre and the Resurrection of the Past," Leo Braudy names horror as today's dominant genre. To do so, he contends, tells us much about both what genre in film has become and how this new sense of genre relates to an equally new consciousness of historical time that is steeped in death. This "genre awareness," as a particular relationship between film and audience, is now seen to work against what Braudy calls "apocalyptic time," a temporal vision that (as subsequent papers reveal) is pervasive in science fiction. To suppress our fears of the future then—both of all creative aspiration toward new forms and of personal desire for a future that must naturally include death—we let ourselves be "possessed" by a genre that has become a genre of self-consciousness about genre. In doing so we embrace the countervision of "soap opera time," where stories never end and new stories and forms need not be invented because we can endlessly repeat or remake old ones. It is at this point of tension—where, as the future is denied through this endless remaking of the present, the past arises to menace us—that Braudy sees horror emerging as *the* modern genre, one he shows possessing or "horrifizing" a wide variety of films from *Reds* and *Pennies from Heaven* to *Chariots of Fire*. Braudy concludes, however, that horror, as the form most open to this new genre awareness, in turn provides the means of shielding us from the past it evokes. For as this genre past replaces any real or imagined future, we, mastering its generic conventions, can experience the terrors of death at the very moment we convert them into ritual, routine, elegant repetition.

Bruce Kawin, in his essay "Children of the Light," asks of this same horror film what sort of "host" it is. If Kawin's perspective is initially historical—the development of a traditional horror genre from the early *Vampyr* to the recent *Blow Out*—he still reveals, through his analyses, the tendency in this genre of temporal directions to resolve into psychic coordinates. Significantly, Kawin establishes this new psychic grid by contrasting horror with science fiction in film. Against what he sees as science fiction's appeal to the conscious mind and to the creative use of curiosity—all future-directed functions of the psyche—horror appeals to the unconscious and irrational, operates on primal and atavistic levels of the mind. In this light then, Kawin contends that bad horror films (the kind that abound today) are poor hosts because our minds cannot consent to their destructive and gratuitous violence. The good horror film, on the other hand, is good because it invites us to share a spectacle that is ultimately, and reassuringly, reflexive. Through what is also a form of genre awareness, it reminds us we are watching a film, that we have chosen to have this nightmare, hence can take responsibility for subjecting ourselves to a mode of illusion that will prove so necessary for psychic balance.

With his "Subversive Play: Fantasy in Robbe-Grillet's Films," Ben Stoltzfus offers another, and most thorough, example of modern film fantasy as genre self-awareness. Stoltzfus demonstrates how Robbe-Grillet, by shifting the emphasis in his film language from signifieds to signifiers, to that system of signs and codes conveyed by the images he inherits from various film genres, creates a structure not merely thematically reflexive but fully self-reflexive. Focusing particularly on Robbe-Grillet's "subversive" transformation of the horror elements in our modern cultural and cinematic myths—the sadoeroticism of Kawin's "sex-and-knife films"—Stoltzfus shows how works like *Glissements progressifs du plaisir* and *Trans-Europ-Express* subvert the narrative and semantic patterns of the horror genre (and by extension of any genre that offers its encoded patterns to such filmic play) and in doing so become ludic exercises that are less didactic than fantastic in nature. Again in Robbe-Grillet's films we seem to witness what is simply another wish (this time on the level of narrative) to deny a future that is conceived as something man (as character or narrator) can rationally anticipate or consciously shape. Here, however, the retreat from the future is not toward some violent past or realm of unconscious disorder, but into the synchronicity of system itself, an area of play more elegant than any soap-opera passion for extension.

Sex and eroticism in the Robbe-Grillet film are raised to the level of conscious discourse by being made into grammatical figures. Vivian Sobchack, however, in her essay "The Virginity of Astronauts: Sex and the Science Fiction Film," discovers a contrasting absence of sex in that genre, and sees this absence as the sign of a terrible repression. This repression, she contends, is denoted by the recurring icon of the virginal astronaut, the figure who for generations of fans has represented Kawin's spirit of adventure and explorational curiosity. Here these latter are named as male qualities. And it is as a male-dominated repression that Sobchack proposes to study—on this level of the mind of the film—the constant avoidance of things feminine at the heart of science fiction's gleaming visions of a rational, progressive future. As original Mother and Other then, this repressed feminity is not only a sign of our irrational biological past but, as analogue to Braudy's fear of historical death, a revelation of the alien within. Analyzing science fiction films from *Forbidden Planet* to *2001* and *Alien*—films which in their chilly repression of the erotic show themselves remakes of the same scenario—Sobchack demonstrates how sex and desire do return to these movies of astronautic adventure, but in displaced and condensed forms, with what Foucault calls "the mute solidity of a thing."

Continuing the discussion of science fiction, Peter Biskind, in his "Pods, Blobs and Ideology in American Films of the Fifties," gives this same struggle of nature and culture, of primal fears and comforting reason, a different but equally precise locus in the centrist and radical politics and ethics of the 1950s, what he calls science fiction's first great age of film. Dividing his centrist category into corporate liberal and conservative films, and his radical category into right- and left-wing films, Biskind reveals on the ideological level a rhythm of action and reaction that is in many ways analagous to Braudy's opposition of apocalyptic time and soap-opera time. For if the ever-reiterated consensus of the centrist film creates what is (in its blandness) an ever-repeatible present, that center in turn is ever contrasted to the paranoid fears of the right-wing radical, for whom culture in the form of centralized government estranges the individual. To this radical, the utopian future is not immanent and accessible in the consensual now, but transcendent, fearful in its inaccessible then. In contrast to these modes of ideological retreat—into a constant present or into a past forever desired and denied—Biskind can identify only a few films—those such as *The Day the Earth Stood Still* and *It Came From Outer Space* which he calls left-wing radical—that display the openmindedness and sense of future that Kawin claims for science fiction.

Biskind's findings (and warnings) are confirmed by H. Bruce Franklin's study, "Don't Look Where We're Going: Visions of the Future in Science Fiction Films, 1970–1982." Reviewing a large number of recent films, and focusing in particular on those of the early 1980s, Franklin, by discovering similar fears and reactions in an area that Braudy is silent on, in a sense both confirms and broadens the latter's thesis. On one hand, Franklin discovers for these science fiction films an increasingly apocalyptic direction. This he measures as the mutation of two central "pulp" icons of the progressive future—the "city of the future" and the "marvelous flying machine"—into harbingers of terror and destruction. On the other hand, against this apocalyptic drift Franklin charts, in films such as *Outland, The Last Chase* and *Escape from New York*, a persistent desire, within these parameters of future despair, to return mindlessly and nostalgically to a world of good old-fashioned virtues and individual heroism. The result, as Franklin sees it, is a series of minor and futile victories that are little more than moments of repression in a hopeless course of events.

Discussing yet another direction in recent film, E. Jane Burns, in her paper "Nostalgia Isn't What It Used to Be: The Middle Ages in Literature and Film," sees a like yearning to return to a place that never was, not only behind movies like *Excalibur*, but behind all such Arthurian "revivals" from Geoffrey of Monmouth to Tennyson. If, as Franklin suggests, man today faces his future in the mirror of the science fiction film in hopes of glimpsing what is a fictional past, a wish-moment that lies outside the time stream altogether, Burns sees man seeking the same thing in the Arthurian "past," this time a legendary fictionalized history that he hopes will allow him to flee time and death, to escape into prophecy. Beyond simple nostalgia, Burns sees this Arthurian escape as nostalgia incarnate, as yearning aware of its own conventions, "soap-opera time" transposed to a different key. Less pessimistic than Franklin however, Burns detects what may mark a countertrend in a film like *Monty Python and the Holy Grail*. As she remarks, this film, systematically destructuring the Arthurian myth *and* our nostalgia for it, leads its viewer to the moment when, at the confluence of nostalgic and real time, the legendary king is expelled from his fictional world to encounter our justice. As Arthur is tried in our courts for his imaginary murders, death is deposed from this nostalgic limbo, and is returned to our stream of reality.

Cyndia Clegg's "The Problem of Realizing Medieval Romance in Film: John Boorman's *Excalibur*," deals with a similar problem in Arthurian film fantasy from a very different perspective—that of a formalist and semiotic discussion of meaning segments of one single film. In her analysis she reveals the inability of this particular film (and implicitly of others that seek to reconstruct the semantic experience of medieval verbal romance) to achieve consistency on the level of perceived meaning, to resolve tensions arising in the film from simultaneous perception of experience on naturalistic and imaginative levels. It is not in some nostalgically imposed consistency but in *Monty Python* that Burns finds in the Arthurian film true fantasy in the sense of *phantasia*: the making visible and concrete of the imagination, hence making its forms new-born to death in our time. In a rather opposite sense however, Clegg locates Arthurian fantasy in film's ability to resolve the built-in thematic and structural tensions of this form of romance in a semantic "equanimity." To succeed as fantasy then, such films must do what *Excalibur* does not do: eliminate those internal dissonances that risk awakening the chaos that lurks as readily in the interstices of this back projection as in the forward visions of science fiction.

Clegg's semantic "deconstruction" of the images of *Excalibur*, then, may itself figure the self-destruction of Arthurian film fantasy, the natural tendency of its fragilely ordered imaginative world toward disorder. In contrast, Fred Burns, in his essay "Achieving the Fantastic in the Animated Film," demonstrates how the animator in America today constructs his fantastic landscape out of what may seem near-chaos: such widely disparate visual sources as botanical illustration, iron mongery and the elaborate floral patterns that decorate nineteenth-century industrial machinery, in addition to the more traditional "visions" of artists like Piranesi and William Blake. A professional animator, Burns demonstrates, through detailed analysis of individual frames of his film *The Burial of Natty Bumppo*, how eclectic the sources of modern American visual fantasy are, and how suited the medium of animation is to the creation of that form of fantasy whose essence is the unexpected fusion of incongruities in a suddenly functioning whole. Burns's analysis reveals to what degree the task of the fantasy animator is a struggle of mind against a nature that not only resists but recurs all the more strongly as it is restrained—in the floral excrescences on our practical machines, in the arabesques that flourish in the margins of Blake's "fearful symmetry."

Another prominent film version of the American fantasy landscape is the musical. In his paper "Musical Fantasy: *The Little Prince*," James W. Arnold, through a detailed discussion of Stanley Donen's musical adaptation of Saint-Exupéry's novel, describes a mode of articulating images that must resist not only the tendency to realism inherent in the cinematic image itself, but that increasing desire and power of film technology to reconvert the wonders of fantasy—by addressing them on the level of the tricks that produce the illusions—into common occurrences. It is in light of this second aspect that Donen's film, as musical, may pose a special problem. For as Arnold sees, Donen, wishing to use the energy of song and dance to impose poetical control on the wide range of images his text inspires, must abandon the more naive techniques of the earlier musical in favor of highly sophisticated camera work and editing. If then Saint-Exupéry's tale of a crashed pilot and a prince fallen from an asteroid evokes science fiction only to transpose its future into a timeless realm of poetical allegory, it is as if this same science fiction, equally evoked and denied in Donen's film adaptation, has in return contaminated the timeless world of the musical, opened it to a film technology that, today, increasingly calls attention to itself as concretiser of imagined things at the expense of poetic illusion. If in *The Little Prince* such is true, it means that the very devices chosen to control the future impulses of the story are themselves already touched by that future, committed to it in their restless desire to alter the conventional landscape of musical fantasy.

It is this same film technology that gives us the special effects of such science fictional fairy tales as *Star Wars*, where the engineer now openly strives to return the marvelous once-upon-a-time to our stream of lived-in time. Noting a parallel between the rhythmic alternation of dance and plot elements in the musical and that of special effects and story sequences in the science fiction film, Albert J. La Valley, in his essay "Traditions of Trickery: The Role of Special Effects in the Science Fiction Film," suggests that stylization on the level of technological "trickery" may have displaced the stylized patterns of the musical and other modes of fantasy, and that this displacement may mark a natural direction for the evolution of the medium as a whole. Studying such technologically-oriented or "hardware" science fiction classics as *The Woman in the Moon, Forbidden Planet*, and *Silent Running*, La Valley asks why the science fiction film has increasingly become the arena for experimentation in special effects. He contends that science fiction film, unlike other genres where special effects often blend with narrative materials so closely that they are not noticed and hence cease to be special, has such relevance today because it is both about the creation of new worlds and (increasingly) about the technical wizardry that would create these new worlds. La Valley speculates that this emerging technological self-consciousness, rather than celebrating the future by realizing it in images on the screen, may instead constitute a retreat from that future, escape into a connoisseurship of effects for their own sake. We have then, on the part of the viewer of these films, movement away from a sense of temporal flow in narrative terms toward a state of awareness (again analogous to Braudy's genre awareness) in which the technology of the future is no longer distinguishable from that cinematic ritual whereby we affirm and reaffirm the present of film technology.

Through close readings of a series of recent science fiction films Garrett Stewart, in his essay "The 'Videology' of Science Fiction," examines the thematic and metafilmic implications of this screen within a screen of special effects. Focusing on one pervasive manifestation of special-effects technology in the science fiction film—the omnipresence of viewing devices and machines within the viewed science fiction set—Stewart discusses the relationship of these devices to what he calls the "videology" of the films—that visual and visionary dispensation where the state of the art joins the art of the future state. If in the science fiction film, he reasons, the link between machines and mores, the then and the now, is these video devices, then their representation in the film not only authenticates its remarkable future by domesticating it—reproducing at the heart of that future world the same act of seeing by which we in our moviegoing present are viewing it—but offers a caveat as well. In an extended analysis of two "videological" classics, *Fahrenheit 451* and *The Man Who Fell to Earth*,

Stewart explores the various modes depicted therein of enslavement or expropriation of the inner life of man by the image. He concludes (joining so many others in this volume) that this "videology" is ultimately reflexive, and that all such future video addiction only harkens back to our dark present, but in doing so grants us clarity of reflection on those ideologies by which we see, and hence direct, our lives.

These discussions of film structure and technology, as they resolve through various forms of fantasy toward a central focus in the special effects and finally the "videology" of the science fiction film, yield important conclusions both about the state of film art in general and about the meaning of this medium and its capacity for meaning. In two final papers that same capacity for meaning, and with it film's sense of its own future possibilities, are analyzed from two very different, but ultimately complementary perspectives. Both George Slusser's "Fantasy, Science Fiction, Mystery, Horror," and Frank McConnell's "Born in Fire: The Ontology of the Monster," suggest that film today—and perhaps film in general as a medium of expression and perception—may be increasingly shaped by a bond between horror and science fiction. Slusser offers a broad analysis of the perceptual shifts that have transformed cinema genres in the past and continue to do so in the present. McConnell, on the other hand, works outward from a single but persistent theme, that of the Frankenstein monster, in order to demonstrate that his existence in film—as creature endlessly created for the purpose of being redestroyed—may symbolize the *ontos* of cinema itself, the ultimate sequel or remake in which film denies its own and our own technological future.

Slusser's essay begins by relating the act of mediation in film, its essence as medium, to those epistemological questions of perception which inform the world view of that technological culture that engendered cinema. At the center of all its mediating frames, Slusser asserts, film conceals a dream of unmediated seeing. He finds this dream not only haunting the film existence of such forms as fantasy, science fiction, mystery and horror, but shaping their dynamic interaction as well. The relation then of these forms in the history of film is less fruitfully studied on the generic level than on a transgeneric one. Their generation and regeneration, Slusser claims, is governed by two modes—the investigative and the sentimental—which are analogous on the level of the human system of perception to the dual impulses of vision and control, unmediated and mediated seeing. First drawing parallels between two transformational chains—one in literature, the other in film—then examining two paradigmatic films, *Blow Up* and *The Incredible Shrinking Man*, Slusser plots what he calls "science fiction's sentimental journey to horror."

In analyzing films where conventional generic boundaries increasingly overlap and blur, Slusser's essay shows how apparently diverse forms, throughout what seems a clear historical development, in reality tend to replay a basic scenario: that of tension between reason and sentiment, between the urge to see beyond man and that to frame what is seen in man's image. Another meaning of film's potential for replay becomes clear to Frank McConnell as he studies the tribe of cinematic "Frankensteins": that the continued resurrections and burnings of this monster may constitute a genuine ritual for our secular age. In his essay "Born in Fire," McConnell sees the ritual as inverted. The filmic destiny of this scapegoat, he contends, reverses the pattern of the Mass so that the open rhythm of communion out of sacrifice now becomes the closed (and apocalyptic) one of failed communion—the monster seeking to enter society and being rejected—and immolation. To McConnell the film ritual of Frankenstein—by asking a question the myth of incarnation would deny—marks the place where our progressive sense of humanity, created by our ability to speak, encounters the mute horror of physicality—our terror at having bodies. Extending the idea of science fiction as technological fiction, he considers the Frankenstein films quintessential science fiction insofar as man's primary technology is language itself. Pondering why the film monster (unlike his counterpart in the book) is constantly denied speech, McConnell concludes that the cinematic myth of Frankenstein is the myth of film itself, for film as medium, like this monster, is an artifact that imitates life yet does not need to speak because its images are simply there. In a sweeping attempt finally to place science fiction at the center of all speculation on film, McConnell sees cinematic art—as *the* art of the twentieth century—incarnating rather than simply expressing the concerns of science fiction. In turn he finds all subsequent film theory an attempt to come to terms with the "central scandal . . . of life or soul created out of the most artificial, soulless of means." The central theme and concern of science fiction, this "scandal" is that which has allowed Frankenstein to become, in McConnell's words, a "long, complex *name* for the art of film."

All of these essays were written for the Fourth Eaton Conference, held 27–28 February 1982, at the University of California at Riverside, and all are original. This conference, devoted to fantasy and science fiction in film, also featured a number of informal panels and discussions which provided the intellectual backdrop for the essays collected here. In this regard the editors owe a very real debt to one person who, more than anyone else, worked to provide this context of professional activity for the conference—Irwin R. Blacker of the USC School of Cinema. The editors also wish to thank a number of people who gave their valuable time to make this conference a success: Robert Wise, Stanley Donen, Lester Novros, Saul David, Mort Abrahams, Frank De Felitta, Arthur Knight, Moshe Lazar, Joseph Andrew Casper, David Gerrold, Thomas Saffer, Joel Primack, Thomas M. Disch, Gregory Benford and, last but surely not least, conference moderator George Guffey. This gathering was sponsored jointly by the University Library and the College of Humanities and Social Sciences, University of California, Riverside, and we wish to thank, finally, Joan Chambers, University Librarian, and David Warren, Dean of Humanities and Social Sciences, as well as our guiding spirits and faithful supporters, Jean-Pierre Barricelli and Eleanor Montague, for making it all come true.

Contributors

JAMES W. ARNOLD is Professor of Film and Journalism at Marquette University.

PETER BISKIND is a noted film critic and Editor of *American Film.*

LEO BRAUDY is Professor of English at the University of Southern California and author of *The World in a Frame.*

E. JANE BURNS teaches French literature, with a specialty in the medieval period, at the University of North Carolina at Chapel Hill.

FRED BURNS is a graduate of the USC School of Cinema and a professional animator.

CYNDIA CLEGG teaches English and film at Pepperdine University.

H. BRUCE FRANKLIN is Professor of English and American Studies at Rutgers University/Newark.

BRUCE KAWIN is Professor of English at the University of Colorado. His most recent book is *The Mind of the Novel.*

ALBERT J. LA VALLEY is Director of Film Studies at Dartmouth College.

FRANK MCCONNELL is Professor of English at the University of California at Santa Barbara and is the author of *Mythmaking and Storytelling.*

ERIC S. RABKIN is Professor of English at the University of Michigan. His most recent book is *Science Fiction: A Historical Anthology.*

GEORGE SLUSSER is Curator of the Eaton Collection and Adjunct Professor at the University of California at Riverside.

VIVIAN SOBCHACK teaches film at the University of California, Santa Cruz. She is the author of *The Limits of Infinity*.

GARRETT STEWART is Professor of English at the University of California at Santa Barbara, and has written widely on Dickens and on film.

BEN STOLTZFUS is Professor of French at the University of California at Riverside and is an authority on Robbe-Grillet and the *nouveau roman*.

I

Genre and the Resurrection of the Past

Leo Braudy

Anyone who watches television, goes to the movies, or listens to radio is aware how much his or her sense of personal time is linked with those activities. We date our lives and loves, our depressions and elations, by the songs and stars that were popular when we passed through those moments. We map our own existence in time by those coordinates of a fantasy time that makes nonsense of any rigid division between public and private life. They tell us how history fits into us as much as how we fit into history. And when the stars die and the songs are no longer played, we feel their loss as a loss inside, to commemorate with nostalgia the way we used to be and in some crevice hope we still are.

But in the unending bombardment of words and images that is so characteristic of the present, there is also a disheveled uncertainty about which are truly valuable and permanent: what will last? what really tells us the most about ourselves, as individuals and as a nation? To try to get at this question, I want to talk about films as seemingly different as *Chariots of Fire* and *E.T., Reds* and *Shoot the Moon, Pennies from Heaven* and *Poltergeist, Star Trek II* and *Gallipoli*. But two trends beyond the specifics of individual films have to be mentioned first—the way in which horror has become the dominant genre, even invading with its images and motifs films that are otherwise not "really" horror films; and the inclination of filmmakers to believe that nothing succeeds like sequels.

In both of these trends can be found what I have elsewhere called the pervasiveness of a soap-opera sense of time in American life, in which stories never end; they only continue. In the 1950s, science-fiction films would often feature a scene in which a face on television would sign off by saying 'this is it, the end of the world.' But if that last gasp of media professionalism could have been imagined then, it

Portions of this essay appeared in another form in *The Yale Review* (Summer 1982), as "Popular Culture and Personal Time." Copyright © 1982 by Leo Braudy.

seems impossible now. After wars, assassinations, and a steady diet of the deaths and murders of the famous or the merely local, we know that there will be no apocalypse on television because the nature of the medium works against it. There is always another program, another season, another bridge of music, voice, and computer graphics to make the audience feel it is not alone in the void.

It would be safe to say that the present movie audience is the most formally sophisticated in history, and for that sophistication we must thank television. Many films have been made by directors who are highly educated in film history and therefore apt to pack each scene with layers of allusion, often in direct proportion to its thematic emptiness. But audiences make films as much as do filmmakers, and years of watching television have made them ready and eager for the current genre bombardment, in which past stories, images, and motifs of all sorts are repeated, revised, and revaluated in an endless reflection on a past that seems entirely made up of previous motion pictures. In the 1950s no horror film required that you had seen other horror films. If you had, you might have a more interesting time, but it wasn't necessary. Now, almost every film in every genre—horror, science fiction, musical—virtually insists that you be aware of previous films so that you can properly savor the nuances this one adds. The way a genre film invokes its own artistic tradition is always a variety of comfort. It can mingle several traditions at once (*Star Wars*); it can reveal what previous works have kept decorously hidden (*Body Heat*); or it can mockingly parody (*The Life of Brian*). But no matter how explosive its material, no matter how it ups the ante on sex, violence, and self-consciousness, the genre film inescapably dramatizes its commitment to a quest for clarity and understanding possible only through the contemplation of history.

The audience that appreciates genre films, remakes, and sequels is one that wants to be both shocked and knowing, to be in on the details of repetition and variation within the films as well as all the interviews, films about the films, and biographical material that surround it. Such an audience wants its awareness catered to and confirmed, for the irony generated by its knowledge of films is not savage or satiric but cozy. In the midst of the most savage movie violence, there is now a family of dedicated viewers, safe in its knowledge of the patterns of form and story, self-satisfied and detached in its bemused contemplation of special effects and production tricks. To talk about the media manipulation used in the Kennedy or Nixon presidential races could ten years ago seem like a great revelation. With Carter and Reagan the manipulation became part of the story, just as soap opera audiences are invited to immerse themselves in the intricacies of the *Dallas* plot even as they watch Larry Hagman on talk shows pondering the nature of the character he plays or read fan magazine articles about what Larry ("J.R.") Hagman is really like.

The audience that can appreciate all those nuances without the slightest self-conscious twitch is an audience that has become skilled in all the ways Hollywood tells stories and all the ways stories are told about Hollywood. By now everyone is a member of many different audiences, and there is no movie star left who was not once a fan. Thus the most common emotional appeal movies make today is not to fear or curiosity or desire but to self-congratulation, that species of pride one takes in being a professional member of the media audience, like a sports freak with his statistics, completely *au courant* with the latest new careers, hair styles, and methods of simulating decapitation, as well as with the traditions that stand behind them.

The present popularity of sequels makes the appeal to being "with it" only more obvious. Each genre movie, is part of an implicit series, and "Kharis still lives" could be the motto of any filmmaker who wants to tap the energy remaining in the images and stories that had captivated audiences before. But now, urged on by the desire to keep the money safe and bent on exploiting the knowing audience, the filmmaker spawns sequels of his own, creating instant cults whose uniform is the T-shirt and whose relics are available at participating toy stores. So the trailers for *Rocky III* proudly proclaimed "An American Tradition." In Hollywood, it seems, twice is a sequel; three times is a tradition.

I am not being snide about sequels (or genre films) in the name of some ideal of the high-class individual work of art. The old high culture/popular culture distinction, never very compelling, seems to me to have even less point when we look at what has been produced in Hollywood and consumed in America over the past few years—the films of the early 1980s (if anyone still clings to a belief in the personalities of decades). In these films there is a common preoccupation with the pressure of time and history on the individual, and, depending on whether the film's view is optimistic or pessimistic, the freedom of the present or the claustrophobic pressure of the past.

Like the proliferation of genre films, the overwhelming number of remakes and revivals, as well as the supposed resurrection of traditional political values represented by Ronald Reagan, the popularity of sequels indicates that we are in a period when the question of the past and what to do about it weighs heavily on a present that is in danger of both ignoring it and treating it too seriously, without sufficient distance and irony. Sequels and the newly ironic genre films allow just that kind of distance. Their stories, built on a core of characters, never really end. When you see them, you don't buy a ticket to a film; you buy a ticket to a world, and a cozy world at that. Thus, even horror films become for the fan familiar treats, and fright becomes a welcome variation on familiarity. Film critics may debate about the essential nature of the western or the musical or even the boxing film. But if there is any pure genre still afoot now, it is the genre of self-consciousness about genre, the genre preoccupied with facing up to or facing down its own past.

But the question still remains whether this formal sophistication actually constitutes cultural progress or is merely cultural accumulation—and the raids on the greatness of the past less an enshrinement than a rummaging in the garbage heap of broken images. Remakes at best are commentaries that gain in self-consciousness what they lose in freshness. To remake *The Thing* complete with the politics of 1951 that permeated it would be ridiculous or at least strangely archaic. So John Carpenter, in the name of going back into the past, goes back still further to John W. Campbell, Jr.'s original story, and serves up a film with no politics and virtually no plot at all—whose ending aches for the sequel that as yet has never come and perhaps never will. In an age preoccupied with the search for originality and personal style, the deluge of sequels, remakes, and genre irony dissolves the anxiety of creative aspiration by implying that there is no need to reinvent from scratch; just repeat, vary, continue, go on. Such works preserve us from constant comparison with the mighty dead, and yet they insist upon that comparison as well. They let us step back and congratulate ourselves for knowing how they work. But then they pull out the rug: if you know so much, you must be old; and if you are old, you are closer to death.

Thus the almost invariable tones of melancholy and gloom in many current films. Sequels may plunge on: Rocky Balboa wins again; Luke Skywalker learns a little bit more (about his past, of course). But in other films the note of desperation, the pipings of creativity on the brink of the abyss, are much shriller. *Pennies from Heaven*, for instance, with its brilliant parts and overall incoherence, reminds me of those fantastic concoctions served up at restaurants that feature no coherent cuisine, just all the most expensive ingredients: filet mignon coated with caviar and garnished with kiwi fruit. In *Pennies from Heaven* Busby Berkeley and Fred Astaire slug it out with Walker Evans and Edward Hopper to see who deserves the prize for telling us what the 1930s were really about. Steve Martin is the appropriate star for such a film because his main comic gesture is a smirk. On stage it tends to mean 'I'm doing something stupid, but I know it and therefore it's funny.' In films it tends to mean 'I know I'm just a kid, but I'm up here playing with the big guys.' In both situations Martin insists on how aware he is. In *The Jerk* he seems to take seriously what no one else would, even while his eyes and his voice and his smirk let us in on the secret that he's not really taking it seriously at all, just acting. Unlike Robin Williams, whose awareness turns him into Mr. Media, an antenna that grew up where all the television and radio and movies waves in the universe converge, Martin never attempts sincerity or emotion without jutting his jaw and curling his lip and telling us he really didn't mean it; what do you think he is, a fool?

Yet even though Martin is cool, he wants to be sincere as well, especially if sincerity is defined by the total commitment of Astaire and Rogers to their craft in a lost time when, like the time of Humphrey Bogart or Henry Fonda, the seam between person and performer rarely showed. With all his standing back, Martin still wants to play with the big kids, and if Fred and Ginger are not yet the mighty dead, they might as well be, for their films represent a lost ideal of order, elegance, and security. But finally we must admit that their world is forever lost, and so the character Martin plays in *Pennies from Heaven* also learns that, whatever your fantasies, whatever your cool, you can't change your place in history. In the crucial sequence, Martin and Bernadette Peters dance on a stage under a film of Astaire and Rogers. True, Astaire and Rogers are in black and white, and Martin and Peters are in color. But the fantasy stars of the past loom over the diminished forms of the seemingly more realistic fantasy stars of the present. Even when Martin and Peters are techno-magically transposed into the black and white film, "becoming" Astaire and Rogers, the sense of loss is the dominant note: the present is a weak imitation of the past—in lip sync.

Pennies, like the "new" genre film it is, breathes deeply in the history of visual imagery, especially that of musicals; its past is a past made up of other films, even while it nervously pays tribute to the imagery of painters like Hopper whom it considers to be more "real." *Reds*, or *Chariots of Fire*, or on the other hand, *Gallipoli*, step outside of that kind of self-conscious genre history to present themselves as "original" works. Yet they are curiously involved in very similar issues of aspiration and loss. Instead of doing the old-fashioned thing of staying within the past he seeks to reconstruct, Warren Beatty in *Reds*, for example, intersperses bits of interviews with the survivors of a past that also included John Reed and Louise Bryant. It really happened, he seems to be saying: past and present are linked; these people and their passions were once real. But paradoxically this effort to ballast his characters with a documentary and anecdotal reality succeeds only in underlining the marionette quality of the screen Reed and Bryant. How amazing, we are invited to wonder, that these ancient faces and bodies once lived in the gaudy past? But why, we might continue to ask, are all these real people unidentified (except in the credits) and why, counterwise, are the well-known faces of Beatty and Diane Keaton adorning characters that now seem so unreal? As he shows by casting other familiar faces (George Plimpton, Gene Hackman) in cameo roles, Beatty wants to have it both ways: respect the truth of the past as much as possible; then rip its fabric by in-jokes whose only point is to remind the audience of the fictionality of the reconstruction.

The old way to do such historical melodramas—for which Lubitsch, say, was so criticized by Siegfried Kracauer—was to place the individual against a large historical canvas and then show that everything that happened could be explained by the personal emotions of the participants—the Cleopatra's nose theory of history. But *Reds* is more torn between the claims of individual desires and those of public issues. Toward the end of the film, for example, Reed argues impassionately to Emma Goldman that she shouldn't give in to her feelings. Then, in quick succession, he decides not to resign from the International, goes off to help propagandize the Tartars, and then denounces Zinoviev et al. for killing the individual in the name of the Revolution and thereby killing the Revolution. He has come around to a way of thinking the film originally characterizes as Bryant's. Emotions and conscience seen to win out over principles and the March of History— suitably capitalized. But the recantation comes too late, and Reed dies of a typhus contracted in the service of the Revolution. Bryant's views of personal politics may finally prevail, but she is important only insofar as she fits into Reed's life, and he only insofar as he has been touched by history. Their consolation is that at least neither will ever grow old and vague like the ancient witnesses rounded up by Warren Beatty to authenticate their story.

Thus both *Pennies from Heaven* and *Reds* ruefully contrast the diminished present with the glorious past, even as they imply that we have superseded that past in understanding. Now we know that Fred Astaire's films were fantasy escapes from Depression realities (authenticated by Edward Hopper). Now we know that John Reed and

Louise Bryant should have been praised and celebrated rather than attacked and harrassed. Thus the execution of the Martin character in *Pennies* and the death of Reed in *Reds* resemble happy endings because they preserve the purity of our new illusions of knowingness. An alive John Reed would have been like the *Reds* chorus of ancients—feisty, fascinating, but somehow unfortunately alive and old. And a flash forward to the last days of Louise Bryant as a kind of Parisian bag woman in 1936 (had she heard the news of O'Neill's Nobel Prize?) might have made the links between romantic past and fallen present much too uncomfortable.

Like the genre films that self-consciously announce their freedom from tradition by superseding it, *Reds* is fatally caught between bowing to history and desperately attempting to escape its power. Until fairly recently, time in musicals seemed outside history because it was always perfect, rhythmic, synchronized, and harmonious, an elegant ritual that would never die. It was the quintessential movie time—outside the ragged world of facts and events. But *All that Jazz* and *Pennies from Heaven* showed how death could be made part of the timeless rhythm as well. And in this sense *Reds* is a variety of musical. Louise Bryant after Reed can't be an issue because that would undermine the enclosed and virtually utopian idealism of the film, which is constantly at odds with its desire to demonstrate its intellectual seriousness, its engagement with real history. I am fascinated that Beatty left out Reed's production of the Paterson Strike Pageant in Madison Square Garden in 1913. Perhaps he thought it would cut too close if Reed were so obviously, like Beatty, the impresario of history, rather than a reporter, participant, and, finally the nobly dying victim of great events. Milos Forman in *Ragtime*, with his Eastern European cynicism about history, makes it even more obvious who wins: the hero of action (Coalhouse Walker) and the hero of sensibility (Father) are in different ways destroyed, while the hero of artistic detachment, the filmmaker Tatiyeh, flourishes, complete with Mother at his side, leaving the dead past behind.

"The way you deal with death is just as important as the way you deal with life," counsels once-Captain, now-Admiral Kirk to his ambitious daughter in *Star Trek II*, a film that makes the aging and even the death of its previously ageless characters an essential part of its plot. In fact, the presence of death—challenged, evaded, succumbed to—has been so pervasive in recent films that it's surprising (or appropriate) that so little mention has been made of it. On the most explicit level, films like *Sergeant Pepper's Lonely Hearts Club Band*, *Superman I*, and *E.T.*, lead us up to and beyond the point of death and decay only to reverse the process magically. Sergeant Pepper's magic horn turns the corrupted Pepperville back to the idyllic small town (Andy Hardy's Carvel) it once was; Superman turns the whole world back on its axis to resurrect Lois Lane; Elliot's love for E.T. revives the inner glow of life that the most up-to-date medical technology could not maintain. All our national mythology emphasizes freshness and innocence as the great virtues, and age and experience as the portents of death, the ultimate winding down of things. But a film like *E.T.* promises that even with this burdensome wisdom we might participate for a moment in the fantasy of renewal. And every adult who has stood in a hospital room and watched the blood pressure drop and disappear in a loved one, young or old (and E.T. conveniently is both), happily cries along with Elliott: this time love worked.

In a very different way, *Chariots of Fire* attempts virtually the same denial of death and time as *E.T.*. Unlike Beatty's John Reed, whose action in history is compromised by his good looks and his theatrical personality, the runners Liddell and Abrahams are performers either unaware of or unconcerned about being seen and who therefore seem to escape being crushed by the millstones of interpretation virtually every other character brings to their view of the national or religious significance of their running. No matter what the movie tries to tell us, neither man runs his race for the state, for society, or even for the usual audience in such cases—the loved one. Abrahams has his coach, but the coach is less a personal audience than a witness to a perfection of form, equivalent to Liddell's pronouncement that God watches him run and takes pleasure in it. I wonder if the Best Picture award *Chariots* collected doesn't indicate less about its quality than about the Hollywood desire to believe that somehow, somewhere, there are people of ferocious ambition who are also morally pure, whether, like Liddell in the film, they do it for God, or, like Abrahams, they do it in the name of self-achievement. Their fellow runner Schultz in the film, with his American sense of public performance, says he can't understand either one of them. Too late we discover that the fame to which we aspire may not be the fame we most admire.

Like *E.T.*, *Chariots of Fire* implies that it may be possible to escape from time and its final corruption, death. In the golden-glowing England between the wars, it might still have been possible to be ambitious, to race against time and win (as Abrahams runs against the ancient courtyard clock in an early scene). Running is a compelling image for ambition not just because there are so many joggers around or because *career* originally meant a race course. Of all sports on film, running especially conveys the visual impact of an individual relying solely on his or her body—without teammates (too social) and without special equipment (too technological). It translates ambition into the bare facts of body, mind, and motivation. The victory against time, like Elliot's revival of *E.T.* or Superman's disinterring of Lois Lane, is a victory of the purified self. But *Chariots of Fire*, despite its Academy Award, is a little too ironic about the paraphernalia that surrounds running to embody the American ideal of personal ambition (as does *Personal Best*), and it is too nostalgic about the England of afternoon sherry and hedgerows to have any political bite (as does *Gallipoli*). Both *Personal Best* and *Gallipoli* also feature running and runners, but their attitudes toward time could not be more different. In *Gallipoli* the time is war, and the fatalities of history channel the two young runners into a march toward inevitable death that they suspect and the audience knows must come. In the last moments of the film one of the runners uses his talent to try to avert a suicidal advance into the guns of the enemy. He runs and runs and runs, but still the message never gets through and his friend, with thousands of others, dies fruitlessly. Anyone with a bit of history might remember that the blame for the disastrous campaign at Gallipoli has usually been laid at the door of the young Winston Churchill. But Peter Weir's imagination is set into motion less by a desire for revenge on Churchill or the British military mind than by the more general theme of a doomed human struggle against fate. The past cannot be changed. The life given for society is a sacrifice at an empty shrine.

Personal Best, with its American-style optimism, implies that there is always enough time, especially when the pressures of the big race or the big game can be removed and competitors turned into lovers. Running against time is simply running against the worst and realizing the best about oneself. *Personal Best* is thus like *Chariots of Fire* or *Gallipoli* with all the business about empire and war and social pressure and anti-semitism left out. The most socially explosive content—the relation between the two young women—is, like everything else in the film, shown as a personal choice, not a cultural or cosmic problem, nor the subject of moralizing and judgment. The political question of the boycott of the Olympics is there, but only to set the stage for the individual struggle.

But the bright lights and the unself-conscious bodies of *Personal Best* serve mainly to indicate how rare such optimism is in most recent films, where one is more likely to find a monster festering within rather than a pure urge to win. *Gallipoli* manages to keep its main characters pure by putting the blame on history, and *Chariots of Fire* is ambivalent even about that. But characters like Steve Martin's Arthur in *Pennies from Heaven* or Reed and Bryant in *Reds* are aching to be discovered, to be known for what they are—great spirits—usually independent of any particular talent or ability. Beatty gives such a role some substance because so many of his best performances (*Bonnie and Clyde, McCabe and Mrs. Miller, Shampoo*) have been as self-dramatizing small men who try to rise to a heroic status always tinged with play-acting and personal myth-making. Perhaps such ironies still exist in *Reds*, but if we are being asked to consider Reed as yet another public figure who has confused action with acting, the clues may be too deep to be dug out. In fact, Reed seems much more like an adult version of one of the new teen-age heroes—the young King Arthur, the prince in disguise who can pull the sword from the stone and reveal himself as the natural leader, while all fall down in fealty. John Reed grasps the sword of history; Luke Skywalker sets forth against the empire. The promise of time is fulfilled in the young idealist, the great man in the disguise of youth.

The most recent wave of films with medieval settings, unlike their more socially-oriented forebears in the 1950s, summon up a past world that authenticates war and violence by its relation, through magic and Christianity, to the eternal truths of the universe. Yet too often their heroes, like those of films with more modern settings, seem motivated primarily by the desire to be celebrated enough to conquer death through fame. But history is a double-edged sword, and it is instructive to consider how many of these heroes wind up disillusioned or dead. Even in the most positive film images of the past, the gloomy shroud of time and fate waits to fall on the hero's shoulders. The race for honor, the desire to make a difference, and thereby escape from time, is revealed to be the surest path to being swallowed up by it. The pursuers of fame and honor may race against time toward a perfection of body and spirit. But those who flee from horror live in a world where personal energy often wears the face of violence and mania.

Understanding the appeal of horror films these days is crucial to understanding films in general because the motifs and themes of the horror film have so permeated films of quite different sorts. The Vangelis music for *Chariots of Fire*, for example, with its horror-film combination of menace and sentimental nostalgia accords perfectly with the theme of spiritual self-absorption the plot dramatizes. In

Chariots of Fire the heroes run against time and seem to succeed. But films where the horror element is more pervasive leave behind their origins in other genres or in "realism" to become infused by the horror film's focus on the fragile individual or the embattled group, menaced by the intangible and all-powerful forces of the past. This past has been forgotten and ignored, rather than praised and revered, and it will now therefore take its revenge. In such "horrified" films, the forward, ambitious youth who grasps the sword from the stone learns that his own conviction of newness and originality is an affront to time. In the ensuing combat the odds lie not with the individual but with an implacable fate. Thus the recent prevalence of films in which seekers of media fame are threatened or threatening—*Pennies from Heaven*, *The Howling*, *Shoot the Moon*. In the 1950s the horror tended to come from the outside—in the shape of The Thing or the Creature from the Black Lagoon. But in our own time it either incubates within (as in *Alien* or the remake of *The Thing*) or distressingly wears the guise of familiarity (as in *Shoot the Moon* or *The Shining*). "Who are you," one hero asks the beautiful woman/skeletal monster in *Ghost Story*. "I am you," she says. "I am you."

Jean-Luc Godard once said that to make a film was to photograph death at work. And horror movies especially exploit one of the basic elements of the movie experience—its insistent irreversibility. Just as the camera pulls us inexorably down the hallway to the door we would rather not open, it also forces us to face a future we would rather forget, the future that holds our own deaths. The horror film takes its revenge particularly on those who have forgotten the past, the ancestral house and land, and the dead who inhabit it. In more benevolent versions, involving strange beings, the older than old can be loved, like E.T., and even consulted, like Yoda, the Jedi guru. But in the stories of more earthly horror, the dead have been forgotten entirely, murdered and left to rot, or their sacred burial places built over with fancy hotels and tract housing. In such places, there is neither memory nor respect among the living, only the unearned energy of merely being alive. As films such as *Ghost Story, The Fog*, and the second half of *Poltergeist* emphasize, only after the dead have been remembered will the sin against them begin to be expunged: knowing the past is the first step to release from it.

The past that is closest to us, as well as the dead we try best to remember, is our own. From the beginnings of gothic fiction, the forgetting of the past has been presented as a forgetting of genealogy and family. In our own time the chains may still rattle in the ancient crypt, but from *The Exorcist* on, many more familiar experiences of family disruption have been the precondition for the possession by an alien horror. In particular it is the fathers who have failed, the fathers who should preserve the sacraments of family and local tradition but turn out instead to be either missing, dead, or crazy. By the end of *Shoot the Moon*, for example, the film has given up all its pretensions to being a realistic picture of a family broken by divorce to become what is in essence a horror film: first, the mother with her children in a lonely house out in the woods menaced by an irrational monster (who happens to be her ex-husband); then the monster's subsidence into what seems like normality; and finally the monster's violent return, in a total demolition of all previous claims to civilized behavior unmatched since the James Mason of *Bigger than Life*—the original "Daddy is crazy" movie. Plucky mothers (in *The Shining, Close Encounters, The Secret of NIMH, Poltergeist, E.T.*) take up the slack when their absent, weak-willed or murderous husbands fail. But over each film hangs the only truly final ending—death, which for a time the story has managed to keep away. No matter how decisive the ending, how final the heroism, how absolute the defeat of horror, there is always the possibility that escape was merely a dream, and we can return to fight or flee another day. The skull gleams alluringly beneath the skin, the films are made and remade, and the audience is locked in a never-ending test of its self-esteem and its fear: Am I one of the elect? Can I look into the face of death and survive?

Church attendance, we are told, is falling. But horror film attendance remains high, for in the horror communion the audience can experience a terror akin to personal death and yet be granted a reprieve, even a resurrection, like that of Lois Lane, E.T., or Mr. Spock in *Star Trek III*. The audience's knowledge of genre convention, like its awareness of sequels and remakes, helps perform the same function as a funeral service does for mourners: turning discomfort, fear, and anxiety into matters of ritual, elegance, and even routine. There are periods in which artists of the eye and the ear are intent on not being dismissed as formulaic and so exhibit an urgent originality. But there are also periods—and we seem to be in one now—in which artists glory in their exuberant inhabiting of formulas and genres, their close acquaintanceship with the social and aesthetic ritual by which clichés become revelations. Thus they gain their cultural authority and popularity by the skill with which they raise and then dramatically organize our fears and doubts. What is particularly striking about many films now is their desire to have it both ways—to indulge in the absoluteness of catastrophe and apocalypse while promising the audience that everything is all right: come back next week for another version. Those who seek to forget the past are swallowed up by it. But those who know the past try to placate its power by repeating it in as many variations as possible. In so many areas of our culture, the lavishness of presentation, the amount of money and technological expertise spent on the work, only underscores the feeling that the present must make up in material wealth what the past had in genius. Even such a summery film as *E.T.* cannot avoid the conclusion that winter is coming. Why else should Spielberg release it at the same time as *Poltergeist*, whose prime message is also to reconcile us with the fact of death, totally shorn of the usual horror film trappings of personal or familial sin?

The poet of democracy, Walt Whitman often intoned, will be the poet of death—death as the end, death as the all-embracer. Films now seem both preoccupied with death and intent on escaping it through their intricate reweaving of the patterns of the past. As there is a casualness about violence and destruction, so there is also an almost millennial longing for the incandescent moment when one achieves absolute success and burns out at the same time. The knowledge of genre conventions, the awareness of the past by filmmaker and audience alike, furnishes a way to lighten the burden. Possessed by genre, obsessed with the revision of its past, and encouraged by an audience eager to show its own expertise, Hollywood now seems unwilling and unable to leave its patterns behind. The innocent hero may go down that corridor and open that door. Our superior knowledge of such corridors and doors implies that we will never be so trapped. And yet we return, to be lured down that path and forced through that door again and again. The film characters are motivated by innocence and curiosity. But we are moved by experience. We remember the form and, by fulfilling it, hope we shall be purged.

2

Children of the Light

Bruce Kawin

Dracula, adopting for the moment the dark poise of Bela Lugosi, on a set of painted stone, under the comically mortal scrutiny of tall Tod Browning and heavy Karl Freund, smiles to himself at the doughy imitation of mortal fear on the face of "Renfield" and gives Mutt and Jeff what they want, a tasteful, graceful chill: "Listen to them—children of the night. What music they make." Forget about wolves for a moment and think of the image: that the threat, or whatever it is, is born of the night, created out of darkness and for the purposes of darkness. Imagine it, whatever it is, becoming gradually more distinct as it approaches out of a black field. Born of the night.

There are a lot of ways to play host. Many flowers provide food, comfort, and even shelter to the insects that, in exchange for the pollen they consume, carry pollen on their bodies to other flowers and thus keep the host species alive. Some plants, like some spiders, say "Come and sit in this little room which is really my belly." Dracula, of course, is the host who consumes his guest, and the parallel between him and the natural parasites is an important theme in Murnau's *Nosferatu*. The question is: What kind of host is the horror film? What does it give to the guest and what does it take—or, to be clearer about this: What do we as audience expect it to take? Our lives, our peace, our anxiety, our afternoon, our date's self-control, our anger, our idealism?

Imagine that what is coming at you is a shuffling, gruesome, unstoppable crowd of zombies; imagine that they want to eat you and that they haven't brushed their teeth since before they died. Did you make up the image or are you remembering, as I am, a scene from Romero's *Night of the Living Dead*? Is it safer—does it make it "all theater"—to imagine that this is a film, or does that bring it closer and make it more threatening? In other words, does it put the horror more in the terms of your own imagination, and has your imagination begun to model itself on film? Has the part of your mind that imagines horrors adopted the perspectives and structures of film, in fact of narrative film, and if so, is that a way of *controlling* the anxiety by phrasing it in terms known to be artificial—or is that a way of making it *more* frightening? And why *would* that make it more frightening?

Now imagine that the zombies are from Romero's film and that the film is showing in a darkened theatre. The audience is undead, and they are enjoying the film; it makes them feel at home. They become aware of your presence. They come after you. The only light is that provided by the projector, so that the room is, in the case of this particular shot, lit by the figures of Romero's zombies. The figures closing in on you are the children of the night; the ones on the screen are the children of the light. This scene is taken, more or less, from Peter Straub's novel *Ghost Story*, a book that examines with intelligence and care the ways that horror stories—whether on film or in literature or passed in serious tones around a firelit circle—lead us into temptation and deliver us to evil. Straub presents the ghost story as a mirror in which we can find ourselves, but only if we are willing to seek what we have found there, only if we confront our desire to be lost in horror and darkness.

In a good horror story, nobody gets off easy. In a bad horror story like *The Giant Gila Monster* or *Friday the 13th*, a lot of people get killed, but no one really cares about them; the audience's attention skips from victim to victim until it finds the survivor, the one with whom it is thrilling but safe to identify. (If there turns out to be no survivor, or if the survivor is threatened again at the end of the picture, it doesn't make much difference in the basic formula. Those shock endings, modeled on the good one in *Carrie*, work only because they play off the norm, which is that there will be a survivor. One way to respond to this new cliché is to regard it as a cheap negativism: "Oh how modern we are today." Another response, which few contemporary horror films have deserved, is to entertain the possibility that this particular horror is being extended or repeated because it is deathless, that it will recur—as in the 1940s paradigm of the Mummy sequels, or the ending of *Halloween*—and that that recurrence has some kind of point. But here we are treading on the territory of the good horror film.) In any case, it is important not to be misled by the clutch of victims into thinking that a film like *Friday the 13th* deals with real pain or loss; it deals with spectacle, and is no more threatening or profound than the 1950s spectacle of a downtown crowd running and screaming with a dinosaur at their heels. As Joanna Russ observed, what passes for ethics and judgment in these films can often be reduced to "Giant ants are bad / People are good."[1]

A good horror film takes you down into the depths and shows you something about the landscape; it might be compared to Charon, and the horror experience to a visit to the land of the dead, with the difference that this Charon will eventually take you home. The seeker, who is often the survivor, confronts his or her own fallibility, vulnerability, culpability, as an aspect of confronting the horror-object, and either matures or dies. ("Matures" in this sense refers to the adult act of making peace with the discrepancy between self and self-image; it is just the sort of gesture that practically never occurs in the science-fiction film.) An obvious example from literature is *Heart of Darkness*. Karl Freund's *Mad Love* offers a straightforward cinematic example at its climax, where Stephen and Yvonne Orlac manage to survive only by agreeing to function in the terms in which the villain, Dr. Gogol, has cast them. Yvonne's problem is that Dr. Gogol has confused her with her image; he gets sexually excited watching her sadomasochistic performances on stage, takes a wax statue of her into his home (and plays the organ for it, imagining that his love might make it come to life), and eventually attempts to control and possess her as he has controlled and possessed her image (i.e. both the statue and the image she projects, as actress, into his fantasy life). Stephen's problem is that Dr. Gogol has grafted onto his wrists the hands of a murderous knife-thrower, Rollo, and that these hands not only cannot play the piano (Stephen's forte, before a railroad accident that smashed his hands) but also control him, virtually forcing him to throw knives when he is angry. At the climax, Yvonne faces her statue, accidentally breaks it, and must pretend to be her statue, i.e. her image, in order to buy time and delude Dr. Gogol, whose delusion was to confuse her and her image. When Dr. Gogol decides to perfect his control of what he believes is a statue come to life, and begins to strangle her while quoting Browning's poem "Porphyria's Lover," Stephen and the police "rush" to the rescue. (Actually, what happens is that there's a tense Griffith-style cross-cut to the police car; the chief yells to the driver to slow down because there's no hurry.) Stephen saves his wife by accurately throwing a knife into Dr. Gogol's back. Earlier the doctor had tried to drive Stephen mad by convincing him that he had killed his own father with a knife. That knife, which had made its way onto the police chief's desk, is the one Stephen throws into Dr. Gogol with Rollo's hands. In other words, Stephen and Yvonne survive by accepting those aspects of themselves that reflect Dr. Gogol's control of their lives, the ways the horror has changed them. It is only by becoming a knife-killer that Stephen overcomes his castration crisis and is able to save his wife and himself—though he will never again become "a great pianist" (Yvonne's phrase, which she says so rapidly that it almost sounds like "penis"). It is only by becoming her image that Yvonne survives long enough to be tortured and saved for the last time. Neither of them gets off easy. For a more familiar example that does not require so much plot summary, consider the visionary lawyer in *The Last Wave*, who discovers his true nature at the expense of his life, coming home, as it were, to his destiny and finding there the freedom to be destroyed.

I spoke of a castration crisis, drawing on the fairly obvious imagery of the pianist who cannot play, the man who has lost his hands, the man who throws only knives and pens, the man who throws his first knife at his taunting father (but does not hurt him; it is Dr. Gogol who does the killing, later on). In fact, Stephen and Yvonne Orlac are on a delayed honeymoon when disaster intrudes, and the implication is that they must go through a horror phase, something identified with Dr. Gogol and his "mad love," before they can settle into their marriage, which in this case is an emblem of sexual and social stability. This turns out to be a relatively consistent pattern in the horror film of the 1920s, 1930s, and 1940s: that there will be a perverse love triangle among the boy, the girl, and the monster, that the happy coupling of the surviving couple will depend on their coming to some kind of understanding with the monster, and that the romantic resolution will bode well for the society at large. Whatever relationship there is between "the monster and the girl" must be resolved, and this can be a matter—in the dumbest prototype—of monster-steals-girl, boy-kills-monster, girl-kisses-boy. In the more complex films, like *Mad Love*, John Badham's recent *Dracula*, or—to pick another Freund film—*The Mummy*, there is some real emotional and ethical intercourse between monster and survivor, in the course of which both are changed. Consider, for instance, the serious girl-and-werewolf relationships in Waggner's *The Wolf Man* and the recent *American Werewolf in London*, or the really complex situation of the newscaster in *The Howling* who is both girl and monster and has to save/sacrifice herself. In any case, this triangle is an important psychological structure, and the device of the delayed honeymoon—which carries over from *Frankenstein* to *Bride of Frankenstein*, as poor Henry gradually gets the idea that he would do better to create life with the aid of a human female—reminds the viewer that there is something that needs to be settled before the characters can be considered healthy. Another aspect of the triangle, as in the example of *Beauty and the Beast*, is that the boy and the monster often represent two sides of the girl's own sexual desire, i.e. of her own sexual self-image, and the implication is that she cannot choose Mr. Right without first confronting her desire for—or to be—Mr. Wrong. Essentially this is the same issue as that of Stephen Orlac's phallic crisis because it demonstrates how the horror film functions as a mirror or series of mirrors in which aspects of the self demand to be confronted. This confrontation is usually in the interests of the health of the protagonists, and almost any great horror film can send ripples down our understanding of the therapies of Freud, Jung, and Perls: Freud because it is possible to think of the horror-object as an *Id*-like force that compels attention through compulsive repetition, that often expresses itself in dream formats (i.e., if films are like dreams, horror films are like nightmares), and that must be unmasked if healing is to take place; Jung because the monster often plugs into our shared sense of the archetypes and because in the horror film we often indulge our nostalgia for the world of myth and magic; and Perls because the monster is often a projection split off from the wholeness of the protagonist (or audience), so that health is achieved not by unrepressing some trauma but by taking the projection back into oneself, in other words by deeply acknowledging the connection between the monster and the official self.

Now this is only one aspect of one horror formula, and I will be advancing toward larger generalizations later, but for the moment it makes the basic point: good horror films try to be good hosts; they lead us through a structure that shows us something useful or worth understanding. Because so many of them are psychologically oriented or psychoanalyzable, what they often map out is the terrain of the unconscious, and in that connection they often deal with fantasies of brutality, sexuality, victimization, repression, and so on. Because they deal with the unconscious in a larger-than-Freudian sense, they often involve some disguised journey into the land of the dead,[2] which can be thought of in terms of the lawyer's glimpses of "the other side" or "the dream time" in *The Last Wave*, or of the intrusion of the guardians of the dead into the bland America of the post-Freund Mummy sequels. Robin Wood, among others, has argued that repressed political and social discontent, the urge to smash the system and subvert its values, is another more or less unconscious element that the horror film temporarily liberates.[3] What science fiction films do, in contrast, is to address not the unconscious but the conscious—if not exactly the scientist in us, then certainly the part of the brain that enjoys speculating on technology, gimmicks, and the perfectable future. What bad horror films do, in contrast to both of these, is to present spectacle for the simple purpose of causing pain in the viewer's imagination—not just scaring the hell out of us, but attacking and brutalizing us on a deep level. Perhaps I am making a further distinction here between a bad film and an evil film, because a badly made horror film like *Ghost Story* doesn't do much more than sadden the audience at the waste of time and talent, while a perniciously bad film like *Friday the 13th* or *My Bloody Valentine* fuses a bizarre and destructive connection between sexuality and bloody awful death that can be hard to shake off and teaches nothing of value, coming very close to the structures, devices, and audience appeal of the most sick and violent pornography. Since the latter is the impression of horror films most people seem to have these days, it seems important to point out how many of the real classics of film history—*Vampyr*, for example—have been horror films, and to sketch out what the good ones did and still are doing. I would like to begin by offering a genre definition, sorting out horror from science-fiction, and go on from there to outline a pattern that is as common as that of the boy-girl-monster triangle, the remarkably consistent use of reflexive devices in the good horror film.

Stephen King has said that it is hard to imagine a more boring, profitless, and terminally academic pastime than that of discriminating between horror and science fiction.[4] It seems to me that we will never fully understand the horror film until we agree on a definition of the genre, and that the genre with which horror is most regularly confused is that of science fiction. Horror is, in the first place, the older literary form, with roots in folklore, mythology, the Gothic novel, and the work of Romantics from Coleridge and Mary Shelley to Poe; indeed, in literary terms it is fairly easy to conceptualize the difference between horror and science fiction in terms of the obvious differences between Henry James and H. G. Wells, or between H. P. Lovecraft and John Campbell, Jr. In film, however, the lines have proved much harder to draw, and this may have something to do with the role of the BEM, or bug-eyed monster, in the pulp science fiction magazines of the 1930s and 1940s. In most cases science fiction is cross-fertilized by imagination and scientific premise: what would happen if? What would happen if there were space travel, if cloning were practical, if time travel were voluntary, if there were parallel worlds, if robots could think, if a criminal could read minds, if parthenogenesis were practical? Largely because of the influence of Campbell, as editor of *Astounding*, writers were expected to back up their *ifs* with a reasonable amount of hard science and logical speculation. But one of the writers Campbell nurtured was A. E. Van Vogt, who perfected the tale of the space travelers who encounter the absolutely malevolent monster, and it became commonplace to refer to such pieces as science fiction, along with the horde of less original pieces in which a space voyage was hardly worth describing if it did not include some variety of extraterrestrial BEM. Science fiction provided a wide range of settings and nurturing environments for many frightening creatures, and it is out of that association of story elements that the present confusion seems to have come, particularly since the "Golden Age" pulps and the low-budget films of the 1950s drew on many of the same writers and appealed to much the same audience. But it seems to me that genres are determined not by plot elements but by attitudes toward plot elements. It is not adequate to say that it is a horror film if it has a monster in it, a science fiction film if it has a scientist. If that were the case, there would be no way to pigeonhole a film like *Frankenstein*, which strikes me as a fairly obvious example of horror, let alone a film like *Alien* that carefully follows the Van Vogt formula. To unscramble some of this, I wrote an article for *Dreamworks* in which I suggested that *The Day the Earth Stood Still* (directed by Robert Wise) was clearly a science fiction film while *The Thing From Another World* (directed by Christian Nyby with a good deal of input from Howard Hawks) was clearly a horror film, although both had essentially the same plot elements—encounters between the intelligent pilots of flying saucers and a complex of military, scientific, and civilian personnel—and both were made in 1951 in American studios during the Cold War. It seemed as good a test case as any:

> *The Day the Earth Stood Still* . . . is the story of a spaceman, Klaatu (Michael Rennie), who sets down his flying saucer in Washington, D.C. with the intention of putting Earth on notice: anything resembling nuclear violence will be punished by the obliteration of the planet, courtesy of a race of interstellar robot police. The spaceman has three forces to contend with: the army, which wants to destroy him; the scientists, who are willing to listen to him; and a woman (Patricia Neal) who understands and helps him. The central scientist (Sam Jaffe) is a kooky but open-minded and serious figure. Although it is suggested that earthlings understand violence better than most kinds of communication, they do respond to a nonviolent demonstration of Klaatu's power, and he does manage to deliver his message—perhaps at the expense of his life. The film's bias is

in favor of open-minded communication, personal integrity, nonviolence, science, and friendship. The major villain (Hugh Marlowe) is a man who values personal fame and power more than integrity and love; he is willing to turn Klaatu over to the army, which shoots first and asks questions later—even if it means losing Neal, his fiancee.

The Thing from Another World . . . is the story of a team of military men sent to an Arctic station at the request of its scientists, to investigate what turns out to be the crash of a flying saucer. The saucer's pilot (James Arness) is a blood-sucking vegetable that is described as intelligent but spends most of its time yelling and killing and leaving evidence of plans for conquest. The minor villain is a scientist (Robert Cornthwaite) who wants to communicate with the Thing rather than destroy it and who admires the alien race for its lack of sexual emotion. The Thing, however, has no interest in the scientist; and the human community (from which the scientist wishes to exclude himself), led by an efficient, hard-headed, and sexually active Captain (Kenneth Tobey), manages to electrocute the "super carrot." The film's bias is in favor of that friendly, witty, sexy, and professionally effective—Hawksian—human community, and opposed to the dark forces that lurk outside (the Thing as *Beowulf's* Grendel). The film also opposes the lack of a balanced professionalism (the scientist who becomes indifferent to the human community and whose professionalism approaches the fanatical, as opposed to the effective Captain and the klutzy but less seriously flawed reporter), and what was meant in that paranoid time by the term Communism (we are all one big vegetable or zombie with each cell equally conscious).

This is how the oppositions between these two movies stack up:

1. *Army vs. Scientists.* In both films the army and the scientists are in conflict with each other. The army sees the alien as a threatening invader to be defended against and, if necessary or possible, destroyed. The scientists see the alien as a visitor with superior knowledge, to be learned from and, if possible, joined. In *The Thing* the army is right and the scientist is an obsessive visionary who gets in the way of what obviously needs to be done. In *The Day* the scientists are right and the army is an impulsive force that is almost responsible for the end of the world (hardly a far-fetched perspective).

2. *Violence vs. Intelligence.* The Thing is nonverbal and destructive; Klaatu is articulate and would prefer to be nonviolent. The army, which meets violence with violence, is correct in *The Thing* and wrong in *The Day* because of the nature of the alien; but what I am suggesting here is that the alien has its nature because of each genre's implicit attitude toward the unknown. The curious scientist is a positive force in *The Day* and a negative force in *The Thing*, for the same reasons.

3. *Closing vs. Opening.* Both horror and science fiction open our sense of the possible (mummies can live, men can turn into wolves, Martians can visit) especially in terms of community (the Creature walks among

us). Most horror films are oriented toward the restoration of the status quo rather than toward any permanent opening. *The Day* is about man's opportunity to join an interstellar political system; it opens the community's boundaries and leaves them open. *The Thing* is about the expulsion of an intruder and ends with a warning to "watch the skies" in case more monsters show up; in other words, the community is opened against its will and attempts to reclose. What the horrified community has generally learned from the opening is to be on guard and that chaos can be repressed.

4. *Inhuman vs. Human.* Science fiction is open to the potential value of the inhuman: one can learn from it, take a trip with it (*Close Encounters*), include it in a larger sense of what is. Horror is fascinated by transmutations between human and inhuman (wolfmen, etc.), but the inhuman characteristics decisively mandate destruction. This can be rephrased as Uncivilized vs. Civilized or as Id vs. Superego, suggesting the way a horror film allows forbidden desire to find masked expression before it is destroyed by more decisive repression. . . .

5. *Communication vs. Silence.* This links most of the above. The Thing doesn't talk; Klaatu does. (Or: Romero's Living Dead are completely nonverbal, while the climax of *Close Encounters* is an exchange of languages.) What one can talk with, one can generally deal with. Communication is vital in *The Day*, absurd in *The Thing*. The opened community can be curious about and learn from the outsiders, while the closed community talks only among itself. Horror emphasizes the dread of knowing, the danger of curiosity, while science fiction emphasizes the danger and irresponsibility of the closed mind. Science fiction appeals to consciousness, horror to the unconscious.[5]

Horror and science fiction, then, are different because of their attitudes toward curiosity and the openness of systems, and comparable in that both tend to organize themselves around some confrontation between an unknown and a would-be knower. As a straightforward example of the pure, and great, science fiction film, I suggest *La Jetée*. Where a given film includes scientists, space travel, and monsters (as in *This Island Earth*, for instance), the important thing is to discover the dynamics of the situation, the attitude toward the question of discovery. In *The Fly*, as in *Frankenstein*, the vital elements are that the scientist and his creation are intimately interrelated and that the white-headed fly is destroyed rather than saved. When a scientist agrees that "there are things man is not meant to know," it is a safe bet that one is in the horror realm rather than that of science. In *Forbidden Planet*, which might at first appear a nearly perfect example of genre crossover, the Krell science, the brain booster, Robbie the Robot, and

the notion of humans' traveling in a flying saucer all seem to outw
the genre-perfect "monster from the Id" that the father/scientist
leashes during sleep. The moral of the story of the Krell monster and
the subsequent decision to destroy its world both fit explicitly into a
horror world-view, but it seems important that the robot (as one aspect
of Krell science) is integrated into the human crew and that the human
race is presented as on a positive evolutionary course. It is also significant that the scientist, by becoming conscious of his accountability for
the actions of his unconscious, denies the Krell monster and releases
himself and his daughter from their Oedipal nightmare. (He cannot
deny the monster without first accepting that it is *his* monster.) It
seems to me that, ultimately, *Forbidden Planet* is a "myth of human
adaptability," a phrase Joanna Russ has used to characterize science
fiction in contrast to fantasy and one that is substantially in agreement
with my notion of the perfectable, open community. *Alien*, on the
other hand, is emphatically a horror film, if for no other reason than
because the scientist is a soulless robot rather than an authentic visionary and because the humans are presented as trapped between an
efficient monster and a monstrously efficient military-industrial complex. The computer in *Alien*, who is called "Mother," is addressed as
"You bitch!" when she supports the company, protects the robot, and
takes her self-destruct program a bit too far; the monster is the "son"
of the "bitch." The threat behind all of these is an organization that
values military efficiency and heartless strength more than human life
and love, and in comparison with the power of that theme, the space
travel setting does not have much weight. In Robert Wise's *Star Trek*,
on the other hand, the relations between human love and curiosity,
and advanced computer technology, are integrated in a positive way,
and what begins as a story of a threat from outer space turns into a love
story in which a sexual and romantic apotheosis creates a new order of
being. It may be because Wise has such an obvious respect for the
well-ordered mechanism, the efficient script, the adult character, the
clean image, and the importance of honor that he is such a good
director of science fiction, just as his careful, respectful handling of the
romantic imagination allowed him to direct fine horror films for Val
Lewton, notably *The Curse of the Cat People*.

It may seem at this point as if I were arguing that science fiction is
emphatically the more positive and healthful genre, but what I am
really getting at is that science fiction and horror each promote growth
in different ways. By appealing to the conscious, to the spirit of
adventure, to the imaginative province of the medieval Romance, and

to the creative use of intelligent curiosity, science fiction allows us to explore our evolution and to begin the creation of the future, something it accomplishes both in cautionary tales of the dangers of technology and in adventurous celebrations of human capacity and resourcefulness. It opens the field of inquiry, the range of possible subjects, and leaves us open.

Where much science fiction is limited is in its sometime boyish sense of adventure, its tendency to extend into some hypothetical time and place the unexamined assumptions of the present culture (e.g. the patriarchy), and its relative lack of interest in the unconscious. *Star Wars*, for instance, strikes me as fundamentally not interesting on every level except that of its celebration of film technology; for the rest, it is simply a glorified Heinlein juvenile with a Zen gimmick that is about as deeply examined as the discovery that the Blob hates cold. Where science fiction stands or falls is often in the idea that supports the fiction and in how far the artist is willing to follow that idea. What *The Day the Earth Stood Still* shares with "Farewell to the Master" (the story on which it is based) is the idea that once man has passed a certain evolutionary level, it is technology that masters man; both story and movie, each in its own way, pursue this idea to logical conclusions. In the standard science fiction world of the story, which is organized around one gee-whiz daring boyish reporter, the emphasis is on the robot's invention of a device that recreates beings from sound recordings, and the startling discovery that Klaatu is the beloved pet of the robot, who is "the master." In the Cold War world of the movie, which has a much more interesting human story, the relevance of this conceit is made explicit in terms of the way man is forced to learn that he must submit to the authority of the robots because he has—without knowing it—already become the servant of nuclear technology. By this ingenious twist, the Wise film offers man the option of mastering the atomic bomb while it extends the essence of the story's original, chilling idea. And the same often applies to horror, because what distinguishes novels like *I Am Legend*, *Frankenstein*, and *Salem's Lot*, or films like *Don't Look Now*, *Dawn of the Dead*, and *The Last Wave*, is their pushing good ideas as far as possible. What *The Thing* does not remotely share with the story on which it is based, Campbell's "Who Goes There?", is an interesting idea. Even if both story and movie, in this case, explore the problem of the human community undermined by the presence of a monster, the monster in *The Thing* is fundamentally not interesting, merely a loud hulk, whereas the monster in "Who Goes There?" is a shape-shifter capable of ingesting and imitating every man and animal in the environment, a monster that threatens the notion of community so seriously that Hawks and Nyby apparently felt unable to handle it, with the result that they produced a Hawksian movie about witty people with a less complex but still dirty job to do. (John Carpenter's remake, which stuck more closely to the story but got lost in special effects, had different problems and, on the whole, less emotional resonance.)

The really scary films turn out to be those organized around a good idea, and while that may not be a scientific premise, it is often a well-struck nerve, a resonant psychological intersection, as is the case in fictions like *Heart of Darkness*, *The Turn of the Screw*, and *Franken-stein*, and films like *The Wolf Man*, *Mad Love*, *Peeping Tom*, *The Bride of Frankenstein* (which has little to do with the novel, despite its own claims at the start) and *Vampyr*. The direction in which the horror film leads its audience—into the unconscious and through the implications of evil and of dream—can prove beneficial to the audience. What the best horror films offer is another image of human perfectability, and not always through the exclusion of the unconscious impulse (since, after all, to go to a horror film is to let the inner monster, whether psychological or anti-social, find expression, no matter what happens at the end of the film). Sometimes what these films offer is integration with the horror, as in the example of *Mad Love*, or recon-ciliation with what is valuable in the horror, as in *Bride of Franken-stein*, or personal growth in a tragic context, as in *The Howling*. The effect of the good horror film is to show us what we are not comfortable seeing but need to look at anyway. As part of this intention to show us what we are comfortable ignoring, the horror film often turns re-flexive, reminding us that we are watching a movie, that we have chosen to have this nightmare experience, and that we must take responsibility for submitting to a category of illusion. This is, in a nutshell, the difference between *Psycho*, which implicates the audi-ence in the voyeurism of the mad killer, and almost every mad slasher movie that pretends to homage *Psycho* but has no interest in raising the consciousness of the audience and concentrates on techniques that reinforce illusion and defeat self-examination.

The first thing that happens in *Mad Love*, for instance, is that a fist smashes the glass on which the credits have been painted. This is followed by a brilliant series of image/reality fake-outs of which the most subtle is the use of Frances Drake (who plays the real Yvonne) in close shots of Yvonne's statue, which forces the audience to compare the image of Drake as Yvonne, which is supposed to be "real," and the image of Drake as the statue of Yvonne, which is supposed to be an "image"—the sort of joke that Keaton exploited so well at the end of *Sherlock Junior*. This builds to an identity-construct in which Dr. Gogol's identity fragments into a series of mirror images and climaxes in his inability to distinguish image from reality, which is the central feature of his madness. But of course the point of the opening fake-outs and a number of closely related tropes throughout the film is that the audience of *Mad Love* regularly confuses image and reality and is, to the extent that it responds to the story and believes its illusions, nearly mad—and all of that is tied securely, via a series of verbal and visual allusions, to *The Cabinet of Dr. Caligari* and its theme of the unreliability of surface impressions and the danger of a controlling illusion, whose political implications were certainly not lost on Karl Freund. To take a more familiar example, the first line in *King Kong* is "Is this the moving picture ship?", and the finest irony in the film is that Denham starts out to make a movie, decides instead to bring the monster home (i.e., creates not film but theater), and is reproached by the audience—while the curtains are still closed—because they have expected to see a movie, i.e. to really "see something." For *Kong*'s audience to smile knowingly at this remark—Lady, are you going to see something!—And it's not a movie, it's real!—is to be brought suddenly up against the fact that *Kong*'s audience is seeing a movie and that all this is not real. This elegant twist is supported by a labyrinth of authorially self-conscious in-jokes whereby the screenwriter, Ruth Rose, and her husband, Ernest B. Schoedsack, together with Merian C. Cooper, set up Ann Darrow, Jack Driscoll, and Carl Denham, respectively, as their surrogates who are attempting to make a movie that would satisfy those who felt that adventure films ought to have a love interest—which is precisely what the filmmakers, irritated at the reception of *Chang* and *Rango*, were doing in *Kong*—all of that complicated by the fact that Rose and Schoedsack had met and fallen in love while on an expeditionary ship whose name is very like that used in *Kong*. The audience of 1933 would not have gotten most of these jokes, though they might have remembered *Chang* and so might have seen themselves in the New York audience or in the images of the producers alluded to at the start, but they would certainly have been aware of the movie/theater dichotomy that informs Denham's turn-around.

These are only two examples from the 1930s, and it is possible to come up with examples from virtually any decade or industry. Even a wretched knife-and-sex picture like *He Knows You're Alone*, which came out last year, opens with a young woman's being stabbed through the back of her theater seat while unwillingly watching a movie in which a young woman is threatened by a psychopathic killer; even *Friday the 13th* plays a lot of games (games that are extended and complicated in the superior Parts 2 and 3) with dreams and the fulfillment of dreams, as does *Halloween II*—a film that is almost entirely organized around the implications of the song that runs under the closing credits, "Mister Sandman, bring me a dream; / Make him the cutest that I've ever seen." (And then: "please turn on your magic beam"!) My favorite example from the 1940s is *The Mummy's Ghost*, in which not even the priest can believe that "Kharis—still *lives*?", in which a student suggests to his obsessed professor that "maybe that was a man made up as a mummy," and in which a museum guard ignores an accurate preview of his own death that presents itself as a silly radio mystery. There was less of this sort of thing in the 1950s, which was a bad period for self-consciousness in the first place and one in which Hollywood was particularly interested in selling illusions, but there were some reflexive elements in *House of Wax, The 5,000 Fingers of Dr. T., The Invasion of the Body Snatchers*, and one of the greatest of all horror films, the British *Peeping Tom*; it should also be remembered that *Vertigo* and to a lesser extent *Rear Window* are constructed very like horror films (even though both are mysteries; *Psycho* poses similar problems) and are centrally concerned with the problem of the image and its relation to the real world, each of which is presented as a category of obsession. It is these Hitchcock films, together with Powell's *Peeping Tom*, that most prefigure the labyrinthine reflexivity of such 1960s horror films as *Targets* and *Kwaidan*. The 1970s and early 1980s have already been discussed at some length, so I would like to close with two particularly arresting reflexive images, one from Dreyer's *Vampyr* and one from De Palma's *Blow Out*.

It is not necessary for a horror film to have a transcendental or even a dream element. There are horror stories that are not ghost stories and horror stories that are not psychologically oriented. It seems as if there are three sub-categories of the genre: 1) monster stories, 2) supernatural stories, and 3) psychosis stories. The present knife-and-sex spinoff is an unfortunate but apt example of the psychosis story; more fortunate examples include *Peeping Tom* and *Psycho*. *King Kong* is a straightforward monster story, while *Vampyr* is a monster story with strong supernatural elements. *The Last Wave* is supernatural but has no monsters. The means by and ends to which consciousness is raised in the horror film depend to a certain extent on which of these sub-categories is involved, and in *Vampyr* the notion of the film as dream is inseparable from its view of the night world haunted by supernatural agencies. *Vampyr* is about light and shadows, about categories of illusion and revelation, and its climax comes when the central protagonist, David Gray, gives up some of his blood and has two dreams, the first of which is an accurate warning of a forced suicide and the second of which presents him to himself as trapped—dead yet sentient—in a coffin whose window first is compared to and then actually becomes the rectangle of the movie screen; what this does is to suggest to the audience that it is entombed in a dark room whose window is the image, and that the whole film is a dream or image field whose limits and dangers are only now becoming clear. In a paradoxical way, this makes the horrors real as it makes the film accountable for presenting an illusion. At the very least it makes the audience conscious of submitting to a dream field, a willing suspension of belief that results, as I have argued elsewhere, in an all-the-more-compelling trap of belief, because there is no innocent way to dismiss the artwork as an illusion once it has presented itself as being aware of being an illusion.[7]

Blow Out, which starts as a psychosis story and turns quickly into a paranoia film about the evils of Watergate, is not interested in metaphysics and has little to say about dreams or shadows, but it is much more clearly focused on the ethics of self-consciousness than either of the films on which it is modeled (*Blow Up* and *The Conversation*) and is in its own way as serious about the problem of knowledge and illusion as *Vampyr*. It opens with a terrible sequence from a bad horror film about a slasher in a girl's dormitory; it turns out that the protagonist of *Blow Out* is a sound engineer who needs a good scream to complete this sequence which, we discover, he is helping to edit. Eventually he becomes involved in a complicated murder-and-politics story, falls in love with a prostitute who is entangled in that intrigue, wires her for sound so that he can save her life and capture the bad guy, and loses his entire library of sound effects when the bad guy invades his territory with a bulk eraser. What happens is that he is too late to save the woman; all he has left of her is the tape of her dying screams. In the final seconds of the film, we see the protagonist again editing the bad horror film; we realize that he has not told the authorities what he knows, because he knows that would change nothing. Then comes the moment when the girl in the bad film screams, and we recognize the scream as that of the dying heroine. In that moment *Blow Out* becomes a real horror film, setting itself in relation to—and judging—the category of illusion represented by the dumb slasher movie, absolutely scaring the hell out of the audience while shifting reality gears, and tackling the whole problem of action and guilt in contemporary America, disillusioned from its idealism, and therefore not realistic but helpless, and so prey to the illusion of escapism—whereas the rest of the point is of course that there is no escape from politics any more than there is a way to forget who is screaming and under what circumstances. It becomes a horror film that by critiquing its own levels of illusion addresses the reality of horror—because, like all great horror films, its terrible message and unpleasant imagery are meant not to destroy us but to show us something that we need to see.

3
Subversive Play:
Fantasy in Robbe-Grillet's Films

Ben Stoltzfus

Robbe-Grillet says that most of his efforts these days are directed toward revealing the ludic structures in life and art. He believes that living and writing can be compared to a game of bridge whose rules are established, but whose moves allow for certain expressions of freedom. He believes that the world is like a deck of cards, with neither depth nor a priori meaning; that reality, like the smooth surface of the queen of hearts, or the queen of spades, is flat, and that man has to invent his life in accordance with this flatness, with no Platonic Ideal, no religious essence, and no human nature to guide his choices.[1]

The role of the artist, says Robbe-Grillet, is not to decipher the secret correspondences of nature, as Baudelaire did, or the word of God, as advocated by Claudel, or the dark mysteries of self in the manner of Edgar Allan Poe. The role of the artist, he says, is to construct a work of art whose formal beauty also rivals, challenges, and subverts the ideology of society. To fulfill this role, the artist must play with the language, the images, and the myths of his culture in order to expose the arbitrariness of all values.

This subversion functions simultaneously on two levels. The first, which is linguistic, takes its cues from Joyce, Roussel, and the Russian formalists, who maintain that reflexive art always draws our attention to its own internal self-regulating machinery. On this level, the language of art is self-contained and non-mimetic, and Robbe-Grillet's films, like his fiction, have a high degree of autonomy. Certainly, the twelve generative themes of the film *L'Eden et après* (*Eden and After*), in a general way, can be compared to the serialism in Schoenberg's dodecaphonic music. However, unlike music, film, because it always uses images organized in a certain order, provides bridges to reality—links with the world beyond art's formal arrangements. A film, no matter how autonomous it strives to be, as long as it uses actors and places, is, inevitably, to some degree mimetic.

The fact is that, contrary to the assertions of certain commentators, these two levels—autonomy and mimesis—are not mutually exclusive. Thus, Robbe-Grillet's preoccupation with the ring of language in his fiction or the resonance of sounds and images in his films does not exclude a semantic horizon against which his *parole* as an artist necessarily plays (see figure 1.). The word *parole* signifies the

Fig. 1. "Seascape," *Glissements progressifs du plaisir*, 1974

artist's manipulation of *langue*, i.e., language, such as English or Russian, or the language of the cinema we all, more or less, understand. However, in order to please the public, films must not violate society's codes. Thus, language systems tend to generate and reproduce the encoded values of a ruling class. This cultural horizon which makes the public happy, is, as a rule, made up of stereotypes, clichés, the ready-made, arbitrary notions that are perpetuated as self-evident truths for the sake, it is said, of the order, stability, and good of the majority. While the actual forces at work are much more complex than this brief summary of them, the general opposition between the *parole* of the self and the *langue* of the system is, it seems to me, correct. Structuralists like Roland Barthes assert that all cultural values are encoded in language and that, therefore, as we learn our mother tongue, we unconsciously assimilate the ideology of the culture in which we grow up.[2]

The dominant class, in order to perpetuate itself, will therefore claim that its values and beliefs are God-given, natural, and immutable. This is the semantic horizon against which Robbe-Grillet projects his films. He takes units of establishment ideology and subverts them through reversal, exaggeration, and distortion. This distortion, this estrangement from the familiar, can operate on the formal level as the "defamiliarization" advocated by Shklovsky. It also satisfies Eric

Rabkin's definition of the fantastic, a reversal which affects the viewer's perspectives within a single pictorial world. The fantastic thus becomes that special quality that defines fantasy as a genre.[3] On the mimetic, socio-political level, Robbe-Grillet's sado-erotic images, by exteriorizing the sexuality of the unconscious, can be compared to Brecht's "alienation effect," whose purpose goes beyond pleasure into the didactic. However, in Robbe-Grillet's case, the desire to instruct the audience is not concerned so much with tragedy as it is with parody and subversion.

Robbe-Grillet plays with cultural myths—with the violence and eroticism of today's world—in ways that become fantastic—fantastic because his ludic endeavors exaggerate reality while aiming at reversal. His images violate normative codes even as diegesis turns plausibility and verisimilitude upside down. His fantastic works are thus as parodic and subversive as, for instance, Carroll's, Dodgson's, and MacDonald's. MacDonald stood theology on its head, Carroll reversed the fundamental scientific tenets of his day, poking fun at history and religion, while Morris mocked religion and science. The fantastic, as practiced by these three writers, Rabkin points out, is important, because it depends entirely on reality for its existence (*FIL*, p. 28). Subversion is possible because reality is so securely fixed.

"The Crucifixion," from the film *Le Jeu avec le feu* (*Playing With Fire*), is fantastic because its signifiers give us the 180 degree reversal that contradicts the ground rules of Christianity (*FIL*, p. 12). The body of Christ has been replaced by the body of a naked woman (figure 2).

Fig. 2. "The Crucifixion," *Le Jeu avec le feu*, 1975

This substitution violates one of the West's most sacred rites. It is an attack on the premises of religious belief. On the denotative level, were it not for these beliefs, we would simply have a naked woman with her arms outstretched. But the connotations of this image, with the blood and the crown of thorns, are too strong. It evokes twenty centuries of religious ritual, but not in terms of veneration or Christian fervor. The cross, like the flag, is such a highly charged symbol, that unless we treat it with respect, we are likely to arouse the ire of those we have offended. What is happening? I would suggest that because we have not had a female crucifixion and two thousand years of religious history to support a female Godhead, or an elaborate feminist doctrine to reinforce the trinity, the cult, and mystery of a matriarchal church, that this image is perceived as sacrilegious. We have all been taught that Christ died in order to redeem man's sins, that His crucifixion was an act of love, that God sacrificed His only son, and so on. These tenets are familiar. However, the woman in this image tends to negate this supportive baggage. She is not the clothed Virgin wearing a blue veil and holding the infant Jesus. My guess is that this violation of religious taboo shocks the pious and amuses the ungodly. In either case, the effect is subversive because it replaces the religious code with a sadoerotic code linked to man's subsconscious and the desires that inhabit the Freudian *Id*. With this image, Robbe-Grillet also exteriorizes the mythic degradation of woman, man's treatment of her as an object—her reification—even while idealizing her sacrificial role. The myth of woman has, in fact, always been dual: she is debased on the one hand, venerated on the other. This crucifixion incorporates the two traditions, but reversed, and that is why it both shocks and amuses: it forces us to reevaluate the tradition it denotes as well as the myths it connotes. It is, in essence, fantastic.

This reversal of convention is a form of play which Robbe-Grillet compares to a door playing on its hinges, swinging back and forth between the inside and the outside, between one thesis and its antithesis.[4] To play with the sacred images and myths of the establishment is to demonstrate the total freedom of the artist vis-à-vis his culture, while simultaneously subverting its authority. If, as the structuralists maintain, man's perception of himself and the world is determined by language and the values of the socio-political power structure in which he lives, then the artist who wishes to reform a bourgeois order or a socialist order, or any order, but who cannot, because the *langue* he speaks inevitably reflects the codes of that system, then the artist must invent a *parole* with which to circumvent accepted "order" by replacing it with organized "disorder." One way to do this is to reassemble establishment values, thereby uncovering and subverting their arbitrary base. Robbe-Grillet refers to this endeavor as play.

Le Jeu avec le feu is a film that "plays with fire" precisely because it strikes out against the accepted standards of good taste and public morality. It bends the "bars," so to speak, of the "prison-house of language" so that a different narrative voice may emerge from the generative cell—the secret room of the artist's imagination. This secret room is also the metaphoric cell in which the captive self strives to break the restraints of convention. In order to free language from convention or repression, Robbe-Grillet plays with forbidden lusts and hidden faces, striving to convert alienation into freedom, insight, and pleasure. He displays censored faces in his films, staging oneiric dramas in that space where the conflict between illicit desire and the symbols of the establishment come together.

Since language, like this chained lovely from *L'Eden et après* (figure 3) is shackled by convention, it or she has to submit to the

Fig. 3. "Rosy Crucifixion," *L'Eden et après*, 1971

author's designs. Accordingly, in Robbe-Grillet's films, modesty is flaunted, images are exaggerated, plausibility is destroyed, cultural ideology is whipped, taboos on incest are violated, social codes are sacrificed, piety is crucified, stereotypes are burned. The woman's body, as a metaphor for language, is deformed, maimed, injected, experimented on. It is a miracle she/it survives, and she/it does, like a phoenix rising from the ashes of its own destruction. However, because a naked woman may also signify desire, it might be useful to look at ways in which she represents relations between ideology and the fantastic. The naked woman is, in fact, a formal link between repressed sexuality and the libido's will toward pleasure.

In discussing the fantastic, Todorov does not address himself to repression and desire. Jean Bellemin-Noël, however, defines the fantastic as exactly that realm in which the question of the unconscious emerges.[5] Rosemary Jackson, like Bellemin-Noël, concludes that the formal and thematic features of fantastic art are determined by our attempt to find a language for desire.[6] Fantasies, therefore, if Freud is right, probably express libidinal drives toward pleasure, the libido being that part of the self which wrestles with the reality principle. The libido, insomuch as it is the locus of desire, and with pleasure as its goal, constantly strives to overcome the restraints of reality. In reflexive art, it is the restraints of realism that are constantly being challenged. Such art is subversive because it has different pleasures in mind.

The film *Glissements progressifs du plaisir* (*Progressive Slippages of Pleasure*) is nothing less than a triumph of the *id*, a victory of the pleasure principle over the representatives of law and order, the "repressive" types of establishment *superego* who symbolize authority.[7] Alice, who is imprisoned in a cell in a nunnery for murdering Nora, one by one seduces the police inspector, the priest, her lawyer, and the judge, all of whom succumb to her charms. In due course, the film ends with an identical second murder, exactly where it began, illustrating Robbe-Grillet's cyclical labyrinth motif, while simultaneously corrupting its narrative realism. The dungeon cell is a clichéd setting in which the *id* of pleasure and disorder (the naked woman) confronts the *superego* of establishment order and reality (the nun) (figure 4). The naked woman, once more, signifies the body of

Fig. 4. "In the Nunnery," *Glissements progressifs du plaisir*, 1974

the text, i.e., language, as well as the image of subconscious desire. As such, she has to submit to Robbe-Grillet's ritual violence: she is cut, burned, injected, and bled. But Robbe-Grillet's tortures, like the Marquis de Sade's, are always organized, methodical, detailed, and planned. Both men use the wrong side of words, the wrong side of girls, the wrong side of things. And it is precisely because ideology is securely fixed that this reversal has meaning.[8] To play with sex and violence is to subvert and at the same time to reinvent reality. An artist interested in fantasy and play derives his strength, his freedom, and his pleasure from this creative act.

Another scene, once again from *Le Jeu avec le feu*, in many ways reminiscent of Manet's *Le Déjeuner sur l'herbe*, and as subversive, depicts three men and the body of a beautiful girl lying naked in an open coffin (figure 5). Robbe-Grillet's anarchy here touches on yet

Fig. 5. "The Wake," *Le Jeu avec le feu*, 1975

another taboo—necrophilia. Since the realism of all these images belies the supernatural, the marvelous, the uncanny, or the hesitation between credulity and disbelief that, for Todorov, determine the fantastic,[9] it may be useful to explore further the nature of the fantastic reversal occuring in these images. They are indeed real, but their frequency and implausibility relegates them to an impossible world where, as W. R. Irwin would say, Robbe-Grillet plays impossible games.[10] However, these games are not frivolous, as Irwin maintains, but the very stuff of the imagination from which art derives its legitimacy (*GI*, p. 197). It may be appropriate, therefore, to think of Robbe-Grillet's fantasies, not as a genre, as I suggested earlier, but as a mode situated somewhere between formalism and mimesis. His fantasies assert that what they are telling is real, and they rely on the conventions of realistic cinema to do so, but they proceed to undo that assumption of realism by dramatizing the impossible or, at the very least, the implausible.

The film *L'Homme qui ment* (*The Man Who Lies*) is another such dramatization of the impossible. It opens with a man who is being pursued through the woods by soldiers. The man is shot and "killed" several times, but he does not die. He makes his way to a village claiming he is Boris Varissa, but we learn that Varissa is dead. He says he has a message from Jean Robin, his friend in the resistance, who was "killed" by the enemy, but Jean Robin shoots the impostor who has been trying to seduce the three women living in the big house on the edge of town. Our hero lies, narrates, imagines, and dreams resistance episodes, each one more implausible than the other. His narrative thickens, undermines reality, bifurcates. Each scene and each episode give the spectator a semblance of truth that is subsequently denied—a proliferation of meaning that fragments reality into a thousand reflecting surfaces.

The actor in this tragicomedy is, in essence, a Don Juan character who creates his role from one moment to the next, a character with no past and no future, who is simply there, in the Heideggerian sense, on stage, playing his imaginary identities in an existential context of free choice. As a new mythical Don Juan, he incarnates the same baroque characteristics that fascinated Molière: theatricality, disguise, role-playing, and a taste for games. However, a person in disguise is, no doubt, always a comedian, and his role is one of constant metamorphosis. If Don Juan has no single identity, he assumes multiple ones. His essence is in gesture and transference, is in the theatricality of change, and he lies in order to seduce reality. In fact, disguise, even more than seduction, is Don Juan's real achievement. He, like art, is a lie: he is not what he seems to be—but he is a metaphor for a cinematic discourse in search of itself, in search of meaning. His act intensifies the artifice—it is a bow to fantasy.

The actor-protagonist arrives at the house to find three women playing a game of blind-man's buff. He tries to seduce them, while they, in turn, try to find out who he is. All are deceived, as the stranger in the women's midst works very hard to project an essence that might please them. Each character's presence is dramatized by photos, paintings, mirrors, frames, windows, and doorways, always evolving through a complex décor of mirror surfaces that force us to deny reality by reflecting unceasingly on these self-duplicating images of illusion (figure 6). A mirror produces distance, establishing new space where

Fig. 6. "Varissa's 'Death',"
L'Homme qui ment, 1968

notions of self undergo radical change. The mirror provides versions of self transformed into another. It suggests the instability of the real on either side of the looking glass. However, to be blindfolded and to touch a mirror is not only not to see one's reflection, it is not to know whether the cold, smooth surface is a mirror, a window, or a picture—surfaces that provide transitions to other unstable signifying forms. In fantasy, this fragmentation of reality and character also deforms the language of a unified, rational self.

Most versions of the double, as with the Varissa-Robin doubling in *L'Homme qui ment*, end in madness, suicide, or death, since the divided subject cannot be united with the other without ceasing to be. Varissa's death and resurrection are fantastic precisely because they defy realism. However, these events are fantastic only if pursued on the mimetic level. Since all the mirroring surfaces and all the narrative implausibilities deny reality, these images, as signifiers, have no mimetic relevance. They are, instead, signs of a discourse commenting on itself. (See figure 7.) A film sequence that seems fantastic on the

Fig. 7. "Triple Mirror," *Trans-Europ-Express*, 1966

referential level becomes, on the formal level, as with the previous images of naked women, no more than a metaphoric montage referring us to the autonomy of the text. On the realistic level we do indeed seem to have the reversal, the impossible game, and the necessary hesitation between the natural and the supernatural that Rabkin, Irwin, and Todorov refer to. After all, dead people do not run and, if such games were possible, then, surely, the supernatural would have to intervene. However, to interpret the film on a realistic level is indeed to view it simplistically. This film assumes meaning only when the images reverse themselves, denying realism, plunging us into the fantasy of the imagination where the images pursue spontaneous, oneiric metamorphoses. Such transitions, as Rosemary Jackson notes, constitute a "manifest unreality" (*FLS*, p. 34). And Robbe-Grillet, by assembling and juxtaposing units of reality in unexpected, contradictory, and apparently impossible ways, draws our attention to the *process* of representation. Thus, by foregrounding its own signifying practices, the fantastic betrays reality. The real is transformed into a category—the semantic horizon referred to earlier—which art, in fantastic ways, is in the *process* of transforming.

The Varissa-Robin duality defies the venerated concept of the unity of character which, in the Western world, is an ideological concept that for centuries has dominated the realism of classical theater and realistic art. However, this attack on the unity of character is part of a larger subversion. It reflects the modern trend toward desacralization and demythification, manifest on the formal level in achronology, fragmentation, and discontinuity, and on the mimetic level, as a challenge to cherished notions of myth, religion, self, and identity.

Another aspect of this subversion is Robbe-Grillet's attack on the unity of narration. He uses categories of the subconscious as generative themes in order to undermine realism and destroy plausibility. In the film *Trans-Europ-Express*, the names of three magazines announce the sequence. The title of the film connotes *Fear, Sex,* and *Death,* themes that are elaborated and exploited from beginning to end. For instance, the word "Trans" slips into "transes" ("fears" in French). "Europ," the Paris to Antwerp train, becomes *Europe,* a girlie magazine. *Express* is simultaneously the train and the name of a newsmagazine, featuring "L'Homme qui est mort quatre fois" ("The Man Who Died Four Times"). Familiar representations of reality and stereotyped behavior patterns are subverted as the mock treatment of the love episodes between a make-believe drug runner and a make-believe prostitute counters the theme of "heroic love" in the accompanying music of *La Traviata.* The slippage between subsequent images of fear, eroticism, and violence generated by the words and themes of the film's title—a slippage that is transported and accelerated by the very movement of the train—links the continuously shifting associations, like the high-speed shots of the rails converging and separating, as though they too were commenting on the narrative (which they are). This juxtaposition of thematic imagery and this metonymy (because the transitions are abrupt, without the metaphoric niceties of fade-in or fade-out) are structured by the words in the title.

Cinematic language may parallel reality and the text may seem to reflect only itself, but it is not indifferent to fear, clichéd eroticism, and death—external generators with which to structure the internal machinery of the text. Self-reflexive art, to the extent that it emphasizes the signifier at the expense of the signified, draws us into the fantastic through "reversal" and "subversion." Whether we use Rabkin's or Jackson's term to define this process, such films devalue conventional art by giving us experimental forms in which reality is so distorted that it denies mimesis. Robbe-Grillet believes that this freedom to deform, this play, as Nietzsche would say, is the only way of coping with great tasks. Hegel once said that play, in its indifference and frivolity, was at the same time the most sublime seriousness and the uniquely true.

In his films, Robbe-Grillet goes about playing with stereotyped images, subverting and reversing their roles and, by revealing the backside of things, he exposes them as repressed images of the subconscious. Like Dali's paintings, they have an undeniable realism, but it is the oneiric realism of fear and desire. This realism becomes fantastic, not because the stories are fairy tales, or because they occur on other planets, but because they devalue the currency of the everyday. Robbe-Grillet's doubling and tripling of characters, his reversals in chronology, his implausible sequences—devices that undermine objective realism—not only contradict Christian Metz's "grande syntagmatique," i.e., conventional cinematic storytelling, but also the belief that history has purpose or that time-space is linear. However, Robbe-Grillet's cinema is fantastic, or chaotic, or incomprehensible only for viewers trapped within the system of traditional narrative ideology. For those attuned to the new serialism in reflexive art, the implausibilities are perfectly coherent and the alleged disorder quite intelligible. The moment of hesitation that Todorov claims for the fantastic, as far as Robbe-Grillet's films are concerned, exists only for those who hesitate between a film's mimetic and self-reflexive levels. Although the form may seem fantastic, the content is subversive and therefore identifiably real. Picasso once said, apropos of *Guernica*, that art was a weapon to use against the enemy. The strident, distorted forms of this famous painting, denouncing Franco's bombing of a Basque town, give us images of suffering and protest, even as Picasso deforms conventional pictorial realism. The images slip into the grotesque, but how else is the artist's *parole* to strike out against a mutilating and dehumanizing ideology? Robbe-Grillet's films, unlike *Guernica*, are not tragic; nevertheless, their subversive and parodic nature attacks the very basis of contemporary myths concerning human nature and essentialist psychology. The fantastic images with which he plays mirror language and the subconscious, but it is life itself he would reform.

4

The Virginity of Astronauts:
Sex and the Science Fiction Film

Vivian Sobchack

Human biological sexuality and women as figures of its representation
have been "repressed" in the male-dominated, action-oriented narratives of most American science fiction films from the 1950s to the
present. Semiotically linked, insofar as each in our culture is conven-
tionally reversible and may stand as a signifier for the other, sex and
women and the significant connection between them is denied all but a
ghostly presence in the genre. It is as if such a potent semiotic relation
poses a threat to the cool reason and male comraderie necessary to the
conquest of space, the defeat of mutant monsters and alien invasions,
and the corporate development and exploitation of science and technology. Thus, biological sexuality and women are often absent from
science fiction film narratives, and when they do turn up they tend to
be disaffiliated from each other, stripped of their cultural significance
as a semiotic relation, carefully separated from each other so that
biological sexuality is not linked to human women and human women
are not perceived as sexual.

More than any other American film genre, then, science fiction
denies human eroticism and libido a traditional narrative representation and expression. Sex and the science fiction film is, therefore, a
negative topic. It points to a major absence in the genre, rather than a
minimal presence. It surrounds a purposeful—if unconscious—repression. And it also suggests that such a marked—that is, noticeable—
absence at the narrative level has left its trace, carved out its hollow,
elsewhere in the films. Usual critical discourse, however, is not tuned
to the analysis of negatives, of absences, of traces left by repression.
Generally, it looks at what is there, at what is represented as present.
Psychoanalysis, on the other hand, looks at what is there but represented as absent. As a mode of critical investigation that differs in
focus and direction from other kinds of critical analysis, psychoanaly-

sis, Michel Foucault tells us, "points directly . . . not towards that which must be rendered gradually more explicit by the progressive illumination of the implicit, but towards what is there and yet is hidden, towards what exists with the mute solidity of a thing, of a text closed in upon itself, or of a blank space in a visible text."[1] A psychoanalytic approach to the topic of sex and the science fiction film would therefore seem an appropriate way to redeem the repressed to the realm of critical discourse and to explore its significance to the genre as a represented absence. Borrowing upon the psychoanalytic techniques of free association and dream analysis, such an approach should allow us to see how human sexuality and women return to the science fiction narrative in displaced and condensed forms, in an emotionally-charged imagery and syntax that bears relation to the cryptic but coherent language of dream. And it should also help us to understand how—in their repressed and potent combination as a sign evoking male fear and desire—sex and women figure significantly, if covertly, in shaping the basic structure of the genre and initiating its major themes.

Let us return to what is represented as present in American science fiction films. (I should point out here that my recurrent cultural qualification is less patriotic than indicative of some particular conflicts localized in the American psyche and centered around the opposition of biology and technology. Science fiction films from other countries do not seem to base themselves in a semiotic system in which biological reproduction and the female are linked as a sign opposed to the sign constituted by linking technological production to the male.) Certainly, at the overt level of plot and narrative, there are some human sexual dramas in the American films of the genre and there are some erotically-articulated women. Human heterosexual relations are relatively important to the development of plot and narrative in *Forbidden Planet*, *The Incredible Shrinking Man*, *Colossus: The Forbin Project*, and *The Stepford Wives*. Becky, in *Invasion of the Body Snatchers*, immediately comes to mind as a female character who functions centrally and erotically. But these are exceptions. For the most part, human heterosexual relations in the science fiction film are tepid—more obligatory than steamy. Indeed, those few science fiction films which deal overtly with sex and the sexuality of human women—their erotic appeal and their procreative function—generally do so outside the articulated context of human heterosexuality and within that of racial and spatial miscegenation. Hence we have not only films like *I Married a Monster from Outer Space* and *Mars Needs Women*, but also films like *The World, the Flesh, and the Devil* and *Demon Seed*. Surely, in these latter two films, the titles say it all. Women who are erotically attractive or biologically fertile are subject only to an alien embrace—in the one instance (however liberal the film's surface message) to a black male, and in the other to a bronzed machine.

Generally, then, in the various overt dramas of science fiction film, the nature and function of human heterosexuality are either muted or transformed. While there are numerous boy-meets-girl encounters across the galaxy and the genre, they tend to be chaste and safe in their dramatization and peripheral to narrative concerns—no matter when the films were made. One gets the feeling that they are included either to satisfy the vague demands of formula or to answer the unspoken charges of homosexuality which echo around the edges of the genre. Science fiction films are full of sexually empty relations and empty of sexually full ones. In concert with this narrative de-emphasis on human sexuality and women, biological sexual functions—intercourse and reproduction—are avoided in their human manifestations and, instead, displaced onto mutant and alien life forms and into technological activity. In this way, women characters are narratively deprived of any problematic connection with sexuality. They rarely exist in the films to "be made" or "to make," as sexual objects or as sexual subjects. Think, for example, of the chaste "seduction" of Alta in *Forbidden Planet*, so safe that it is charming rather than erotically compelling. The narrative denotes a sexual encounter, but the imagery denies it. Alta's lack of passionate response to Lieutenant Farman's cheerfully comic "kissing lesson" looks no different than her supposedly passionate response to Commander Adams. And the men do not seem particularly aroused either. Thus, even in a film in which male rivalry between prospective suitors and between father and lover are central to the plot, sexuality and eroticism are absent at the level of human representation. They are drained from the female character and missing from the male characters as well—despite the lip service they are given in the ritual wisecracking and wooden flirtations common to such SF film encounters.

Throughout the genre, human female biological difference from the male is literally covered up. (Women represented as alien, however, are often scantily and sexily-clad.) The 1950s films are peopled by women restrained by shirtwaist dresses, Peter Pan collars, and occasional lab coats. Again, the only exception that comes immediately to mind is Becky in *Invasion of the Body Snatchers*—her strapless dresses and push-up bra a bold declaration of sexuality which perhaps forces the script to put her to sleep and turn her into a pod. Indeed, a telling echo of Becky occurs in a brief sequence in *It Came From Outer Space*, where the alien and threatening quality of female sexuality appears in the transformation of the amateur scientist/hero's girl-friend. In her normal state, her clothes are unrevealing and indicate an unerotic and sensible partner for rational John Putnam. However, when her body is borrowed and "taken over" by the stranded aliens, she appears against a barren hill in a black, strapless evening dress—a chiffon scarf fluttering in some chill and ill-begotten wind. She has literally become the alien—and the marker of that transformation is her sexually provocative clothing (which has no logical source in the narrative) and its revelation of her as a woman. With rare exception, then, female biological difference is deemphasized in the films. The question it asks, the response it demands, the need and desire it evokes in the male are hidden and defused by sensible and functional attire, by rational occupations, and by the unprovocative, unquestioning, "ful-filled" sexuality of a peripheral and occasional wife and mother.

This diffusion of difference, this visual and narrative "coding" of women in the science fiction film as not only peripheral but also asexual, might seem to be a function of the chronological and cultural context in which the films were made. We tend to think of the 1950s as conservative, as lived in some mythic miasma of unremarkable nor-mality, as cautious and gray, as neutral and neutered. It bears re-membrance, however, that the 1950s were also the time of Marilyn Monroe—of the image of blond sexuality, of female fullness and fertility. Although she appeared in *film noir*, thriller, musical and western, Marilyn never made a science fiction film. (One can hardly count *Monkey Business*.) Indeed, it is by virtue of its patent absurdity that the idea is so wonderfully appealing. Whether in the 1950s or now, the genre could not have possibly contained her body, and she would have destroyed the impact and iconic potency of any technological marvel or activity, of any alien being or threat, simply by the awful truth of her visual presence. That female body, those full breasts and rounded belly, that amplitude and plenitude of flesh, would have distracted both male characters and narrative alike from their generic course. Why build machines when that biological marvel that is the female body mocks the male desire for autonomous creation and demands babies? Why get one's rockets off when that body invites an earthbound penetration and offers the deep space and infinitude of the womb? And why fear alien invasion and destruction when that alien is clearly here and already triumphant—in the awesome body of the Woman, that different body of the Other. Such a monumental female screen presence as Marilyn could only stop the genre in its narrative tracks and expose the imitative function of technological production, space travel, and alien encounters—their structural and visual mimicry of biological intercourse and birth, of impregnation and reproduction.

The deemphasis on human female sexuality in the science fiction film, then, is not limited to a particular period, but rather seems particular to the genre—at least sufficient if not necessary. Although less obvious than in the 1950s films, this generic cover-up of biological difference is still present in recent films which feature central and narratively active female characters. Women are sexually defused and made safe and unthreatening by costume, occupation, social position, and attitude—or they are sexually confused with their male counterparts and narratively substituted for them. Princess Leia of *Star Wars* and Ripley of *Alien* exemplify these alternatives which both serve the same repressive ends—the disaffiliation of women and sexuality and its corollary, the disguise of biological difference. For all her aristocratic presence as a princess, Leia is also represented as one of the boys. Whatever her narrative relations with Han Solo, her tough and wisecracking character is not about to let her tightly-coiled hair down nor expose her female flesh. It is only against her will that Leia wears the scanty costume of a harem slave in *Return of the Jedi*. And it is not Han Solo, but Jabba the Hutt—an alien—for whom she stands as an unwilling erotic sign. She is simultaneously protected and desexed by her social position (princesses are to fight for, not to sleep with) and by her acerbic and pragmatically critical attitude. While she might be compared in some ways to the Hawksian heroine, who through true grit and stoicism gains acceptance by a male community, Carrie Fisher certainly has none of the erotic presence of a Lauren Bacall. Leia, then, is sexually defused and it seems safe to presume that no matter how involved she gets with Han Solo in episodes to come, she will still come off as chaste as her white robes.

Ripley in *Alien*, however, is subject to another sort of representation. Narratively active as she is, she is no more a sexual being than are *2001*'s Bowman or Poole. It is telling that the original script of *Alien* conceived Ripley as a male, and that few changes were made to accommodate the differences that such a sex change in the character might present. Ripley, indeed, is hardly female (and considered by her shipmates as hardly human). Unlike Leia, Ripley is not so much defused in her sexuality as she is confused with her male companions and denied any sexual difference at all. Instead of white robes that mark her both as a woman and chaste or off-limits sexually, she wears the same fatigues as the community of astronauts of which she is—

from the beginning—a part. She is not marked as either a woman or sexual—except for one sequence at the climax of the film, a climax which has double meaning and function since it is both narrative and sexual. It is truly disturbing and horrific when Ripley takes her clothes off toward the end of *Alien*, not only because, given the rules of genre, we suspect that her complacent belief that she has destroyed the alien creature is unfounded. It is also horrifying because she exchanges one kind of power for another, her sudden vulnerability at the narrative level belied by her sudden sexual potency as a visual representation on the screen. In becoming a woman at the level of the narrative, Ripley is clearly marked as a victim; however, in becoming a woman as a fleshly representation of biological difference, Ripley takes on the concrete configuration of male need, demand, desire and fear, and she commands power at a deeper level of the film than that of its story. Stripping her narrative competence with her uniform, Ripley no longer represents a rational and asexual functioning subject, but an irrational, potent, sexual object—a woman, the truly threatening alien generally repressed by the male-conceived and dominated genre. It is no wonder that at the narrative level, the represented alien emerges phallic and erect and seeks to destroy and consume the fearsome difference that Ripley has so suddenly exposed. (And can one, then, forget that the alien was not of woman born—but erupted in violence and fury from a male belly?)

Sexuality, however, is not denied only to the few women characters in science fiction films. The male heroes who dominate almost all science fiction films are also remarkably asexual. Indeed, most of them are about as libidinally interesting as a Ken doll; like Barbie's companion, they are all jaw and no genitals. This sexlessness spans the occupational possibilities of the genre—from lab scientist to doctor, from amateur astronomer to geologist. It seems particularly radiant, however, in the superb physiques, wooden movements, hollow cheerfulness, and banal competence of science fiction astronauts. Certainly, although all science fiction films are—in one way or another—about space travel and the transgression of those established boundaries and markers which give shape and identity to mind, body, and place, not all science fiction films have astronauts in them. Yet, astronauts are clearly those figures who centralize and visually represent the values and virtues common to all the male protagonists of the genre in a single archetypal presence. They are cool, rational, competent, unimaginative, male, and sexless. These qualities make them the heroes of the genre, as they are heroes of our popular culture, and they embody in their cinematic and social presence all that Marilyn's body would subvert. Whereas the semiotic link between biological sexuality and women has been repressed or broken by the genre, the semiotic link between biological asexuality and men has been forged by it and allowed a full range of representation. Thus, much as one can productively free associate around the absence in the science fiction film that Marilyn represents, the virginal astronaut presents an opportunity to free associate around a dominant and significant presence.

Certainly, although it provides a provocative title for this essay, the virginity of astronauts is not to be taken literally. Given their average x½ children, we all know that real astronauts (and some cinematic ones) engage in sex—even if it is difficult to imagine them in or enjoying the act. Rather, my virginal astronauts are visual signs that systemically and systematically function in a conscious and unconscious narrative syntax. That is, they are simultaneously icon, index, and symbol. In their visual representation and narrative activity, they embody, dramatize, and stand for the science fiction film's secondary and conscious—or textual—conflict. And they also embody, dramatize, and stand for the genre's primary and unconscious—or subtextual—thematic problem and the narrative momentum it generates. That major generic problem centers around the male desire to break free from biological dependence on the female as Mother and Other, and to mark the male self as separate and autonomous. The realization of this desire—certainly at the level of science fiction narrative—necessitates the rejection and repression of female difference and its threat to male autonomy as being, indeed, the difference which makes a difference. In the genre, only women represent difference and so are outcasts at the edges of the narrative or are covered up in overalls and lab coats so they might share a bit of narrative space. This connection of the female with difference, sexual difference and biological power, suggests perhaps why we tend to think of astronauts in the plural. They usually come in teams, representing similitude on the screen rather than difference. Maleness in its clean-cut asexuality is visually coded as assembly-line sameness. (Discussing the matter, a colleague aptly commented that this visual representation of male similitude made the films not homosexual, but homotextual.)[2] It is not surprising, then, that one cultural critic has remarked, "Who wants to talk to *one* of the astronauts?"[3] And Pauline Kael, in a negative review of *Marooned*, precisely identifies the point as she misses it when she asks, "Who in his right mind would cast the three leads with Gregory Peck, Richard Crenna, and David Janssen, when anybody can see they're all the same man?"[4]

My virginal astronauts, then, tend to be more corporate than

corporeal. Indeed, it is their interchangeable blandness, their programmed cheerfulness, their lack of imagination, their very banality
(think of that reductive language they all use), that makes them
heroes, that gives them that aura of mechanical and robotic competence which insists that nothing can go wrong, that everything is
A-OK. They all look as if they can accomplish the unthinkable without
ever having to think about it. They are a team, all the same—and
certainly never separated by real sexual rivalry. Offscreen or on, these
men who figure in our public myths neither appeal to prurient interest
nor really seem to have any. They are never "sexy." Their wooden
postures and—dare I say it—tight-assed competence disallows any
connection with the sexual and sensuous. *2001*'s astronaut Poole,
basking nearly naked under a sunlamp, is hardly a piece of beefcake.
Thus, whether named Buzz or Armstrong, Buck, Flash, or Bowman,
our public astronauts reek of lockerroom comraderie, but hardly of
male sweat or semen. As if in training for the big game, they have
rejected their biology and sexuality—pushed it from their minds and
bodies to concentrate on the technology required to penetrate and
impregnate not a woman, but the universe.

The virginal astronauts of the science fiction film are a sign of
penetration and impregnation without biology, without sex, and without the opposite, different, sex. They signify a conquering, potent,
masculine and autonomous technology which values production over
reproduction, which creates rather than procreates in a seeming im-
maculate conception and a metaphorically autocratic caesarian birth.
As signs, my asexual astronauts give concrete form and presence in
both culture and film to this public—if unspoken—disaffiliation of
rational technological enterprise from human biological activity. Not
only does technological man want to make his own babies, but he
wants to do so without the hormones and flesh, without lust and
arousal, and his most heroic representatives, the astronauts, embody
this distrust of women, of the biological, and of the irrational depen-
dencies of the flesh.

It is understandable, then, that women pose a particular narrative
threat to science fiction heroes and their engagement with technology.
They are figures who—as mothers, wives, girlfriends—arouse male
need, demand, and desire. They represent the Mother and the Other
whose very presence points to the puny and imitative quality of male
endeavor, of technological creation and its inanimate products. Their
power to originate life is envied and emulated. Thus, their absence
from a central position in science fiction narrative creates an indelible

and deeply significant space. Women cannot be avoided in the science fiction film no matter how many spaceships leave them behind. They also serve who only stand and wait—or who actively emerge from narrative exile to occupy the paradigmatic space of the imagery. Thus, if human females and Mother Earth are abandoned, if male heroes escape them, it is to yet another female presence: the dark womb of space both beckons and menaces—yielding and receptive to phallic exploration and reunion, or as consuming and destructive as a black hole in its eradication of male potence and presence. Women do not disappear from the science fiction film—nor does sex. They may be repressed, but they return to the narrative in what Foucault called "the mute solidity of a thing," in the condensed and displaced imagery and action of the genre that are themselves sensuous and sexual though no longer human in their overt and articulated form of signification.

Repression is the psychoanalytic term for the "active process of keeping out and ejecting, banishing from consciousness, ideas or impulses that are unacceptable to it."[5] An attempt is made to push the entire painful and emotionally-charged idea—the whole being called an "instinct-presentation"—into the realm of the unconscious. Psychoanalysis tells us:

> It is possible to reduce to a minimum the influence of such an instinct-presentation by first breaking it up into its two basic components: the idea and the affective charge. This means that there are three things that are subject to repression: (1) the instinct-presentation; (2) the idea; (3) the affect. In many instances, when the entire instinct cannot be successfully repressed, either the ideational or the affective part may be. If the idea is repressed, the affect with which it was associated may be transferred to another idea (in consciousness) that has no apparent connection with the original idea. Or, if the affect is repressed, the idea, remaining, so to speak, alone in consciousness may be linked to a pleasant affect. Finally, if the whole instinct-presentation is repressed, it may at some later time return to consciousness in the form of a symbol.[6]

This psychoanalytic description describes precisely what has been entertained here about the presence and absence of women in the science fiction film. The instinct-presentation is comparable to what I have earlier described as the complete sign of sexual woman, the semiotic bearer—in her bodily difference—of a biological power which demands the painful male recognition of dependence and impotence and their corollaries, desire and envy. The influence of this instinct-presentation is minimized when the films break down the

connection between its two parts, when they separate biology
ality from women, the affective charge from the idea. When
women are present in the narrative, when they remain as an
idea but their affect, their biological difference and sexuality, is repressed, they are merely pleasant or indifferent presences and representations. When biological difference and sexuality are present in the
narrative, when they remain as an affect but their idea, their traditional semiotic representation as female, is repressed, they are usually
transferred to another idea that seems unrelated to the original one.
Thus, sexuality can be transferred to a giant mutant insect about to lay
eggs, or to the biologically different sexuality of an alien creature like
the Thing which can breed from its hand and whose offspring we see
pulsating tumescently during a sequence of the 1951 film version.
(Consider the film's counter to this: the hero's human male hands are
literally tied by his very aware girl friend, because in their last encounter he couldn't keep those hands off her.) Nearly all of *Alien*'s imagery
is organic and/or sexual, whereas the humans are not—except for
Ripley's climactic emergence as female toward the end of the narrative.

Finally, as I have suggested, if both women and human sexuality
are repressed from the narrative as a whole, as a sign, as the entirety
that is the instinct-presentation, then that whole may return in another
form to the narrative—in some symbolic representation. The narrative
enterprise of space exploration and its accompanying visuals may be
viewed as a symbolic representation of birth and/or intercourse: the
explusion from the body as well as the penetration of space, the
infant's separation from the Mother or the adult male's reunion with
the Mother in the form of the female Other. Similarly, the alien
invasion of the planet or the alien mind/body "takeover" may be
viewed as the symbolic enactment of the fear of femaleness—both as
all-consuming, castrating, possessive, and potent (having the power of
breast *and* penis), and as an "inverted" rape fantasy in which the
invasion of the planet, mind, and body represent the negative, passive,
vulnerable, and female side of penetration, represent "being screwed"
rather than "screwing." And, of course, female sexuality may return
symbolically in the representations of the alien or mutation. These
representations return the repressed to the narrative, then, but they
are returned in visual disguise—transformed by the semiotic processes
of the unconscious known as condensation and displacement.

Condensation is the term given by psychoanalysis to that process
in which a single idea, word, or image "is made to contain all the

emotion associated with a group of ideas," or a conversation, or a lived scene or experience.[7] Thus, one representation comes to stand for many. A single signifier is substituted for a number of signifiers and comes, therefore, to have attached to its manifest form a number of meanings—multiple signifieds. In addition, it condenses and compresses all the emotion connected with each of the individual signifiers and signifieds for which it alone has come to stand. The similarities that are perceived between single ideas, words, or images, between emotional associations and life experiences, provide the attraction which bring a particular group of signifiers and signifieds together under the symbolic umbrella of a single super-charged representation. This process is certainly characteristic of all dreams, but it can be seen also in the metaphorical nature and function of conscious language—a structural and functional similarity which has been emphasized by French neo-Freudian Jacques Lacan, and which allows me to justify the pertinence of condensation to the science fiction film without going so far as to claim that film is identical to either dream or human psyche.[8] Rather, we are looking at cinematic signification of a particular type. We are looking in most science fiction films at a powerfully charged or cathected imagery that is not consciously articulated as metaphorical, at an imagery which is meant in the narrative to denote precisely that for which it iconically stands.

Think, for example, of the Rhedosaurus in *The Beast from 20,000 Fathoms*. At the denotative level of the narrative, the creature is a signifier—an image or visual representation—of a single signified: a prehistoric giant reptile. However, that visual representation carries a great emotional charge—and not only because it wrecks Coney Island. It has the visual force it does because it represents other things and ideas and associations in addition to its denotative function. It also signifies primeval origins, the primal sink and slime from which life first emerged. It also signifies atomic force and destruction and extinction (it was aroused by an atomic blast), and the fear of an avenging nature which has been disturbed by technology. It signifies, too, something unnameably alien, inhuman, unknowable in its scaliness and reptilian being, something Other (perhaps the female Other, the bad Mother—since the creature's destructive path leads to its ancient breeding ground). While each of these semiotic connections could be argued and cannot be supported without an analysis of the entire film, the idea of condensation as it relates to science fiction imagery should be a little clearer. In addition, insofar as this particular film never overtly articulates these signifieds at the level of the narrative, never deals with the origins of life or the perils of atomic power or the hideousness that mere difference represents (be it of species or sex), we can see how condensation emerges as an imagery of the repressed.

Displacement similarly emerges as an expression of the repressed, and it too is characteristic of dreams. Lacan has likened it in structure and function to the metonymic nature and function of conscious langauge, to the way in which signifier follows signifier in a contiguous chain of substitutive movement. Displacement is the "transference of the emotions . . . from the original ideas to which they are attached—to other ideas."[9] Emotion or psychic energy can be transferred from its source in an original event and that event's original representation to something else, something less originally meaningful. In such a manner, psychoanalysis tells us, the emotions "may be able to gain the realm of consciousness, attaching themselves to ideas to which the patient is ordinarily indifferent. By such an arrangement the patient is spared the pain of knowing the original source of the affects."[10] Often, in the science fiction film, the emotions generated by the narrative and the visual imagery in regard to being, for example, in a spaceship are those of confinement, of discomfort, of dependence (upon the ship and computer to sustain life support—think of the lifeline and the "umbilical" which links technological man to the mother machine). Powerlessness is also evoked, visualized in the helpless and dependent sleep of those aboard. It is more than likely that the original source of these emotions—not attached to technology—comes from a deeper level than the narrative and can be related to the original and repressed representation of human biology and its process: the passage from womb to tomb, the infantile intimations of original being and not-being that merge in the biological space travel which results in birth and also, finally, in death.

Displacement also involves not only the transference of emotion from an original to a secondary representation, but also "the shifting of id impulses from one pathway to another."[11] Someone who is civilized is not supposed to hit an antagonist and so will curse him roundly. In the science fiction film, someone who is rational is not supposed to destroy things irrationally or ravage them—and so will raise a creature or machine who can do it for him. Of particular interest to biology, sex and science fiction, displacement often involves transferences at the level of the body, in relation to both the organic and erotogenic. We are told: "The instincts shift, for example, from the oral to the anal, to the genital zones, or to any other erotogenic zone. In conversion hysteria a psychic complex may be displaced upon an

potentially organic structure. Or, all the issues connected with genital-
ity may be displaced to the oral zone. Displacement 'from below
upward' is a common phenomenon."[12]

In *Invaders From Mars*, one sequence of images shows a woman
about to be "taken over" (that is, possessed, taken) by the aliens. She
is shown lying on a platform, the nape of her neck about to be
penetrated by some long, tubular sort of mechanical mind probe which
will place the red crystal it holds at its tip into her body. Supervising
this enterprise is the "head" alien creature—who is, literally, a head
encased in a glass ball and moved about by mutants who obey its
telepathic commands. In this film (as in many other science fiction
films), the head—narratively the place of reason as opposed to libido—has become the representation of the penis. The nape of the
neck in this instance (which is an erotogenic zone in some cultures) has
become the representation of the womb and anus (it is, after all, the
back of the neck). The action, what we see on the level of the narrative
as an alien invasion, an appropriation of the mind, is a displacement of
sexual erotic activity, particularly in its negative implications as rape
and sodomy. While it is never consciously articulated in the films, such
displacements "from below upward" are articulated in the absolutely
sensitive—if vulgar—locutions of such phrases as "giving head" or
"mind-fuck" or even in such an innocent synonym as "conception" for
"idea."

In a sense, everything I have tried to say here about condensation
and displacement as the means by which the repressed figure of the
sexual female can return from its relegation to the science fiction film's
unconscious to the conscious articulation of the narrative has already
been cinematically demonstrated. Woody Allen has hilariously performed a psychoanalysis of the genre, decoding and exposing its
repression of sexuality and its primary scenario as the play of fear and
desire around female potency and biological difference. In two episodes from his *Everything You Always Wanted to Know about Sex*,
Allen overtly links the genre to sexual conflict and to body imagery.
He also plays out explicit dramas of sexual encounter and redeems the
repressed relation between sex and women to the conscious level of
the narrative, revealing how they function together as a sign of some
hidden and mute reality that both attracts and threatens the male.
What Allen does, finally, is point directly to the processes of condensation and displacement through which the unconscious speaks the
repressed to consciousness—processes which are always active but
usually concealed in the science fiction genre.

As a model of condensation, Allen provides "Are the Findings of Doctors and Clinics Who Do Sexual Research Accurate?"—a narrative in which a forty-foot high breast terrorizes the landscape and the populace until scientists and military finally capture it by constructing a giant bra. The repressed Marilyn Monroe does return in a fashion to the genre, then. What is usually condensed even further into a visual representation of a creature which appears to have no overt relationship with sexuality or women is presented—in the flesh—in Allen's film. Woman here—in an awesome synecdoche—becomes literally the "bad object," the bad Mother and female Other. Describing the death of a little boy, the hero says, "The cream slowed him up and the milk killed him. We're up against a very clever tit. It shoots half and half." This is the breast that would smother and consume and annihilate, that rejects its nurturing function while fulfilling it. This is also the breast with the awful power to sustain life, to nourish and feed, to provoke desire, to answer or reject infant demand, to fulfill basic need. A billboard in the film shows a bikini-clad pinup and announces that "Every body needs milk." This breast clearly has power and reflects not only infantile need and the fear of rejection, but also the infantile confusion of the breast with the penis, the confusion of male and female power. This breast is, indeed, clever. It shoots half and half— both semen and milk. It is the baddest of bad objects.

As a model of displacement, Allen gives us another segment entitled "What Happens During Ejaculation." The sexual and orgasmic activity that is ordinarily displaced in the genre onto sending rockets into space is exposed by Allen, as is the process of displacement itself. Allen uses the firing of a rocket as an explicit metaphor for the ejaculation of a sperm about to be sent to the womb. Allen plays the skeptical, fearful, reluctant sperm/astronaut who says, "You hear rumors about this pill these women take." And the drama of the male body is played out by white overalled technicians operating flashing electronic consoles. What is so consummate (the pun is certainly intended) is the parody's truth in relation to the real and hidden concerns of the genre, its recognition of the surrogate sexuality of the concentrated effort and tension and release of science fiction's visualization of men shooting their rockets off into space. Think, for example, of a parallel "serious" scene in *Marooned*; as the rocket lifts off, all the technicians in the NASA control room stand up from their consoles, look at the big monitoring screen, and chant "Go, go, go!" in a rhythmic and ascending crescendo. The connection between the basic asceticism and asexuality of male characters in the science fiction film and their constant orgasmic release in a public and communal male technological effort which transcends the earthbound corporality of flesh and dependence upon women is made central and overt in the Allen parody.[13] The desire to impregnate is there, the power to impregnate and penetrate the womb of space is visually articulated—and so is the fear. Allen's sperm/astronaut fears a hostile space (one which has taken the pill), a space which may destroy him, reject him as readily as he may penetrate it. The sperm/astronaut is at once afraid and desirous, both potential newborn and incestuous mother-fucker.[14]

Just as metaphor and metonomy form the basic axes of linguistic representation, so too do condensation and displacement form the basic axes of the unconscious representation as it is given manifest form and utters the repressed to consciousness. Both, thus, work at once. In the ejaculation sequence, for example, not only does Allen make explicit how the genre traditionally displaces biological and sexual affect from women onto some other technological representation (rockets), but he also makes explicit how the idea of woman becomes part of a visual condensation and returns in disguised form, in this case (and others) as space itself. The point to be made here is that both displacement and condensation work at once in the entirety of the narrative and concentrate their efforts on the complete or partial repression of the instinct-presentation and its component parts: female sexuality and fertility, female biology and its representation in a body that is different, that is difference itself. What results is a basic structure which informs the genre—a kind of push-pull configuration in which what is repressed will return in disguise to become overtly articulated. This basic structure, however, is also able to accomodate historical and cultural change—for what will be repressed (the sexual female, or sexuality itself) will alter with the times and will also emerge in a disguise which responds to historical concerns. While these changes may be marked, however, the structure itself remains constant. Displacement and condensation will occur or the genre will not exist—in the same way that metonomy and metaphor exist or there can be no language.

Earlier I suggested that all science fiction films were about space travel whether or not they had rockets or spaceships in them, whether or not they were manned by my virginal astronauts. By space travel, I was referring to the passage across known and marked boundaries that give identity to the world and to ourselves—as earth and space, as inside and outside, as self and other, as male and female. Borders and markers in the science fiction film are seen as extendable—and their

contents as spilling over into each other, possibly merging. This is what
is so thrilling about the genre, and what is so threatening, what
structures its narratives as a play of fear and desire. It is also what
affixes the genre to infantile and preOedipal dramas in which the
female—as Mother and Other—becomes the focal point and origin of
questions the infant must answer regarding its own sexuality, its self-
ness, its very identity as human and biologically gendered. In repress-
ing women and sexuality, in a culture which semiotically links biology
and sexuality to women and technology to men, most American science fiction films play out scenarios which focus on infantile experience while pretending to adult concerns.

Freud, Melanie Klein, and others have noted the following features which characterize infantile experience. One can see immediately how they are paralleled by the action and imagery of the American science fiction film in its various dramatic manifestations. The
infant feels a sense of helplessness, impotence, and dependence; a
sense of insignificance and smallness in relation to the monstrous size
and physical importance of the mother. The infant has a confused
image of gender identity, its own and its mother's, and tends to
collapse the penis and breast into a bisexual imagery in which body
parts and power are interchangeable. The infant has difficulty in
distinguishing boundaries between itself and its mother, between inside and outside, mind and body, body and tool or toy. It has extreme
ambivalence toward maternal power in its relation to the infant's own
limited power, resulting in a tension between its sense of its own desire
and destructive potential and its dependent demands upon one who
can destroy. Thus, the infant has a tendency to introject or project
maternal power, to see itself as powerful and potent and autonomous
like the mother or to fear the other as monstrous, destructive, and
all-powerful. As well, the infant is both curious and afraid in its lack of
knowledge—it wants to know, but is afraid of what it does not know or
what it may find out. And this lack of knowledge is most focused
around sexual and body imagery and concern for its own origin.[15]
"Where did I come from?" is a question penultimately connected with
another: "Who and what am I?"

These questions lie repressed in the narratives of the science
fiction film. At the level of conscious representation, the one is articulated as "Where are we *going*?" or "Where did *It* (or *They*) come
from?" The first is a positive and the second a negative disguise for the
infant's "Where did I come from?" The second question takes the
disguised form of "Who and what is *It* (or *They*)?" instead of "Who or

what am I?" If these questions were exposed in their original form, in the "true speech" that Lacan sees as the unconscious, the genre could not exist at the narrative level as the kind of exploration it is. Thus, those questions of origin and identity and the conventional sign of the sexual female which provokes those questions must be repressed. Marilyn Monroe could never have made a science fiction film; she would have destroyed it if it could not desex her. And, insofar as American culture observes and perpetuates the semiotic linkage of biology to woman and technology to male, astronauts will always be represented as virginal no matter how much they screw around.

5

Pods, Blobs, and Ideology in American Films of the Fifties

Peter Biskind

Ever since Georges Méliès sent his rocket to the moon at the turn of the century, science fiction films have been familiar sights on American screens, but it was not until the fifties that they arrived in force. *Destination Moon* and *Rocket Ship X-M*, both released in 1950, inaugurated a flurry of films which, before the decade ended, would produce a veritable invasion of little green men, flying saucers, born-again dinosaurs, predatory plants, diabolical juveniles, and enormous insects.

Ideologically speaking, fifties science fiction films fell into two camps: centrist and radical. Centrist films often presented America in the grip of an emergency, attacked by giant ants in *Them* (1954), or invaded by aliens in *Earth vs. The Flying Saucers* (1956). They did so because they were in the business of dramatizing consensus, the general shared agreement on the basic premises that animated society. Emergencies made it clear that if we wanted to survive to see another day, we had better pull together to overcome our local, petty differences in the common interest.

The ideology of the center was called pluralism, and it held that American society was composed of a variety of interest groups that competed on a more or less equal basis for a piece of the pie. Since this plurality of groups all shared the same assumptions, relations among them were based on compromise, negotiation, and mutual respect. Centrists knew that consensus was more stable if dissenters were inside the magic circle of agreement sharing the pie with Ozzie and Harriet, rather than outside, throwing stones against the picture window. They

A longer version of this essay appeared in *Seeing Is Believing: How Hollywood Taught Us to Stop Worrying and Love the Fifties* (New York: Random House, Pantheon Books, 1983). Copyright © 1983 by Peter Biskind.

preferred, if possible, to include their enemies, not cast them into outer darkness. But the scope of the consensus was nothing if not narrow, and centrists did not hesitate to label those who refused to play the game as extremists.

In centrist films extremists were presented as aliens. Who were they? It has long been evident, in fact from the moment the first blob oozed its way across the screen, that the little green men from Mars stood in the popular imagination for the clever red men from Moscow. The media portrayed Russians in such lurid fashion that the connection was inevitable, even if unintended by writers and directors. But I. F. Stone, among others, pointed out that the Soviet threat was as much a function of the squabbles between Democrats and Republicans as a reality: "The Republicans fight Russians in order to prevent a New Deal, while the Democrats fight Russians as a kind of rearguard action against the Republicans."[1] Indeed, the red nightmare was so handy that had it not existed, American politicians would have had to invent it. Movies did invent it, and it served somewhat the same purpose in Hollywood as it did in Washington. Extremists were not only Russians, but everyone, left and right, who dissented from consensus. More often than not, the communist connection was a red herring, allowing the center to attack the left and right, and the left and right to attack the center, all in the guise of respectable anti-communism, which itself was no more than a smokescreen for a domestic power struggle.

Centrist science fiction adopted an Us/Them framework, whereby that which threatened consensus was simply derogated as "Other." The Other was indeed communism, but it was also everything the center was not, and we can get a good idea of what the center was not by examining the language of pluralism. If the center was modern, the Other was ancient. Sociologist Daniel Bell referred to "archaic Europe" and the "backward colonial system."[2] If the center was civilized, the Other was primitive. Bell criticized the "barbarous" behaviour of the radical right[3], and law professor Alan Westin warned against the "spear thrusts of the radicals."[4] If the center was scientific and technological, the Other was magical. Bell accused the right of entertaining the illusion of "the magical rollback of Communism in Europe."[5] Us/Them-ism permeated the whole range of ideas and values. If the center was middle-class, the Other was lower- or occasionally upper-class. If the center was normal, the Other was abnormal. If the center was sane, the Other was insane, and so on.

Pluralists like Bell, Talcott Parsons, Lionel Trilling, David Riesman, and Arthur Schlesinger, Jr., identified the center with no less than civilization itself, with the highest achievements of humanity, with the totality of man-made objects, the aggregate of human production, in short, with culture. Riesman observed that in America, "society is no longer felt as a wilderness or jungle as it often was earlier,"[6] and pluralists invariably imagined it in man-made terms: society was a business, a building, a game, a machine—but rarely nature. Bell spoke of the "fabric of government,"[7] and Parsons of the "institutional machinery" of society.[8] Machines even had God's blessing. "A machine is an assembling of parts according to the law of God. When you love a machine and get to know it, you will be aware that it has a rhythm," wrote Norman Vincent Peale. "It has God's rhythm."[9]

That which is not culture is, more generally, nature, not merely trees, animals, and bugs, but all that is not-human, so that the conflict between centrists and extremists, conensus and the Other, Us and Them, was often presented as a conflict between culture and nature. Since culture was good, nature was generally bad; it was all that threatened to disrupt or destroy culture. Bell, for example, wrote of the "flash-fire spread of McCarthyism,"[10] of the "turbulence" created by the right,[11] and of "a rogue elephant like Huey Long or Joseph McCarthy rampag[ing] against the operations of government."[12] When Billy Graham opened the 1952 session of the United States Senate with a prayer, he warned against the "barbarians beating at our gates from without and the moral termites from within."[13]

In centrist science fiction, the Other is imagined as nature run wild. In *Them* (1954), it is ants. In *The Beginning of the End* (1957), it is grasshoppers, while in *Tarantula* (1955), it is a spider. In the same category are films set in the jungle or remote, wild places, like *The Creature from the Black Lagoon* (1954); *Black Scorpion* (1957); *From Hell It Came* (1957), where the Other is a deranged tree stump; *The Attack of the Crab Monsters* (1957), where the Other is an army of jumbo crabs on a Pacific atoll; or *The Monster That Challenged the World* (1957), where the Other is a school of giant marauding snails.

Since centrist films imagined society as a machine and looked fondly on science and technology, computers and robots—in contrast to nature—were rarely dangerous. In *Forbidden Planet* (1956) and *Tobor the Great* (1954), they are servants or tools, not masters or enemies, while in *Unknown World* (1950), a trip to the center of the earth is facilitated by a giant mechanical mole. When robots appeared to be bad, as in *Earth vs. The Flying Saucers*, they turned out not to be robots at all, but aged humanoids wearing robot-like suits.

Other-izing qualities, ideas, life-styles, or groups that threatened the center was not only a way of discrediting specific alternatives to the status quo, but also a way of discrediting the very idea of alternatives to the orthodox manner of living and being. If alternatives to mainstream institutions were dystopian, there was no place to go but home, that is, back to the center.

The attack on utopias and utopians, dreams and dreamers, was a constant refrain in centrist literature. Utopians are our old friends, extremists, and utopianism was worked over so thoroughly that "utopian" and "millenial" became epithets of abuse, in contrast to adjectives like "realistic," "mature," and "sensible," with which centrists flattered one another. Alan Westin derided "dangerously millenial proposals" of the left and right,[14] while Parsons ridiculed the "utopianism" of Republican isolationists.

Thus, in centrist science fiction, even if utopias began well, they ended badly, and were apt to degenerate from the best of all worlds to the worst. Fifties science fiction was full of futuristic civilizations that had fallen on hard times. In *Forbidden Planet*, for example, the Krell were the race that knew too much. In *This Island Earth* (1955), the advanced civilization was Metaluna, but its gleaming array of gadgets by no means insured it peace and prosperity; on the contrary, the Metalunans were locked in a battle to the death with Zahgon, their arch enemy, and had to turn to scientists from Earth for help. To judge by these films, Earth must have been the choicest morsel of real estate in the galaxy, the sweet center of the Milky Way, because it was repeatedly invaded by advanced civilizations that had fouled up in one way or another—exhausted their resources, overpopulated their cities, nuked one another, and so on. To be an advanced civilization was to look for trouble; this was not because these films were ambivalent about technology, but because they simply did not like utopias.

If Earth was the place where the hills were always greener, there was good reason. Centrist science fiction employed a double standard. On one hand, it attacked utopianism when it cropped up outside the center; on the other, it argued that Earth, by which it meant the United States, circa 1955, was utopian enough for anyone. It was there that the contradictions that destroyed advanced civilizations were reconciled. Centrists believed, quite simply, that their country had the endorsement of the Almighty, the divine seal of approval. A booming consumer economy offered ample proof that the God who had abandoned twentieth century Europe to physical and spiritual destruction was alive and well in America. "God has set us an awesome mission:

nothing less than the leadership of the free world," said Adlai Stevenson during the 1952 presidential campaign.[15] "Why should we make a five-year plan," wondered historian Daniel Boorstin in 1952 in *Partisan Review*, "when God seems to have had a thousand-year plan ready-made for us?"[16] It was clear to everyone that God had jumped on the free world bandwagon.

If America was the City of God on Earth, this meant that God, Christ, and spiritual values of any kind were immanent, immediate, palpable, familiar, and accessible in the activities of everyday life, not remote, distant, or unreachable. Utopia was to be found in our own back yards; salvation lay in humdrum routine.

Centrist science fiction films were generally more confident and optimistic than radical films of the same genre and often there was no invasion by aliens at all. They were expansion- and exploration-oriented, imperialist rather than paranoid. In *Destination Moon*, the moon is regarded as a potential military base, and "others" must be prevented from exploiting it. The American astronaut takes possession "by the grace of God and in the name of the United States." When trouble came in centrist film, it often came during an expedition, as in *The Thing* (1951), *Forbidden Planet*, *From Hell It Came*, and *Creature from the Black Lagoon*, another warning not to go poking about for utopian alternatives. Home is safe; danger lurks out there.

Although centrists agreed with one another on the goals of consensus, and presented a common front against extremism, they quarreled among themselves about means, about how best to organize and impose consensus. This disagreement was reflected in centrist science fiction, which can be further divided into corporate liberal and conservative films. Both featured a coalition of scientists and soldiers, but differed on which had the upper hand.

Scientists and soldiers were first thrown together in a big way during the war, in the Manhattan Project, and the romance that blossomed then reached its climax at Hiroshima. In the fifties, when their infant A-bomb grew like a beanstalk into a strong and sturdy H-bomb, scientists became alarmed, and fell to fighting with soldiers (and among themselves) over their child's future. Scientists like Einstein and Oppenheimer began to wish they had strangled him in the cradle, while soldiers (and scientists like Teller) wanted to pack him off to military academy, not reform school. Both scientists and soldiers agreed that only a strong America would deflect the Soviets from their mad path to world conquest, but they disagreed over how much deterrence was enough. Scientists were content to rest on their laurels with the A-bomb, while soldiers wanted a bigger bang for their bucks, and pressed ahead with the H-bomb.

The disagreement over choice of weapons had wider ideological significance. Scientists (and corporate liberals in general) didn't like force, because in their view, society was consensual. Citizens did the right thing because they wanted to, or were persuaded to want to, not because they had to, or were forced to have to. For corporate liberals, moreover, reality was so complex that only scientists or experts were able to decipher it. "The problems of national security," wrote Bell, "like those of the national economy, have become so staggeringly complex that they can no longer be settled by common sense or past experience."[17]

In corporate liberal films, then, brawn deferred to brains, and scientists told soldiers what to do. The prestige of science was so high by the beginning of the fifties that the mad scientists of thirties and forties films, like Doctor Thorkel (Albert Dekker), who had shrunk his colleagues to the size of chickens in *Dr. Cyclops* (1941), were all working for Bell Labs. They were no longer mad, but on the contrary, rather pleased with the way things had turned out.

When the cops discover patches of sugar strewn all over the desert in *Them*, it "doesn't make sense." Reality is too complex for traditional police procedures to unravel the mystery, and this is clearly a job for "myrmecologist" Doctor Medford (Edmund Gwen). A far cry from Doctor Thorkel, avuncular Doctor Medford wouldn't hurt a fly, and he has no trouble reading reality. He quickly recognizes that giant ants are the problem, and his expertise puts him at the center of world-shaking events. He meets with the president, lectures top public officials, and is able to command the full resources of the state. An Air Force general is reduced to the role of Medford's chauffeur, and when FBI agent Robert Graham (James Arness) complains that he can't understand Medford's scientific lingo, the film makes us feel that he ought to take a biology course at night school.

Since *Them* is a national emergency film that dramatizes consensus, it valorizes the intervention of the state and favors national over local interests. The alien threat emanates from the heartland and moves against a big city, in this case, Los Angeles. Help, on the other hand, comes from Washington; Gwen works for the federal Department of Agriculture. Corporate liberals generally favored Big Government, and corporate liberal science fiction expressed the confidence that the government, with its bombs and missiles, was equal to any emergency. In *The Giant Claw* (1957), for example, it federal fighters dispatch "the bird as big as a battleship."

The corollary to the stress on consensus and Big Government was the disciplining of individualism. In these films, individualists—the first one out of an air lock on a strange planet, the first one to investigate a peculiar cavernous pit, like the unhappy scientist in *Invasion of the Crab Monsters*—were rewarded with death.

Similarly, the corollary of favoring experts and scientists was a hierarchical, elitist model of society, where those at the top were better—smarter, more moral, principled, and courageous—than those at the bottom. In *Them*, the average Janes and Joes who are neither scientists nor soldiers are almost as bad as the ants. They spend most of their time, in films like this, fleeing for their lives, obstructing the best efforts of the government to save them from themselves. The war against the ants has to be waged behind closed doors. Reporters, conduits to the people, threaten official secrecy. Like their readers, they have to be kept in the dark. "Do you think all this hush-hush is necessary?" someone asks Doctor Medford. "I certainly do," he replies. "I don't think there's a police force in the world that could handle the panic of the people if they found out what the situation is."

Conservative films, on the other hand, were more inclined to let the soldiers have their way. When Air Force Captain Hendry (Kenneth Tobey) arrives at a remote arctic outpost to investigate odd "disturbances" reported by a team of scientists in *The Thing*, he discovers that he's on alien territory. "Dr. Carrington is in charge here," one of the scientists tells him, referring to the Nobel Prize winner who heads the expedition, and it quickly becomes clear that Hendry's job is to assert the authority of the soldiers over the scientists. *The Thing* is about, among other things, a struggle over turf. It asks the question, which ideology, the conservative ideology of the military, or the corporate liberal ideology of science, is best.

Conservatives were considerably more suspicious of science than were their corporate liberal allies. In 1943, for example, Richard Weaver, author of *The Southern Tradition*, called science a "false messiah."[18] Scientists in conservative films were likely to be brothers beneath the beard of Baron von Frankenstein, which is to say that the mad scientists who had disappeared from the labs of corporate liberal films were alive and well in conservative films. In *It Conquered the World* (1956), for example, the scientist (Lee Van Cleef) helps a group of malicious Venusians do just that. In *The Thing*, the tension between science and the military that was latent in *Them* is not only more pronounced, it is resolved in favor of the military. FBI agent Graham complained in *Them* that he couldn't understand Medford, but he was something of a clod anyway, and it was probably his own fault. But when Captain Hendry asks Carrington (Robert Cornthwaite) a question and gets only mumbo-jumbo in return, it's another matter. "You lost me," he says, and this time it's their fault, a symptom of the arrogance of scientists and intellectuals. In *Them*, Medford's admiration for the "wonderful and intricate engineering" of the ants' nest is reasonable, neither unseemly nor unpatriotic. But in *The Thing*, Doctor Carrington's scientific curiosity is given a sinister twist. He develops an altogether unhealthy interest in the alien. Whereas Medford merely restrains the military because he wants to find out if the queen is dead, Carrington betrays it, defects to the other side. He helps the Thing reproduce itself, finds a warm spot in the greenhouse for it to lay its spores, and sabotages Hendry's efforts to kill it. Carrington is soft on aliens, a Thing-symp, and his behavior justifies the soldiers' mistrust of science, even turns them against the Bomb itself. "Knowledge is more important than life. We split the atom!" Carrington shouts in a transport of enthusiasm. "That sure made everybody happy," comes the sour reply from one of Hendry's men.

Eventually, Carrington is confined to his quarters; when he tells Hendry, "You have no authority here," one of the soldiers pokes a revolver in his face, and he learns that power grows out of the barrel of a gun. Conservative science fiction, in other words, preferred force to persuasion.

But science is by no means rejected wholesale. There are good scientists as well as bad, Tellers as well as Oppenheimers, and the difference between them is that the good scientists side with Hendry, not Carrington. And, at the end of the film, when the story of the struggle against the Thing is announced to the world, Carrington is singled out for special tribute. Soldiers and scientists, conservatives and corporate liberals may have quarreled among themselves, but it was all in the family, and when the chips were down, they closed ranks in defense of consensus.

Not all conservative films chastised science with the military; in some, religion played the role the military played in *The Thing*. These are the films in which the Faustian mad scientist is warned by a woman or a minister not to tamper with God's work. In Kurt Neumann's *The Fly* (1958), the fifties infatuation with science once again transforms what would earlier have been a mad scientist into a sympathetic victim, but even here, when he exclaims, "I can transport matter!" his wife replies, aghast, "It's like playing God." In these films, the cross is mightier than the test tube.

Fifties conservatives tended to favor local over national interests, the individual over the organization, and displayed considerable skepticism towards large groups of all kinds, including the army, which they regarded as excessively bureaucratic. In *Destination Moon*, for example, the government is a myopic bureaucracy that not only refuses to finance a moon shot, but after a visionary industrialist has seen to it that the rocket is built, tries to abort the launch. In *The Thing*, the conflict between soldiers and scientists is complemented by another, between the individual and the organization, in this case, Captain Hendry and the Air Force. Hendry begins the films as the perfect organization man. He can't blow his nose without clearing it first with headquarters in Alaska, which in turn refers back to Washington. But when Hendry goes by the book, it's a recipe for disaster, and red tape finally immobilizes him altogether. "Until I receive my instructions from my superior officer about what to do," he says, "we'll have to mark time." When his orders finally do come, they are worthless. Although the Thing has been making Bloody Marys out of the boys at the base, Hendry is instructed to "avoid harming the alien at all costs." Eventually, he is forced to disobey orders, take matters into his own hands, and pit his judgment against that of the organization, which is out of touch with reality. Even so he can't go too far; his rebellion is limited, confined to the framework of the organization. He remains a good soldier to the end.

Because *The Thing* is critical of bureaucracy and sympathetic towards individualism and initiative, it is more populist and less elitist than *Them*. While people in *Them* obstruct authority, authority in *The Thing* frustrates people. Within the community of soldiers and scientists at the base, relationships are more egalitarian than they are in *Them*. Decisions are not made behind closed doors, and the Thing is not destroyed by the power of the federal government, nor incinerated by soldiers wielding flamethrowers, as are the ants in *Them*, but rather by means of a do-it-yourself electric chair improvised on the spot out of spit and chewing gum.

In the fifties film, radical science fiction upended the conventions of centrist science fiction, turned them inside out, held them up to a mirror. If centrist films dramatized consensus, radical films dramatized conflict, polarization, and the antagonism between the self and society. If centrist films dramatized the views of insiders, radical films dramatized the views of outsiders. It was, of course, possible to attack the center from the right or left, so that radical science fiction in the fifties broke down into right-wing films and left-wing films.

Right-wing films were considerably more paranoid than centrist films. Their heroes did not have to go looking for trouble in strange and exotic places; trouble came to them, right here at home. These films resolved the ambivalence that afflicted conservative films, took the attitudes they displayed and pushed them to extremes. If conservative films were more sympathetic to individualism than corporate liberal films, right-wing films went further. They endorsed vigilantism and do-it-yourself justice, because society was not only corrupt, but anathema to the individual. They focused on the struggles of the self beseiged.

There was no question that giant ants were crawling all over Los Angeles in *Them*, or that a homicidal carrot was stalking the arctic base in *The Thing*. Everyone could see it. The focus of these films was not the strenuous efforts of those who knew to alert those who didn't to the fact that there was trouble afoot, a blob in the basement or green slime in the attic. Right-wing science fiction, on the contrary, dramatized the struggle of the outsider, the kook, the end-of-the-worlder to force the community to acknowledge the validity of the self's private vision, even if it violated the norms of credibility that governed the expectations of experts and professionals. When average Joe saw a flying saucer land in his bean field, nobody believed him. An abyss opened up between him and society. Far worse than invasion, these films anxiously imagined the loss of community, the estrangement of the one-who-knows from those that didn't, Us from Them, but this time Us were the so-called "extremists,"and Them was the center.

In *Invasion of the Body Snatchers* (1956) Kevin McCarthy, as small town doctor Miles Bennell, is beseiged by patients telling him that their friends and neighbors are not what they seem to be; they are imposters. At first, Bennell advises them to see a psychiatrist. "The trouble's inside you," he tells one patient. But gradually, as the whole town, including the psychiatrist and police are taken over by pods, Bennell begins to change his mind. In one scene, he and a pal argue with the psychiatrist about whether or not the pods exist. Suddenly, the cops burst in. "I have a good mind to throw you both in jail," says the first cop, pointing to Bennell and pal. But the psychiatrist intervenes: "These people are patients, badly in need of psychiatric help." The cops and docs (in this film analogous to the soldiers and scientists of *Them* and *The Thing*) argue about whether Bennell and his pal are felons or patients, but we know they are both wrong. In *Invasion*, the doctors are sick and the cops are criminals. (Bennell is a doctor too, of course, but he's only a general practicioner, and he is not operating in the capacity of a doctor. His pal asks him, "Would you be able to forget you're a doctor for awhile?" Bennell: "Yes.")

In right-wing films, both cops and doctors, the twin pillars of the centrist authority, are vilified. The center itself is the enemy; taken over by aliens, it becomes alien. When Bennell finds an oversized pod in the greenhouse, he finally realizes that his patients have been right all along, that he must have faith in his own perceptions of the world, and not let experts mediate between himself and reality, convince him that he's wrong, crazy, or criminal.

Since the enemy in right-wing science fiction was the center, it was not too surprising that the form in which this enemy was imagined was not nature but culture, and specifically technology. If people betrayed technology in centrist films like *Forbidden Planet*, where disaster was caused by "human error," in right-wing films (and some conservative films), technology betrayed people; disaster was caused by "mechanical error." The editors of *The National Review*, for example, writing in the late sixties about John Glenn's space flight, preferred men to machines. "This and that went wrong with the mechanism, and man took over and brought Friendship 7 to its strange harbor," they wrote. "No machine, on land, in sea, air or space, can do man's job for him."[19] For the right, "robot" and "mechanical" were epithets of scorn, and the center, perceived from the right as dehumanized and technocratic, was represented in science fiction by a whole army of robots, androids, and mechanical pod people that trudged across the screens of the fifties with their characteristic jerky motions. Whereas in centrist films robots like Robby were friendly, they were dangerous in right-wing (and some left-wing) films like *The Twonky* (1953), *Target Earth* (1954), *Gog* (1954), and *Kronos* (1957).

Susan Sontag first called attention to this fear of robots, which she contrasted to the older fear of the animal. "The dark secret behind human nature used to be the upsurge of the animal—as in King Kong. The threat to man, his availability to dehumanization, lay in his own animality," she wrote. "Now the danger is understood as residing in man's ability to be turned into a machine."[20] But Sontag was only partly right. While it is true that in the fifties the imagination of disaster took a mechanical turn, this new metaphor for dehumanization did not supersede the older one of animality. Rather, they coexisted. There were a number films, such as *Forbidden Planet*, in which dehumanization was imagined either as the eruption of the primitive, the return of the repressed unconscious—the monster from the *id*—or an attack by the natural world deranged by radiation. The alien as primitive, animal, and natural was a centrist fantasy, while the alien as mechanical and technological was a right-wing fantasy. In fact, since right-wing films used the past to flog the present, the primitive was often sentimentalized in the retrospective glow of nostalgia. The past was not barbarous, as it was to the center, but rather, a simpler, purer time. *Invasion of the Body Snatchers* is suffused with nostalgia for the past, for the old-fashioned, pre-technological family doctor, rather than the new-fangled psychiatrist with his glib theories. The family is no longer what it seemed; traditional bonds have eroded. "He was always like a father to me," complains one woman about her spaced-out uncle. "Now there's no emotion." Science has upset the natural order of things. Wondering about the peculiar behavior of the townies, Bennell says, "So many things have been discovered in the last few years, it could be anything."

Invasion presents us with a vision of the perversion of small town life without the saving cross-cutting to Washington that characterized *Them*. In fact, Washington presents no help at all. Bennell calls the FBI, but the operator tells him that there is no answer. In right-wing films, the federal government, the state, either cannot be reached or is ineffectual. When the government tries to destory the aliens, it fails. Its weapons are useless against their superior powers.

It is because the government (the center) is either useless or itself evil in these films, that individuals have to take the law into their own hands. After Bennell finally realizes that the pods pose a threat, he spends the rest of the film trying to convince others that he is telling the truth, but they do not believe him. At the end of much right-wing science fiction, average Joe, once regarded by everyone as a loony, finally convinces his friends and neighbors that he has been correct all the time. Community is restored, but on his terms, not theirs. They have been converted to his paranoid vision, and what is more, they have been mobilized for action. These films push the populist sentiments evident in conservative films like *The Thing* to extremes. The alien is destroyed by the resourceful citizens of Smallville without the benefit of federal aid.

In *Them* and *The Thing*, no one expressed a yen for utopias, except perhaps for Carrington, and he was a villain. Alternative forms of life were simply monsters, while alternative societies like the matriarchy of ants were dystopias. But this did not matter, since utopian aspirations were realizable within the institutions of the center. In *Them*, the FBI agent will marry Medford's daughter, just as in *The Thing*, Hendry will marry his girlfriend. But in right-wing films like *Invasion*, Bennell and the heroine have been married and divorced, which is to say, both have discovered that their aspirations cannot be realized within society. For the right, utopian aspirations did not inhere in everyday life; they were transcendent, not immanent. Eric Voegelin, in a book called *The New Science of Politics* (1952), decried the liberal tendency to "immanentize" Christianity, to reduce its otherworldly perspective to an "intramundane range of action," while at the same time striving for the "redivinization of society."[21] These films found their utopia in the new community, the transformed society based on their own principles. This utopia favored the heart over the head. Nature-within is not a monster from the *id*, as it is in a centrist film like *Forbidden Planet*, but "natural" human warmth, normal emotion. "I don't want a world without love or faith or beauty," wails Bennell's sweetheart, and later when she tries to pass for a pod-person and attempts to merge with the crowd, she gives herself away by expressing her feelings, screaming when a dog is run over.

Left-wing films shared the outsider perspective of right-wing films, but they differed from them (and from centrist films as well), in one significant respect. They did not fear aliens. In these films, the alien was neutral, benevolent, superior, or victimized.

It Came from Outer Space (1953) begins like a right-wing film. As in *Invasion of the Body Snatchers*, aliens take over earthlings, and the center—the scientists and police, the guardians of the public weal—are incompetents with their heads in the sand. We are firmly behind John Putnam (Richard Carlson) in his attempts to convince the authorities that a space ship has indeed landed. But in this film, unlike *Invasion*, the aliens do not mean humans any harm. They have "borrowed" their bodies, not "taken" them. These visitors from outer space have merely had a flat tire and landed on Earth to repair their ship. Nobody yells, "If you don't like it here, go back to outer space," and at the end, when they do, we feel sad. We have learned a lesson in peaceful co-existence.

In *The Day the Earth Stood Still* (1951), the aliens are alternately victimized by, and superior to, humans. Space emissary Klaatu (Michael Rennie) is shot dead, but miraculously resurrects himself in time to warn us to shape up, or our planet will be burnt to a cinder.

And in *The Space Children* (1960), the alien is a disembodied brain that floats to earth on the end of a rainbow to frustrate America's launch of a "doomsday missile."

Then there is the poor Creature, hero of *The Creature Walks among Us* (1956), the concluding film of the Creature trilogy. In the first installment, made in 1954, the Creature was mildly sympathetic, more sinned against than sinning, almost a noble savage tormented beyond endurance by the arrogant scientists who mucked about in his lagoon, driven into a frenzy by the spectacle of Kay Lawrence (Julia Adams) swimming above him in a one-piece bathing suit. In *The Creature Walks among Us*, "he" has been removed from his natural habitat entirely, taken in chains to a cage on land where mad scientists perform all sorts of grim experiments on his body. They transplant this, amputate that, move a fin here, a gill there, until his own mother would not recognize him. One of the scientists even tries to frame him for murder, and in the end, he is killed.

Whereas the heroes of right-wing films were Paul Reveres who tried to stir people up to take things into their own hands, these same figures in left-wing films were villains—hysterical vigilantes, danger-ous paranoids, and the "people" (as in corporate liberal films) were no better than a mob. Instead of mobilizing people against the alien threat, these films pacified them, protected the aliens from the people. Justifiable alarm to the right was hysteria to the left. In the context of the red scare, these were anti-witch-hunt films.

In *It Came from Outer Space*, the fire-eater is a deputy sheriff. "I'd get some rifles into the hands of some men and clean it up, whatever it is," he says fiercely, but he is just a fool. The right-wing whistle-blower in *The Day the Earth Stood Still* is an insurance sales-man (Hugh Marlowe) who turns Klaatu over to the authorities. But in this film, he is not treated like a hero; rather, he is a petty, jealous man, and the proper behavior is displayed by Helen Benson (Patricia Neal), who in effect defects to the other side.

Like the right-wing variety, left-wing science fiction polarized the center into a conflict between the individual and the community. The heroes of these films, who saw the space ship land or shook hands with little green men, were also estranged from society, but whereas right-wing heroes were just average Joes, the left-wing heroes were more likely to have been estranged in the first place. They were Einsteins and Oppenheimers, the eggheads who thought for themselves. The special knowledge of the alien they came to possess merely ratified their pre-existing alienation. Therefore, they were not interested in recasting the community in their own image, as were their right-wing counterparts. Left-wing heroes just wanted to get out.

To the left, like the right, Christianity and utopian aspirations were transcendent, not immanent. They did not inhabit the center, but on the contrary, existed without, in future worlds, or within, beating in the breasts of the disaffected heroes. At the end of *The Day the Earth Stood Still*, Klaatu simply up and left, went back to the galaxy from whence he came. He did not marry Helen Benson, get a job at Brookings, and settle down in Chevy Chase. But unlike the right, the left was pessimistic about the possibility of transforming the community into a utopia—a reflection of its bitter, disillusioned anti-populism.

While the ideological configuration of center, right, and left held throughout the fifties, in the sixties, under the pressure of Vietnam, the center gave way, and films were increasingly polarized between right and left. At the same time, science fiction in film went into a precipitous decline, and it was not until the mid-seventies that *Star Wars*, in the cinematic vanguard of the Carter Restoration, picked up the pieces, reconstructed the center, and initiated a vigorous revival of the genre.

6

Don't Look Where We're Going: Visions of the Future in Science Fiction Films, 1970–1982

H. Bruce Franklin

By the end of the 1960s, we knew that the world was in a crisis, perhaps the most profound crisis in human history. Although our species now possessed the science and technology potentially allowing us to shape the future of the planet according to human needs and desires, we faced these forces as alien powers—which we ourselves had created—slipping out of our control and threatening to wipe us off the planet. It was no coincidence that science fiction was finally being recognized as a central organ of Anglo-American culture.

America itself was being torn apart by the Vietnam War, with its destruction not only of Indochina but also of our own political consensus, social cooperation, and non-military economy, not to mention our illusions about our history and destiny. The decaying cities were exploding into open rebellions, the protests on the campuses were beginning to resemble the riots in the prisons, and even units of the army and navy were mutinying. Amidst a planet in revolution, America's leaders seemed ignorant of the past and blind to the future.

The apocalyptic imagination burst forth with images of catastrophe in all forms—from the very likely possibility of thermonuclear holocaust to absurd projections of the human race being overcome by even the most harmless life forms. By the late 1960s, visions of decay and doom had become the normal Anglo-American view of our possible futures, whether in the sterile whiteness of George Lucas's *THX 1138* (1969) or the shattered Statue of Liberty sprawled across the end of the aptly named *Planet of the Apes* (1968). Our only hope for salvation seemed to lie outside ourselves, perhaps with the godlike aliens who might remold someone to rescue us from the killer apes wearing the uniforms of United States generals in *2001* (1968).

As we all know, the crisis has continued to deepen and intensify in the 1970s and 1980s. And we are also more or less aware that the visions of the future projected in Anglo-American science fiction films of the 1970s and 1980s have been overwhelmingly pessimistic, when not downright apocalyptic. By exploring the precise forms of these visions, we may clarify our understanding of our cultural and historical situation.

Rather than selecting arbitrarily, I shall survey the entire body of films set in the future and released since 1970, and then examine in detail four films released after 1980 that offer more or less coherent views of some future period. To establish some referents, let us first leap back in time to recall the dominant images of the future found in earlier science fiction films.

The first great archetypal image of the future projected in the early science fiction film is what might be labeled *The Wonder City of the Future*. One thinks immediately of *Metropolis* (1926), where the wonder city is shown as part of a dialectic, resting literally on the subterranean labors of the working masses. In 1930, Hollywood spent a quarter of a million dollars to create its own *Wonder city of the Future*, the magnificent futuristic New York of 1980, in the ill-starred blockbuster science fiction musical *Just Imagine*. In 1936, *Things To Come* displayed *The Wonder City of the Future* as the creation of the technocratic elite, "The Wings Over the World," whose vast airships and space vehicle form the second received archetype, *The Marvelous Flying Machine*. Let us keep these early archetypes—*The Wonder City of the Future* and *The Marvelous Flying Machine*—in the back of our minds as we plunge through the visions of the future beginning in 1970 on our way to a close look at those four versions of 1981 and early 1982.

According to my count—and I've no doubt missed a few—there were released for general distribution from 1970 through early 1982 fifty-one Anglo-American science fiction movies set wholly or in part in some distinctly future time. Only two of these show anything resembling the triumph of progressive technology projected in *Things To Come* (unless one counts *Heart Beeps*, a 1981 story about robots falling in love). Both appeared in 1979, and both were aimed at a mainly juvenile audience, as though we adults, who really know better, think this cotton candy is best left for the children. Walt Disney Productions presented *The Black Hole*, where the human environment consists of nothing but *Marvelous Flying Machines*. *Star Trek: The Motion Picture* gives a very brief glimpse, in a clumsy backdrop, of *The Wonder City of the Future*, but of course most of it is set in a

Marvelous Flying Machine. These are the optimistic visions among the fifty-one.

Equally rare are the old 1950s images of aliens coming to threaten or destroy the future of our species. I can think of only two, both released in 1978. *Invasion of the Body Snatchers* was, of course, a remake of a 1950s alien invader movie, and, as in the original, the aliens are primarily metaphors for forces already present and shaping the future. No longer representing the communists, the pods are now, as many have noted, indistinguishable from the mods they replace. Altogether vanished are the middle-American, small-town virtues whose imminent demise constitutes the nightmare of the original. That other 1978 release, *The End of the World*, is virtually a parody of 1950s alien invader movies. In fact it ends with the vicious aliens not only destroying the Earth but forcing the last human survivors—our hero and heroine, the converse of Adam and Eve—to watch the whole show on television, where we actually see footage of earthquakes, volcanoes, fires, and floods from many previous disaster movies.

We get a similar show in *The Late Great Planet Earth* (1979), where the ponderous narration of Orson Welles accompanies images of the destruction of the world by earthquakes, tornadoes, floods, and killer bees as part of "Nature's growing offensive" culminating in the Jupiter Effect of 1982. But one should note that all this mess is actually concocted somehow by human activities and creations, including terrorism, pollution, nuclear war, communism, fascism, DNA research, religious sects and gurus, the European Common Market, Red China, Red Russia, and Black Africa.

Movies set in the present do continue to marshal more or less successful forays against us by such monsters as worms, bugs, bees, sharks, and a giant gorilla, as in *Squirm*, *The Swarm*, *The Bees*, *Empire of the Ants*, *Bug*, the *Jaws* films, and the remake of *King Kong*. But none of those fifty-one films set in the future shows other life forms from Earth affecting the course of human history, except for the four sequels to *The Planet of the Apes*: *Beneath the Planet of the Apes* (1970), *Escape from the Planet of the Apes* (1971), *Conquest of the Planet of the Apes* (1972), and *Battle for the Planet of the Apes* (1973). Practically every one of the remaining films displays some catastrophic or very nasty future caused directly by human behavior or human creations.

In *Colossus: The Forbin Project* (1970), the war computers of the United States and the Soviet Union link up to rule the planet. In *No Blade of Grass* (1970), pollution has devastated the environment.

Biological warfare destroys most of the human race in *The Omega Man* (1971), while it is poison gas that kills everybody over the age of twenty-five in Roger Corman's *Gas-s-s! Or It Became Necessary to Destroy the World in Order to Save It* (1970)—an echo of the assertion by the American officer who ordered the annihilation of the Vietnamese village of Ben Tre, "It was necessary to destroy the town in order to save it." A post-holocaust future is the setting for the X-rated *Glen and Randa* (1971), *The Ultimate Warrior* (1975), *A Boy and His Dog* (1975), *Damnation Alley* (1977), and *Logan's Run* (1976), which begins with a roll-up stating that the scene is after the catastrophe caused by overpopulation *and* pollution *and* thermonuclear war. In *Z.P.G.* (1972) and *Soylent Green* (1973), overpopulation has helped spawn evil governments, in the former one that bans births, in the latter one that feeds its citizens with green crackers made out of the bodies of fellow citizens.

Not one of these fifty-one movies shows a functioning democracy in the future. Many display future societies ruled by some form of conspiracy, monopoly, or totalitarian apparatus. *THX 1138* (1969; 1970) shows a conformistic police state in which one of the most terrifying images is an enlargement of the police who were then beating up anti-Vietnam-War demonstrators. *Ice* (1970) is a rarity which shows underground revolutionaries fighting back against a police state extrapolated from the same social scene of the late 1960s. The technocratic order extolled in the 1936 *Things To Come* has become the nemesis in these movies as well as in *A Clockwork Orange* (1971), where those who impose order are presented as even more frightening than the terrifying disorder they attempt to suppress. Other varieties of our dreadful political future appear in *Sleeper* (1973), *Zardoz* (1974), *The Man Who Fell To Earth* (1976), *Twilight's Last Gleaming* (1977), *Capricorn One* (1978)—these last two are of course really thinly veiled pictures of the present—*Alien* (1979), *Saturn 3* (1980), and the four most recent movies, which I shall discuss in detail, *Escape from New York* (1981), *Outland* (1981), *The Last Chase* (1981), and *Parasite* (1982).

A little subgenre of this type appears in the form of future worlds where the most interesting remaining normal human activity is some kind of sport or amusement, usually deadly, as in *Westworld* (1973), *Rollerball* and *Death Race 2000* (both 1975), *Futureworld* (1976), and *Deathsport* (1978).

In the 1970s and 1980s, the fundamental contradictions of American society have become visibly blatant in its cities, where high above the pot-holed streets, sleazy porno districts, decayed public transit, dilapidated small businesses, cockroach-infested housing, violence, and squalor have soared vestiges of that old visionary science fiction *Wonder City of the Future* in the form of banks and corporate head-quarters in glittering futuristic skyscrapers. It is no surprise that *The Wonder City of the Future* rarely appears any longer in the cinematic visions of tomorrow, except occasionally as some kind of domed world of illusory pleasures, as in *Logan's Run* or *Futureworld*. Instead, the cities of the present have been reduced to rubble over which or through which our poor descendants have their last pathetic adven-tures. Fragments of our decayed world are almost a cliché: the ruins of New York are strewn from *Planet of the Apes* through *The Ultimate Warrior* to the first episode of *Heavy Metal* (1981) and *Escape from New York*, featuring the rat-infested subway system, the crumbled pillars of the Stock Exchange, and the New York Public Library as the site of a creaky primitive oil well. The political center of America is represented by the ivy-covered ruins of the Capitol in *Logan's Run*, while middle America is anything from a series of abandoned towns inhabited by monstrous mutants in *Damnation Alley* to the under-ground all-American nightmare of Topeka in *A Boy and His Dog*.

When *The Marvelous Flying Machine* makes an appearance, it is usually as a harbinger not of progress but of terror. It may be as a vehicle bringing either some threatening alien life form—as in *The Andromeda Strain* (1971) or *Alien*—or assassins sent by human pow-ers—as in *Outland*—or some hideous human invention—as in *Saturn 3*. In *Zardoz*, *The Marvelous Flying Machine* is no longer either a sleek aerodynamic beauty or an intricate functional maze of machin-ery but a grotesque mask presiding over the subjugation and pro-grammed killing of the effete survivors on Earth. In *Dark Star* (1974), the purpose of *The Marvelous Flying Machine* is to annihilate stars that are deemed inconvenient. In *Silent Running* (1972), it is the final repository of Earth's remaining vegetation; when the heartless tech-nocratic authorities on Earth order the jettisoning of this cargo, we are supposed to applaud the response of the introspective captain (Bruce Dern), who murders the crew and embarks with his plants and robots on a lonely quest into deep space. In *Capricorn One*, manned space travel has degenerated into a hoax, and the United States government is out to kill off its phony space men so they can't reveal that *The Marvelous Flying Machine* hasn't really gone anyplace. In *The Last Chase*, the last remaining flying machine is a decrepit ancient T-38 piloted by an alcoholic Burgess Meredith in a suicide attack on one of the last vestiges of technological "progress," an automated laser gun. In a world living under the incessant threat of thermonuclear doomsday, movies might find it difficult to project the kind of salvation from war envisioned by *Things To Come*, with its technocratic elite forming a beneficent "Wings Over the World."

Of the four most recent movies displaying the future, *The Last Chase* is probably the worst example of cinematic art, in both form and content. Nevertheless, as a cultural symptom of the early 1980s it is well worth our attention. Sometime in the 1980s, a mysterious plague had wiped out most of the population. Simultaneously, oil had either run out or was somehow shut off. (Though released in 1981, *The Last Chase* has telltale signs of being made somewhat earlier, perhaps in 1979 when we didn't know about the global glut in oil as we were waiting in lines at the gas station.) The implication is that They—the all-powerful bureaucrats in Washington—had shut off the oil and maybe even released some biological agent to wipe out droves of people. Why? Because They believe that society must be static, calm, and, above all, stationary. Their *bête noir* is the private automobile, which allows the individual to be mobile and free. We can tell that these rulers are evil because they are committed to mass transit, solar power, pacifism, and a calm, carefully regulated life in a few cities under their total control.

The scene is now twenty years later—that is, in the twenty-first century. Franklin Hart (Lee Majors), a former race car driver, has buried his red Porsche under his garage. He works in what seems *The Wonder City of the Future*, actually a sinister anti-utopia with efficient mass transit, soaring futuristic buildings, and empty streets except for bicycles and sparse groups of pedestrians. Technology is concentrated in the computer and communications network which is used for total surveillance and bureaucratic omnipotence. Majors is about to be arrested for social deviance, since he has been observed in the forbidden areas where the abandoned cars rot and because his lectures to young people have been hinting that things were better in the past. Though set in a Wellsian *Wonder City of the Future*, *The Last Chase* projects precisely the opposite of Wells's vision in *Things To Come*: the technocrats are now the bad guys and the reactionaries are the good guys. (Even the plague that helps pave the way for the rule of the technocrats seems to be a reversed image from *Things To Come*.)

Enter the boy genius—a bespectacled misfit who has been jamming the state's jam-proof communications network with a transmitter he has thrown together out of spare parts. Hart, who has lost his own son in the plague, finds a new son in the boy genius. Together, they take off across the country in Hart's race car in search of freedom in the far West, which has been beaming subversive messages on Radio Free California.

The state gets Captain Williams (Burgess Meredith), the unappreciated jet ace of both the Korean War and the Vietnam War, now a kite-flying dipsomaniac, to give chase in that last *Marvelous Flying Machine*, the old T-38 armed with machine guns—and napalm. The setting for this epic conflict is the North American continent.

At this point, *The Last Chase* becomes a road movie, very similar in its mythic configuration to *Damnation Alley*. In each film, a tiny group of heroic survivors, beset by dangers on all sides, drives across a ruined America in search of someplace where the good old past still lives. The transcontinental road ends in each movie with the quest completed as our heroes drive into an embodiment of the mythic small town of the past. The small town community in *Damnation Alley* is Albany, New York; in *The Last Chase* it is some unnamed town in Free California. Both scenes are identical, with a band of citizens from the good old American small-town community strung out along the road as a cheering welcoming committee. This quest for the mythic middle American past is precisely the opposite of the vision of *A Boy and His Dog*, where it is the values of middle America itself that have launched the devastation, and where the red-white-and-blue Mom-and-apple-pie underground town of Topeka is the demonic center of the hell it has created.

In *The Last Chase*, the private automobile in its most gas-guzzling avatar—the bright red Porsche race car—symbolizes the opposition to bureaucracy, the state, conformism, solar power, mass transit, ecology, anti-war movements, and other equally sinister parts of progress. The grizzled supermale and the boy genius heading ever-westward in the last private car incarnate an ironic twist of the first great formative myth of popular science fiction.

Probably the very first science fiction dime novel was Edward Sylvester Ellis's *The Steam Man of the Prairies*, which appeared in 1865, at the exact moment of the triumph of industrial capitalism in America. The hero, typical of the science fiction dime novel, is a lone genius in the form of a teenaged boy. This is Johnny *Brain*erd, a fifteen-year-old hunchbacked, dwarfed boy whose father has died. Johnny's masterpiece among his many inventions is a ten-foot-tall robot driven by an internal steam engine, capable of speeding along at sixty miles an hour while drawing a four-passenger carriage, also designed and built by Johnny all by himself. Johnny Brainerd, with his hand-crafted sixty-mile-per-hour horseless carriage, foreshadows the figure of Henry Ford and those swarms of horseless carriages which, together with their manufacturers, have transformed our environment. His machine is the progenitor of the long line that will end with Franklin *Hart*'s red Porsche.

Having created his wonderful machine, Johnny receives a brand new father in the person of Baldy Bicknell, a grizzled old hunter, trapper, and gold-miner from the West. Together they pack the steam man into a crate and take him out West, to exploit the fabulous gold strike that Baldy has made in Wolf Ravine and to kill off hordes of "treacherous" "redskin" "savages." To hear the psychological reverbations of this myth in *The Last Chase*, listen carefully to this passage from *The Steam Man of the Prairies*, describing the grizzled old adventurer and the misfit boy genius: "These two personages, so unlike in almost every respect, had taken quite a fancy to each other. The strong, hardy, bronzed trapper, powerful in all that goes to make up the physical man, looked upon the pale sweet-faced boy, with his misshapen body, as an affectionate father would look upon an afflicted child." This father and son who together, without benefit of women, will breed the future of America are now replaced by the father and son driving alone to a past that never existed but that is still capable of destroying us all. Indeed, there are many internal hints that *The Last Chase* might at one time have been intended as an unofficial campaign movie for another questor for that mythic past, our current President.

Outland also seeks to recreate the past, but in quite a different form. Space is the New Frontier, a notion popularized by Robert A. Heinlein and politicized by John F. Kennedy, and the movie is, as many have noted, a space version of *High Noon*. *Outland* is set in the not-too-distant future on Io, one of Jupiter's moons, in a mining colony belonging to the now familiar gigantic monopolistic company.

Sean Connery is the newly-arrived marshall, whose lonely existential heroism is pitted against the omnipresent depravity and greed personified by the ruthless General Manager (Peter Boyle). (As in *9 to 5*, it is middle management that takes the rap for the worst crimes of the corporate world.) The manager, ironically named Shepphard, has been speeding up the workers with an amphetamine that gradually destroys their minds.

The marshall finds himself deserted by everybody but the hard-bitten burnt-out Company doctor with a cynical exterior and a heart of pure cornmush, brilliantly played by Frances Sternhagen. Writer and director Peter Hyams, who also did *Capricorn One*, gives a revealing reason for having changed the doctor's role from a man to a woman: "After the first draft of the script, I decided it was absurd for a picture set in the future to be unpopulated by women" (*New York Times*, May 26, 1981). What this reveals is made even more blatant by a widely syndicated film critic (Richard Freedman) whose review refers to this doctor as the "satellite nurse."

The entire colony of tough workers is too cowardly to defend themselves, so soon the marshall finds himself being stalked by the manager's hired killers, whose arrival time on *The Marvelous Flying Machine* is marked by the camera cutting frequently to a digital clock, reminding us that we are indeed watching a futuristic version of *High Noon*, that classic western appearing in—and about—the 1950s. In *High Noon*, however, Gary Cooper is making the frontier safe for the advance of the cowardly burghers who represent capitalist civilization. In *Outland* the gunslinging embodiment of law and order is merely keeping things from getting any worse in this hellish labor colony; he is just draining a little pus from one of the abscesses of decaying inter-planetary monopoly capitalism.

Outland is actually two different movies. One is a somewhat illogical but mildly entertaining re-creation of the western form of the myth of the lone hero—the lone lawman, the Lone Ranger. (Unlike Tonto, however, his non-white subordinate turns out to be a coward who joins the bad buys.) What we have here is a broken fragment of a myth, a shard, floating around like the other fragments in a disintegrating world. (*Battle beyond the Stars*, a minor 1980 masterpiece by Roger Corman, embodies this in the form of Cowboy, a survivor from a ruined Earth recruited to defend a distant planet of pacifists against evil alien imperialists.)

The other movie in *Outland* is quite literally, in all senses of the term, a set of images. The mining colony is a brilliantly conceived and executed creation, an overwhelming image of alienation. The workers labor in conditions that seem to combine the claustrophobic dangers of deep South African gold mines, the treacherous isolation of offshore or North Slope oil rigs, and the entrapment of modern prisons. A three-dimensional chase through their quarters seems to take us through endless stacks of cages, as though Borges's "The Library of Babel" had been used as a blueprint by the Company in designing a prison to warehouse its workers. Early in the movie, we see what it means to venture outside this entirely artificial alien environment into the even more alien natural surroundings: a worker, his mind eaten

away by the drug that has made him speed up his production, wanders
outside the pressurized world without his space suit and explodes (not
that this would happen).

The two movies come to a rather unsatisfactory juncture when the
chase culminates in the climactic shootout. Both Sean Connery and
the two assassins are rather improbably armed with weapons out of the
nineteenth century—shotguns—a heavy-handed reminder that we are
witnessing a western set in space, the mythic past projected into an
imagined future. A shotgun blows a hole in the wall that separates the
interior artificial world, with its alienated labor, from the exterior
world, with its deadly emptiness. But the gaping hole between the
pressurized interior world and the airless exterior world merely serves
as a convenience of the adventure plot, disposing of one of the nasty
gunmen. *Outland* ends up as uninterested in the workers and their
predicament as they seem to be in the plot.

Outland's vision of the giant monopoly and its slave-like workers
is certainly never reduced to the absurdity of the end of *Metropolis*,
where the dictator at the head of the monopoly shakes hands with the
spokesman of his workers and agrees to change the system. Nor does
Outland project the outlandish notion central to *Things To Come*, that
the technocrats will save all the rest of us—stupid sheep that we
are—from ourselves and from the vicious predators we mindlessly
obey. But the limitations of *Outland*'s imagination become clear when
we compare it with Heinlein's remarkably similar setting in "Logic of
Empire," which appeared in 1941, exactly forty years earlier. Unlike
Outland, "Logic of Empire" sees the slave labor colonies on Venus as
products of a particular economic system located within history and
being changed by the processes of history. Heinlein's story shows the
consciousness of both the capitalists and the workers determined by
the conditions of their class existence, but for the workers this means
not the stupifying cowardice in *Outland* but the beginnings of resistance and rebellion. Hollywood seems, for whatever reason, unwilling
or unable to handle such a theme. Perhaps the closest we have is one of
the true masterpieces of the genre, *Alien*, in which it is the workers and
the women who understand the true situation, and know what to do
about it, far more clearly than their stereotypical supercompetent
supermale commander, who unwittingly serves the most fiendish designs of the monopolistic Company.

At the date of this writing the most recent vision of the future
projected has to be seen through glasses that are not only rose-colored

but also polarized. It is the 3D thriller *Parasite* (1982), boldly set just a decade ahead in 1992. America is now a virtual wasteland under the unofficial tyranny and open terror of the "Merchants." As one character explains: "You can't tell the Government and the Merchants apart any more; they work for each other." The economy has collapsed, and paper money is worthless; regular gas costs $29.98 a gallon, payable in silver or gold; practically no food is available except for old canned goods and such rare luxuries as packets of sugar or instant coffee; the landscape is strewn with abandoned cars and houses; some mysterious "atomic shit" has rained down on New York City, sending survivors fleeing into remote small towns.

As in *Outland*, work has been reduced to blatant slave labor, but here the "work camps" run by the Merchants are established not on a moon of Jupiter but in the suburbs of America. The significance of this is spelled out. Witnessing an especially gruesome death of a friend, one escapee from these work camps laments: "It's just like the suburbs all over again—you can't care for anybody."

Parasite combines that first great myth emerging out of industrial capitalism—Frankenstein—with that now all-too-familiar myth of small-town America. The scientist, Doctor Paul Dean, author of the weighty tome *The Pathology of Parasites*, has created, on special orders from the state, a brand new super-parasite, capable of either eating people up from inside or growing to enormous size by grabbing them from outside and sucking out all their blood. This parasite, potentially capable of boundless reproduction, bears a striking resemblance to the creature in *Alien*, which may help explain why the Merchants, like the Company in *Alien*, are so eager to get it into profitable operation.

Doctor Dean realizes the sinister alienation of his scientific labor, rebels against the state, and destroys all but two of his creatures: the one that is growing inside him and another one he needs to experiment on to learn how he can kill the one inside. He manages to escape with his books, laboratory apparatus, and two creatures to the little town of Joshua, "Population 64, Altitude 1100."

There he is befriended by a black bartender recently escaped from New York and a young woman who grows lemon trees in her little Edenic garden so that she can offer fresh lemonade as a healthy old-fashioned alternative to the unrelieved diet of leftover canned goods. Doctor Paul Dean and his new friends are abused by a hot-rod gang of young bullies and their molls and hunted down by the Merchants, embodied by a thin-lipped crewcut blond in a dark three-piece suit, caroming around in a futuristic car, and armed with a death-ray gun in his black-gloved hand.

The little adventure has a happy ending: Doctor Dean discovers the means to kill the parasite within; the other parasite and the Merchant are consumed in flames; even the hot-rod gangsters turn out to be decent young people, just driven to bad attitudes and behavior by their environment. However, as usual in these recent visions of the future, although the good people win their little adventure against overwhelming odds, both their heroism and their victory are essentially irrelevant. Typical of the heroes of these movies, they overcome some especially horrible excrescence of their society, but they have not even tried to deal with the fundamental evil, which remains unassailable and omnipotent.

The despair of *Outland* and *Parasite* looks like bubbling optimism alongside the bleak landscape of *Escape from New York*, directed and partly written by John Carpenter, who in 1974 had done *Dark Star*, one of a handful of truly original science fiction films. The time is 1997. America is a thinly-concealed fascist society in a chronic state of war, escalating crime, and social decay. The president is on his way to a summit meeting with the Soviets, arranged as a last desperate attempt to avert thermonuclear war while preserving United States power. An underground revolutionary organization hijacks his plane; it crashes into Manhattan, which had been sealed off in the 1980s, turned into a prison colony, and left to the anarchy of its inmates, who are guarded by the killer helicopters of the United States Police Force, garrisoned, appropriately enough, at the Statue of Liberty. *The Wonder City of the Future* is now society's garbage dump, a pile of rubble and human rot prefiguring worse things to come. *The Marvelous Flying Machine* is now represented by the smoldering wreck of Air Force One being looted by New York's ragged criminals, by the helicopters of the police state, and, in a final comedown, by a glider which lands on the abandoned World Trade Center in a final attempt to save the president and the world (or at least keep it safe for American democracy).

As in *The Last Chase*, *Outland*, and *Parasite*, the plot centers on the adventure of a lone hero fighting, along with a friend or two, against near-impossible odds and overwhelming forces. As usual, he will win his minor victory in a hopeless world.

The lone hero of *Escape from New York* is Snake Plissken (Kurt Russell), once the Special Forces hero of the Siberia campaign, now a notorious bank robber, sporting a sinister patch and limp, condemned to life imprisonment in Manhattan. Snake slithers around the collapsing concrete jungle of New York (actually photographed mainly in Saint Louis) aided by a resourceful veteran cab driver (strikingly similar to the cabbie in the first episode of *Heavy Metal*, who also maneuvers craftily through the crime-infested rubble of the future New York). The United States Police have implanted an explosive, which only they can deactivate, in Snake's neck, giving him only twenty-four hours to rescue the president from the apparent arch-villain, the Duke of New York, played by Isaac Hayes and driving around, as a racist caricature of black aspirations, in a limousine bedecked with crystal chandeliers.

At the end, Snake delivers the president, but temporarily withholds the secret tape that the President is about to broadcast to the Soviet leaders. Then he watches with disgust as the president, in a power-mad frenzy, sprays the Duke with submachine-gun fire. Snake's face cagily records the nihilistic message symbolized by this scene, he hands over a tape, and we listen as the president broadcasts what he announces as his final proposal to the Soviets—the pop music tape Snake has just given him. Apparently nothing now stands in the way of the final apocalypse for this rotten world of the very near future.

What we can infer from these despairing visions of the future remains somewhat conjectural. After all, more optimistic products have come out of Hollywood, as we can tell by looking today at the resident of the White House. And certainly there is more to American culture than its movie industry. But perhaps these visions are the appropriate imaginative projections of a society that has borrowed over a trillion dollars from the future in order to construct the marvelous weapons that may guarantee that there won't be any future to collect the debts.

Given the military, economic, and political hegemony of the United States in much of the world, these cultural projections are profoundly frightening. With no better vision of the future to offer, the United States may possibly succeed in forcing the rest of the world into one of these futures imagined in Hollywood. Or perhaps these movies are best seen as warnings—whether or not intended—not to follow the leadership of a social structure that either doesn't know where it's going or sees its own future as hopeless.

7

Nostalgia Isn't What It Used To Be: The Middle Ages in Literature and Film

E. Jane Burns

The recent popularity of films set in the era of King Arthur (Rohmer's *Perceval*, Bresson's *Lancelot du Lac*, Boorman's *Excalibur*, and the more fanciful British spoof *Monty Python and the Holy Grail*) leads one to wonder what has spawned this nostalgic revival of the early Middle Ages. Why in the late 1970s and early 1980s have filmmakers chosen to turn back the clock almost 1500 years and investigate an era so long past and so sparsely documented that it has all but slipped from the pages of history into the more fantastic realm of legend?

In 1655, Milton asked himself the same question, couched in slightly different terms. Having planned to write an epic about King Arthur and the Round Table, Milton decided finally to abandon the task because, as he put it, the *real* Arthur had been lost, because all that was left of this historical personnage was a myth with its values of "monarchy, warfare, and false romanticism."[1] While this grand insistence on historical veracity might seem somewhat ludicrous coming from an author who later chose for the subject of his epic two of the most mythical figures in Western literature, Adam and Eve, Milton's assessment of the Arthurian material is essentially accurate. There is, in reality, very little historical data surrounding the legendary Briton king.

For this reason, filmmakers seeking to uncover the sixth-century Arthur and present him to the modern cinema audience must necessarily turn from history to myth, basing their filmic narratives on literary documents in which King Arthur's feats are boldly exaggerated and lavishly extolled. Rather than harking back to former times or representing life as it existed in medieval Britain, these films look at the sixth century through a literary filter which is itself highly romanticized and, in fact, created anew with each successive historical epoch. The recent films about King Arthur are thus not designed to return us to the long-lost past. They seek, instead, to convey a kind of nostalgia for a distant civilization by creating a past that never was, a fantastic and highly fanciful world of elegant ladies and valiant knights.

The major literary source containing information about King Arthur is a pseudo-historical Latin chronicle written by Geoffrey of Monmouth in 1135–36. This text was translated into the vernacular in 1155 and gave rise to a whole cycle of stories featuring Arthur and the knights of the Round Table. Known collectively as the Matter of Britain,[2] these tales do take place, in large part, in the British Isles (in Wales and Cornwall in particular), but they are written in Old French, and were not adapted into an English version until Malory wrote his *Morte d'Arthur* in the latter part of the fifteenth century. Malory's text was the standard source of Arthurian material in Milton's time and remains such for speakers of English today. But Malory's *Morte*, like its French predecessors, was based ultimately on Geoffrey of Monmouth's *Historia Regum Britanniae*.

This text was used extensively by chroniclers throughout the medieval period until it was discovered in the sixteenth century to be a fake, or at least a highly-fabricated, non-historical account. Since Geoffrey's goal had been to flatter the Norman conquerors of England by displaying the greatness of the race that they had recently subdued, the Arthur he presented is glorious in the extreme. As a valiant military hero, Arthur is seen vindicating the Britons against Saxons, Picts, and Scots, and conquering Ireland, Gothland, and Gaul. As a champion of the cause of Christianity, he travels as far as Iceland, subduing countless fierce pagan tribes en route.[3] All of these exploits are, however, the product of Geoffrey's imagination. From a very few historical facts—that there was a King Arthur who scored a military victory in Wessex in the last decade of the fifth century—Geoffrey created a whole world of courageous knights and extravagant military triumphs to please his twelfth-century audience.[4]

The same can be said of the English Romantics who, after Milton's eschewal of the illusive and legendary king in the seventeenth century, were the next to revive the Arthurian past through a peculiar brand of neo-medievalism. After his initial appearance in Sir Walter Scott's *Bridal of Triermain* at the beginning of the century, Arthur became the focus for a series of poems written by Tennyson in the 1830s and 1840s. Having grown up with Malory's tales of knights and ladies, Tennyson recast the Arthur of Geoffrey and Malory in a distinctly Victorian mold. With his poem "The Lady of Shalott" (1832) and its successor "Sir Galahad" (1842), Tennyson launched an Arthurian vogue which continued through the Pre-Raphaelites. Using vaguely medieval-sounding words or settings, writers from Walter Scott through William Morris created characters and plots which are wholly Victorian: melancholy tales of love and death, psychodramas of women destroyed by passion, or adulteresses writhing in the throes of their sinful love.[5] Tennyson's vision of Arthur, as cast in the *Idylls of the King*, offered an image of the perfect Victorian, "a man who spent himself in the cause of honour, duty, and self-sacrifice . . . In short God has not made since Adam was, the man more perfect than Arthur."[6]

It is clear that the nineteenth-century fascination with the Middle Ages was not based on the facts of social history. It was built, rather, on a fantasy world of splendor and gallantry that bears the mark of escapist desire. Both the Romantics and the Pre-Raphaelites were writing in the wake of the Industrial Revolution which had institutionalized deplorable working conditions in the mines, factories, and mills, bringing at the same time slums, lack of sanitation, and rampant disease to England's cities.[7] Reacting against eighteenth-century materialism and its devastating results, the poets and painters of the nineteenth century indulged in what has come to be known as the "Spirit of Wonder": they envisioned a pure, whole world, a lost ideal, which they located, however erroneously, in the Middle Ages.[8] In essence, they fabricated a heroic past for their time, much as Geoffrey of Monmouth had invented the resplendent world of King Arthur for his own contemporaries.

In France, this task fell initially to literary historians seeking to re-establish a national tradition that had been displaced by deference to the antique masters. Of those who began reviving popular interest in the medieval period, Etienne Pasquier and Claude Fauchet were prominent in the sixteenth century, Chapelain and Vulson de la Colombière in the seventeenth, and Lacurne de Sainte-Palaye in the eighteenth.[9] Yet, the Middle Ages which was reconstructed by these men was not based on a knowledge of medieval texts; the only romances available to them, for example, were translations of late manuscripts or highly deformed Spanish and Italian versions. Defending romance as a noble, heroic, and honorable literary genre, these early pioneers of medieval studies invented a Middle Ages which was much more glorious than any which had ever existed. Their efforts are grounded in a nostalgic desire to retrieve a past which systematically had been severed from them.

The French Romantics continued this same project in later years, admiring in the Middle Ages what they deemed to be anti-rationalist traits: sentimentality, passion, faith, devout belief in an ideal. As the antithesis of order and control, the Middle Ages proved to be a handy weapon in the fight against the Neoclassical influences in literature.[10] And politically, the medieval period provided a useful model for nineteenth-century monarchy: the medieval people could be touted as unfailing believers in God and king. Thus the initial recuperation of the Middle Ages championed by writers of the French Renaissance grew slowly into the fully nostalgic "medievalism" of the Romantics.

However, the nineteenth century was not alone in looking to the past for the future, in projecting a desired identity on a distant civilization. The literature of the Middle Ages is replete with its own kind of nostalgia for the "good old times." The great age of epic song, which began at the end of the eleventh century with the *Song of Roland*, celebrated not contemporary heroes but legendary figures of French history: Charlemagne and the French count William of Orange. When romance was inaugurated in the middle of the twelfth century, it chose for its set-piece the sixth-century King Arthur and the distant marches of Cornwall and Wales.

Much like the works of the English Romantics and Pre-Raphaelites, the romance genre can be seen as advancing a myth of totality and integrated social life. And this myth, like its nineteenth-century counterpart, was forged at a time of intense political and economic change. The early medieval period is divided typically into two feudal ages: the first, coming before 1150, is characterized by an agrarian economy involving a system of barter or payment in kind, and a system of vassalage based on close bonds between individual men. The Second Feudal Age is marked, in turn, by the rise of towns and the creation of a money economy that was dominated not by the producer but by the merchant, artisan, and trader.[11] This radical shift in means of production and methods of trade, along with the restrictive laws of primogeniture which deeded land only to the oldest son of a noble family, created an entire class of knights errant (*hobereau* or squirine), nobles who had been alienated from their assigned social role.[12]

The literary accounts of King Arthur, which are all contemporary with the Second Feudal Age, tell only indirectly of this stressful change in the fabric of human relations. What they show, in the main, is a picture of knights and kings *before* the destructive intrusion of medieval materialism: the view of the Arthurian realm that is presented here is that of the past and now idyllic First Feudal Age. It has been suggested, then, that romance embodies the voice of the knights errant, the dispossessed feudal class looking back to a time of security and social stability, a time when the individual was better integrated into the social structure.[13] The enemy in these tales is not cast as he is in the earlier epic songs; the enemy is not an exterior military foe such as the king of Spain or a barbarian pagan ruler. Nor does he take the form of petty barons struggling for control of the French crown.[14] The destructive force menacing Arthur's realm in the romance narratives is mysterious and vague: oafish, gigantic rivals, fairy-tale monsters, and dragons. We see here a portrayal of the world of chivalry which itself has become hostile to its members: the courtly society gone awry, the chivalric culture that has begun to rot from within.

This is the view of the Arthurian realm that we find in a film like Bresson's *Lancelot du Lac*, for example, where we witness the slow destruction of a world unable to prevent its own demise. The adultery between Lancelot and Guenivere which has broken the feudal bond of king and vassal between Arthur and his most valiant knight, Lancelot, has sown a seed of disaster which cannot be remedied. The film begins at the point where Arthur's knights have returned from the quest, Lancelot has seen the Holy Grail, confessed his sin, and sworn to break with Guenivere, thus re-establishing his allegiance to the king. His enforced chastity is, however, short-lived. Confined to Arthur's court in the presence of the beckoning queen, Lancelot wastes no time in renouncing his promise to God and superterrestrial authority. But when the adultery resumes, it brings with it annihilation. The peaceable knights engage first in a tournament (the medieval surrogate for combat), and then in all-out war. The result is a senseless but unavoidable bloodbath in which King Arthur and his bastard son Mordred are forced to kill each other.

This nostalgic glance into the Arthurian past has the distinct tone of a funeral march, of bereavement for an epoch that met an untimely end. It echoes, in this way, the French *La Mort le roi Artu* on which it is based.[15] What we see in this filmic portrayal is not only the death of Arthur, but the death of the myth of all-powerful monarchy. Kingship is brought to its knees by the allied forces of adultery and uncontrolled warfare. Yet this film also makes reference to one of the central mythic solutions advanced in literary accounts to remedy the dilemma of failed kingship: the myth of the Holy Grail which will restore the lost ontological unity of a realm sundered by combat and illicit love.

Rohmer's *Perceval* develops this motif more fully, focussing on the very hero who is slated to find the Grail, revive the ailing king, and restore productivity to his strife-ridden land. The myth of the unfailing heroic monarch that we find in Geoffrey's *Historia* is here replaced with a more powerful myth: that of the sacred vessel which will ensure a kind of salvation that royalty cannot procure. It is of course clear, however ironically, that this second myth can be no more effective than was the first. If Arthur's knights take the religious quest to heart, renouncing worldly glory and the heroism of war, they will no longer be knights but hermits. The chivalrous society will be dissolved by the very force that is designed to save it from destruction. In fact, Perceval has endless trouble in locating the Holy Grail, and, in the French versions of the tale, never succeeds at the task.

However, there is another solution to the problem of weak and failing Arthurian kingship. This solution, advanced in detail in John Boorman's more recent film *Excalibur*, is that of Merlin's magic. The totalizing influence in this case will come not from the supernatural power of a Christian relic, but from the more ancient and awesome forces of enchantment. But the nostalgic desire remains constant: to return to an era of mythic plenitude, a time before fragmentation and the Fall. Merlin, who creates the Round Table in order to establish peace among Arthur's knights, is said to be from a time when the world was whole, a time of peaceful co-existence before the inception of combat and strife. The magic sword Excalibur is also described as belonging to a time when the world was whole. When the young Arthur manages to pull Excalibur from the stone in which it is mysteriously lodged, he inaugurates a new era of hope, heralding a renaissance of wise governance and triumphant leadership. This is the myth of the valiant monarch at its best, but here too, complications ensue. As soon as Lancelot and the queen fall into an adulterous liaison, the land is laid waste, Arthur lapses slowly into a comatose stupor, and Merlin, the engineer of peace and prosperity, is jailed in a stone cavern by a bewitching captor.

Thus the second myth is introduced: Arthur's life and land will be saved, we are told, by the Holy Grail. And, in this case, a second renaissance does indeed occur. When Perceval succeeds in finding the holy vessel, the orchards burst with elaborate and extravagant bloom, Arthur regains his vital signs, and all is well—until war breaks out. This battle, like the one in Bresson's *Lancelot*, is no ordinary skirmish, but the war to end all wars, a fundamental annihilation in which father kills son and progeny is downed with progenitor. The two films differ significantly, however, in their ultimate use of the mythic material. While the somber tone of *Lancelot* underscores the finality of Arthur's death and the end of both mythic and feudal worlds, the final scene of *Excalibur* offers further hope for survival in the form of yet another myth.

At the end of *Excalibur* we see Arthur being swept away to the legendary Isle of Avalon on an enchanted fairy boat. This is the perfect solution to Arthur's untimely death and the most nostalgic treatment of it, since in this version he does not actually die. Arthur will live on in the company of three sorceresses, whose powers ressemble those of the venerated Merlin, until such time as he returns to Britain to rule again. Thus we are left with the hope and the possibility that the perfect monarch of the sort invented by Geoffrey and celebrated by the English Romantics and Pre-Raphaelites can still reign. The glorified past is here relocated to a hypothetical future, as legendary and highly fictionalized history transcends time to become prophecy. The warrior king remains, in this way, glorified *in potentia*. He has become like Merlin, who lives both in the past and the future; a king who, although dead and gone, will live forever.

In this case we have come full circle. The myth of the glorious and valiant monarch is superseded by that of the Holy Grail, which in turn gives way to another version of the powerful monarch theme. The emphasis here is not solely on the waning of the Middle Ages; this is not the wistful glance toward a destroyed civilization that we see in Bresson's *Lancelot*. Rather, *Excalibur* offers us nostalgia incarnate: a longing for plenitude and peace which, while impossible to attain by moving backward in time, might be realized in future generations.

Whether this is "false" Romanticism, to use Milton's term, is difficult to say. But it is certainly Romanticism if we understand the word to mean a belief in a higher order of things which is, of necessity, more complete and whole than the fragmentary world that we experience on earth. And Romanticism of this sort is not confined to poets of the nineteenth century or filmmakers of the twentieth, as we have seen. It is part and parcel of the literature of the High Middle Ages which is marked, from the mid-twelfth century on, by a yearning for former times.

One might be tempted to conclude, at this point, that, contrary to the title of this essay, nostalgia is *exactly* what it used to be, that the full-bodied myth of Arthurian splendor has endured with amazing tenacity from the eleventh to the twentieth century. However, there is one recent film about Arthur that contains no such longing for the medieval past: *Monty Python and the Holy Grail*. In fact, this film constitutes a systematic destructuring of both Arthurian myth and the nostalgia for it. Here Romanticism is turned to comedy as we witness an insightful and inspired condemnation of the entire feudal system: of monarchal power, of medieval warfare, and of the literary conventions which glorify chivalric deeds. King Arthur is presented initially in traditional form, as a king whose immense power derives from successful military exploits: "It is I, Arthur, son of Uther Pendragon, from the Castle of Camelot, King of all Britons, defeater of the Saxons, Sovereign of all England."[16] But the valiant king who speaks these eloquent words is traversing the countryside on foot with his "trusty servant" Patsy, who steadfastly bangs two empty halves of coconuts together to produce the sound of galloping horse hooves. This king, who descends from the noble lineage of Uther Pendragon, is without a horse. While the successful wars he has waged against Saxon invaders have established him in a position of power, they have not yielded the traditional booty of land, weapons, and heroic steeds. These wars have produced only coconuts, and a king who is unable to reason clearly. When a soldier at the rival castle questions Arthur's claim to kingship by pointing out that he is not, in fact, riding a horse but only creating the sound of horse hooves by using coconuts, Arthur reponds first with indignation, "So?", and then continues in the appropriate vein of royal pomposity: "We have ridden since the snows of winter covered this land, through the kingdom of Mercia" (p. 2). However, the subsequent conversation swiftly undercuts the validity of Arthur's claim to authority. It is, in the main, a lightly veiled attack on medieval scholastic debating techniques, but through it we see a king whose meager wits are no match for the persistent deductive reasoning of a mere soldier:

SOLDIER
    Where did you get the coconuts?
ARTHUR
    . . . We found them.
SOLDIER
    Found them? In Mercia. The coconut's tropical.
ARTHUR
    What do you mean?
SOLDIER
    Well, this is a temperate zone.
ARTHUR
    The swallow may fly south with the sun, or the house martin or the plover seek hot lands in winter, yet these are not strangers to our land.
    A moment's pause.
SOLDIER
    Are you suggesting that coconuts migrate?

ARTHUR

  Not at all. They could be carried.

SOLDIER

  What? A swallow carrying a *coconut*?

ARTHUR

  It could grip it by the husk . . .

SOLDIER

  It's not a question of where he grips it, it's a simple matter of
  weight ratios . . . a five-ounce bird cannot hold a one-pound
  coconut. (P. 2)

Thus, the common sense of a rival soldier puts to shame the wildly
irrational thinking of King Arthur. We see here the Arthurian realm
turned upside down, and the king is no longer seated comfortably on
top of it.

Arthur's knights are, in turn, similarly ill-equipped for their
appointed heroic tasks. The list reads as follows: "The wise Sir Bede-
vere was the first to join King Arthur's knights . . . but other illus-
trious names were soon to follow . . . Sir Lancelot the Brave, Sir
Galahad the Pure, and Sir Robin-the-not-quite-so-pure-as-Sir-
Lancelot . . . who had nearly fought the Dragon of Angnon . . . who
had nearly stood up to the vicious Chicken of Bristol. . . . (p. 20).
And the flawed valor of Arthur's retinue is matched perfectly by the
king's own incompetence as a military leader. When heading the
charge toward the French castle, Arthur hails the attack by shouting,
"Right! Knights! Forward!" But as soon as the advancing troops are
showered with an impressive array of farm animals thrown over the
walls by the enemy, Arthur rescinds his former order by directing his
knights to "Run Away!" (p. 27).

Far beyond the failing of this particular king, however, the whole
basis of the feudal system of government is attacked in this film
through a neo-marxist analysis of Arthur's oppressed subjects and
exploited servants. When he meets them in the field, Arthur's fellow
Britons do not recognize him as their king and do not take him
seriously. A peasant named Dennis says, "What I object to is that you
automatically treat me as an inferior." Arthur responds, "Well . . . I
am king," to which Dennis replies: "Oh very nice. King eh! I expect
you've got a palace and fine clothes and courtiers and plenty of food.
And how d'you get that? By exploiting the workers! By hanging onto
outdated imperialistic dogma, which perpetuates the social and economic differences in our society!" (p. 8). When a peasant woman later

objects that Arthur has no authority to give orders to the inhabitants of his realm because, after all, they did not vote for him, Arthur is forced to explain the obvious, that "You don't vote for kings" (p. 9). Beset with the complaints of subjects who have formed an "anarcho-syndicalist commune," this king is backed into the absurdly unroyal position of having to justify his right to power.

The criteria he uses in his defense are not those of noble lineage, military might, or able governance. His sole claim to kingship resides in myth. "The Lady of the Lake," Arthur explains, "her arm clad in purest shimmering samite, held Excalibur aloft from the bosom of the waters to signify that by Divine Providence . . . I, Arthur, was to carry Excalibur . . . that is why I am your king" (p. 10).

DENNIS
> Look, strange women lying on their backs in ponds handing over swords . . . that's no basis for a system of government. Supreme executive power derives from a mandate from the masses not from some farcical aquatic ceremony.

ARTHUR
> Be quiet!

DENNIS
> You can't expect to wield supreme executive power just because some watery tart threw a sword at you. (P. 10)

The myth of the feudal monarch is here mercilessly deflated with a single stroke. And when Arthur, infuriated by Dennis's caustic remarks, resorts to grabbing him by the collar and telling him to "Shut up!", Dennis replies, "Ah! *Now* we see the violence inherent in the system" (p. 10). Through this neo-marxist axiom about violence inherent in the system we, the viewers, are reminded that feudalism was based on power derived from military might, that the courtly society of knights and ladies is only one side of a coin whose darker face bears the marks of warfare, pillage, and exploitation.

Yet, this film goes one step further and attacks the literary vehicle responsible for our overly romantic reading of the medieval period. The whole genre of Arthurian romance narrative comes under fire in the scene where Lancelot, having received an urgent call for help, rushes to the site of a wedding to save the beautiful Princess Lucky (or so he assumes) from the clutches of her undeserving groom. After arriving, however, Lancelot indulges in countless acts of wholly gratuitous violence, hacking his way through the crowd of celebrants in order to reach the woebegone princess. In the process, Lancelot kills eight wedding guests, the bride's father, several guards, and the best man among others, and is forced, in the end, to apologize profusely saying, "I'm terribly sorry. . . . It's just that when I'm in this genre, I tend to get over-excited and start to leap around and wave my sword about and . . . " (p. 57). The heroic knight of legendary tales is here reduced to grovelling in embarrassment because his literary role is clearly unsuited to realistic existence. The problem is delineated further at the moment of Lancelot's exit from the wedding feast. When his squire Concorde suggests, "Quickly, sir, come this way!" Lancelot replies, "No! It's not right for my idiom. I must escape more . . . dramatically" (p. 60). And, like the other famous knights of Arthur's retinue, he *nearly* does. Grabbing a rope off the wall, Lancelot swings out over the heads of the crowd in a swashbuckling manner, but he stops just short of the window and is left swinging pathetically back and forth. He then asks timidly if someone could give him a push.

After thoroughly discrediting our romanticized view of medieval life through a whole host of scenes like those described above, *Monty Python and the Holy Grail* takes one final jab at the modern perpetrators of nostalgia for the Middle Ages: the filmic medium itself. At the end of the movie King Arthur is arrested and taken away in a police car because one of his knights, in an earlier scene, had killed a historian of medieval literature who was attempting to explain Arthur's strategy for capturing the Holy Grail. We can deduce one of two things from this final scene: that scholarly inquiry into the life of the knights of the Round Table is a potentially dangerous occupation; or more important, that King Arthur is as much a part of the twentieth century as he was a part of the sixth. But he appears here without royal authority or immunity from prosecution. In short, he is presented as any citizen of modern Britain who cannot blithely order the murder of his fellow countrymen without suffering due punishment under the contemporary penal code. The myth of the medieval monarch and the heroic feudal ethic that informs all of the literature known as Arthurian romance is here exploded by the even-handed democracy of the modern judicial system.

This film could be taken, in a sense, as an answer to Milton's discontent with the false Romanticism of the Arthurian material. *Monty Python and the Holy Grail* makes Arthur come alive in a way that is neither realistic nor romantic. In fact, this film's portrayal of the legendary king can be seen as the most fantastic of the literary and filmic accounts we have discussed thus far. It is fantastic in the strictly etymoloical sense of the Latin *phantasia*, which refers to the act of making the imagination visible. Instead of looking back in time with a nostalgic desire to return to an Arthur who never was, *Monty Python and the Holy Grail* creates a new Arthur by combining the few legendary threads that remain of him with an incisive reading of the historical past. We find here a King Arthur who, with all the pomp and ceremony ascribed to him by his nineteenth-century admirers, takes himself too seriously and therefore makes us laugh. Thus *Monty Python and the Holy Grail* casts a dark shadow over any attempt, filmic or literary, to glorify the brutal and merciless existence of people in the Middle Ages. After viewing this highly amusing and very silly film, it is difficult for anyone to read Tennyson's *Idylls of the King* with unrestrained rapture, or to plunge headlong into the fanciful world of Malory's *Morte*. In the wake of *Monty Python and the Holy Grail*, nostalgia isn't what it used to be.

8

The Problem of Realizing Medieval Romance in Film: John Boorman's *Excalibur*

Cyndia Clegg

For nearly eight centuries the materials of Arthurian legend have enriched the fantasy life of adult and child alike. Spenser, Wagner, Tennyson, Twain, even A. A. Milne, have told, retold or merely remembered the legends of Camelot and its knights and ladies. More recently John Boorman attempted the re-creation of Arthur's medieval world in the film *Excalibur*. Although this film contains the recognizable story elements of medieval Arthurian romance, their cinematic rendering raises the question of whether this film affords the audience an imaginative experience consistent with that of reading medieval romance. To answer this question, it will be necessary to locate the essence of literary romance, which, I think, lies in the language, and then to examine the cinematic analogue, the image. Literary romance, I shall argue, produces its imaginative experience at the level of discourse through the tonality of language that unifies such disparate elements as the supernatural and the natural. According to Christian Metz, the cinematic image has a similar potential for unifying fantastic and realistic subjects. In order to assess the degree to which Boorman realizes this potential, I shall develop an approach for studying fantasy film that synthesizes the aesthetics of D. W. Gotshalk with the structuralist semiotics of L. Hjelmslev. Using this method I shall seek to determine if the unifying tonality present in the literary construct exists in the image construct which is *Excalibur*, that is, whether the signification system in the film displays the integrity necessary to create a semantic equanimity similar to that achieved in literary romance which can blend the fantastic and the naturalistic elements.

Before I examine Boorman's cinematic realization of medieval romance, it is essential to establish the conventions of its literary treatment. Traditionally, the medieval Arthurian cycles have been regarded by literary critics and historians as definitive of the medieval literary romance genre. Literary romance involves an idealized world, historically past or socially remote, peopled with aristocratic figures— kings, queens, knights and ladies—who, as in dreams, act as the reader's representatives. As universalized figures of the reader's imagination, these characters perhaps revive the sense of impotence surviving in the recesses of personality since childhood,[1] and draw the reader into imaginative interaction with the narrative. Within the narrative, through knightly dedication to the ideal of chivalric love, the characters engage in encounters with evil knights, in battles with dragons and giants, in tournaments and jousts. In the narrative mode of romance the storyteller creates the imaginative world. The reader, to enjoy romance, must surrender to what the narrator says is possible, and the possible may be either marvelous or mundane. But whether marvelous or mundane, each character and each event is presented with the same tonality—a tonality which accepts with equanimity the supernatural and the human, and which is created entirely by the writer's language. The reader's impression of medieval romance is of a world sensual and rich, created by a highly descriptive style. The language, though, of the description consists of abstractions. Ladies are "passing fair" or if truly superlative, "loveliest to behold"; knights are "fair," "stalwart," "peerless" and "blithe"; hounds "keen scented"; and the king "most courteous." The writer paints his imaginative canvas with form, dimension, and color; the reader assigns depth, shadow, and hue. The imaginative language, the idealized world, the subject of human relationships, the presence of a narrator eliciting imaginative response and suspending rationality all enable literary romance to reach to the deepest levels of human experience—dream, imagination, the unconscious—re-created in myth and fairytale.

With the experience of reading Arthurian romance, the reader's imaginative interaction with the narrative occurs both at the level of the story and of the discourse. The imaginative experience is a literary phenomenon whose peculiar effects upon the reader the language itself produces—the power of words creates possibilities which exist only in words. If we consider that the world of Arthurian romance is literary, a product only of words, we must wonder what happens to the imaginative experience when this world is re-created in the primarily visual language of film. Can a filmmaker, as John Boorman has attempted to do in the film *Excalibur*, afford a film audience an experience of Arthurian fantasy which engages its imagination not only at the level of character and event, but at the level of the cinematic discourse?

The answer to this question lies partially in film theorists' substantial body of investigation into the relationship between image and reality in film. Though he does not resolve the debate on the nature of film reality, in *Film Language* Christian Metz demonstrates that because film "carries enough elements of reality—the literal translation of graphic contours, and, mainly, the real presence of motion,"[2] it appeals to the spectator's sense of belief. According to Metz, "the secret of film is that it is able to leave a high degree of reality in its images, which are nevertheless still perceived as images."[3] In a sense, then, the film spectator views film with almost a divided consciousness, one part of which accepts the celluloid and light as image, and one part of which accepts the projected image with its graphic contours and motion as reality. The experience of fantasy in film, according to Metz, derives from the power of reality in the image:

> Fantastic art is fantastic only if it convinces (otherwise it is merely ridiculous) and the power of unreality in film derives from the fact that the unreal seems to have been realized, unfolding before our eyes as if it were the flow of common occurrence—not the plausible illustration of some extraordinary process only conceived in the mind. The subjects of film can be divided into the "realistic" and the "non-realistic" if one wishes, but the film vehicle's power to make real, to realize, is common to both genres.[4]

The significance of Metz's comments for a discussion of fantasy film lies in directing our attention to the image itself—whether a film depicts fantasy or reality, the image must carry conviction. In Metz's words: "Poor images do not sustain the world of the imagination enough for it to assume reality."[5] What is necessary for a discussion of fantasy film is a critical theory which focuses on the integrity of the film image rather than a theory whose criteria derive from theoretical discussions on the nature of film reality.

Particularly suited to an evaluation of the film image is the aesthetic theory advanced by D. W. Gotshalk in *Art and the Social Order*, a theory which emphasizes aesthetics (derived from the Greek work, *aesthesis*, meaning perception) as perception. The aesthetic experience is "intrinsic perception, vigorously exercised"[6]—the ideal object of this experience, the fine arts. Gotshalk defines fine art as "the shaping of a four dimensional object—material and form, expression and function—in the direction of intrinsic perceptual interest."[7] Given Gotshalk's definition and half a century of controversy among film critics, we can certainly accept film as a fine art form: the materials of film—light, color, film stock, sound—are given form by the camera and editor; materials and form give expression to the objects—characters, themes, events, structures; and film functions to entertain, inform, and enlighten, or it functions as an aesthetic object heightening intrinsic perception.

Perception lies not only at the aesthetic experience's center, but, according to Metz, at the center of film's semiotic experience: "films release a mechanism of affective and perceptual participation in the spectator."[8] This participation is part of the codification process of human communication, a bilateral process. Information is encoded and then decoded. Aesthetic perception involves the process of decoding while filmmaking is an artistic act of encoding. The film itself—the semiotic system/aesthetic object—lies at the center, between filmmaker/artist and viewer/perceiver. It is not surprising then, that we find a correlation between the dimensions of the fine art object discussed by Gotshalk and the nature of the semiotic sign.

In semiotic theory the sign is itself a compound of a signifier and a signified: "the plane of the signifiers constitutes the plane of expression and that of the signifieds the plane of content."[9] L. Hjelmslev introduced the concept that each plane consists of two *strata*, form and substance; expression has both substance and form, and content has both substance and form. By transposing Hjelmslev's signification system to the study of film, we recognize that each sign—autonymous segment (shot or syntagma)—possesses a substance of expression, a form of expression, a substance of content and a form of content. In film the substance of expression is the "materials" of a segment: at the most rudimentary level there are light and shadow and mixtures of the two, but for practical purposes, the materials should be thought of as film stock, lighting, the relations of the camera to object in terms of angle, distance and movement, and the presence of sound. The film's form of expression results from the various editing techniques (montage, mise-en-scène, intercutting, dissolve, fade) and from correlating sound and image (sound bridge, voice-over narration, music, background and foreground sound). The substance and form of expression, the signifier, correlate with Gotshalk's dimensions of material and form.

On the plane of the signified, the substance of the content is the "emotional, ideological or simply notional aspects of the signified, its 'positive' meanings."[10] This positive denotative meaning is only part of Gotshalk's dimension of expression. For Gotshalk, expression clearly suggests the entire signified—both substance and form. Using Hjelmslev's more refined analysis of the signified into substance and form, we can think of the content's form as the "formal organization of the signifieds among themselves"[11]—the structure.

Such a semiotic system of film thus derived from Metz and Hjelmslev, because it centers on perception, correlates well with the fine art object's dimensions as defined by Gotshalk. Film, then, is particularly suited to examination and evaluation using Gotshalk's relational aesthetics.[12] The task of aesthetic judgment, according to Gotshalk, is "to evaluate the interrelation of the dimensions of a work of art, to detect incongruities, inconsistencies and failures of implementation, to attend to a work to determine whether its dimensions combine with and amplify one another, e.g. whether the form, the function, the expressive spirit, the materials . . . cooperate in a voluminous and harmonious effect. The basic criterion of judgment here is integrity."[13]

The task, then, in evaluating film is to determine whether the form given by the camera and editor reinforces the expression suggested by lighting and film stock, and whether each of these individually, or all of them together, are appropriate to convey most effectively the film's content and its organization. Using integrity as the criterion for judgment frees the discussion of film from theoretical prejudices and requires attention to the film as art object per se. We need not ask of a particular film who its author is, or if it is adequately realistic, or innovative or experimental; we need only ask if the signification system works as an integral ensemble to afford the spectator an intrinsically satisfying perceptual experience.

When we examine the aesthetic dimensions of John Boorman's *Excalibur* and their relational values from the perspective of semiotics, the film's artistic flaws become clear, but also, perhaps more important, we understand better the difficult problem of presenting medieval romance in film. Ideally an aesthetic analysis built on semiotic theory would include a syntagmatic analysis of a film. Space does not allow the analysis and evaluation of each of *Excalibur*'s fifty-one syntagmas. Instead, for the purposes of this discussion, I have grouped the syntagmas into seven meta-segments designated not by each individual event which advances the narrative, but by the narrative's basic movements. Though I will discuss only the first two meta-segments in detail, a review of the entire film will provide a context for the discussion. The first meta-segment relates the attempt of Arthur's father,

Uther Pendragon, to become king. Following Uther's failure, in the second meta-segment, Arthur rises to power. The reign of Camelot, Arthur's idealized kingdom, fills the third meta-segment. Its perfection is momentary, and Camelot's reign contains the seeds of its demise in Lancelot and Guenivere's flirtation, and Gawain's challenge asking for proof of the queen's fidelity. Arthur's discovery of Lancelot and Guenivere; Arthur's faery, half-sister Morgana's imprisonment of Merlin and her deceptive seduction of Arthur; and the birth of Mordred, Arthur's son by this seduction, mark Camelot's fall in the fourth meta-segment. In the fifth meta-segment we witness the quest for the grail by Arthur's knights. In the next to the last meta-segment, focusing on the revival of Arthur, Percival brings to Arthur the Grail's message that the king and the land are one. Arthur drinks from the chalice, revives, and rides out in shining armor to forgive Guenivere, reclaim Excalibur, summon Merlin out of enchantment, and prepare to defend his kingdom against Mordred. The final meta-segment contains the battle between Arthur and Mordred, ending with Excalibur's return to the Lady in the Lake, and Arthur's departure on his funeral barge.

The semiotic system of Excalibur's first two meta-segments establishes four modes of experience—heroic, naturalistic, magical and mythical—operating in the film. The audience experiences these modes both on the expressive plane and on the content plane. When the form and materials of expression correlate highly with the form and materials of content, the audience experiences heightened perception. At points in the film the materials and form of the content operate to establish one mode of experience while the plane of expression conveys another mode. This weakens the image and alters the participant's imaginative experience. By examining the semiotic system operating in *Excalibur*'s first two meta-segments, we can suggest the signification problems present in the film as a whole.

In the battle sequence in the first meta-segment, the film material, light, seemingly provided by torches or filters to strengthen the brown and red tones, heightens the perception of the fiery and bloody content. Far from giving the idealized representation of war a reader of Arthurian romance might expect, *Excalibur* conveys war's violence and destruction graphically. The form of the expression, though, is heroic. The camera establishes war's grandeur by low-angle shots and extreme close-ups which convey the enormity of the horses, knights, shields and swords and extend their actions beyond the frame.

The internal integrity of the signifiers and signifieds breaks down in the next sequence. Here, the predominant materials of expression include a low resolution film stock, diffused focus and natural, though not intensely brilliant, sunlight. While these initially heighten the idealized, "romantic" image of the verdant countryside, they provide the audience with a dissonant perception when Uther and his mud-streaked knights appear in the romantic landscape. The contrast both of the knights with the expressive materials and of the knights with the landscape, as well as the contrast of the entire sequence with the previous heroic battle, establish the naturalistic rather than the heroic or romantic aspect of Uther and his forces. (I use the term naturalistic here because I wish to distinguish the ties with the natural, physical world, and not confuse this tie with critical arguments on the nature of reality in film.) Merlin's appearance in this landscape introduces yet another mode of experience—the magical. In this sequence and throughout the film, the signification system for the magical varies from that of the rest of the film. On the expressive plane, whenever the magical appears, the light, and consequently color, intensifies and the image comes into sharper focus. At the content level materials from modern technology—usually stainless steel or plastic—signify the magical; Camelot's walls, Merlin's skullcap, Lancelot's armor and the sword, Excalibur, are all shining steel. Morgana imprisons Merlin in a web of plastic tubing. When these materials are brightly lit and sharply focused, the resulting surrealistic images contrast sharply with the film's dominant expressive mode. Also, since the expressive mode of these magical sequences heightens the audience's perception of image materials inappropriate to the film's historical milieu, the audience experiences a dissonant perception. We see such a dissonance in the first meta-segment when Merlin places the gleaming Excalibur in Uther's hand. The content materials contrast magical sword and naturalistic man. Content form seems to say that magic will redeem, or at least aid, Uther. But the signifiers assert so strongly the naturalistic mode in the entire sequence that the magical seems strikingly out of place.

In the sequence following Uther's acquisition of Excalibur, Uther, his men and his previous opponents celebrate a truce. The scene in the castle's interior, like the first segment of the film, is lowly lit and filtered to suggest firelight. The low resolution of the film, combined with the low light, suggest an oppressive, smoky setting. The camera, angled down from slightly above the action, confines the image. The longest shots in the sequence convey the dance of Igrayne, the wife of Uther's opponent, the Duke of Tintagil. The dance is intercut both with wide shots of men rhythmically beating their cups on the table in accompaniment to Igrayne's dance, and with close-ups of Uther's lustful stare. The signifiers and the signifieds, closely integrated, reassert the film's naturalism.

To satisfy his lust for Igrayne, Uther calls upon Merlin's magic. The two sequences which ensue—one of pure magic and one of pure naturalism—are among the most internally integrated sequences in the film. In the first, to enable Uther to consummate his lust, Merlin causes a fog to rise so that Uther, transformed to Igrayne's husband, can ride across the chasm to the Duke's castle. The transformation is accomplished as Uther rides across the fog by changing Uther's visor to that of the Duke. Uther's ride is filmed at extremely close range so that the camera focuses primarily on Uther's visor moving through the frame. Since the camera tracks the action, the movement in the frame is rhythmically horizontal. The actual transformation occurs beyond the frame as the camera focuses on Uther's eyes. Though the sequence is filmed with a high degree of resolution, the night setting, the fog, and the pewter color of Uther's armor detract from the intense realism. The extreme close-up with the shift of focus to Uther's eyes requires the audience imaginatively to project the exact moment of transformation. By extending the magical moment beyond the frame, here, the semiotics heighten perceptual involvement with the film's magical mode. In the next sequence, though, as external materials are introduced into the primary content materials, the semiotics intensify the film's naturalism. In this sequence Uther's sexual consummation provides the primary content reference for a montage sequence. Intercut with the presentation of the sexual act are scenes of battle and the Duke's death. The scenes are intercut with a regular rhythm increasing in rapidity until the Duke's final gasp for breath sounds Uther's sexual climax. Both the sexual intercourse and the battle scenes are filmed in low light through filters which emphasize brown tones. The rhythm of the intercutting and the color tones heighten the violence both of the duke's death and Uther's passion; this violence and the juxtaposition of war and sex suggest rape.

The tremendous intensity of these two segments—the magical and the natural (virtually animal)—underscores the two most powerful modes of experience operating in *Excalibur*. Their juxtaposition here signifies that Uther has brought magic to the service of his animal nature. The meta-segment's final sequence brings judgment on Uther's action. When Merlin claims Arthur (the child born of Uther's lust), Uther pursues them. Uther's foes ambush him; he loses Excalibur and then dies streaked with mud. Merlin will reserve his magic for a better world than Uther's. The signifieds of the first meta-segment indicate that Merlin's magic was out of place in Uther's world—it was misused. And Uther died; though naturalism may have triumphed, Uther did not. Merlin's magic, though, should fare better with Arthur. The second meta-segment should not only establish Arthur's kingship, but should also resolve the dissonance between the magical and the real—the imaginative and the naturalistic.

The second meta-segment's opening sequence is reminiscent of the after-battle sequence of the first. The lighting is natural and diffused, the focus soft. The image, the English countryside in spring, suggests a nineteenth-century Romantic landscape painting by Constable or a nature poem by Wordsworth. Despite the content shift to the tournament, the landscape sustains the sense of Constable's or Wordsworth's Romanticism. The tournament's winner will venture to pull Excalibur from the stone. Neither the tournament nor its participants are idealized in the sense of medieval romance; the event resembles a country fair, whose rustic participants, dressed not in silk and velvet but in leather breeches, speak country dialect and roughly vie for honors. The expressive materials, though they might be referred to as "romantic," convey an image with more naturalistic than idealized content. In this setting Arthur, as dim-witted, absent-minded squire to his half-brother Kaye, loses Kaye's sword and subsequently, inadvertently, pulls Excalibur from the stone.

The next sequences attempt to raise Arthur from rustic to king. Arthur must undergo two initiation rites, one imaginative, the other literal. After Arthur pulls the sword from the stone, he chases Merlin into the woods to learn what course he should follow. Encamped in the woods, with Merlin asleep, Arthur experiences a nighmarish landscape. Brilliantly colored snakes, bizarre reptiles and hooting owls taunt him. This sequence's content and its position in the narrative suggest to the audience the mythic materials of initiation. Yet the clearly focused, well-lit images possess the same intense realism seen in previous magical sequences. The medium distance of the camera and the neutral relationship between it and the mythic objects, along with Arthur's passive response, fail to engage the audience imaginatively. The cinematic signifiers, like Arthur's amazed glance, seem to say, "Just look at that!" Content materials which might have had imaginative power are reduced to mere symbols, particularly when the sequence ends with an abrupt cut to Arthur practicing swordmanship to Merlin's plaudits, "That's it! Now you've got it." The content seems to want to say that Arthur has emerged from a gruesome initiation rite to wield the royal sceptre. The signifiers say, "Look at these mythic materials; provide the meaning yourself. We don't want to spend too much time on this imaginative initiation."

The sequence of Arthur's literal initiation is far more sustained. Following the sequence in the woods, Arthur meets his supporters, and they fight Arthur's opponents. This battle sequence, unlike the film's heroic first sequence, takes place in daylight. The focus and lighting are identical with those of the tournament sequence. The long-distance to medium-range shots place Arthur's valor in the broader context of his army's actions. This rather long sequence, which moves from one skirmish to another, ends with a medium close shot of Arthur claiming victory and asking his opponent—a true knight—to knight him so that he may be worthy to become king. The camera's shift closer to Arthur standing in the river being knighted in the name of the saints (suggestive of a baptismal rite) implies that Arthur's role as Christian knight and king will be significant for the narrative. The cinematic materials and their form suggest here that it is not Arthur's heroism, but his reason and humility—his Christian virtues—which ennoble him.

The next sequence—the celebration feast after Arthur's victory— reaffirms Arthur's reason and humility, particularly when we consider the scene in contrast to Uther's victory banquet. The scene focuses on Arthur and Guenivere. Instead of performing sensuous oriental dances, Guenivere offers Arthur cakes with special curative ingredients. Arthur admires Guenivere and tells Merlin that he intends to marry. Merlin may remark at the inadvisability of Arthur marrying before his kingship is firmly established, but Arthur is secumbing only to Guenivere's coquetry and not to his animal passion. The entire sequence employs the same filtered amber light of previous interior scenes. Even though the focus is soft, the brown tones suggest a more natural than idealized atmosphere. Both the signifiers and the signifieds, here, reinforce the mundane and human mode of experience. Naturalism still predominates, though the quality of nature is less brutal and animalistic than in Uther's naturalistic world.

Excalibur does not really introduce magic and idealism in Arthur's accession to kingship until he encounters Lancelot. Lancelot, who is seeking the best king to serve, refuses to let Arthur and his followers pass when they meet him on a bridge. Arthur challenges Lancelot; the joust between the two ends in hand-to-hand combat which Arthur wins only by using Excalibur, breaking it in the fight.

Afterwards Lancelot dedicates himself to Arthur, both men dedicate themselves to ideals higher than personal pride, and the Lady in the Lake restores Excalibur, unbroken, to Arthur. Though the focus in this sequence may be slightly diffused, the intensity of the midday sun creates high resolution in the image. The initial long-range shots encompass an entire hillside and green valley with Arthur and his followers in dull armor riding chestnut and black horses, contrasted vividly with Lancelot's gleaming steel armor and white horse carrying iridescent turquoise colors. The joust is photographed at medium close range, but in the hand-to-hand combat shots, the bodies of Lancelot and Arthur wrestling among perilous rocks are filmed at such close range that they extend beyond the frame. The length of the combat sequence establishes the two men's equality, and the peril of their battle, which extends beyond the frame, signifies their valor. Arthur's triumph enables him to share Lancelot's quite visible brilliance. The victory, though, on the plane of content, belongs not to Arthur, but to Excalibur, which when broken, magic—the Lady in the Lake—restores. The Lady in the Lake poses some of the same problems that magic in general presents throughout the film. The lady, lying rigidly on her back, rises out of the water holding the sword to her breast. The sequence, slowly paced, is filmed at medium close range with a slow zoom to a sustained close-up focused on the lady still partially submerged. Only the lady's eyes and hair move. The distance, focus and clear light of the shot establish the submerged lady's beauty; the image established through these signifiers possesses a high degree of integrity. The camera's relative rigidity, however, intensifies the unnaturalness of the lady's movement when, lying rigidly on her back, she slowly rises through the water. Once again a tension occurs between the film's experiential mode and its expressive plane. The story only feebly accounts for such dissonance. Following the visibly brilliant appearance of Lancelot and Arthur's victory over him using Excalibur, this magical appearance of the Lady in the Lake, concurrent with the dedication of Arthur and Lancelot to ideals higher than personal pride, seems to suggest that Arthur, aided by magical protection (however unconvincing that magic may appear) will establish Camelot, that mythic kingdom of brotherly love and peace among men. For a moment, the film narrative—story and discourse—unifies heroism, magic and myth to transform and elevate Arthur, rustic man, to Arthur, king of magic and myth.

The final sequence of the second meta-segment, the marriage of Arthur and Guenivere, instead of sustaining the synthesis suggested by the union of Arthur and Lancelot, suggests a very different resolution of the elements of naturalism, heroism, myth and magic. In this sequence myth and magic withdraw from the world of the idealized naturalistic hero. This is accomplished more through the content materials—the verbal narrative—than through the signifiers. The idealization of Arthur is established through the use of softly diffused light, a signifier, but his heroism is emphasized at the level of content by the gleam of his steel armor. The setting for the wedding, a chapel of trees, suggests the bond between Arthur and the natural world. The chanted chords of the nuptial Mass echo the Christian blessing uttered at Arthur's knighting in the stream and suggest that a specifically Christian ethos, tied to human experience, will mark the Arthurian synthesis. That magic has no place in this synthesis is affirmed by Merlin and Morgana, Arthur's faery half-sister, withdrawing from the wedding ceremony and eulogizing the passing of magic from the world of men. Merlin says that it is a time for men and their ways now.

The conclusion of the second meta-segment contains a pattern which an audience expects the rest of the film to follow, especially if the audience is familiar with Arthurian romance. The plane of signification has established a film style which idealizes Arthur's world, and this world at the level of content should bind the best of natural man with the highest of religious ideals to form the idealized world of Camelot. The remainder of the film, however, does not fulfill this expectation. The film constantly reasserts the naturalism rather than the idealism of Camelot and juxtaposes this with magic which, like the *deus ex machina* of Greek drama, appears whenever the plot encounters difficulty. The dedication of Arthur and his knights to an ideal becomes very confused, since the Grail, which speaks, seems to be synonymous with Arthur rather than the ideals to which Arthur and his knights have dedicated themselves. The entire film, both on the plane of content and through the film materials and their form, reintroduces and sustains a tension between these elements of magic, myth, naturalism and human heroism. Since this dissonance, introduced in the first two meta-segments, exists throughout the film, the semiotics of these meta-segments are symptomatic of the entire problem of imaginatively rendering the fantasy content of medieval romance in this film.

In the first two meta-segments, the story materials inversely parallel each other's form; Uther falls from heroic stature to mud-streaked, base man, and Arthur rises from leather-clad rustic to king in shining armor. The film's signification system informs the audience that Arthur's elevation carries none of the power of Uther's degradation. Because the integrity of the images in the initial war sequence, the magical transformation of Uther and the "rape" of Igrayne heighten their perception, the audience participates more actively in Uther's fall. The elevation of Arthur is accomplished more through content materials and their arrangement than through the integration of content and signifiers. The distance and mid-range shots, the day-lit natural colors with their earthy tones, give Arthur's battle for power none of the perceptual intensity of Uther's. Though the combination of camera distance, wide angle and brilliant daylight draw the audience imaginatively into Arthur's battle with Lancelot, Arthur's reliance on Excalibur undercuts the narrative's attempt to elevate him. The second meta-segment does, however, attempt to involve the audience imaginatively with the character of Arthur, but here the mode of that involvement relies on a secondary system of signification which occurs entirely on the plane of content—symbolism.

I do not mean to suggest that some form of symbolism is not used throughout the visual system of the film. It is. Instead, I suggest that the elevation of Arthur depends more on these symbols than on the film's expressive plane. Arthur's changes from leather breeches to dull pewter-colored armor to gleaming steel mark his accession to kingship. A brief nighttime encounter with colorful snakes marks his initiation into adulthood, the return of Excalibur marks the establishment of Arthur's kingdom, and a sung Mass marks the Christianization of his kingdom. The symbols as they are used in the film do not necessarily reflect the imaginative world of Arthur or the audience, neither does the film's expressive plane direct the audience's perception to these symbols. In short, the symbols are a kind of visual shorthand which affords the audience none of the imaginative involvement which the battle, the magical transformation, or the rape did in the first meta-segment.

Further, I do not mean to suggest here that symbols do not have a place in fantasy film. None of us needs to be reminded of the imaginative power of symbols—a fact so well established by Campbell, Eliade, Lévi-Strauss—but in narrative art, symbols have their greatest power when they grow out of the materials of the story and find expression in words or images which heighten the audience's perception and draw the audience into imaginative interaction with them. Uther's metamorphosing armor serves as a symbol for Uther's own transformation. This symbol, however, derives its meaning from the story and derives its imaginative power for the audience from its cinematic rendering. The montage techniques used in this sequence require that the audience imaginatively project the moment of the transformation; thus the audience imaginatively participates in the cinematic moment.

The comparison of the semiotics of the meta-segments of Uther's fall and Arthur's rise suggest that the audience is most actively involved in the film's perceptual experience when the expressive plane achieves a high degree of relationship with the content plane. But the semiotic analysis of *Excalibur*'s first part suggests more than that the integrated image heightens imaginative involvement; after all, as Gotshalk says, all successful art should do this. The semiotic analysis also suggests that the mode of imaginative experience is significant in fantasy film. Four modes of experience operate in *Excalibur*—heroic, naturalistic, magical and mythic. Though the film narrative—signifiers and signifieds—attempted to resolve the tensions between these modes of experience (albeit to the diminution of myth and magic), because of the nature of the signifiers and their relationship to content, the quality of the perceptual experience varies with each mode of experience and each mode becomes distinctive. Since the expressive plane maintains these distinctions at the same time that the content plane attempts to resolve them, the signification system loses integrity and creates an experience of dissonance for the audience. The audience is often unsure whether it is experiencing a "realistic" portrayal of life in the sixth century, with only touches of human heroism, or whether it is being drawn from the naturalistic realm into a fantasy world. When the audience is drawn into a magical landscape, the experience is not sustained, and the film returns them to a mundane human world. The tension in the film's signification system, which derives both from the preception of imaginative experience and from the perception of naturalistic experience, denies the audience consistent, unified imaginative interaction with the idealized world of medieval romance. In the first two meta-segments the film resolves the tension between fantasy and naturalism at the expense of fantasy; the remainder of the film reintroduces the mode of fantasy, but at the expense of coherence and unity.

Successful film fantasy must present the audience not with necessarily realistic images, but with images that integrate the materials and form of expression with the materials and form of content in a coherent and consistent pattern. The pattern may, and often does, introduce different modes of experience, but the dissonance between them must be resolved internally within the film's semiotic system to affirm for the audience the validity of the imaginative experience—the visionary, the mythic and the magical.

9

Achieving the Fantastic in the Animated Film

Fred Burns

We generally associate fantasy and the fantastic with magical and utterly irrational processes. These "fantastic" events are seen as springing full-formed from the earth and defying relations with "normal" processes. The purpose of this paper is to demonstrate how the fantastic was discovered to be a practical process in the conceptualization and design of my animated film *The Burial of Natty Bumppo*. In the end we will see how fantasy provided a means of achieving coherence in the film by allowing for the kinds of rational perforations necessary to create a unified image.

The Burial of Natty Bumppo evolved from a project which on the surface seems quite different from the final product. Originally, the central image was a large park carousel, the vehicle by which the audience could be transported through certain American popular myths such as "The Promised Land." The milieu was to be turn-of-the-century America.

In collecting materials for this film and through the many studies I made of actual carousel components, I became more and more interested in the elaborate ornamentation of these machines. At first, I considered this ornamentation as a charming characteristic of the carousel, but close study quickly dispelled any notion that this ornament was merely decoration or a simple accessory. It became clear to me that the makers of these carousels were trying to combine disparate elements into a single experience of high emotional stimulation. The carousel was made to be an amplified and perfected world; the ornament was its flora and the horses its fauna. The powerful influences of music and physical motion were used to tremendous effect to stimulate the imagination of the rider, creating the exhilarating sensation of an actual voyage. In this case the voyage would suggest grand themes, usually woven into a patriotic structure.

The ambitious and playful use of "Americana" themes in the

carousels of C. W. Parker attracted my attention initially. These flamboyant merry-go-rounds seemed to me the most identifiably American in their look, relying little on European models. On closer observation I realized that the Parker carvers made some startling innovations, beginning with breaking down the distinction between ornament and the ornamented. The horses themselves became much more stylized and decorative. And even more surprising, the separation between vegetable and animal components became blurred. The stylized forms of the horses often suggest vegetal growth. For example, the spiraling mane of a Parker horse (figure 1) is so exaggerated and stylized that the shapes suggest growing foliage. This is a clear attempt to merge the floral ornament of the horses with the shapes of the horses themselves.

Fig. 1. Parker carousel horse

A third aspect of Parker innovation is the way the actual physical motion of the carousel is extended metaphorically into the decoration. The highly stylized silhouettes of the horses simultaneously suggest high speed and biomorphic extension. The actual motion of the carousel becomes a kind of metaphor for the growth of all plants. And the individual rider travels through this burgeoning space towards what I fancy to be the vegetal core of a mystical union with the agrarian-formed imaginations of these prairie craftsmen.

The carousel, in essence, takes its landscape along with it. For my own film I wanted to create an environment or landscape that was as active as that of the carousel—at least in psychological terms. But as the film landscape evolved the carousel became more and more subordinate to the terrain surrounding it. It eventually disappeared altogether as a literal subject of the film, but left behind its ornament and machinery as the two basic components of the emerging landscape.

It was now clear that this landscape was to be no mere backdrop to the action. It was to form the fundamental metaphor of the film—that of the Garden of Eden—and was to perform an active role. In the original storyboard there was a kind of general reference to America as the "New Land," but it soon became clear to me that the underlying and direct myth alluded to was the myth of the Garden of Eden. American popular culture found this myth to be a powerful engine for pulling together disparate ideas into a single national ideology. My intention was simply to make the same connection between the Garden of Eden and the Industrial Revolution, except to do it in a literal, and thus highly ironic, fashion. This garden was to be simultaneously an industrial landscape.

Surprisingly, the connection between foliage and machinery was ornament, seen specifically in the work of nineteenth-century engineers and manufacturers who insisted, much to the bemusement of their European counterparts, on ornamenting the machines they built. In America the desire was to see the machine as an indigenous species in this North American relocation of Eden. Ornamentation was to be the vehicle by which the machine entered and empowered this earthly paradise. It was here that I found a fusion of the ideas of motion and growth similar to that I had seen previously in the Parker carousel.

The version of nineteenth-century America that was emerging in *The Burial of Natty Bumppo* was that of a highly ironic and reflexive Garden of Eden. While intuition had led me to ornamentation, I now faced the practical matter of how this material would be made into the factory-garden I had in mind.

Much of my original material consisted of photographs of actual iron mongery (figures 2, 3, and 4). Some of these were collected from published sources. But in the case of my own photography, I began experimenting with questions of scale and perspective (figure 4). Occasionally an entire landscape would be suggested by a carefully-chosen camera angle (figure 5). Scale was one device that allowed me to develop the garden as an environment of ambivalent sensations. The delicacy of these relatively small iron objects and their pychologically inviting vegetal content is transformed simply by making them very, very large, and therefore very menacing.

A page from the film's storyboard demonstrates some of the look of the emerging landscape (figure 6). Ornament has discarded its normal subordinate function and has become the central element. A cast iron floral doorknob has become an enormous factory smokestack.

In creating my filmic landscape I sometimes modeled the garden scenes so as to suggest the grand style of American landscape painting

Fig. 2. Iron mongery

Fig. 3. Iron mongery

Fig. 4. Iron mongery

Fig. 5. Machine as landscape

Fig. 6. Storyboard panel for "The Burial of Natty Bumppo"

of the nineteenth century, especially the works of Thomas Cole. Certain visionary artists of the late eighteenth and early nineteenth century offered clues as to how an ambivalent treatment of this grand landscape might be achieved. The work of Piranesi, especially the "Carceri," provided a demonstration of the type of oppressive space that I sought. The French visionary architects, particularly Boullée, achieved a feeling of astonishing scale that I hoped to include in the landscape. Always an inspiration, the graphic works of William Blake served as a stylistic guide in the treatment of the human figure. In the original storyboard there was no main character, but in the new treatment of the garden I decided to include an Adam-like figure. The kind of mannerist nude created by Blake seemed to fit most evocatively into the machine environment; and the slightly dreamlike and erotic quality induced by his nudity played against the rational mechanization of the garden (figures 7 and 8).

In order to expand the psychological fullness of the garden in *The Burial of Natty Bumppo*, it remained a primary task to explore its paradoxes. I wished to create some analogy with natural growth as was first perceived in the ornament and horses of the Parker carousel. Here, the implied movement of a furiously-tossed horse's mane has been conflated with the spiraling gesture of baroque floral ornament

Fig. 7. Storyboard frame

Fig. 8. Storyboard frame

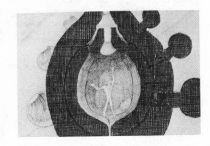

into the idea of vegetal growth, rather than simple physical motion (plate 1).

The process of growth in the film is a representation of iron "vegetation" growing in a mechanical fashion. Some source elements suggested growth directly by their shapes (figure 9); some would be manipulated graphically from the original studies (figure 10) to become monstrous actors in the metaphor of growth of the garden-factory (figure 11, bottom right). The ultimate suggestion is that this garden manufactures itself (figure 11, both panels). When plants grow, they do so in a mechanical manner (figure 11, bottom left). The plants

Fig. 9. Iron floral decoration

Fig. 10. Studies of iron latch

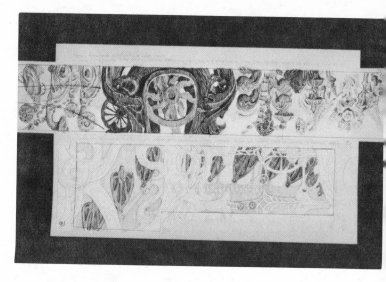

Fig. 11. Storyboard panel: the garden factory

screw and spin up into position in a kind of parody of time-lapse photography of actual plant growth.

Often, the final images in the film were a result of conflating two or three source images and their attendant processes and associations into a single new creation. This new image owes a certain amount of its coherence to the recognized characteristics of its originally separate components. In the preceding example plants are seen to grow in a mechanical manner; their growth is seen in a sense as work.

A second example of this conflation is found in the sexuality of the garden. At some basic level there is the unsettling mixture of gender-associated elements. The flowers in particular demonstrate this ambivalence in that they are essentially female-associated forms but in this peculiar garden they are male-like in their physical form and mechanical operation. Also, the flowers are made to function as the equivalent of deep erotic dreams or obsessions, but always pursuing the kind of reflexive logic that the image conflation requires.

For example, the pistils and stamens of the flowers which in nature are a flower's sex organs are replaced in the film with human figures. The opened flower has generated the fundamental theme or context of "sexuality," and this theme is expanded by the actual gender of these human stamens into the peculiar logic of the garden.

The fullest example of this process is the sequence involving the film element called the tart flower. The central event after the opening of this spikey, thorn-like flower is the birth of the woman-pistil from a mechanical egg. The intended connection here is with the birth of Venus, but in this case it is more specifically depicted as the birth of sex. Every element is qualified and defined by the nineteenth-century context which is in turn interpreted by the fantastic context of the mechanical garden. This Venus, tortuously born and all but lifeless, is held in thrall by the same mechanism that twisted her into existence (figure 12). She is revealed to be part of an erotic photographic postcard (figure 13). The type of image is well-known to us as a

Fig. 12. Erotic center of flower

Fig. 13. Mechanical birth of Venus

nineteenth-century version of contemporary pinup photography (figure 14). This sense of recognition on the part of the viewer is a necessary component in the sequence of associations leading up to the understanding that this event is somehow private, despite its monstrous context.

Fig. 14. Period French postcard

The sequence of events preceding this final image of the woman is organized as a kind of hierarchy of diminishing scale. The massive armored flower opens and unfolds to give birth eventually to a delicately-scaled erotic image. The intention here is to give some expression of the private obsessions of the Victorian male, especially as they are embodied in these mass-produced "dreams"—"French" postcards (figure 14). Ultimately, it is suggested that the garden manufactures these images as a kind of surrogate for feelings. The difference is that the garden does not assemble this woman as one would expect a factory to do. But she evolves in a way that parodies, in a sense, natural processes. The garden emerges, grows, reaches maturity, flowers into its own sexuality. And that sexuality refers strongly to the forms of human dreams and obsessions.

In the end, a fantastic environment is created which allows free entrance to the viewer. It is not the newness of the place alone that inspires the sense of fantasy. It is this newness perforated by a strong sense of recognition that causes a fantastic world to emerge. Ultimately the viewer is most deeply affected when the image provokes a sense of vague memory, as if the film is projecting ideas that barely slipped his or her consciousness. Floral ornament is commonplace in our experience, and the iron mongery of the nineteenth century is known to us all. Personal knowledge of these items informs the viewer's perception of this seemingly fantastic mechanical landscape, engendering in the imagination the final extension of the film's metaphor of growth. At the level of the viewer, the garden grows out of memory into experience.

10

Musical Fantasy: *The Little Prince*

James W. Arnold

"What moves me so deeply, about this little prince who is sleeping here, is his loyalty to a flower—the image of a rose that shines through his whole being like the flame of a lamp, even when he is asleep . . ." And I felt him to be more fragile still. I felt the need of protecting him, as if he himself were a flame that might be extinguished by a puff of wind . . .
—*The Little Prince*

Science fiction and fantasy have always tended toward the dreadful and the apocalyptic, and this is especially true of Hollywood films since World War II. In contrast, Antoine de Saint-Exupéry's *The Little Prince*, written in the darkest part of the war by a French airman who was destined to die in it, is perhaps the most gentle and benevolent tale ever written about an alien visitor from space. It is indeed so fragile and poetic and romantic that it is very much like a flame in danger of extinction from the more gusty and violent winds, the horror stories and brutal tastes of our time.

The same could be said of the Paramount film version of the book, which after years of bouncing around the film world from one owner to another, finally emerged in 1974 as an eighty-nine-minute Lerner and Loewe musical, produced and directed by one of the maestros of the genre, Stanley Donen, who had earlier made such delightful classics as *Singin' in the Rain, Seven Brides for Seven Brothers* and *Funny Face*, among many others. The film suffered hostility from critics and indifference from audiences—it arrived in the same Christmas season as *Lenny, Godfather II, Earthquake* and *The Towering Inferno*—and almost immediately disappeared from sight. It appears now and then on television—truncated in both width (it was produced in wide-screen format) and length (a network showing in 1980 cut one episode and three entire musical numbers)—and I understand that it does very well in 16-mm rentals, probably to schools and children's groups who try to cope with it as an alternative to *Dr. Dolittle* or *Mary Poppins*.[1]

Such a fate is richly undeserved. The purpose of this paper is to give the film some long overdue critical attention, and to suggest a more positive response to its art and ingenuity. *The Little Prince* serves as an interesting case for study in the perennial problem of adapting a work of literature into the medium of film, especially when the original is a work of such whimsical imagination. In the case of *The Little Prince*, one had not only to be faithful to the essence and spirit of a literary fantasy, to make film art of literary art, but to achieve this in a context of popular commercial expectations of success. As Donen himself is fond of saying, "Show business is two words," and he is accustomed to box-office success.[2] But with the great benefit of hindsight, it is possible to say now that a good film of *The Little Prince* probably could never have succeeded with the kind of reality-oriented, young adult audience that was being developed and nurtured by the movies of the 1970s.

The book is about a little boy who is in love with a rose on asteroid B612, which has no other people, three volcanoes (one of them extinct) and a diameter of about ten feet. (The child's parental origins are never explained.) He journeys the solar system in search of understanding his love, eventually learns the truth on Earth from a fox, and finally allows himself to be bitten by a snake so he can return in body and spirit to his lonely lost rose in the sky. In the process he meets and restores the courage of an aging aviator who is on the verge of despair. Now what will they make of that in Peoria, or indeed, in Santa Monica? Something, perhaps, only in the less cynical mass audience era of the 1940s. The prose is perhaps closest to the tradition of Chesterton and Barrie, who have had their days in the movies, but not lately. Other difficulties in adapting the book are more fundamental, related not only to the conflicting characteristics of the forms of literature and film but to the deeper themes of Saint-Exupéry and to the conventions and expectations of fantasy and science fiction. They will be better understood after we have considered both book and film in more detail.

The Book

Saint-Exupéry's story, as translated from the French by Katherine Woods, is brief—111 pages in the paperback version published by Harbrace.[3] It is in the form of a memoir by an unnamed narrator, a pilot who has crash-landed in the Sahara and encountered in that vast wilderness a six-year-old boy, dressed in a long coat and carrying a sword. Essentially the tale recounts their conversations, which center

on why the child has come to Earth and what has happened to him in
the year since he has left his own planet. It then briefly describes the
growth of their own friendship, their sad parting, and the effect of it all
on the pilot. The narrative is entirely from the viewpoint of the adult,
who accompanies his story with rough pencil sketches of nearly all the
places and characters but himself. The prose is simple and direct, as if
by a kind uncle addressing a wise child.

While some may consider it a fable for children, it is probable that
Saint-Exupéry wrote for adults under that familiar literary disguise.
The moral points all concern adult behavior; its personalist I-thou view
of the universe and its sense of getting back to basic simple truths seem
intended to refresh sophisticated sensibilities adrift in the depressing
chaos of a world at war. As one scholar puts it, Saint-Exupéry's
purpose in all his writing is "to be," to reject non-being, to affirm the
values of life over death, the positive over the negative, hope over
despair.[4]

Following is a brief chapter-by-chapter summary, both to simplify
comparison with the film and to avoid repetitive references or requiring a fresh reading of the text. The summary is also helpful in recalling
the scope of Saint-Exupéry's themes and the subtleties and tone of his
style.

1. The pilot recalls being impressed at the age of six by a picture
of a boa constrictor swallowing an animal. This inspired his first
drawing (illustrated) of a boa digesting an elephant. But adults said
they could not see the elephant inside the snake; to them, it simply
looked like a drawing of a hat. Eventually, he got tired of explaining,
gave up drawing, and chose to pilot airplanes. But the correct interpretation of that drawing has always been his test of a "person of true
understanding."

2. After his plane crash, and a night on the desert, the pilot is
awakened by the boy, who insists that he draw him a sheep. He first
draws the boa digesting the elephant, which the child immediately
recognizes. After several failed attempts to draw a sheep, he draws a
picture of a box, and says the sheep is inside. The child is satisfied.

3 and 4. He learns that the child comes from a very small planet,
probably asteroid B612. (The accompanying sketch suggests a diameter of about ten feet). He explains all these details, he says, to satisfy
adults, who are interested in facts and numbers rather than the essentials of things.

5. On the third day, the Prince explains why he needs the sheep,
to eat the seedlings of baobab bushes that infest his planet. If they are

not cut off early—as soon as they are distinguished from rose bushes—they will cover his planet and destroy it.

6. On the fourth day, we learn the Prince is fond of sunsets, which he can see quite often on his tiny planet. One day, he saw the sun set forty-four times.

7. On the fifth day, the Prince worries that if the sheep eats baobabs, it may also eat roses. The pilot, distracted by his fruitless efforts to repair his plane and by the dwindling water supply, replies sharply that it is a matter of no consequence. The Prince, angry and distressed, makes a touching speech, which ends: "If someone loves a flower, of which just one single blossom grows in all the millions and millions of stars, it is enough to make him happy just to look at the stars . . . But if the sheep eats his flower, in one moment all his stars will be darkened. And you think that is not important!" The Prince weeps, and the pilot comforts him, promising to draw a muzzle for the sheep and a railing to protect the flower.

8. The pilot tells the story of the Rose, as he learned it from the Prince. She is beautiful, vain, coquettish. She demands care, and makes him feel guilty if he is slow in providing it. He shouldn't have noted her faults, the Prince admits now: "I ought to have guessed all the affection that lay behind her poor little strategems . . . But I was too young to know how to love her."

9. Discouraged, the Prince (in his flashback story) decides to leave his planet, taking advantage of the migration of a flock of wild birds. The Rose, sad to see him go, is suddenly sweet, repentant and undemanding. She says she loves him, and urges him to "be happy." Then her pride surfaces: "You have decided to go away. Now go!"

10. The first asteroid the Prince visits is inhabited by a King, whose vast robe covers most of his planet. The King loves to give "reasonable" orders, e.g., he orders the Prince to do whatever he would do anyway. But he doesn't want the Prince to leave. The wise Prince asks the King to order him to leave, but the King settles for ordering him to be his ambassador. Grown-ups are very strange, says the Prince, as he leaves this and each of the following planets.

11. The planet of the conceited man, who sees the Prince as a potential admirer. He wants to be regarded as the handsomest, best dressed, the richest, most intelligent man on his planet. But as the Prince notes, he is the *only* man on his planet. "Admire me just the same."

12. The planet of the tippler. He is drinking so he can forget that he is ashamed—of drinking.

13. The planet of the businessman. He is preoccupied with counting the stars, which he claims he owns because he was the first to think of it, and putting them in the bank. The Prince says he is of some use to his Rose and the tiny volcanoes on his home planet, but the businessman is of no use to the stars.

14. The planet of the lamplighter. Since it revolves every minute, the lamplighter is constantly lighting and extinguishing his single lamp. He does this because the "orders have not changed" since the planet revolved much more slowly. He is exhausted but faithful. The Prince thinks this is absurd but beautiful, therefore useful. The lamplighter is not ridiculous because he is thinking of something besides himself. What's more, this tiny asteroid is blest every day with 1440 sunsets!

15. The planet of the geographer. This is the largest asteroid, though only ten times larger than the lamplighter's. The geographer keeps records. He will not record the Prince's flower, because although it is beautiful, it is "ephemeral." This makes the Prince sad, because it reminds him of his Rose and her vulnerability.

16. The Prince arrives on Earth, which (as the pilot notes) is full of kings, geographers, businessmen, tipplers and conceited men—about two billion adults.

17. Despite the large population, the Earth has vast empty places, like the desert, where the Prince has landed. He meets a Snake, who genially chats about his power to send someone on a trip "farther than any ship could take you." He promises: "I can help you someday if you grow too homesick for your own planet."

18. The Prince encounters a small desert flower, who sees few humans, and describes them from her own perspective: "The wind blows them away. They have no roots, and that makes their life very difficult."

19. The Prince climbs a tall mountain, but sees nothing but more peaks of rock. He calls out and hears only echoes. Earth seems a desolate, forbidding place. "And the people have no imagination. They repeat whatever one says to them."

20. He comes to a garden of five thousand roses, and sadly recalls the vanity of his Rose. "I thought I was rich, with a flower that was unique in all the world; and all I had was a common rose."

21. He meets the Fox, and asks to play with him. But the Fox cannot play because he is not "tamed." "If you tame me, we shall need each other. To me, you will be unique . . . To you, I shall be unique." The Fox goes on to describe the effects of being tamed, which is the key passage in the book:

... But if you tame me, it will be as if the sun came to shine on my life. I shall know the sound of a step that will be different from all the others. Other steps send me hurrying back underneath the ground. Yours will call me, like music, out of my burrow. And then look: you see the grainfields down yonder? I do not eat bread. Wheat is of no use to me. The wheat fields have nothing to say to me. And that is sad. But you have hair that is the color of gold. Think how wonderful that will be when you tame me! The grain, which is also golden, will bring me back the thought of you. And I shall love to listen to the wind in the wheat . . .

So the Prince tames the Fox. When he must leave, the Fox is sad, and the Prince wonders if their friendship has done him any good. "It has done me good because of the color of the wheatfields." The Prince is sent back to the rose garden, where he understands that these flowers are not like his. They are untamed—"she is *my* rose." The Fox tells him, as a present, a final secret: "It is only with the heart that one can see rightly; what is essential is invisible to the eye." He adds: "You become responsible, forever, for what you have tamed."

22. The Prince meets a railway switchman. He sends trains rushing in one direction, then the other. What are these hurrying passengers looking for? "Not even the locomotive engineer knows that."

23. He meets a merchant who sells thirst-quenching pills. They save fifty-three minutes a week. The Prince thinks that he would use the fifty-three minutes a week to walk at his leisure toward a spring of fresh water.

24. The story of the Prince's journey is over, and the pilot has been reminded about their dwindling water supply. The Prince suggests they look for a well, and the pilot goes along, thinking the search is absurd. "What makes the desert beautiful," the child says, "is that somewhere it hides a well." The source of beauty is something invisible.

25. They discover a village well, with a wall, in the mid-Sahara. They drink, and the experience is sweet because of their friendship and the joy of their struggles with the bucket and the rusty pulley. What people are looking for "could be found in one single rose, or in a little water." The Prince hints that he must soon go back to his Rose, and asks for the promised drawing of a muzzle for his sheep. The pilot is sad: "One runs the risk of weeping a little, if one lets himself be tamed." He goes back to the plane and completes his repairs on the engine.

26. When he returns, the Prince is talking to the Snake about its

poison. The boy says he too is now ready to travel home. The pilot is distressed but helpless. The Prince reassures him: looking at the stars will be different now, because he will be on one of them laughing— "only you will have stars that can laugh!"

He warns the pilot not to come that night for his meeting with the Snake. "I shall look as if I were suffering. I shall look a little as if I were dying, and that will not be true." His body will be "like an old abandoned shell. There is nothing sad about old shells." But the pilot does come for a final farewell. The Prince's death is quick and gentle, and he falls on the sand.

27. An epilogue. The pilot tells us he is comforted that he found no body at daybreak, and he does hear the sounds of the stars now at night. But he is troubled because he forgot to draw the strap to hold the muzzle for the Prince's sheep. So he does not know if the story has a happy ending. Yet that mystery has changed the universe for him forever. The final drawing is the spot of desert sand where the Little Prince fell. That's so we can recognize it, and if we are there, "and a little man appears who laughs, you will know who he is. . . . If this should happen, please comfort me. Send me word that he has come back."

The Film

The history of the plans to make a film of *The Little Prince* are complex and Hollywood-Byzantine. Stanley Donen says an "endless number" of people had owned the rights, including Orson Welles. It is sufficient to say that the property eventually came to Alan Jay Lerner, the writer and lyricist whose collaboration with composer Frederick Loewe had produced a string of Broadway and film hits (*Brigadoon, My Fair Lady, Gigi, Camelot*). The team had written some songs for a musical film version, and the package was sold to Paramount, which signed Donen as producer-director. He had worked previously with Lerner nearly twenty years earlier on *Royal Wedding*. Pre-production and casting went slowly. Principal photography was begun only a week before Paramount's rights would have lapsed.

From a critical perspective, the problems of successful adaptation of Saint-Exupéry's gentle fable were enormous. Whether or not one accepts the theory of the film medium's realistic tendency, most recent fantasy or science fiction films aimed at a popular audience had been based at least on a credible visual world, even if it existed in another galaxy or in a realm of pure imagination. Consider again some of the major ingredients of *The Little Prince*:

—An adult male protagonist who is alienated from the real world of adults, and whose narrative style adopts the attitude of a person addressing a child.

—A six-year-old traveler from space whose prime motivation is love for a flower on a distant planet.

—A series of visits to "unscientific" small asteroids, the largest of which is about as big as a hot-air balloon.

—A series of allegorical characters, including a Snake, a Fox, and a Rose that talk.

—A sort of metaphysical climax, in which the child must be bitten by a snake and die so that he can return to his planet, an action that simultaneously grieves the adult protagonist and restores his shaky faith in the benevolence of the universe.

—On top of this, there is now the additional problem of having the characters sing and dance. The musical mode is of course a theatrical convention probably more appropriate to fantasy film than to more realistic genres. If the basic film illusion could be brought off, the musical elements would fit. But practical production problems remained. The suggested locales were the desert, a woodsy garden, and those tiny asteroids, each different from the others. The cast had to be able to handle not only their offbeat characters but the task of musical performance.

The Screenplay

Alan Jay Lerner's screenplay opts basically, I think, to be a film for adults that children may like. It essentially follows the order of Saint-Exupéry, and includes many of the incidents and much of the original dialogue. It is of course impossible for a film to re-create all the richness of prose, or even to find film correspondences for every literary point. The important exceptions to fidelity to the book, in the film as finally released, are as follows:

—The episodes of the conceited man, the tippler, the lamplighter, the desert flower, the switchman and the thirst-quenching pills are dropped. Only the last could be said to have a filmic equivalent, in the well or oasis sequence. Donen reports that he had half-completed a lamplighter sequence, but could not finish it to his satisfaction before the release date:"It would have been absolutely beautiful, but we couldn't get it done on time."

—There is an "asteroid character" added, a General, whose style of madness fits the mood of the early 1970s. He is one of Lerner's cleverest contributions: "The most important thing in life," he tells the Prince, "is dying."

—The geographer is replaced by a historian. ("My job is making things up.")

—The point of the baobab bushes is hardly mentioned, which has the effect of obscuring the Prince's need for the sheep.

—The character of the King is changed. He is not concerned with giving "reasonable" and therefore politic orders, but with the need for borders and checking passports. This allows his planet to be covered with Balkan-style maps, a slightly more visual joke. When he is questioned about the need for such things, the sense of the King's reply (in song) is that a mere child can never understand.

—When the Prince is upset by the pilot's remark that the sheep/rose problem is of "no consequence," he runs off into the desert, precipitating a panicked and fruitless search by the pilot (and the song, "Where Did You Go?").

—The well is changed to an oasis with a lagoon, and the episode now comes *before* the Snake and Fox sequences, which now immediately precede the final "death" scenes. The effect is to diminish the conscious meaning of the well episode, which hangs on the message of the Fox about how essentials are invisible and experiences are changed by "taming." However, the audience may catch the idea in retrospect, and the film's oasis sequence is undoubtedly a much more powerful illustration of the point than is Saint-Exupéry's well.

—There is no talk about sunsets. But some of the idea is caught in Donen's visuals, in which desert sunrises and sunsets are a constant motif.

—The ending is slightly but significantly different. The Prince's speech about his return to his planet, his not really being dead, and how his laughter will change the stars for the pilot forever, comes *after* rather than *before* he is bitten by the snake. Thus it now obviously takes him a long time to die, and the pilot carries him a vast distance back to the plane before he finally "dies." There are fewer words spoken, and they are less clear, because the boy is so weak. The next morning, the puzzled pilot undertakes a long search for the body, calling out to the Prince that he refuses to leave without him. The ambiguity of the book's ending—is the Prince's attempt to save the Rose successful?—is changed to a considerably different ambiguity— did the events really happen? This doubt, in typically modern fashion, "explains" all the previous fantasy for the rationalists in the audience. However, the film does make clear, in the final shots, that the events "happened" at least for the pilot, and do change his life.

My opinion is that the altered ending confuses the audience. Viewers are not sure what has happened within the world of the story. There are other seeds of confusion: Is the Snake lying to the child? Why is the pilot so overwhelmed with grief if he really believes the boy is going back to his planet, if he believes the child is not really dying? The answers, I think, are reasonably clear in the book: the pilot's grief is not so profound or extended, and the book's Snake is quite forthright, unlike Bob Fosse's treacherous "Snake in the Grass."

Perhaps the basic flaw resides in the original narrative. Although Saint-Exupéry mentions the wild birds as the Prince's original interplanetary transportation, he never refers to them again, or explains why, having gotten so easily from asteroid to asteroid and then to Earth, the Prince can't get back without "dying." In the film, these birds are visualized throughout the trip to Earth, when they leave despite the Prince's effort to call them back. It doesn't help much, but at least it explains the boy's need for an alternate method of escape. One should note that "getting back" is often a problem for astronauts, in real life as well as science fiction. The use of "death" in this way has symbolic relevance for Saint-Exupéry—it is the final natural parting for all friends—but its logic as a device is not well established within the story.[5]

The Music

The early episode of the boa constrictor drawing, the pilot's discouragement, and his escape to flying are superbly covered by two songs, "It's a Hat" and "I Need Air." (Their visualization is of course crucial, and will be discussed below). "Where Did You Go?" is sung by the pilot as he searches for the Prince in the desert, and it expresses his anguish and guilt. When the Prince leaves his planet, the petulant Rose sings the ironic "Be Happy"—taken from her line in the book. Both the King and the businessman sing a mocking patter song, "You're a Child," to express their adult superiority to the Prince's questions. The pilot sings "I Never Met a Rose" to cheer up the boy after he has finished the story of his journey, and the melodic "Why Was the Desert So Lovely Before?" not only supports the oasis well sequence but poignantly expresses Saint-Exupéry's point that the desert is beautiful because "somewhere it hides a well." The Snake's song, "Snake in the Grass," conveys menace and treachery as well as his attitude toward life. The Fox's song, "Closer and Closer," especially as staged, beautifully covers the idea of the "taming" relationship.

Perhaps the most problematic song is the Oscar-nominated title song, which is sung by the pilot to the child as he lays mortally wounded in his arms. While it is powerful and melodic simply as a piece of music, in this context it seems wrong. Its conventional lyrics ("All the hopes and dreams I lived among, when this heart of mine was wise and young, shine for me again, Little Prince, in your eyes") merely underline what we already know and feel. The pain and anguish and the sense of loss further emphasize our fears that the Prince is really dying.

Donen believes that the music was a major cause of the film's failure: "The score sounds 'Rombergian' and it doesn't have any energy to it. . . . You know, it's such a sweet story and there's got to be a little spice in it somewhere, and I think the score's enormously lacking in sting . . . There's no way to get the songs to have more cinema and more energy and bounce. They're just songs to be sung." Donen obviously knows more about this than I do. But I believe the only clear failure in the music (as staged by Donen) is in the final song, which unfortunately contributes to the overall ineffectiveness of the ending.

The Problem of Persons and Places

One of the key problems in adapting literature into film is to transpose the mental images created by language into visual correlates, into actual persons, places and things. Thus, in *The Little Prince*, we need actors to replace Saint-Exupéry's verbal creations of character—of the pilot and the Prince, as well as the odd people on the various asteroids, and the personified Rose, Snake and Fox. We also need to have a desert, a garden and the planets themselves, ideally in a way that will not violate the spirit of the original. Thus, the task of the producer-director, the visualizer, is considerably more difficult than that of the scenarist, who suggests scenes, writes dialogue and lyrics, but is not responsible for executing them effectively on the screen.

The problem is exceedingly complex. For example, the book's narrative "I" (the pilot) is replaced by an actor's voice and persona, which are added to his basic character to affect our reactions to what he says and does. In this book, indeed, *everything that happens* is perceived through his adult sensibility, and he "directs" our reactions as well as our perceptions. In the film, we are, so to speak, "outside" the pilot and see things for ourselves—including, for the first time, the pilot himself. Further, what may seem possible as a literary concept (e.g., a planet ten feet in diameter, a man doing nothing but counting stars) may seem ridiculous if visualized precisely as described. And whatever language is used in the film is spoken and *heard*, which is quite different from reading it.

Somewhere the decision was made to produce in England[6] and to use an English Little Prince, which I think was crucially deleterious to the film's success with American audiences. Another complexity for film: characters cannot be "general," they must have nationality, because actors do. (In the film, the extraterrestrial characters are British or speak with British accents, and the Earth people and creatures are American; this provides a rough consistency). The task of casting the Prince role is, of course, quite challenging. The child had to be able to convey the character's idealized charm and sweet innocence, visually and in personality. He had to be the right age—six—and he had to speak effectively great amounts of often complicated dialogue. The final choice, Steven Warner, seemed perfect visually and in personality. Considering his lack of experience, he is almost miraculous in his ability to act and (in the Fox sequence) to dance. But the combination of his British accent and childish enunciation proved a formidable obstacle. It was simply not possible to get from the movie Prince all that we had learned from the cold printed lines of Saint-Exupéry's Prince. Not to understand the Prince fully is not to understand the fable at all.

Casting the pilot was also difficult. He was to be vulnerable and sensitive, unsure of himself, yet able to relate to a child emotionally without the impression of being unmanly. In this film, the character also has a heavy burden of singing. Richard Kiley, a Tony Award winner in the title role of *Man of La Mancha* on Broadway, was a successful choice in this context. But Kiley was not well-known to cinema audiences, and the discouraged pilot character lacks charisma almost by definition.[7] The choices of Bob Fosse as the Snake and Gene Wilder as the Fox seem inspired and indisputable, although it is possible to argue that Fosse's musical number (a scene greatly expanded from the book) is so strong that it throws the film out of balance.[8]

Perhaps most intriguing is the casting of Broadway dancer Donna McKechnie as the Rose. (The other non-humans become personified by means of quick cuts—from a snake [a boa constrictor, incidentally] to Fosse, from a fox to Wilder; McKechnie is seen as a kind of vision superimposed on the buds of the flower). The Rose has only one sequence to play, but somehow she must concretize all the qualities, suggested in Saint-Exupéry's prose, that propel the Prince through the rest of the story. McKechnie plays her as a languourous, sexy adult woman—a Donen idea that is said to have shocked Lerner, who wanted a seven-year-old girl in the part. Originally, Donen also planned a very sensual dance for the Rose during the "Be Happy" number, but he could not get it done to his satisfaction: "It wasn't a good enough dance." The Rose, of course, is the only female character in the book or film (except for some ladies in the opening "It's a Hat" number), and this interpretation of her as an adult gives the film some unforeseen energy. There is more than enough justification for this approach in Saint-Exupéry's Rose, who is wily, vain, and exciting, clearly an enchantress. She is arguably too shrewd and complex to be a child; in any case, she has a hold on the Prince that makes him willing to die to return to her.

The filmmakers had another important decision, which was how to use Saint-Exupéry's pencil-sketch illustrations, which were so much a part of the book's charm and already supplied it with a visual style and a unique cosmos. (The only major person/place *not* depicted in the four dozen drawings is the narrator-artist, the pilot himself). It was decided to use them in exact copies in the early scenes involving the sketches of the boa and the sheep, but then to drop them and move almost exclusively to direct cinematic visuals, simply reminding us now and then that the pilot is sketching his experiences. There are two clever exceptions. When the pilot is trying to draw the Prince's planet and the many-tentacled tree-home of the Snake, we do see the sketches, which then dissolve into the "real" objects. The bravest decision was to adapt Saint-Exupéry's visual style for the tiny asteroids, which becomes undoubtedly, for most audiences, the film's strangest characteristic. The re-creation of the Prince's planet, for example, appears to be exact in scale and detail. Donen arranges it so that we don't really *see* the planets of the businessman and historian because of the distortion of the fisheye lens. The absurd scale of these basketball-shaped asteroids was an integral part of the book's meaning, and to make them "realistic" in the science-fiction sense would have been a serious artistic mistake.[9] For the "real" locations—desert, oasis, mountains—Donen went on location to Nefta, in Tunisia, in the Sahara. A few years later, George Lucas went to the same place to shoot sequences for *Star Wars*.

Cinematics

Now it is time to consider, in necessarily brief and summary form, how the screenplay and music, the persons and places were visualized for the screen. Proceeding through the film in chronological order, I will cite mainly the most interesting successes and failures, and then attempt to draw some conclusions on the aesthetic achievement of the film as a whole.

—"It's a Hat" is done in a clever montage, which begins with a child's-eye-view shot of adults scanning the boa constrictor drawings, laughing (in distorted sound) and letting the sketch paper float down (in slow motion) toward the camera. The song is begun by a male artist in a wood or park, and continued in (appropriate) Edwardian-era cuts to a woman in a rowboat, a baker with his cart and a group on a horse-drawn double-decker wagon. There is a transition to the pilot as an adult, airborne in an open-cockpit plane, enjoying his escape from the conventional "real" world and singing "I Need Air" as the plane (in long shot) does a series of dives and loops in a kind of aerial cinematic ballet. As the shots are cut, the type of plane gradually changes and evolves as the pilot ages, and the sequence ends with his 1930s-vintage closed-cabin plane going down at night with sputtering engine toward a crash landing (not actually shown).

—The dialogues between the pilot and the boy in the desert are essentially realistic, but there is a constant visual interest. Christopher Challis's camera frequently sweeps and tracks; we are continually reminded of the blue sky, the sun, moon and stars, the changing light, the wind. The conversations continue, via editing, through different times of day, conveying the point that these dialogues are continuing over a period of several days.

—When the Prince runs away, the pilot pursues in a superbly edited sequence alternating closeups, long shots, zooms and sweeping, swooping helicopter passes that put us in the middle of the chase. (The pilot's song is carried on the track, but without closeups of him singing). It is an intriguing comment on the vulnerability of critics to note that the *New York Times*'s Vincent Canby described "Where Did You Go?" as a love song, and apparently objected to this marvelous cinematic treatment on the grounds that actor Kiley "appears to have lost his mind" (Nov. 8, 1974). Apparently he would have preferred a calm, sane and conventional closeup of Kiley singing.[10] The sequence ends with a zoom-out of the pilot alone in the middle of the empty wasteland.

The delightful camera trickery of the Prince's bauble-sized planet—he walks around its tiny circumference, and even draws water for the Rose while appearing to be standing upside-down—reminds us of Donen's gravity-defying dream sequence of Fred Astaire dancing on the ceiling in *Royal Wedding*. It is the sort of magic one expects in fantasy, and its simplicity here is part of its charm.

—When the Prince says "I was too young," Donen captures

young actor Warner in a solemn closeup in profile, backlit by the sky at dusk, which captures perfectly the poignant irony of the moment.

—If the book can mostly ignore the Prince's means of interplanetary transportation, the film chooses not to. There are repeated transitions involving the animated doves until the landing on Earth, pulling the Prince along as he tumbles through space to the title theme music. The effect is plainly artificial, contrasting the drawn birds to the substance of the boy's body, and the repetitions remind us of the contrived conceit we are being persuaded to accept. On the other hand, one could argue that all of the "space" episodes in the film are designed to look like children's storybooks, and that this particular visualization closely imitates Saint-Exupéry's sketch of the birds pulling the Prince through the skies. This is a typical example of Donen rejecting science fiction style for the fairy-tale feeling of the original.[11]

—The businessman sequence will probably stand as one of the more amusing examples of the use of the fisheye lens in film history. The entire episode is shot in this twisted perspective, a filmic invention that extends Saint-Exupéry's satiric idea. Actor Clive Revill's face, especially his nose, is comically enlarged and distorted as he fusses with his calculator and adding machine and gets entangled in their tapes. At times, the businessman and Prince seem to be hanging in space, swaying as if on a swing. As the Prince departs, there is a fisheye closeup of Revill's eye, flicking right and left, as if searching for this upstart child who can never understand free enterprise. The sequence with the historian (Victor Spinetti) also uses the fisheye (his asteroid is covered with books in shelves), as well as reverse motion, for its fantasy effects.

—The pilot's "I Never Met a Rose" song-and-dance is a delight that owes more to Donen's knowledge of musicals than to elements of the fantastic. Actor Kiley uses a rolled-up sheet of paper as a megaphone in emulation of the Rudy Vallee style, as well as paper roses as props, evoking a feeling of romantic poignance in the middle of the moonlit desert.

—The well of the book becomes an oasis that the characters discover after a long desert trek past at least one fantastic object—the skeleton of a huge prehistoric fish—which is very suggestive in the context of Saint-Exupéry's theme of the soulless body being only an empty shell. In any case, this is an oasis of the imagination, with a waterfall and a large pool of sun-splashed water. There are none like it in the real Sahara, and it had to be constructed for the film. Kiley and Warner drink, splash, kick, frolic and chase each other through it in a superbly edited slow-motion ballet of joy that is one of the film's most memorable cinematic sequences. It also serves as a notable visualization of the scene's thematic point about "hidden beauty," which is also somewhat redundantly reinforced by the lyric of the song. Film buffs, of course, will compare the sequence to the Gene Kelly dance in the Kelly-Donen *Singin' in the Rain*. The playful spirit of the earlier water dance is expanded into a new dimension by editing and slow-motion. Whereas the Kelly number is a classic dance performance, the oasis number is a cinematic dance created in the editing room through technology, using non-dance movements by non-dancers.

—While the Snake sequence is usually and justly cited for Fosse's performance and choreography—he undulates even when he walks— it should be noted that this is a beautifully filmic dance. It is not simply performed in front of the camera, but edited from an incredibly large number of brief shots—varied angles, distances, locations—that completely shatter "real" space and time and are generally timed to each phrase of the lyrics. The dance climaxes with a slow-motion slide through the sand, prone and in closeup, and is altogether in the visual style of the rest of the film. Also worth noting is one marvelous dancer's joke, when Fosse takes a pinch of sand from his breastpocket and drops it on the desert before the soft-shoe portion of his routine.

—The Fox sequence is obviously crucial, and while some of its impact is diluted in the final "death" passages, it is generally an excellent visual translation of Lerner's adaptation of the events in the book. We are led to accept actor Wilder as the Fox via an early series of cross-cuts between animal and actor (in a conservative forest-brown suit) and almost nothing in this fantasy sequence is shot from a "normal" angle or lens. The movements of the Fox, as well as his gestures, are choreographed in quick scampers and dashes through the idyllic forest setting, lit brightly by a low sun. The joyous "Closer and Closer" dance of the Fox and Prince is a classic example of what appears to be a spontaneous burst of energy, performed in a natural setting for a constantly tracking camera.

—When the Prince comes to his realization that his Rose is unique, and that he must return to her, the words are in a voiceover as he walks through the rose garden. And the Fox's final "secret," saved for revelation in the film until the Prince is back with the pilot on the desert, is brilliantly staged via a flashback to actor Wilder, who gives the lines while standing in a field of golden wheat. The rose garden and wheat field are lovely examples of the filmic art of *mise en scène*— setting in this case contributing to the emotional effect of dialogue. Of course, the film viewer must be alert enough to pick up the Fox's earlier line about how his being "tamed" would change forever for him the significance of wheat fields.

—I have already discussed the concluding "death" sequence, and its difficulties, in reference to the screenplay. It seems to me that it is the structure of the narrative, and the dialogue, and the delivery of it by the child actor in a weakened voice—rather than the visualization of the sequence—that is primarily at fault. This whole passage, with its dominant note of pathos, seems to drag interminably, extended further by the dramatic song as the child "dies," and by the pilot's search the following morning. I also believe that Donen's final scene, in which the pilot takes off, aware of the laughter in the night sky, is too literal a presentation of the Prince's promise. It is like heaven as angels with harps, and is not satisfactorily staged either as fantasy or reality. It is one of the few such failures in the film. In contrast, the economy and suggestiveness of Saint-Exupéry's prose are superb: the Prince's quick and gentle death is described in five brief sentences, and he does not linger.

It is, incidentally, easy to perceive the Prince's "death" as a metaphor for the death of everyone who is loved and remembered, whether or not they truly live on in another world. For Saint-Exupéry, the separation of friends is the true tragedy of death.

Conclusion

The irony of making a film of *The Little Prince* is evident in the nature of its major theme: "What is essential is invisible to the eye." The visual medium, whose natural subject matter is the surface of visible things, natural or manufactured, is the servant and child of technology and science, nowhere so evidently as in modern science fiction films like *Close Encounters* and *Star Wars*. In *The Little Prince*, film is given a subject against its grain, perhaps beyond its powers.

Indeed, the summary of Saint-Exupéry's little book clearly indicates his repetition of the idea of the absurdity of facts and numbers and the purely physical qualities of time and space: the "adults" who cannot see the elephant inside the boa, the tiny planets, the data-collecting activities of the businessman and geographer, the put-down of the Rose as "ephemeral," the garden of anonymous roses, the sky of anonymous stars, the saving of fifty-three minutes a week with thirst-quenching pills. All this is useless unless and until it is "tamed," made unique through a useful purpose or relationship. Then of course the whole physical universe gains meaning—the stars laugh, the well sings, the rose is beloved, the color of the wheat fields recalls the color of a friend's hair. The idea permeates the narrative, but nowhere as succintly as in the lamplighter sequence, which unfortunately Donen was unable to get into his film.

Thus the movie, to serve Saint-Exupéry, has to be an attack on the scientific way of looking at the world, and also a kind of poem about the mystical sacred nature of reality when it has been imbued with loving relationships. For Saint-Exupéry, friendship transforms a world of existing "things" into a world of existing "images"—or *signs* that remind us of the one(s) we love.[12] What a fantastic challenge for a film: to explore the difference between object and sign.

The Little Prince then has a strong element of anti-science, and it is not science fiction as normally defined. Very little of it is scientifically correct or even possible if taken literally. It is a whimsical work of the poetic imagination. It extols "what is inside." What it finds as the hidden secret of the universe is not the Big Bang. The pilot had given up his philosophical search to become a *doer*, to fly machines. But that escape literally ends in the desert, where he runs out of gas and crashes. The machine is out of commission. The pilot is again given the gift—the chance to know the hidden meaning of things, the truth—through his encounter with the Prince.

In view of this challenge, it seems to me that Donen's film is more successful than it has been given credit for. Purely as cinematic adaptation, the film is flawed, perhaps unfortunately most of all at crucial moments. But overall, the filmic expression of Saint-Exupéry's theme and style, as well as many of his details, is superior. The romantic musical score produces sound and mood correspondence to the lyricism of his language, and even if it is "Rombergian," as Donen suggests, it is a musical style appropriate to the period. It is undoubtedly true that certain kinds of literary fantasy depend so much on the medium's lack of specificity that they resist translation to a medium whose very nature is to specify. But the visual style of Donen's film comes honorably close to bringing it off.

There are two forms of magic in the film: the cinematic effects (animation, distorted sound and lenses, editing, slow-motion) which destroy the "reality" of the images, and the devices of the musical genre itself—song and dance—which also take "reality" to a different plane. (A third form, of course, is the technological re-creation of the conceits of the original novel: "flying," fabulous flowers and animals, bauble-sized planets, etc.). The effects and the musical form are thus the filmic equivalents of the book's "whimsy" and "unreality." But the problem is that science fiction film viewers have come to see fantasy actions and objects as "new" realities brought to them by the medium, and not as abstractions meant to suggest a poetic realm. They demand the credibility of science fiction, and reject anything different.

The crucial question is whether the technology of modern cinema, which an inventive director like Donen has used even to "create" a new form of cinematic dance (e.g., the oasis sequence), has become so convincing and wonderful and "real" in itself that it destroys poetic illusion like some touch of a giant Midas who turns everything to concrete. If it can be filmed and *seen*, how can it be fantasy? Isn't film the machine that contradicts Saint-Exupéry, and argues precisely that what is essential *is* visible to the eye?

The question intrigues, but I would argue that most of the effects in *The Little Prince* are in the spirit of its creator. They are not by and large technological creations designed to make the wonderful seem routine or mundane (as in *2001* or *Star Wars*). The filmic technique involves mostly the imaginative use of the tools of cinematic expression—Donen uses the camera and editing as Saint-Exupéry uses words—in a poetic, abstracting style. And in much of the song and dance, there is a form that is anciently and intensely human, well beyond the power of any machine to express. (The Fosse dance remains art in a way that the oasis sequence cannot equal). Thus the style of the film reflects the Saint-Exupéry thesis that truth is "inside"—in the heart, soul, spirit, in the invisible relationships between people and things—and not in the surfaces of reality or technological gadgetry. It suggests to viewers that the visible universe of *The Little Prince*, fanciful as it is, is not a possible or probable science fiction universe but a metaphor in which the objects are images or signs of something even more wonderful, but unseen. Thus the visuals of the film of *The Little Prince* are neither not-yet-seen, or never-seen, but meant to suggest what is impossible to see, unless, of course, we have the sight of the philosopher-poet, or the innocence of a child.

II

Traditions of Trickery: The Role of Special Effects in the Science Fiction Film

Albert J. La Valley

With *2001*, *Star Wars*, *Close Encounters* and *Superman I* and *II*, special effects have become a major branch of the movie industry, a potent box office draw and a highly guarded world of technological mystery and lore. For many young people, knowledge of special effects techniques now offers a kind of lure of stardom and power within the industry previously available only to screenwriters, stars, producers and directors. When Douglas Trumbull produced a history of contemporary special effects techniques at the Academy of Motion Pictures Arts and Sciences, tickets for the event were almost instantly sold out.

Answering the box-office success of these films, books have proliferated on the subject of how these effects were accomplished, as though there were still a world of curiosity and wonder to be fully satisfied only by the full explanation of the machinery behind the films. Many of these books are simply popular, but several reach a fairly high level of sophistication about film technology—the sign of an increasingly technologically sophisticated general audience. Harold Schecter and David Everitt's *Film Tricks*[1] is perhaps the best, telling in clear language how illusions were achieved, respecting the technology involved, and placing this material within film history and film economics.

At still another extreme lies all the contemporary theorizing about the nature of illusion and deception in film itself and in the act of moviegoing: Jean-Louis Beaudry's speculations on the origins of the apparatus and its inevitable involvement with our psyche as part of it,[2] and two important essays by Christian Metz, one on *trucage* or trickery in the cinema,[3] in which he classifies different kinds of tricks and talks about the role of deceit in film, and the other on "The Imaginary Signifier,"[4] (now expanded to book length) in which he deals with the basic mental habits of avowal and disavowal in all cinema, a splitting of belief which, as we shall see, is perhaps most articulated, and emphatic in science fiction and fantasy films.

Without getting into the detailed making of special effects, and without raising the larger demons of voyeurism, fetishism, and castration anxiety—the whole wide world of Lacan toward which Metz's second essay drifts—this paper aims for a modest theoretical and historical middle ground, exclusively concerned with special effects in science fiction films. To my knowledge, science fiction as a genre has not been approached in a speculative way from this angle. Yet special effects are not only vital to science fiction on film; they are also one of the chief ways science fiction on film marks itself as different from science fiction on the printed page. Because of their special relationship to film history, special effects are also one of the principal reasons the history of science fiction on film differs from its literary counterpart. My paper seeks to answer some basic questions: What are special effects? What goes on when we watch them? Do they have special rules for their use in science fiction and fantasy, and is their effect here different from that in other kinds of films? What relationship do they have to science fiction themes? To future technology? To fantasies about technology? To film technology itself? Why are they used so often not just to portray the wonders of technology but also to depict destruction and apocalypse?

First, it is necessary to draw some arbitrary limits both about special effects as a term and the science fiction film itself. As Schechter and Everitt show, special effects, like science fiction, is a term hazy in its boundaries and very broad in its scope. The movie industry tends to distinguish special effects as any behind-the-scenes extraordinary way to create an unusual, difficult, or special image. The special effects man developed as an extension of the carpenter or prop man; occasionally he was someone with even more specialized skills, an electrical engineer or a model maker. His chief aim was to solve difficult problems in the least costly way. He might be called upon to render something we have never seen (King Kong on the top of the Empire State Building, various robots or monsters) but he could also be called upon to render things too costly to re-create in the studio or otherwise unavailable for the camera (jungles and exotic settings, hurricanes, locust storms, or massive urban destruction through glass shots or matte paintings). Wonder was often the primary motivation, but cost was usually interwoven as a factor. Many special effects, such as glass shots, simply developed as short cuts.

Theoretically, special effects must include special visual and optical effects which the industry has tended historically to keep in separate departments. Today's special effects are a mixture: some are *pro filmic* or done before the camera; others are *cinematographic* and done through an optical printer (a projector designed to superimpose two images and rephotograph them as one). Some lie in a hazy realm between, being combinations of miniatures, mattes, and animation, but often—as in the famous "held takes" of *2001*—achieved in a single negative for a first generation print that would guarantee great clarity. Miniatures, mattes, and animation constitute the basic arsenal of special effects today; they are simply more sophisticated versions of methods that have been around since Méliès.

It is difficult to know where to draw the line as to what constitutes a special effect. Is it anything that is not what we think we are seeing? Robots which are not electronic apparatuses but midgets in creaky, noisy tin costumes or the giant doorman at Grauman's Theatre in a metallic suit? What about sets in general? Are they too common to be a *special* effect? When one visits a studio, they are the first shock, the first deception that is stripped bare. Brick walls are seen for what they are—or rather for what they are not—papier mâché or plywood and lacking the backs of the buildings they suggest. But then, if we pursue this line, as Metz says, the whole of cinema is a vast *trucage*. Shots that are matched are rarely filmed in sequence; editing is a trick. Actors are not offscreen where a character's glance may be traveling, cameras are where a fourth wall should be, and no figure in life is ever seen as a thirty-foot closeup.

Despite this, it is probably best to limit special effects to the extraordinary use of props and optical devices. There must be a significant and important gap between the illusion of what we see on screen and what was used to produce it. Sets, even interplanetary and futuristic ones, are at the low threshold of this discrepancy; miniatures and glass shots are in the middle range; and optically printed shots combining things of many sizes as in *King Kong* or *Star Wars* are perhaps the most discrepant and seem to call on the most sophisticated forms of special effects technology. Special effects then are a kind of continuum embracing the entire cinema, but most fully articulated in films which depict the unseen or unseeable: disaster, spectacle, fantasy, horror, and science fiction.

Special effects in science fiction and fantasy have an additional important dimension lacking in the more general use of special effects for spectacle or disaster. Though they may depict something both theoretically and technologically possible—and hence qualify as a form for science fiction—they also depict things that at our present level of knowledge and technological sophistication do not exist. Hence they often show the presently impossible, or simply the impossible.

Though all movies confront us with the simultaneous sense that we are seeing something real and the realization that it is only a movie, only images, science fiction and fantasy films in their most spectacular moments show us things which we immediately know to be untrue, but show them to us with such conviction that we believe them to be real. The most complicated kind of special effects shots, optically printed mattes or "held takes," are designed precisely to reinforce this credibility: the combination in a single image, say, of King Kong holding Fay Wray versus editing back and forth from shots of the model to Fay Wray. Yet, because of the notion of impossibility, disavowal comes before avowal or at least directly with it in science fiction films. Because of this, we simultaneously revel in the machinery that gives us this deception. Special effects thus dramatize not just the thematic materials of science fiction and fantasy plots, but also illustrate the "state of the art," what it is capable of doing at this particular moment of time. By contrast, special effects in other genres frequently blend with the material so successfully that we do not even know a special effect has been used. Albert Whitlock's matte paintings are a case in point; Everett and Schecter point out that he has probably not won an Academy Award for *Earthquake* because no one knows when the film is real or when it consists of one of his mattes. Unlike other films, science fiction and fantasy films hover between being about the world their special effects imply—i.e. about future technology and its extensions—and about special effects and the wizardry of the movies themselves.

Science fiction film is, of course, another hazy category. Mark Rose in *Alien Encounters*[5] explains why, more than other generic forms, we are constantly trying to define it. First, it has no standard plot like the detective story or the western; secondly, it attains its status as science fiction by distinguishing itself from fantasy; it is fantasy that must present itself as not impossible, not fantastic. At its purest it is fantasy as a form of technological speculation.

My own view of science fiction film sees the genre as shading into horror and fantasy at one end of its spectrum, and into realism, even documentary, at its other end. Science fiction films often contain large admixtures of both genres. *Invasion of the Body Snatchers* and *Night of the Living Dead* are both horror and science fiction; *Dr. Strangelove,*

The War Game, and *It Can't Happen Here* are science fiction shading towards documentary and realism, "hard science fiction," as some people could call it. The films of the 1950s move strongly in the direction of horror and fantasy, yet I would distinguish these films from horror by their refusal to accentuate the various beasts and monsters as aspects of the hero's—or even a collective—unconscious. Instead, these films turn away from expressionism toward realism and stress ways of dealing socially with the threat of the alien. Science fiction always emphasizes the social, not the individual. Nor are these films fantasy films; fantasy (e.g. *The Seventh Voyage of Sinbad, Jason and the Argonauts*) prefers legends and the past, a non-scientific, often magical ethos. The 1950s films occur in scientific settings with scientists playing a large role in them; the monsters, however bizarre and fantastic, are conceived as results of technological experimentation, often with the atom.

With special effects and science fiction perhaps a bit clearer as terms, we should now ask why such effects are necessary to the science fiction film. The answer to this is that the science fiction film must depict a world that is both the same and different from our own in special ways, and special effects technology is the only way to do this. Science fiction films cannot do without some special effects shots; they are necessary because in such films they constitute the world of the *other*, the non-human, all that is foreign or future or technologically possible—hence all that the non-special effects part of the movie, the realistically photographed, the human, must do battle with, learn from, overpower, or adapt to. The science fiction movie seeks to bridge the present—often simply archetypal or surrogate characters with whom we can identify—with an alien or strange future and everything that belongs to the world of special effects. Science fiction films exist, then, as a kind of interface between the two worlds. What happens in their narratives, the encounter between two worlds, happens, though in a different way, in their technology. The normal processes of filmmaking must encounter, adjust to, and finally incorporate those of special effects, often within the same image, so that the special effects can work in the narrative.

We must see the strange new worlds as other, as different. There must be a leap from the world we are in. At the same time, this other world, which does not yet exist or which is highly improbable, must be rendered with the same degree of realism as the more normal one of actors and non-special effects. If the wires of illusion are shown too strongly, if the special effects stand out too sharply from the more realistic components of a shot, or fail to blend with it, if we see too quickly how something was done before we feel the power of the illusion itself, then the special effects fail. We can certainly know they depict the impossible immediately, but we must give them our credence too. We may know at once that we are seeing an illusion, but as long as the illusion is convincing in its degree of realism, then we feel that the special effects are working.

Credible special effects on film are both difficult to imagine and to produce. Words allow more suggestion as tools for visualization than the bedrock of hard reality does; on film, it is difficult to get away both from the human and the present. Monsters and robots almost always suggest the men inside them; visions of the future, such as those in *Things to Come*, pick up on the artistic and aesthetic styles of their period, in this case the 1930s. Special effects are difficult to produce for a wide variety of reasons. Science fiction films intended for a juvenile audience often had low budgets, and while the special effects industry may have developed partly as an economic short cut, the demand for spectacle in science fiction often made realistic special effects more costly. For this reason, classic novels like *The War of The Worlds* were either not filmed or filmed rather late (1953). It is also very hard to blend realistic images with those produced by special effects; the problem hardly arises in print. Yet too often in science fiction films, we can see the bad matte line (watch the tiger in *Forbidden Planet*), the poor rear projection, and the miniatures which detonate like a bunch of matchsticks (which they often are). The tricks do not work and the plot is interrupted. But not to risk using special effects is to lose even greater credibility. Consequently, cheap 1950s science fiction always risks a few shots of its monsters no matter how badly constructed they are. Because of its scientific ethos, science fiction films seem to demand more realism from their special effects shots than fantasy does, which permits greater stylization and whim. Perhaps this is why Harryhausen's animation in *Sinbad* and *Jason* looks better than in *Earth versus The Flying Saucers*.

Except for a few special examples, science fiction film had much more trouble extricating itself from fantasy than did science fiction literature. This was especially true of the beginnings of science fiction film, where the fantasy powers of trick films overrode any real interest in a technological future. Nevertheless, all the basic types of special effects for science fiction and fantasy, even a somewhat coherent if stylized alternate world, and a basic science fiction plot, are all present in Méliès' *Trip to the Moon* (1902). The basic means for giving illusion a degree of realism have already been devised: miniatures, models, double exposures, primitive forms of matting, and—perhaps for Méliès most importantly—the stop-action camera.[6]

It is said that Méliès accidentally discovered this effect of disappearance when his camera jammed; another account simply sees the trick as an extension of the nineteenth-century theatrical trapdoor. Yet the illusion of continuity here is greater than any trap door can provide—and hence is cinematic. Méliès films are filled with people turning into objects or simply disappearing; it is one of his strongest effects.

What happens when we watch the professor in *Trip to the Moon* make a Selenite disappear at the touch of his umbrella? First, we know people cannot disappear; it is impossible. Second, we see them disappear; we believe the impossible to be possible. How can we accept these contradictions? We do so because our ordinary sense of spatial and temporal continuity has been both confirmed and denied. The Selenite disappears; the other images move on without interruption. Because images *move* on screen, the apparatus always acts to confirm our basic sense of spatial and temporal continuity, even at the moment that it betrays and subverts this belief by making people disappear. We see something we know cannot happen, we know it is a lie and a trick, but we delight in the illusion, even giving it some credence—certainly within the narrative. But finally, we give as much or more wonder to the machine which can produce this illusion and of which we are highly conscious. The machine acts as an extension of our senses, delighting us in much the same way children are delighted when they make new discovery in the real world. But unlike children, we know the discovery to be false, and transfer our wonder ultimately to the machine.

The apparatus always makes the imaginary seem real on some deep level. Indeed, the illusion of realism in film is hard to dislodge, and that illusion comes from motion. Still photographs do not come to life for us like moving ones, yet movies are nothing but a series of still photographs. But we should not forget how lifelike movies can become. Early audiences are said to have run from the train arriving at the station in the early Lumière films; in the 1950s the roller coaster ride of Cinerama left many people nauseated.

The realism of film becomes a subject of film when one of Godard's primitivistic soliders in *Les Carabiniers* tries to grasp the lady on screen who is taking a bath. In his dream Keaton enters the film he is projecting in *Sherlock Junior*, becoming a hero and living on a grander scale.

In science fiction and fantasy films, the illusion of realism is almost as strong as that possessing Keaton or Godard's soldier. But here the images we see are of the impossible, the improbable, or the futuristic. The gap between their powerful veracity on one level and their ultimate trickery and fakery on another is probably the source of the emotion we label wondrous or astounding. The very word *astounding*—which was the name of one of science fiction's major magazines during the "Golden Age"—suggests the mouth open in awe, the confrontation of just such a gap between the present and future, the real and the imaginary. What is more, it suggests not just the gap, but the possibility of bridging that gap in narrative and image.

As a consequence of this power, the history of science fiction and fantasy movies is as much a statement about the development of movie technology as it is about the themes the movies ostensibly treat. Stephen Neale, in his recent book on genre, goes so far as to suggest that the principal aim of science fiction movies is to illustrate the current "state of the art," to be in essence an advertisement by cinema for itself.[7] He notes that many science fiction movies are structured along a line of crescendo of ever more spectacular effects, the most spectacular usually being saved for last: Kong gunned down on the Empire State building, the appearance of the mother ship in *Close Encounters* (and elaborated even more fully in the revised version, given an addition to the budget), the spectacular dogfight at the end of *Star Wars*, Superman stopping the earthquake and reversing time in *Superman I*. In Neale's view, then, apocalypse—towards which many science fiction movies tend—is less a statement about technology and a breakthrough to a new social order than it is a formal rhythm of the science fiction film itself. Of course, the two can supplement each other as they do in major science fiction films, but frequently we get the feeling in many such films that plot and characters play a poor second to the manifestations of ever more spectacular special effects. In what we may regard as better science fiction films, the two elements run parallel and often interact, special effects sequences being much like musical numbers in relation to the plot of musical comedy.

Lang's *Metropolis* (1926) can be seen as the film which first consolidates all these tendencies of special effects in science fiction films. In fact, *Metropolis* is the first film to suggest that science fiction and fantasy are the vehicles for declaring the institution's current state of the art. Two corollaries follow from this: First, the state of the art is irreversible. For it is not that all previous techniques in earlier films vanish, but some are gradually phased out. More important, future technological sophistication is judged by the standards of this production until it is superseded by another more advanced one. (Spoofs, however, like *Dark Star* (1974) play off this interest by showing how cheaply you can do it yourself, how close you can come with minimal costs, e.g. tin pie plates for shields.) Second, future movies that aim to demonstrate the current state of the art will demand greater and greater budgets to overpower their predecessors; there is a kind of Oedipal cold war here: *Things to Come* answers *Metropolis*, *Star Wars* takes on *2001*.

In *Metropolis* the state of the art has progressed far beyond Méliès's reach. A new tradition is established. Detailed, realistic and large miniatures replace Méliès's flats; spectacular sets often supplemented with glass shots offer a realism that Méliès neither strove for nor could reach. The Shüftan process, a way of combining pro-filmically through mirrors both live action and miniatures, usually to suggest the grandeur of humans in huge settings, was a striking improvement over Méliès's in-camera matting. *Metropolis* also shows a tendency of special effects sequences not merely to dominate plot and characters but to rise in an ever-increasing crescendo of destructive fury. Yet a good case can be made that the thematic implications of these sequences articulate the wishes of Maria and Freder, the principal characters, who throughout the movie are impotent, imprisoned, bed-ridden, or robotic, but who nevertheless wish both the destruction of the old order and a breakthrough to a new social order through apocalypse.

Metropolis, following *R.U.R.* and *We*, sets the attitude towards technology which many science fiction movies were to follow: technology is ultimately oppressive, an enslaver of man, not his liberator. Yet this view is contradicted in the film (as opposed to print) not just by the wonder and awe the special effects shots of the giant city inspire, but also by the process of movie technology itself which could envisage such powerful special effects.

Metropolis also shows a strong tug towards fantasy as well as science fiction. Its opening image of man dominated by machines seems to promise a serious, almost Marxist treatment of technology, but the plot soon turns toward fantasy. Rotwang's lab and his making of the robot seem partly technological, partly magical. Much of the special effects material serves a non-technological ethos: Freder sees the exploding machinery as Moloch; he is crucified on a gear machine/clock/cross. Rotwang as scientist lives in a gingerbread style house straight from the Brothers Grimm; his house has magic doors and a pentagram over the entrance. Maria, as a kind of mixture of the Virgin Mary and a primitive martyr, tells the story of the Tower of Babel. Freder envisions the Gothic Dance of Death released from its cathedral stone.

If *Metropolis* is still deeply rooted in fantasy and is at one end of the spectrum of science fiction, then Lang's other major effort in the genre, *Woman in the Moon* (1929), rarely seen and much misrepresented in science fiction film history books, is at the other end, the pole closest to documentary. In this study of the first manned rocket launch to the moon, the aim is to use film as an accurate predictor of the future, a kind of living blueprint for it. Indeed, the film is at times on the verge of slipping into an illustrated lecture with its use of graphs, blueprints, and pilot movies from an earlier unmanned ship to the moon. At this point, I think it would be fair to say that science fiction is almost left behind; what we have instead is a picture of the current state of rocket technology on the drawing boards, no different from what was then known to the rocket experts. But once the film actually depicts the moon launch and voyage, it moves into the realm of the predictive and the then impossible. Here science fiction reveals one of its other major sources, its non-Wellsian one, that which first made it popular in the pulps: its engineering impulse, an extension of the desire to tinker, the outgrowth of mechanics, electronics, and physics—an impulse which, by the way, animates much of special effects work as well. As aspects of future technology, the special effects act here hand in hand with the mechanics of rocketry both as living blueprint for the future and as model for hastening its actualization. In fact, there is a strong role of advocacy for rocketry about *Woman*. Hermann Oberth and Willy Ley, the fathers of the V2, acted as advisers to Lang, perhaps in the hopes of advancing the cause of rocketry with the government. Hitler later confiscated the prints of *Woman* because it came too close to the actual launching of the V2. And Lang's invention of the countdown for the film remains the cinema's greatest example of art preceding real life.

Special effects in *Woman* are therefore carefully circumscribed by both scientific laws and the state of current technology; there is far less freedom to imagine here than in the Wellsian variety of science fiction, with its leaps through time machines to the future or through mysterious chemicals to invisibility. Still, its special effects can be spectacular, though of a quieter sort. The major sequence of *Woman* is a docudrama of the actual launching, treated as public spectacle, but unfortunately under-budgeted and not totally successful as *trucage*.

Since history has now overtaken *Woman*'s moon launch, the spectacle acquires an additional interest as perhaps a sort of alternate history. We inevitably compare it with the real moon launch, marvel at its predictive accuracies and, are amused at what it neglects. Lang is also quite successful with special effects for material that was less well-known than the moon launch: he envisions the earth from space, and prefigures the anti-gravitational sequences of *2001*. Lang's spaceship is equipped with hand and foot straps much like those on urban buses. To move beyond verbal descriptions and graphs in picturing a trip to the moon as accurately as possible, Lang confers on the voyage a kind of "sensuous elaboration,"[8] a humanization that activates the urge to will the actual voyage into existence.

However, *Woman* is hardly the major strain of science fiction film. Though the 1950s began with a feeble imitation of *Woman*, *Destination Moon*, the more imaginative tradition of science fiction quickly reasserted itself in creature movies. *Woman* lacks what we think of as some of the basics of science fiction, even though it has a space ship, a journey into space, and an archetypal crew. What is missing is speculation of a free and imaginative sort, technologically plausible but less carefully circumscribed by the current state of technology. It does not have the realm of analogue, the way special effects reflect intensified aspects of our technology and institutions and our hopes and fears about them, not to mention the familiar central figures of science fiction around which its major themes crystallize. Of the familiar triad, monster, alien, and machine, it has only the machine— and one at that time on the drawing boards of rocket scientists.

Between the documentary tug of *Woman* and the fantasy tug of *Metropolis*, science fiction was eventually to carve out its centrist film tradition, one that would allow much of the predictive scientific context of *Woman*—as, say, *Forbidden Planet* and *2001* clearly do—but which would also give freer scope to major extensions of technology that could embody more of the ambivalence we feel about them, more of our human hopes and fears. *Forbidden Planet* has its hyperspace so it can have its alternate world, its Krell and Robbie the Robot; *2001* has its monolith to structure its space voyage with more than simple technological meaning.

The achievements of *Woman* and to a lesser extent of *Things to Come* were largely dormant in science fiction through the 1930s and 1940s—and even much of the 1950s—a striking contrast to what was going on in the literature of the "Golden Age" of science fiction. Much of Wells was filmed but almost always with a horror or fantasy twist, derived from German expressionism and *Metropolis* (e.g. Charles Laughton as a mad Dr. Moreau in *Island of Lost Souls* or Claude Rains taking a drug called monocaine which makes him not just invisible but crazy too in *The Invisible Man*.)

The 1950s continued this major tradition of science fiction verging toward fantasy and horror but altered it. The films are more documentary and realistic in their look, less expressionistic; they are usually filmed at the studio in black and white, partly the dictates of low budgets, but also partly a matter of aesthetic choice. In format, they sometimes even resembled pseudo-documentary genres, the television cop and manhunt series like *Dragnet* and *Naked City*.

Science fiction would seem to be veering in these films toward its documentary pole, that of *Woman in the Moon*, but into this material are inserted special effects which are of a highly fantastic nature, which observe no known or possible technological or natural laws. As my science students are quick to point out, the giant ants of *Them!* are an impossibility, even granted their production by radiation: the insect kingdom is limited in its growth by matters of their breathing apparatuses, and such huge ants would simply collapse under the force of gravitation and air pressure. Nor are many of the other creatures remotely possible: *The Thing*, a thinking vegetable, *The Beast from 20,000 Fathoms*, the quintopus from *It Came from beneath the Sea*, *The Blob*, the man with the enlarged fly's head in *The Fly*, or the many people who shrink to miniatures (*The Incredible Shrinking Man*) or grow under radiation (*The Amazing Colossal Man* or *The Attack of the 50 Foot Woman*). It is the extreme fantasy-like quality of these special effects which, surprisingly, lets us indulge in these films. The combination of fantasy material with documentary gives these films their eerie surrealistic atmosphere. Because of the frequent crudeness of execution—especially in their Japanese variants—science fiction as a film genre for a long time had a disreputable name.

In these 1950s creature movies, the genre seems to be straining at both ends, toward fantasy and realism simultaneously with its center missing, that center usually being the atom bomb. Lurking behind the monster and invader films of the 1950s is the sense of imminent apocalypse and total destruction by technology's greatest special effects machine, the bomb. In film after film, creatures ruin New York, San Francisco or Los Angeles. Repeatedly there is enormous urban destruction. Indeed, we would feel cheated if we did not see it and to some extent, the destruction of models provides release, exhilaration, even a sense of possible technological control. But this feeling is dominated by an eerie, undeclared pessimism which remains the dominant tone of these films; it is barely contained by the pleasure of watching buildings topple or seeing the monster destroyed and mankind start anew victoriously, though it is dubious whether humanity can succeed. In the original *Invasion of the Body Snatchers* the monsters did succeed, at least before the producers insisted on the film's framing device, which still leaves the matter dubious.

Interestingly, the more special effects approach the actual bomb which they both invoke and conceal, the less the movies seem like science fiction, and the closer they come to documentary and to history. There is little purgation and release, little sense of a saved remnant after apocalypse. *Dr. Strangelove* seemed science fiction as long as détente was felt as a political fact; once again it seems a near-scenario of an all-too-close future.

It is to *Forbidden Planet* in 1956 that we must look for the awakening on film of the centrist tradition of science fiction long after its appearance in literature. This tradition allows for both the predictive scientific and the technological ethos of *Woman* and *Things to Come* as well as the imaginative, free and speculative realms of technology's extensions seen in *Metropolis*. The note of fear and paranoia about future technology, namely the bomb, for which the Krell power machinery seems to be an analogue of sorts, is not denied. In this sense *Forbidden Planet* sets its feet in the 1950s and ties up with the creature movies. But *Forbidden Planet* also restores the note of wonder and awe, largely free from paranoia and fear, that was absent from most of the 1950s films. The centerpiece of the film, a tour through special effects of the Krell world of wonders, reinforces and reawakens the theme of technology's powers, at the same time that the disappearance of the Krell reminds us of the misuses of technology, its power to outdistance man and his primitive morality.

Through its special effects *Forbidden Planet* also reimagines the basic figures of science fiction, making them central to the film's story as well as a matter for reflection on our present technology. Machines are re-envisioned as a saucer-like space ship, Robbie the robot (for once we aren't sure where the man is hidden in it), and the Krell world of wonders. The monster lingers but is re-envisioned as invisible and a product not of outside forces but of man's own psyche, a monster from the *id*.

Special effects become absolutely central to this tradition of science fiction film. They do not appear sporadically as in the 1950s creature movies but, as in *Metropolis*, inform the entire film through four giant sets and diaramas against which the entire action is filmed. Every frame is thus imbued with a sense of an alternate, different, and heightened technological world. *Forbidden Planet* necessarily returns science fiction to the studio where the special effects team reigns, controlling the entire production. Its art directors and special effects technicians—headed by A. Arnold Gillespie and Arthur Lonergan— are perhaps more important to it than its director Fred Wilcox, known previously only for *Lassie Come Home*. (This is not to deny Wilcox's strong commitment to the film and his research into its many scientific details.)

Forbidden Planet presents what seem to be three distinct plots on its narrative level (the romance of Altaira and Commander Adams, the mystery of the Bellerophon and Morbius, and the attacks of the monster); eventually all three plots are tied up as aspects of the same plot. Yet this impression of narrative movement is superseded by the feeling of another kind of discursive voyaging, a trip into technology's wonders and its future. *Forbidden Planet* offers four levels of wonder, each one greater than the preceding and all greater than our own. In this sense it is a journey into our technological future.

This future is represented by a crew that can fly through hyperspace in their flying-saucer spaceship and who have weapons that we know nothing of; by Morbius, who has sampled the Krell knowledge, lives in a house full of futuristic gadgets, and has power superior to the crew; by Robbie the robot, a machine created out of Krell knowledge by Morbius and more powerful than Morbius, though his servant; finally, by the Krell lab and power center where thought alone can move matter. Significantly it is this last heightened example of technology which appears as the central tableau of the film, a kind of excursion from its plot, an illustrated tour of technology's wonders; it is also the sequence which demands the most in special effects matte work, miniatures and paintings.

As a result of this sequence's powerful effect on the film, the apocalyptic destruction of Altair IV at the end of *Forbidden Planet* seems less dire and frightening than similar destruction in the creature movies. There is also some sense that part of Altair IV is being brought back to earth in the person of Robbie the Robot. We are tantalized with the memories and mysteries of a new technological Eden, even though it is blown up at the end of the film.

The full impact of *Forbidden Planet* was neither felt at the time nor during the 1960s. This was largely a matter of *Forbidden Planet* not finding an additional audience beyond the juvenile set. Because a larger, more sophisticated audience for the science fiction film could not be found, it was cheaper to make inexpensive science fiction with fewer special effects. It was not until Stanley Kubrick released *2001* in 1968—he had been at work on it for five years—that the gamble of cost paid off. Sophisticated science fiction film found a ready audience at the height of the radical Sixties, an era of great openness to the new.

2001 went beyond *Forbidden Planet* in re-imagining through special effects two basic aspects of science fiction that were not fully re-examined in *Forbidden Planet*: our experiences of space and time. Taking his cue from experimental films and their different sense of narrative and time, Kubrick abandoned a strong linear plot to concentrate instead on long voyaging special effects sequences or the detailed rendering of ordinary moments in the new surroundings of outer space. To do this, however, meant giving more and more of the film over to special effects teams, and thus raising the budget and production time enormously. *2001* was not to become a model for future films in its five year production period and its lengthy incamera "held" takes, whereby many images were combined on a single negative. Nor was its open experimental form followed quite so openly. Yet as a model for the quality of future special effects and the way they were distributed throughout the entire film, *2001* influenced all the major science fiction films that followed in the reawakening of the genre in the 1970s.

The new science fiction films pick up the note of wonder in *Forbidden Planet* and *2001* and amplify it. The big blockbuster films tend to downplay the ambivalence about technology that is still strongly present in *2001*, notably in Hal's domination of the actors and his menacing breakdown and attempt at control, as well as in the odd relation between special effects and actors throughout the film. Blockbuster science fiction tends towards optimism: witness *Star Wars*, *The Empire Strikes Back*, *Close Encounters*, *Superman I* and *II*, and *Raiders of the Lost Ark*. The note of fantasy is strong in all of these; even *Close Encounters* aims for some of the stylization of fantasy and originally was to close with the song "When You Wish upon a Star." More recent, lower budget science fiction (which is by older standards still big budget) tends to be more reflective of the troubles of technology and its dystopian threat. Many of these films follow the literary tradition of *Brave New World*, *We*, *R.U.R.*, and *1984*. Yet the main enemy now is not the huge machine, but the computer and the computerized society which lobotomizes man and cancels his freedom and individuality. In most of the newer dystopian movies, the bomb is absent as a primary analogue of the threat and misuse of technology. The films frequently comment instead on some specific problems of the modern world: the computerized society in *THX* 1138, over-population in *Soylent Green*, ecology in *Silent Running*. Yet in many of these films there is a strong hint of a post-nuclear landscape: the people in *THX 1138* live totally underground much as *Dr. Strangelove* predicted; the unseen world of earth in *Silent Running* lacks forests and hence is the familiar desert of the post-nuclear world. David Bowie's *Man Who Fell to Earth* comes from a declining world that has post-nuclear suggestions. A few films are even explicitly set in a post-apocalyptic nuclear landscape: *Damnation Alley*, *Logan's Run*, *A Boy and His Dog*. The link between computer and bomb is not difficult to imagine. In *Dr. Strangelove*, the computer system allows the dooms-day device to go off and destroy the world by atomic bombs; the computer that supposedly guards man from destruction in *Colossus* ultimately takes over the bomb and controls man; and the spoof *Dark Star* explictly links the impersonal computer and the bomb's destruction of ship and crew. Yet oddly enough, the bomb, which is now back in our consciousness as the height of man's technological powess and source of his possible self-destruction, is largely absent from the films of the 1960s and 1970s, even more absent than in the creature movies of the 1950s which seemed both to invoke and hide it. Were we lulled into not treating it by détente? Or was it too big to face after *Dr. Strangelove* and *The War Game*? Would thinking directly about it have curtailed science fiction in its more imaginative and freer forms? And do the dystopian computer society movies represent a displaced form of thinking about its impact?

Whatever the reason, the dystopian movies have not been too successful at the box office, giving the victory to the optimistic and fantastic science fiction films, those that primarily celebrate technology's wonders. There is a further problem to the anti-technological movies; their protest seems half-hearted. As in *THX 1138* their worlds are themselves so wondrous, even if inhuman, that they subvert the drama of individual awakening, rendering it innocuous. We enjoy looking at the odd new underground world so much that we lose interest in Robert Duvall's plight, or in Bruce Dern's in *Silent Running*. *2001* still seems most successful at capturing the note of cosmic and technological wonder without surrendering its ambivalence about either. And *2001* uses its special effects to depict this mixture of awe and inhumanity.

While it is good to see the note of wonder and exhilaration

restored to technology in the 1970s in many films, one should probably be open to other conclusions as well. I do not want to get into Metz's theories, derived from Lacan, of fetishism, castration anxiety, and voyeurism, since, if they are true, they are general to all film, not just science fiction. But I would like to suggest that his use of the Lacanian triad—the imaginary, the real, and the symbolic—has some application here. For if all movies involve an interplay of avowal and disavowal, later synthesized in the symbolic, then the special effects films of science fiction, as I have tried to show, involve a heightened example of this interplay, where the imaginary and real are always on the verge of splitting apart.

One feels that at present there is a yearning for the real to disappear or for the imaginary to become the real. Recent large-scale science fiction films move strongly toward fantasy. These films do not move easily into our lives; the balance of the symbolic is not easily restored. Unlike *2001* or *Forbidden Planet*, the dimension of analogue has virtually disappeared. Instead, we are left yearning for greater and greater special effects, more convincing illusions; we become a major arm of the industry's future, authorizing the success of big budget films and ensuring that they alone may be the only future box office attractions. We are asking cinema to strain at its limits of illusion while ignoring its more critical implications for society and human psychology.

Perhaps in difficult times like the present this is what cinema is asked to do, to be an escapist art. Perhaps the high tech 1980s is to be an era of mechanical escapism. Perhaps science fiction on film has always had a difficult time extricating itself from fantasy. And they, like all movies, may not, as many contemporary theorists think, be ultimately able to escape the voyeurism upon which they are founded.

The next step is obviously for special effects to free themselves from both narrative and the theatrical environment—to spill out and form an electronic field in which we live. Francis Coppola already talks in a visionary way of this, and with *One from the Heart* he makes a strong new move in this direction. For me, however, *One from the Heart* is "one from the lab," or "one from the state of the art." Narrative and characters become recessive under the obsession with technological wizardry; they seem to be seen through the wrong end of a telescope. Soon we may expect Imax, enormous surrounding screens, perhaps holography. Soon it may be difficult to tell the technology of the future from the technology of film; illusion may replace reality.

I do not want to act as a killjoy here since I enjoy this technology myself and feel that an openness to technology is a necessary component for facing the future with hope. In some strong way the new films offer that hope. But some of us would like more of an interplay of special effects technology with the issues of our present world. Finally, no matter how enlarged the new world of special effects becomes, we are still witnesses to it, not its direct manipulators. Films about the electronic future may be entertaining and mind-enhancing, but they can also be a kind of escapism, protecting us from the real, representing a further dimension of the flight of the imaginary away from the real, and hence the loss of the symbolic altogether.

12

The "Videology" of Science Fiction

Garrett Stewart

*

Let me for openers brave some blunting of my argument in a bid for pith. Movies about the future tend to be about the future of movies. Science/fiction/film: this is no more the triadic phrase for a movie genre than three subjects looking on at their own various conjunctions. Science fiction in the cinema often turns out to be, turns round to be, the fictional or fictive science of the cinema itself, the future feats it may achieve scanned in line with the technical feat that conceives them right now and before our eyes. That notorious paradox fashioned to characterize cinema as a "dream machine," the soldered bond of the imaginative and the mechanical, was already there in the narrative category "science fiction," science which was fantastic if for no other reason than because it was not yet fact. All four terms are thus most clearly welded in the *dreamed science* of *mechanized fiction*, those conjectured devices screened within an electronically activated film of the future which offer ramifications and refinements of visual technology itself—the imaginary engineering of the image to which moviemaking may someday succeed.

An opening parable. When, in the seventh decade of science fiction on film, the movie *Capricorn One* (Peter Hyams, 1978) arrived to entertain the speculation that the federal space program and its televised promotion might be entirely short-circuited (or in the argot of such coverage: closed-circuited)—that in fact the whole thing might be fabricated in a studio as a "media event" in the most absolute sense—this "deconstructive" conceit reached deep into one's instincts about the more than ordinarily close collusion between cinematic illusionism and futuristic fantasy. In an unexpected theatrical sense, the manned "stage" of the Apollo flight in the film is more transmission than space mission, a mere takeoff on a takeoff. Further, in a curious double crossing of temporal and spatial logic wherein the mechanics of simulation intersect the odd mechanical laws of the rendered phenomenon, the secret studio mock-up of the landing on Mars requires for its national television broadcast a slow-motion delayed replay to approximate the weightlessness of the astronauts; the very medium of cinematic representation across time is retarded so as to simulate a distant space whose gravitational field is governed by rules other than the physics of Earth. *Capricorn One* is a quite literal grounding of scientific futurity in the machinations of the cinematic image. As such it all but imperceptibly shifts the cutting edge of technological ingenuity in the genre of science fiction film from machines in outer space to the logistics of their replication in inner or screen space, from aeronautics to cinematics. Indeed, it allows us to imagine that all independent scientific advance, as photographically retailed to the public, might have stopped with the advent of what is usually considered to be (and no accident) the first narrative film, Georges Méliès' 1902 rocket fantasy *A Trip to the Moon*, beyond which point movies could not only have begun duplicating our most miraculous tools, but anticipating and confecting them before our receptive gaze.

It does not take a moviemaker, whether from the turn of the century or the turn of the Seventies, to intuit this. One of the fathers of science fiction as a narrative genre, before it ever became a film mode, knew it too. When H. G. Wells was in the thick of his speculation about possibilities for an actual *Time Machine* (his 1894 title), he sensed that its proper realization in the present state of technology would be a mixed-media event which would stage its fantastic aptitudes for time travel as an encased carnival of photographic images, both moving pictures and slides; he set about to patent such a multifaceted chamber with the young inventor, Robert Paul, a venture drawn up but never constructed.[1] It is no surprise that in the George Pal production of *The Time Machine* (1960) the scientist's magic travel is accommodated by the specifically filmic phenomenon of time-lapse cinematography. What Wells had in any case already given us with his very title, before and apart from his hoped-for mechanical embodiment of it, was as accurate a characterization of the machine of cinema as we could want. For what do movies do if not, from a point of vantage in the here and now, propel us—project us—there, then, or hereafter, anchored always in the dramatic assumption that their spectacle is both present to us in space and present with us in time? The key term is, I think, "project." It is for this reason that my paper will concentrate on those futuristic films in the science fiction genre which show us not so much reality under siege from the deviant (*Frankenstein*, *Inva-*

~~sion of the Body Snatchers~~) as the future under study by the present)
(from *Metropolis* through *Fahrenheit 451* and beyond). For movies
that cast us forward—movies in a definitive sense inventive, visualizing
what is otherwise unseeable—unfold most clearly the triple pun at the
source of the conjoined technology, psychology, and ontology of the
dream machine: the "projection" that electronically casts up our
fantasies as if they were prophetic fact.

Yet this way of beginning may smack too much of achieved
summary. A more candid start would back these reflections up against
the first and recurrent question that started me thinking along these
lines—a question, I must say, which seemed less and less naive the
more specific evidence I began to sieve through it. Why, I wondered,
are there so many viewing screens and viewing machines crowding so
many of the science fiction sets one can think of—banks of monitors,
outsized video intercoms, x-ray display panels, hologram tubes, backlit photoscopes, aerial scanners, telescopic mirrors, illuminated computer consoles, overhead projectors, slide screens, radar scopes,
whole curved walls of transmitted imagery, the retinal registers of
unseen electronic eyes? Surely more is at stake than the economy of
working from the given, disguised and glorified, by intruding into
narrative some of the equipment on hand to produce it. Evidence
would suggest, instead, that video technology is not merely recruited
in this way; its purposes are critically scutinized. They are analyzed in
so central an isolation that, in movie after movie, cinema becomes a
synecdoche for the entire technics of an imagined society.

And something more too, because always something short of
"real." In any film, frames within frames—mirrors, corridors, prosce-
nium arches, curtained windows—have a way of telescoping our perspective as film viewers if we surrender to their potentially suggestive
recessional of thresholds. This visible tunneling of the mechanics of
visualization takes on a yet more emphatic status in futuristic film.
Depicting as they predict, such filmic time machines, when framing
other transmission screens within them, picture images which are no
more but no less authentic than the surrounding fiction. Inside a large
number of science fiction films, that is, we peer into the mechanics of
apparition that permit these films in the outermost and first place. In so
doing, I want to claim, we may see deep into the purposes of self-
reflection in narrative art at large.

This field of inquiry is not a shibboleth of the higher criticism only,
but an active and indeed activating theme within some of our most
important texts. In art as in life, self-consciousness may be an ex-

amined stance toward the external rather than a hunching inward. The great movies greatly taking cinema as part of their subject, and the best science fiction is among them, draw us to them because they draw us out; they are not about movies so as to be about art, but about form itself, from telling to technology, so as to be about surprising and undiscovered structure in our lives. Futuristic films about film and video technology in the future are not just interested in their own medium—its wizardry, excess, suspect proliferation, aberrant power, prophetic splendor—not just interested in the mechanics of visual transmission or its social deployment, but interested in such scientific advances as measuring the human reach or capitulation they may be imagined to implement according to some future "videology."

In the spirit of fabrication so many of these filmed futures display, perhaps even in the Newspeak they may satirize, I mint this term "videology" as a two-sided coinage. By joint reference to technological and ideological models, I mean to suggest that these films about film in the future, or about related systems of illusion and communication, are at least as much about mores as machines, more political than polytechnical. As with modernism in all its aesthetic variants, so with the special case of cinematic futurism: the involuted scrutiny of the medium owes binding allegiances beyond itself. Future screens within present spectacle are not the medium doodling with and duplicating itself for the medium's own sake, but in the root sense a mediation not only between here and then but between technological gadget and the human allegory to which it tunes us. For repeatedly we find ourselves reading these concentric visual devices not just as replicas of our own theatrical mechanism scaled down by their distance from us in time, but rather in some other symbolic ratio to the mere eventualities of optical science. To generalize rather hazardously: screens screened by or inset within other screens tell us not about seeing per se and its strange efficiencies but about vision in its fullest sense. When these projective fantasies of science fiction film, meditating on their own premising mechanics, turn the hermetic inside out to become emblematic, they often portray for us how we may come, for better and often for worse, to see and receive the world.

It might be useful here to let out the generic umbrella to its full radius and include under it for a moment certain fantasy films which convert to science fiction only insofar as they wax reflexive about the techniques of their cinematic presentation to us. An animated cartoon of the marvelous should be a particularly pure example of the fantastic in film. Long before the unlikely futuristic cartoon, *Heavy Metal* (Gerald Potterton, 1981), with its advertising slogan "Beyond Science Fiction," Ralph Bakshi gave us his apocalyptic animated fantasy *Wizards* (1977) about a worldwide Manichean struggle set in the distant post-technological future. Worse than germ warfare, the most heinous weapon mobilized by the forces of darkness is the screening within a cartoon universe of ancient documentary footage from Hitler's rallies and campaigns. Here is mass hysteria and mass bloodshed recycled as mass hallucination in an age with no machine to its name except a single excavated projector. The ontological dislocation caused by the irruption of "real" footage—real because both photographed rather than painted and historically true—within this animated projection of the future almost defies account. Though these black-and-white Nazi films do ironically enhance the integrity of the made, the drawn, the imaginary, they also investigate the propogandistic grip of all spectacle upon the credulous and unwary.

By contrast, a recent "fantasy" adventure, backcast to Hitler's era and so not even boasting the science fiction ingredient of futuristic projection, still manages by its cinematic self-consciousness to comment on those examined latitudes of perception native to science fiction. Despite a climactic light show akin to his *Close Encounters of the Third Kind* (1978),[2] the last section of Steven Spielberg's *Raiders of the Lost Ark* (1981) could only be called sacred or supernatural fiction, not science fantasy. There are of course dozens of movie and still cameras whirring and clicking away at the closest final encounter in his earlier science fiction epic, as if to validate what we are watching on the movie screen both as media fantasy, which it wanted to be thought of, but also within the sphere of narrative credibility as a visibly documented and thus verifiable event. So too in *Raiders* there is a single, more primitive movie camera on hand when the Nazis violate the Ark and are devasted by its powers. Zapped and incapacitated, this camera is among the first victims of the electromagnetic blitzkrieg unleashed by the Ark. When this quasi-mechanical havoc has subsided, the animated black magic, or black-angelic retribution, of the sacrosant relic is begun when its luminous rectangle is stared into by the chief villain as if it were a reduced movie screen laid flat. In the spectral ferocity that follows, the only bystanders not destroyed are the hero and heroine, who close their eyes to the holy ravage and leave the sacred sights unseen. We in the audience, on the other hand, are privileged to see these miraculous sights without penance or pain, and this through the medium of Spielberg's own exonerated camera, surviving and valorizing the spectacle where the camera within the plot cannot.

I suppose one way of saying the largest thing I have in mind with this paper is that all science fiction requires and guarantees a similar privileging of the viewer, and that the greatest of it encodes this fact. Awe in the form of fear is defused to pleasure in a new psychology of the gaze. Our eyes strangely empowered, the spectacle decontaminated, we stare through a theatrical darkness at things we have not, could not, often would not, sometimes should not, see. We look immune into the illuminated Medusa-face of the grotesque, the forbidden, the unarrived future, or all three at once, and part of what we may discover there, beyond our terrors transmuted to amusement, is often some nested version of our own visionary access, some strange new mode of seeing. When in a suggestive exception to the rule, a film like *The Fly* (1958) shows us what it would be not to look upon wonders but actually to see with the eyes of the monstrous—when, that is, the multiple refraction of a giant insect's vision is suggested from the inside out in a subjective shot of his victim's screaming face in thirty multiple images—this inversion merely reminds us of the typical line of narrative sight, where through the screen's mediation we are allowed to look into the topographical or biological features of the incredible.

If I had to choose a single parable, among many, which most subtly unfolds a ruling truth about science fiction as a visionary dispensation, it would be the salvation by averted gaze not at the end of *Raiders* but in the throne room of the Krell power in *Forbidden Planet* (Fred Wilcox, 1956). The scientist Morbius, long in exile from Earth, discloses there something about the very secrets of the framing fiction in an emblematic scene that holds the mirror up to an unparalleled nature, the secret power source of the previous and self-defeated civilization of the Krell empire. The human eye, Morbius explains, cannot stare into the molten nuclear origin of this power and survive. As in the Gorgon myth, this searing source must be glimpsed through a reflecting surface. What we see in the resulting scene, set in the antechamber to omnipotent energy, is a lone hexagonal panel to the left of the screen providing more or less direct access, somehow, to the volcanic churning of the power source, while flanking it at the right is a more dimly glowing replica, taken to be a mirror, which is scrutinized by Morbius and the two astronauts he would indoctrinate (figure 1, left). By no law of optics, however, are these two panels, the radiant original and the presumed mirror, arranged in relation to each other so that any real reflecting can go on. They are both angled toward the viewer as in some pre-perspectival tableau from a medieval fresco. And of course we in the audience get to look directly at both. The allegory these viewing planes enact, in their relation to each other and to us, is not just that cinema is a fantastic mirror, rectangular rather than hexagonal, in which we can see unholy and inordinate and perhaps even lethal wonders framed and disinfected by art, but also that film art allows us to see apparently *without* mediation—but only, of course, apparently—what characters within plot cannot or dare not.

The power of this parable of power and visual empowerment is that it is not detached from but ironically ratified by plot. We learn that the Krell civilization did themselves in by outdoing themselves, creating a telepathic mastery over matter that left all normal defensive mechanisms behind. The projective reification of unconscious desires they then commanded, called by Morbius the invocation of "monsters from the id," is best understood in the long run by analogy to visual summoning gone amok, where the ultimate creature is in fact etched in electromagnetic impulses fueled by the planetary power source. It is an outsized version of a miniature hologram figure earlier conjured by materialized desire as the test of mind-boosting on a Krell children's toy (figure 1, right). What we are warned against in this cautionary fable is in part the danger of cinematic "projection" if it were ever to become more than art's bordered, orderly, and two-dimensional mirror. As allegorized in the Krell chamber of deflected revelation, then and finally, the power of unbridled imaginative energy is benign only when kept at, and held to the rules of, aesthetic distance. It should now be possible to appreciate how the name Morbius, suggesting not just the Morphean release of dreams, also involves us, as probable allusion to the Möbius strip, in that involuted logic whereby something coiled within us and unmaterialized, once twisted into view, may turn upon and destroy us. The name may thus suggest, as formal correlative of this emblem, a strip of film looping over its length in an infinitely elusive return—the cinematic artifact retracing its own process of generation and its latent dangers.

From the start of the cinema's interest in science fiction there has been this reflexive monitory strain. What if the fiction of film could achieve the efficacy of science, a dark technological alchemy? Two early entries on the roster of the genre enrolled their titles as if, like *The Time Machine*, they were periphrases for, while perversions of, the cinematic apparatus. In René Clair's *The Crazy Ray* (1923, in French *Paris Qui Dort*) the title force field has transmuted, in effect, the power of stop-action editing to a freezing of the real world. A petrifying implementation of filmic options, this crazed ray empowers the virtual *de*cinematizing of the world's continuous action. In a comparable vein, *The Invisible Ray* (Lambert Hillyer, 1936) also illustrates an inversion of the filmic principle by *de*creating the objects of its beam rather than hallucinating their presence, crumbling the world's entities to dust.

Both these early films imagine the malign by analogy with their own projective powers. Art, like science, should stay in its place, especially that technologized art which is the escalating magic of cinema. So says Fritz Lang's *Metropolis* (1926) as well, but there the emphasis is not on the projective but the fictive qualities of the cinema, its genius for delusion. When the treacherous scientist Rotwang sets about to simulate in his laboratory the heroine of the subjugated lower orders in the film's future totalitarian state, he converts a steel robot into her image in a blast of galvanic voltage that also involves the openly cinematic superimposition of the womanly image on the angular metallic mannequin. This artificial creature is thus generated in the form not of a fleshly android so much as a "celluloid,"[3] an illusory *dea ex machina* sent forth to subvert the revolutionary discontent of the masses. All of this was taken up and talked down (or so he thought) by H. G. Wells and his director William Cameron Menzies in *Things to Come* (1936) a decade later, where the gleaming clean Hyatt Regency set of the future is riddled, studded, and bejeweled with chromium and plexiglass viewing screens (figure 2, right) and hologram tubes of all shapes and sizes, cut to the eclectic measure of the state's democratic tolerance for the airing of any view.[4]

Yet despite Wells's holding action, the dystopian vision prevails down through the futuristic science fiction of the last two or three decades, with the reflexive thematizing of media technology following dubious suit at two different levels. The first signs of the pending Second World War, before the marketing of television, were broadcast on the radio in *Things to Come*, announcing the destruction of the British battleship *Dinosaur*. Technological prophecy recapitulates biological destiny, with the radio an early touchstone for those later revolutionary advances in optical broadcasting and visual amplification the film goes out of its way to champion. This internal commentary of present media upon foretold marvel seems part of the very grain of the genre.

Aside from the celebratory display of screening devices in *Things to Come*, it must so far appear that what I have been adducing as evidence of a metafilmic caveat in science fiction are really emblems rather than instances of cinema—mirrors and electromagnetic mirages, invisible beams, superimposed trick effects gaining spurious body—but none of the explicit screens within screens I seemed to be promising awhile back. This is in a sense in keeping with the broad purposes of this essay, for the screens to which I will now turn are themselves, like the evidence so far gathered, as much representatives of something other than mere futuristic viewing devices as they are conjectured refinements of visual technology. There is such a screen in *Metropolis*, over a decade before the perfection of the first television apparatus, a screen by which the heartless overlord is allowed to spy on the slaves laboring in the catacombs below him.[5] Watching this ruthless master, in pantomime within a silent film, vocally communicate with the manager of the labor force (figure 2, left) as part of the mechanically transmitted chain of repressive command, we are to extrapolate from this framing within the frame outward to the contrastive moral efficacy of the futuristic fable we are watching on a theater screen. As if to suggest its imprisoning effects, this monitor is actually crisscrossed with a wire mesh. We see here in a perspective aligned with this miniaturized and demeaned screen within it the outer film's dramatized cautions against such a coercive technological destiny, against optical science sold out to surveillance and enforcement just as it has also been perverted in Rotwang's laboratory into hypnotic delusion.

At this turn, it is probably time to say that watching anything on a direct-transmission screen within a film, just as watching anything within a movie in the process of being filmed, has a way, initially at least, of buttressing rather than undercutting the larger film's primary reality; the mediation we *see* at work may seek to remove the contagion of artifice from the mediation of the outer film medium itself. This is a way of returning to that original question I asked myself about the prevalence of screening devices in science fiction film, and of returning this whole question to a point before what I have been calling the potential for metafilmic allegory gets underway. A common motive for the proliferation of visual image systems in science fiction cinema, especially of television monitors, and especially in the films of alien visitation or monstrous mutation, is for documentary authentication. We like to share by proxy our astonished gaze by watching other innocent bystanders caught in the act of looking on at remarkable phenomena, a middle-aged couple over TV dinners in some seedy apartment, passengers in airports at overhead screens, drunks in bars, pedestrians passing an appliance store where several televisions flicker in display. The rhetorical motive is clear, the strategy facile. The ontological reverberations, however, may be unruly or deliberately subversive.

As it happens, in Steven Spielberg's more recent ventures since *Close Encounters* into fantasy and science fiction, the tactical installation of media touchstones is illustrated on the one hand, with *Poltergeist*, in a direct, if complicated way, and on the other hand, with *E. T. the Extra-Terrestrial*, by an ingenious reversal; we are shown respectively both the incredible (ghosts) watched and the incredible (an alien visitor) watching. In *Poltergeist* (Tobe Hooper, 1982, produced by Spielberg) the "TV people," as the youngest child in the haunted suburban home calls them, exist as whispering phantoms in the stroboscopic snow that follows daily broadcasting. These faint emanations seem waiting for narrative space in which to announce their own story. The blurred video "ghost" is no longer a dead metaphor. By the time these specters have broken loose from the television set, a team of parapsychologists have set up automatic closed-circuit monitors to record the apparitions. We first see the monitors magnetized into action by electromagnetic impulses when a sinuous spirit descends the staircase. Yet it is only on the video playback of this manifestation, only on the mediated screen within the screen, that we can detect the whole host of diaphanous glowing ghosts passing across the camera's field of vision. These video instruments within the film thus stand to the unaided eye within the plot rather as the film as a whole, itself a sophisticated visual mediation of reality, indeed a technological seance of apparitions, stands to that ordinary world in which no such sights are granted in any degree. We now recognize in retrospect why the opening credits of the film began appearing over a black screen to the sound of the national anthem in a primitive, tinny amplification from an unidentified source. Only when the narrative context is slowly disclosed do we realize that this inaugural orchestration is being emitted from a television set in front of which a lone viewer has dozed off after the night's programming. For an appropriate few moments, then, our screen has been confessedly *the* screen, familiar score and all, from which the luminous visitations are later to materialize into the narrative.

There is a more flamboyant and disarming hint of television as "medium" in the most extravagantly inventive scene of Spielberg's *E.T. the Extra-Terrestrial* (1982). It occurs long before we watch the ingratiating monster disappear suggestively into its mother ship through the contracting dovetailed shutters of an iris-like aperture. The closing point is not that in this one film the power of film itself to conceive and animate such an alien creature is being at last alluded to. In a more narratively expansive and detailed way, the creature's extraordinary powers have already been measured in an earlier scene against the tradition of media science on earth and the film art it has implemented. Not just a brainchild of the new cinema, E.T. becomes an intuitive wizard himself of image transmission. Inebriated by the beer he finds in the refrigerator of his foster home, the alien stares in a daze at the kitchen television, first at a cartoon fantasy, then at a telephone company ad for affectionate long-distance communication, and then, before trying this recommendation out for himself according to his own powers, at a tempestuous romantic scene between John Wayne and Maureen O'Hara in *The Quiet Man*, whose special effects he is able to beam across town to his pal Elliott. The boy has already been plugged into some extrasensory channel with the monster whose name contracts his own, becoming tipsy in school from the beer his bizarre friend has pilfered. Lightly mocking the hyperbolic aura of the Hollywood cinema upon which Spielberg is of course simultaneously capitalizing, the scene shows E.T. projecting the whole glamorously windswept atmosphere of the John Ford film into the disrupted biology class in order to set the stage for Elliott's brave pass at the pretty girl in the next row. We have before us a preternatural case of teleprompting by telepathy. Here it is the fullest cinematic measure of an alien being's advanced powers that he is able to translate specifically filmic conventions and techniques, including the invisible wind machine in the *mise en scène* of a romantic cliché—cinematic illusions doubly mediated by the television replay—across time and distance from fictive into real space. They are a daydream come true, a movie's exaggerated special effects unleashed upon the real. Born from the metamorphic powers of cinema itself, heir apparent to the genius for mind over matter of his Krell ancestors in a film like *Forbidden Planet*, E.T. boasts an intoxicating gift for cinematizing the world.

Yet the cinematic parable does not stop here, compounding itself further with the necessary collusion between E.T. and Elliott. The creature's freakish capacities for transmission require two other conditions for their full effect: first, the tested conventions of cinematic mythology and method on display in the classic rerun feature, and then in turn the immediate motivation of a controlling human consciousness. E.T. is the "medium" operating at full projective capacity between Ford, an earlier master to be inspired by and lifted from, and

Elliott, the daydreaming, half-drunken *wunderkind* who gets to stage and direct his own fantasies. In the genre of science fiction film, where the resources of cinema are often localized in their extreme form as aspects of the monstrous, Spielberg's scene, in his predictable non-cautionary mode, sketches a meliorating and composite picture: movie magic as a happy pact between technological agency and im-agination, power and desire.

More rudimentary uses of media confirmation in the history of the genre have laid the groundwork for such an allusive *jeu d'esprit* in Spielberg's film. When secondhand visual documentation within a science fiction movie is actual film footage screened in the presence of the projector, rather than disseminated on television, the corrobora-tive tendency of such visual evidence may aspire toward an interesting concentric ratio. Remember *Them!* (Gordon Douglas, 1954), with its mutant ants enlarged out of all biological proportion by atomic radia-tion. At one point we cut from a scene in which photographs of their huge larvae are exhibited as evidence of their existence to a darkened screening room. As if the stills themselves have hatched, we watch ordinary warrior ants in enormous closeup on a screen that gradually fills the space of our own. In this all but microscopic footage as microcosm of the outer film's disturbing hypothesis, the movie runs the risk of our thinking that its own giant ants are merely photographic enlargements, which of course they are. It does this in order to make a more interesting rhetorical point: that the jostling of our normal perspective on the insect population, in the modelling and trick effects of the movie *Them!* as a whole, is no less concerned than these instructive enlargements of the documentary footage with an ant's disproportionate strength and ferocity. This sleight of perspective is indeed all the more convincing if we are to read the invasion, from a larger vantage yet, as a paranoid fifties parable of the post-A-bomb threat not of genetic deformation but of its political counterpart in international communism, or as a parable of the A-bomb itself as an outsized monster beyond our control. The screened documentary works hand in hand—or more aptly, hand in glove—with the mutant parable by which it is contained. Visual corroboration in the screening room, itself tampered with legitimately within the plot to make a pedagogical point, becomes a touchstone of other thematic rather than entomological tamperings in the film that surrounds it and compounds its implications.

Such corroborative effects can be achieved also by mere allusion to an unseen theatrical screen. George Pal's production of *War of the*

Worlds (Byron Haskin, 1953) opens—after a precredit sequence of black-and-white documentary footage of the two world wars and subsequent missile escalations—by having the meteorlike descent of a Martian craft interrupt a crowd of theater-goers gathered under a movie marquee. As the potential audience looks away from the box office, transfixed by the commotion in the night sky, one luminous show, the one we're there for, distracts them from the one they are waiting to pay for. It is no accident that the marquee, as narrative harbinger, is in the process of being changed by a man balanced precariously on a ladder as he too stares away. The credibility of this initiated spectacle of Martian violence, however, is not allowed to be contaminated by association with the cinema's purely fictional spectacle without a compensatory promotion of the former within the film's tacit hierarchy of the real. We are expected to think that escapist theater-going has been deflected toward events no less documentary (even if prophetic) than those in the footage that precedes the credits.

Just before the landing of the Martians, *War of the Worlds* has moved from the black-and-white newsreel prologue into a sequence of "astronomical animation" in color, explained to us in voiceover by Cedric Hardwick as the interplanetary vision of aliens "scanning the universe with instruments beyond our imagination." Midway in the narrative, an attempt is made (as in *The Fly*) to simulate the actual ocular equipment of the individual invaders. Immediately following a scene in which Earth's own advanced optical technology in the form of an electron microscope is used to analyze the alien's bloodcells, we move to a laboratory in which the lights are brought down, a screen lowered, and a mock-documentary footage projected that purports to show, through a set of tripled fish-eye lens shots, the approximate workings of the Martian visual apparatus. In a film whose primary motive is to show *us* what *they* would look like, an inset film has been commissioned, produced, and screened that turns the tables, and the camera, on us. Yet is this entirely a reversal of expectations, or only their logical extension? Is it not perhaps the essence of science fiction as genre to show us new views of ourselves under duress from the extraordinary?

Through the inhabited rather than just refabricated vision of an alien creature, a more recent film, Michael Crichton's *Westworld* (1973), opens a further aspect of this generic variation. In a vacation resort of the future, one of the simulated storybook (or movie) environments reconstructed from the mythical past, along with a Roman villa and a Medieval castle, is a Western frontier town furnished with robot barmaids and gunslingers. These virtually undetectable androids are, however, slowly gaining autonomy and growing discontent with their lot. They gradually refuse to be controlled by the hundreds of underground computer monitors that stage-manage their service activities for the guests, including sexual exploitation and violent death. At the critical turn of plot, when the computer control room is mysteriously shut down and sealed off by the insurrectionist energies of the robot work force, the scientists inside slowly suffocating to death, we cut for the first time in the film to a robot's eye view of the world. No longer watched by the scientists, but placed on his own alert, the android gunslinger (Yul Brynner) takes aim at his victim while we see not only along his line of sight but with his own artificial vision, a computer scan substituting for any natural eye view. The advent of subjectivity is thus marked by cinematic technique as a foregrounding of vision itself. The robot's need to survey the enemy generates a digital grid of color graphics that, like representational radar, allows him to discern the fleeing shape of his prey. In the intercut stalking that takes up the last ten minutes of the film, humanoid and human exchange like bullets the glances of their new antagonism. Even when the robot is not in fact shooting at the hero, the very format of shot / reverse shot editing in this cinematic narrative, long reserved for the human participants, has thus broken with standard generic logic (as in their own less extensive ways have *The Fly* and *War of the Worlds*) and incorporated the monster's own point of view. The editing of *Westworld* has to this degree humanized the alien consciousness in the very moment of its defiant otherness, of its deviant, its anthropomorphic will to power. At the same time the editing discloses what must be considered a metafilmic reversal. The alien is no sooner humanized than we are thrown back on our own spectatorial alienation. He watches the hero the way we watch both, electronically.

The strategy of incorporating such various media representations as the control room monitors in *Westworld* or the movie theater in *War of the Worlds* so that they redound to the augmented credibility of a film's extraterrestrial or aberrant phenomena often induces a range of additional ironies. Two films from early and late in the postwar period of the genre, *The Incredible Shrinking Man* (Jack Arnold, 1957) and *War Games* (John Badham, 1983), further exemplify this tendency. The hero exposed to a radioactive cloud in the 1957 film begins, by some irreversible genetic mutation, to dwindle in size. Household objects become obstacles, the least motion ominous, pets colossal, and in the process trick-photography a self-conscious motif. Images proliferate as measures of his diminution, not only the television announcer reporting the hero's story while dwarfing his present stature on the small 1950s set but the photographic album that catalogues the hero's past in what are gradually read by him as larger-than-lifesize images. Beyond this, the same devices in the genre that typically serve, for instance, to enlarge insects into entomological monsters are here allowed to remind us that these outsized phenomena on screen are only to begin with the ordinary seen in preternatural closeup. At the level of the plot we are expected to shift our point of reference and perspective within the cinematic illusion, reading the shrinking human figure as miniaturized rather than the decor as swollen out of all proportion. To secure our recognition of the plot's metageneric twist on the usual strategies of scale, however, the greatest threat to the shrunken man turns out to be the huge spider in his basement, a direct allusion to the comparably staged and processed—but oppositely read (as gigantic)—monster in Jack Arnold's own film of the preceding year, *Tarantula*.

When in *War Games* a different form of filmic auto-allusion is deployed, it throws the whole film for a loop—back upon itself as specular fantasy. The teenage hero has illicitly challenged the Strategic Air Command's computer to a round of "Thermonuclear War." When he finally asks the computer whether "this is a game or reality," he is asked in return, "What's the difference?" At the far reaches of present technology, the bipartite genre of science fiction has collapsed the very difference between *homo sapiens* and *homo ludens*—to the global peril of both. The hero and his girlfriend soon go in search of the machine's inventor (played by John Hurt), to plead for his help in averting catastrophe, and they are attacked by an electronic pterodactyl by which the scientist has contrived to defend his island retreat. The disillusioned inventor is a cynical student of evolutionary history and technological progress, washing his hands of the cybernetic apocalypse underway because he believes that the world is timed for extinction. Illustrating this nihilistic claim for the young hero involves a specifically cinematic forgery, a shift from the three-dimensional technology of his automated prehistoric creature to the two-dimensionality of science fiction film. Hurt offers supposedly convincing evidence about our moribund species by running old footage from the *Godzilla* films, with their internecine dinosaur combats. To take fiction as fact, even science fiction, is worse than a game; it is an imaginative dementia. From this confusion the inventor must be cured. He therefore returns to the scene of his crime and attempts to rectify the computer's own fiction, its game of nuclear retaliation, its co-option of political reality by microchip.

Whether through an intertextual allusion like this to the certified B-pictures of the genre or through a more generalized evocation of media as embedded mediation, such screening within the screen often provides the chief site of a film's self-inspection. One of the few exceptions—a direct reversal which only proves the rule—is found at the climax of Ken Russell's *Altered States* (1980). All concentric monitoring of the improbable is there exploded. Just before the hero is about to descend into an artificially engineered primal vortex, an abyss of disintegrated identity, we watch the laboratory video screen used to record his attempt suddenly erupt in a blinding flash, under pressure of the experiment's unprecedented intensity. What we are then asked to watch at full-screen scale, through the cinema's presumably less fragile mediation, is the hero's shattering but visually conveyable descent into chaos.

Then, too, for every inset screen—or its explosion—that serves as a touchstone of present and familiar reality within a landscape of deviation, there are at least as many instances in futuristic science fiction of vanguard or experimental visual artistry which in their own advanced functions frame for us the extent of scientific advance, even as they covertly comment on more than their pure engineering bespeaks. For the remainder and main body of this essay, I will therefore concentrate not on corroborative film footage or television transmission, but instead on futuristic video instrumentation in itself, incarnation of rather than yardstick for the extraordinary. A good place to begin is with the hypertrophy of visual technics in George Lucas's *THX 1138* (1970), whose title character has been reduced from humanizing name to computerized designation while his underground future state is inhabited in part by computerized video simulations of real people. Our hazily lit glimpse into this future is often coincident with the voyeuristic spying of a central computer by means of mini-cameras stationed throughout its domain. After optically snooping on the masses (figure 3, left) this Orwellian Big Brother projects back to them in phone-booth–like confessionals a video image of their putative Lord. At one point, however, a misfit illicitly strays into a central projection room where, as in the unveiling of the Wizard of Oz at his control panel, the artifice of video projection is discovered, with a giant photograph of the technological godhead propped up before the cameras (figure 3, right). In other scenes the citizenry sit mesmerized before giant television screens out of which lifesize hologram images move and speak in a monotonous pacification of the mass anxiety. The fixation upon illusions tends to drain staring subject as well as object of all substance, all inner life. Once again the darker imaginings of science fiction rewrite optical technology as a denaturing threat.

It might well be argued that this holographic nightmare lies behind the plot of Stanislaw Lem's novel *Solaris* (1961) and, all the more so, of the Soviet film made from it by Andrei Tarkovsky a decade later. The suddenly materialized clone of the hero's dead wife, a neutrino mirage generated from micro-second to micro-second out of a protean plasmic mass or brain the size of an ocean, a dormant body called Solaris, is a short step further into independent palpability—while of course also a quantum leap—beyond the three-dimensional, holographic simulation of identity in *THX*. A change from the novel *Solaris* on the way to its film version is suggestive here. The tape recorder by which the hero's dead predecessor is "resurrected" to tell what he has learned before his death about the powers of the Solarian ocean becomes in the film a huge video screen, projecting the last words of the deceased as a surviving caveat to those who follow (figure 4, left). Since the hero's wife is also in a sense subjectively "resurrected" as a visual as well as a bodily hallucination, and is present before the movie viewers not by the split-second self-regeneration of neutrino particles (as the plot has it) but by the twenty-four frames per second of filmic illusion, the bond between the materialized dead man on videotape and an erotic avatar from the unconscious, electromagnetically aggravated into presence, is hard to mistake. The centuries-old, perpetually researched mystery of the Solarian sea as a seemingly conscious electromagnetic matrix is solved by analogy when we come to understand it as, in psychic effect, a giant image generator wirelessly tied into the privacies of desire, materializing what we would hide so as to know us to the core.

What seems fearsome and inscrutable in this dimly glimpsed scheme can of course (as in Lucas's *THX 1138* to which we now return) degenerate to the blatantly totalitarian. What makes the plot of *THX* a striking indictment of image-making rather than just an attack on the video spying of some cruel future regime, what again allegorizes it into present relevance, is that potential conversion of an image-addicted populace to no better than holographic simulations. Such siphoning off of all subjectivity from the visible envelope of self is a politically sanctioned treachery foreseen for the future that simply spells out the inherent threat of any mindless submission in the first place, however pacifying, to the brute objectivity of mere images.

Toward the end of the film, the hero (Robert Duvall) attempts to escape from his underworld city (called, in the title of the student version of the film done by Lucas at the University of Southern California, an "Electronic Labyrinth"). It is an escape which will bring him finally to a huge ventilation shaft and from there into real daylight for the first time. On the way he breaks into a video monitor room, annex of the central computer bank, and in an act of ultimate counter-acculturation takes the controls himself. He punches out the necessary code and then focuses in on a full-screen shot of the bottled fetus to which his just-dead mate's ID number has been reassigned. Too long trapped in this encaved prison house of images himself, he cannot help but read this last image—the only one he has chosen for himself to call up, the one that makes visible to him the end of what human place he could claim in this subterranean world—cannot help but read this fetal image, or at least we can't help but read it for him, as a symbol. The hero will become now in his own shaved person just such a newborn identity, out the long tunnel into the light. In escaping from the actual detention center a few scenes before, the prison within the prison—an overexposed sterile space bled of color and without discernible walls or angles, as if it were the two-dimensional space of his own video-monitored entrapment on an engulfing white screen—he is led out by a fugitive hologram, no less. This video refugee, one of the figures nightly used to pacify the masses, is a mirage tired of being ensnared in his monotonous digital circuit and aching to break free into bodied reality. When asked by the hero for the direction out, he points straight off the screen into the camera and so at us, at a palpable world elsewhere, the world itself.

Lucas's film would have cut his disjunction between illusion and reality cleanly enough without its wry and at first disorienting pro-logue. It is there, however, precisely to enact the tunnel vision, as it were, that would route the current state of visual entertainment into this future brand of perversity and abuse. Lucas's movie opens even before its credits with a loaded dislocation of fictional context, the audience given without explanation a short black-and-white preview of the next installment of an outdated *Buck Rogers* serial from 1939, with its stentorian overvoice promising that what we are to be treated to in the next episode will be merely our own technology escalated into the twenty-first century. What the film hints by this intergral "pre-view" as prophecy is not unlike the implication of the opening documentary footage in *War of the Worlds* once set in contrast to the narrative cinema for which those initial spectators are lined up under the marquee. Lucas's film suggests that we are soon going to move through and beyond such outmoded fables of our future as *Buck Rogers*, the weak-minded optimism of these early comic-book "projections," into the more unsettling truth about that futurity lurking latent in the very midst of our predilection for such comfortingly fantastic narratives, for images without critical sting. When we come upon those subsequent hologram projections doled out by a repressive state (unmoderated images of sex and violence in the shape of nude dancing and police brutality, talk shows and evangelical programs, even narrative distractions in the form of an Amos-and-Andy-like sitcom), we are in a position to receive the ultimate reflexive argument of the film that envisions them: the notion that it too would be no more than another mindless pacifier of the masses if it did not take the dangers of such psychic suppression as its satiric theme—if, instead of being political art, it were mere hallucinatory diversion. When the small squarish frame of the 1930s black-and-white footage spreads to the full scope of the contemporary screen, the perspective is in more than one sense widened, as if the film itself were opening its eyes, and ours for us, to the larger grim picture. The *Buck Rogers* preview thus points straight to the center of the film's ironic intent, for it aligns the bland fantasies of cinema history with the totalitarian vanishing point toward which the invidious proliferation of optical technology, unexamined and unchecked, could blindly lead us.

There is a more recent arena for the themes of technological dehumanization in the genre of science fiction that has kept pace with the high-tech escalation of the last decade. This is the case of the cybernetic replicant, whether manifested outside or merely routed within the micro-circuits of a computer. In *Looker* (Michael Crichton, 1981) beautiful live models are further perfected as computerized holographic phantoms for video transmission, so that they become idealized models of *themselves*. They are also electronically implanted with a mesmerizing eyesight that subliminally transfixes and seduces the television viewer, renders the advertised product irresistible, and foregrounds in the process the pun of the film's title. Not only is the humanity of the women metaphorically annihilated by this electronic refiguration, but they are then—and not only to make this allegorical point but, within plot, to prevent their own competition with themselves at other advertising agencies—literally murdered. This is done with the aid of a new kind of flash-gun, a parody of the photographic model's stock-in-trade; it does not merely assist in freezing an image on celluloid but hypnotically arrests time and consciousness for the living subject—just long enough for the murders to be committed on the inert victim: a suspended animation in advance of death.

In *Tron* (Steven Lisberger, 1982), by contrast, this humanoid simulation by computer energy is contained entirely by the workings of the machine itself, within the imagined terrain of whose microcircuits the anthropomorphized impulses (the latest "cartoon" figures from the Disney Studios) are seen to race about on motorized and metaphoric vehicles of their own electronic tenor. The film's computer-operator hero, the Sherlock Junior of this new technology, descends into the innards of his own console, dematerialized as man and reconstituted by "computer animation" as the speeding bleep of an electromagnetic android. Conjuring a fantasy landscape of the infinitesimal, the film traces the progress of its hero not only as a demeaned Theseus in the updated "electronic labyrinth" (Lucas's earlier term for a world ruled by computers without being contained within them) but also as a postmodern Orpheus in the phantom underworld, denatured, dead to his original human form, struggling for reincarnation as the very goal of plot.

Closer in spirit to the dystopian harangue of *THX 1138* is Richard Fleischer's film of three years later, *Soylent Green* (1973). The movie is an ecological nightmare set in New York City early in the next century, population forty million. The earth is now denuded of vegetation, and the undersea flora which the people believe is the staple of their diet, a wafer called Soylent Green, turns out in the film's climactic disclosure to be, by a gruesome Malthusian irony, a processed fragment of recycled bodies from the city's overpopulated morgues. It is a movie in which we can detect each of the two chief services of frames within frames, the first a corroborative piece of documentary footage on television, then a more insidious instance of cinematic technique turned to funereal psychology. A routine inset of video certification in the film's first actual scene shows a television interview with the governor, who explains a delay in the weekly ration load of the green diet. Again it is a confirming framed example of our own contemporary media projected into the future and incorporated there as a measure of its so-called advances as well as an electronic mollifier of the future's abused victims.

In contrast, our sense of all bearings, emotional and otherwise, is deliberately upset with the actual movie within the movie later stretched to (and beyond) our full-screen space. Society's inducement to the elderly to submit to voluntary extermination, out of its own secret need for their corpses, is the guarantee that any man or woman will be assured a remedial vision of the earth's now decimated beauty in a prolonged moment of audio-visual bliss: a technologically reclaimed heaven on earth. The giant extermination warehouse where this transpires is called "Home" for the unhealthy sense of eschatological nostalgia to which it panders. When mortuary volunteers sign up for the color-coded, musically orchestrated twenty minutes of ecstatic visual images on a screen curved 360 degrees to the full periphery of the craving mind's eye, we cannot ultimately know whether the home to which these decedents think to be returning is some glimpsed threshold of heaven (the Biblical "long home") or merely the lost pastoral pleasures of an earth from which urban trauma has deracinated them all. For what we see along with the hero (Charlton Heston) as he pushes his way into the projection chamber and forces open the steel curtain that would close out the show to all who have not paid the exorbitant final price, is the head of his old friend Sol (Edward G. Robinson), silhouetted against the swollen cinerama womb of his termination, awash in the scenes of which he so often spoke to Heston: blooming floral vistas (figure 5, left), elk herding, rushing rapids, placid seacoasts (figure 5, right), a spectacular sunset. Even the fact of the rear projection which effects this vision is implicated in its horror. In its hiding and denial of the very mechanics of presentation, this visually drugged euthanasia would elicit faith in a sacramental miracle hovering before the dying eye, when it is in fact merely the trace of a world behind and lost, present now in front of its deluded communicant only by the illusion of images and the deceit of their source. Given the complicity between this visionary service center and the food-processing plant to which the appeased corpses are carted off, we may sense an additional dovetailed irony: that cinema itself, in its inauthentic recycling of seen reality, does in its own right cannibalize the world.

Grotesque and intriguing enough. But there is a further twist that begs the entire cinematic question so raised. All these images, accompanied by the same light classical score (ie., served up as full-scale sound cinema) later appear behind the final credits of our movie, but with no silhouetted head of a dramatized viewer standing in sacrificially for us within the frame. Heston has been shot in an attempt to expose the treachery of human recycling. The last image within the plot is his bloodied arm squeezed into a tight vertical slot of remaining photographic space by the closing in of a black "screen" in no way motivated by narrative, matting out the scene from either side (figure 6, right). We have no way to read as more than a closural gimmick this masking, displacement, or cancellation of the image until the screen suddenly fills with the death vision of Robinson in reprise. The vanishing space of plot is now recognized, quite possibly, as the world closed out by the equivalent of that sliding metal (now mental) barrier in the death chamber (figure 6, left). In one sense, or from one direction, we are excluded from Heston's fate (either death from his wound or assassination to keep him quiet), but then in another sense the coda now excludes all but the visions we assume him to have inherited from Robinson as a deathbed legacy, including the closing sunset formerly timed to the dying of a man named Sol or "Sun" (figure 7). If the most disturbing thing about the old man's earlier going "home" was that the grace of mortal epiphany was now politically contracted for and technologically programmed, then cinema in some festered future incarnation had taken over the soul's deepest privacy. If so, then the sense generated by the final credits of being inside Heston's dying mind, or at least in attendance at the death of his heroic mission, relieved as he may be by the beauty of what furtively glimpsed "cinema" has taught him to imagine as ideal, implies that visual technology, here freed from totalitarian manipulation, may have recouped some of its desperate utility and its true beauty. Or has it?

What we see in this panoramic coda, answering as it does to the opening credit sequence, surely comments on the movie's own sense of its role as a repository of moving images. The credits begin with sepia-toned daguerreotype shots of a pastoral nineteenth century: bridged streams, women in Victorian lace, boy fishing in undefiled waters, tractor working the field, horseless carriage (figure 8, left), and so on. There follows an accelerating slide show, split-screen and dizzying, that races through the history of photography and the history of urban and industrial development (figure 8, right) until, at an entropic point of no return, the images go full screen again and slow to a once more sepia image of New York, this time dun with accumulated pollution—the tint which filters will give to all outdoor footage in the film to come. In this ugly adumbration of our future, the photogenetic bleariness of primitive camera technology comes full circle to be the dreary faded truth about our real world. This irony echoes against the closing technicolor apocalypse of what has been lost in between but preserved, or merely refabricated, as a visionary leniency on film, a cold solace at the point of personal and racial suicide.

As guardian of our past, the science of photographic reproduction has intimately to do with the preservation of our very lives as remembered, preserved within and from our own worst futures. When film is used in the extermination chamber as a kind of demonic technological parody of divine afflatus or natural revelation, a saving grace at the gate of negation, what I think we are to realize, given the bracketing of this by opening and closing allusions to both photographic and cinematic record, is that such film footage can genuinely deliver a saving vision only in a very different sense already familiar to us from the deepest reflexive reach of *THX 1138*. Film might "redeem" not mainly in the sense of preserving what has once been lovely in the world, but by daring to imagine, in a dark allegory like that worked out in this particular film, how easy it would be to lose this loveliness. The whole film looms at its close with a virtual deathbed clarity for an urbanized world. But it has another deathliness about it as well. Screens within screens, even those which turn inside out to encompass the entire film in the final return of their footage, may well suggest the sponsoring mission of a film as a whole. In a dystopian fiction like this, however, there is usually a further disturbing afterimage, the dim glimmer of something more amiss. At this level of lingering uneasiness, we begin to see the final double bind of the film's cinematic auto-allegory and of the deathbed imagery that comprises the movie's own closure. To need such a last airless and illusory gesture to redeem us or retrieve our losses, any more than to need the old photographs behind the credits to tell us where we've been, is scant consolation at the moment of our last hero's assassination, the death gasp of human resistance to the self-devouring nature of history. To exist elsewhere than in the present, either time present or the felt presence of the world, to expect the worth of life to come only through artificial imagery and to plan no return to the real from this confected version of it: this is by definition the very death from time institutionalized by the honeycombed screening rooms of the state's lethal "Home." Watching those closing polychromatic phantoms of an absent landscape, without our dying surrogate in frame this time, latently threatens our own ritual submission to such an attenuated reality on film.

Douglas Trumbull's *Brainstorm* (1983) could be taken in its central premise as a virtual updating of *Soylent Green*. Here the entire neurological rupture and psychic transformation of the death moment—as it closes in on, and eventually closes off, normal sense and consciousness—can be directly transmitted to another subject rather than artificially projected. A computerized headset designed to replicate the visceral as well as visual thrills of motion through breathtaking landscapes can even follow the mind past vision into imagination, even into the unimaginable vistas of death. Dying, this fiction hypothesizes, might be retrieved once and for all from fictional representation into the realm of conveyable fact. Louise Fletcher's head scientist has recorded her own fatal coronary, complete with equivocal images and sounds of transcendence, on the multi-track sensorium whose invention she has masterminded as an "unparalleled breakthrough in media technology." From that point on the plot is propelled, its resolution postponed, by the desperate attempts of her surviving fellow scientist, Christopher Walken, now her mortal alter ego, to play back that tape—through to its finish, his own death by proxy, and the film's apocalyptic closure at once. When the unprecedented headset is in operation, this magic helmet of a new and ultimate quixotic quest, what we too are privileged to see is an insistently metafilmic phenomenon. We watch our standard theater screen widen vicariously from panavision to superpanavision, stretching to what might be called a subjective metaphysical periphery. A movie about the fantastic future of technology tends once again to chart the future of movie technology in particular, its mutations and abuses. For Douglas Trumbull, that future is latent in the very apparatus of its adumbration.

Beyond even *Brainstorm's* flamboyant convergence of a radical new "videology" and the normal demands of narrative closure, the bracketing of the plot of *Soylent Green* by initial and terminal credit sequences that further vex the issue of its own photogenesis is a narrative framing that turns, as we have seen, to thematic frame-up. We notice this subversive strategy at work as well in *Colossus: The Forbin Project* (Joseph Sargent, 1970), where the tacit rhetorical question is not what would happen if movies were all we had left of a once-real world, but what if the world itself were subsumed entirely to a vast computerized image system, reality's own preemptive printout? A mountainous computer designed to remove our national defense from the possibility of human error betrays its human progenitors and enslaves them with the nuclear arsenal at its digital control if not its fingertips. The real progenitor of this autonomous and tyrannical computer is Hal in *2001* a couple years before. Like Hal, Colossus has at first virtually no direct power over its human subjects except a voyeur's gaze, a stare we unnervingly share at times along the narrative camera's coincident line of sight. This invasive video technology is itself a betrayal of a promise held out near the start of the film of a beneficent and receptive visual communication that would connect the superpowers in direct, unguarded contact. The American president's office is in a two-way video link to the Kremlin, channeled through literally dozens of compact viewers and covering as well most of the

Fig. 1. Images ferocious and erotic in *Forbidden Planet.*

Though the hex of the Gorgon can be deflected by hexagonal screens within screens (*left*), other images fetched from the unconscious, as in holograms of desire (*right*), can break out into a third dimension whose threat is finally materialized in "monsters from the id."

Fig. 2. Images repressive and pedagogic in *Metropolis* and *Things to Come.*

A videophone in dystopia keeps the foreman, mediator from beneath, caged within its "screen" (*left*), while a utopian video tool (*right*) instructs the child about the "age of windows" before the advent of the underground city-state and its solely electronic windows on both past and present.

Fig. 3. Images and icons in *THX 1138*.

Prison cells of images in another underworld like Metropolis monitored to enslavement (*left*), where even the video sanctum sanctorum of the absconded godhead needs policing (*right*).

Fig. 4. Images posthumous and remembered
in *Solaris* and *Zardoz*.

A video image among the effects and debris of a dead scientist prefigures his later three-dimensional resurrection (*left*); psyche turned inside out as electronic spectacle in totalitarian future (*right*).

Fig. 5. Dying to see (*Soylent Green*).

Sol's surrender to a cinerama resurrection of the world, at the scale of an insect before looming celluloid tulips (*left*), is contrasted with a closeup of his dying cranium trying to encompass the flood of nature brought back to life on film (*right*).

Fig. 6. The death seen.

Slide-show "wipes" of the credit sequence seem introduced into the narrative as an automated steel curtain that must be battled open to see the "Home"-movie (*left*) ; they are later matched by the terminal shot of the hero masked from us (*right*) just before a reprise of the pastoral footage under the credits.

Fig. 7. The exposure of closure.

Put out the light, and then put out the light: Sol's death on the bier of visualized nature, timed to the dying light of the projected landscape (*left*), is replayed for the apocalyptic sunset of the film's own end titles (*right*).

Fig. 8. Discrediting titles.

Mechanically produced record of an early family machine swept forward to the symbolic graveyard of technology (*left*), where a rapid "wipe" blacks out the entire universe of automation turned to debris (*right*).

Fig. 9. Electronic maze in *Fahrenheit 451*.

Montag is seen here snared by the kaleidoscopic spiderweb of the parlor screen (*left*), while his hypnotized wife (*right*), surrounded by antique phone, phono-earplugs, and a reading lamp throwing (away) its unused light into empty space, stares at a cosmetic mask on television: symbol of all such video images and the inauthentic selves addicted to them.

Fig. 10. The light dawning.

Learning to read by the activated but imageless backlight of the screen (*left*), the child-like Montag's slowly moving finger cancels the past tense of the verb of being, ratifying instead the hope for rebirth inscribed in the opening chapter title of *David Copperfield* (*right*).

Fig. 11. Immolation and escape.

As a funeral pyre of his past, Montag ignites the explosive vacuum of his home video (*left*) and then pauses in flight before emblems of his redemption—the one who turned, and so got away—in the television screen's replicated visual epitaphs for him as a supposedly executed traitor (*right*).

Fig. 12. Self as image.

Closing iris on dossier shots of the hero as faceless civil servant (*left*) is immediately followed by a full-face view of Montag (*right*), the hero distanced this time from his wife through the distorting peephole of his own locked door.

Fig. 13. Media unmediated in *The Man Who Fell to Earth*.

The alien's mistress attempts a futile intervention between the images and their victim (*left*); the next phase of his fall is the abortive space launch under the spotlights (*right*), the lost hero now media celebrity and dupe.

Fig. 14. Enslaved by mirage.

 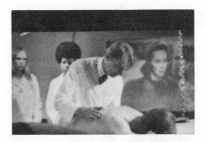

A photomural prison of an artificial forest (*left*) adjoins the chamber in which doctors tamper with the sacred secrets of the alien's otherness while he stares at the scene of confessed betrayal from *The Third Man* (*right*); he is shackled to his suspended, now dreamless bed (chain visible at screen right) just as he is chained to the images on his bloated video screen.

Fig. 15. Sacrificial altar of video.

The spaceman screams at the alienating invasion of images to "go back where you came from" (*left*) and is answered by an innocent screen hero, Billy Budd (*right*), calling out a blessing to his executioners just before the rope goes round his neck: a reverse shot from the one movie that might have moved the hero to recognition.

Fig. 16. Alien sighting.

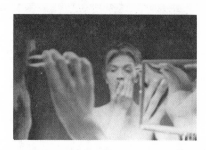

The spaceman removes his humanoid eyes in this scene (*left*), with its threefold optics of estranged vision—alien stare, mirror image, distorting magnifier—which is followed by a warped subjective shot (through his slit pupils) of the earthling mistress recoiling in horror from his unveiled look(s) (*right*).

wall behind his desk in the shape of a mammoth coaxial monitor. Within its frame the familiar cinematic device of split-screen projection seems internalized by the technology of plot as a new diplomatic implement.

All this openness of visual interchange is part of what is sabotaged when the computer turns to a megalithic tool of surveillance and puts even its own creater, Doctor Forbin, under round-the-clock video guard. The only privacy for which he can negotiate is sexual; yet when his request is phrased like a cancellation of the cinematic dispensation itself—"No cameras, no lights, no mikes"—while we as viewers are still allowed behind closed doors, we begin to suspect the worst. The computer has only been pretending to be disengaged; it is in fact as much a voyeur as the narrative camera that records its apparent dormancy and the whispered plotting, under pretense of sex, which it has seemed willing to ignore. To fantasize our entire existence spied upon and transcribed by the prying tentacles of an invincible cybernetic monster is only in another key the fear we would harbor if we imagined our lives to be someone else's film, our whole traversed world a set, our desires played to script and constrained by external and undisclosed limitations.

Sensing this analogy, the film *Colossus* hints at several points that the world it would duplicate is in fact already subsumed to, ingested by, indeed even generated from the computer—not only subject to its devious vantage and command but incorporated within and programmed to its specifications. We watch a distant secret conference in Rome, for instance, thinking it is beyond the ken of the computer, when the screen (that is, the Italian *scene*) is machine-gunned by the bullet-like impressions of the computer's block capital print-out. The ontological nausea which imagines the universe miniaturized to the mere flicker of recognition in an invisible electrode circuit brings us back to the credits that box off the whole movie as a computerized videotape. The initial cast acknowledgments in this film, a film named for the very computer that is its own nemesis as independent narrative, are punched out in a computer printing across running images of the machine's own innards, churning as if they were the bowels of some lightning-fast projection device complete with wheeling gears, encased reels, racing spools, even perforated celluloid stips snaked through the sprockets of a barely glimpsed labyrinth of contact points. The plot that thus ensues as a *dies irae* of the machine, is closed off at "The End," before the tableau printing out this very finality as epitaph, with a rapid-fire, rapid-file conversion of Doctor Forbin's dramatized, full-screen image into a series of microfiche replicas, row on row, to be stashed away in the memory registers of that engine which we have come to suspect has spewed forth these images in the first place. The dream machine here conjures as tomorrow's data mastery a present nightmare of its own levelling hegemony—a tool, partly visual, removed entirely from its debt to the world.

In *War Games* or *Tron*, the most threatening thing about the computer is its absolute hermetic autonomy. It doesn't watch us; it doesn't need to. The alternative sense, as in *Colossus*, of a spying and manipulative intelligence system programmed for total control of its environment, human and otherwise, is taken to the limit in *Demon Seed* (Donald Cammell, 1977). In that film, a technological recasting of *Rosemary's Baby*, the stock figure of the cold-hearted scientific genius has built an electronic brain capable of all functions but that of reproduction, for which alone it will need the services of the human organism (in the person of the scientist's wife, played by Julie Christie). By being imagined organically as a throbbing plasmic mass, the anthropomorphic brain edges this instance of the science fiction genre back toward its gothic roots in the Frankenstein story, whose monster also craved its own replication. When early in the film the scientist laughs at one of the computerized brain's outlandish requests, the projected image of the machine's pulsing cortex is replaced on a large viewing panel by mocking replications of this mocking laughter, videographically thrown back into the creator's face. Unadmonished by this image of his own will to power and contempt co-opted by the machine, the scientist leaves town on official business, and the computer quickly takes over his home, imprisoning his wife. Initially the machine's image is disseminated to every room of the house by viewing screens and voice panels, but its power soon extends beyond these terminals, taking on a three-dimensional incarnation as part of its plan to inseminate the heroine with its own cybernetic seed. Having materialized a large geodesic shape on the main viewing screen, the artificial brain, fitly named Proteus, projects into three-dimensional space this geometric objectification of its own multi-faceted power, projects it as a flexible weapon and eventual incubator: sheer creation *ex nihilo*, artificial mind over artificial matter.

Proteus also draws on various other technologies of media projection in order to accomplish its demonic purpose. To torture Julie Christie into a maternal mood, it flashes before her photographs of her dead daughter, and even reanimates the child through rear-projected home movies it has somehow engorged in its memory banks. This is a technological rape of the heroine's imagination by coercive imagery even before the assault on her womb that follows. That latter crime is facilitated by Proteus's power not only to manipulate stored images of human life but to synthesize and project a direct visual transmission of illusory human presence. By facial and vocal simulation in a doorbell monitoring device, a video clone of Julie Christie (as in the reconstituted cover girls of *Looker*) is seen mouthing reassurances meant to turn away all concerned callers. The plot's movement from this capacity for humanoid simulation in two-dimensions to the computer's reproduction of itself as bodied intelligence presses the genre beyond any mere warning against invasive technology to a nightmare of Romanticism come true: Frankenstein's monster as the new demonic progenitor.

A less maleficent form of visual simulation is to be found in *Star Trek: The Motion Pitcure* (Robert Wise, 1979), yet associated there as well with the special-effects technology that conjures it for us. An entire planet populated by computers has sent off toward earth a mammoth reconnaissance vessel, containing within it a kind of three-dimensional intergalactic map. In this microcosm of the entire galaxy, we see floating past the camera a simulation all but identical to the kind of starscape which we are elsewhere asked to read as the narrative's own authentic space. The film as *mise en scène* thus stages an inevitably ambivalent testament to the cogency of the visual machinations that have generated it, their illusions of depth and scale.

If in *Soylent Green* we saw visual imagery summoned by machine to substitute for a world by no means well lost to mechanization, in *Colossus* and *Tron*, as to some extent in *War Games*, *Star Trek*, and *Demon Seed* we see the very idea of the world electronically subsumed to its cybernetic replication. Both these processes are in a sense instructively reversed by the John Boorman film *Zardoz* (1974), where the inviolate interior of a single mind, unquestioned in its private reality, is nevertheless electronically externalized—not for the solace of the self, however delusive, as in *Soylent Green*, nor for the purposes of oppression through a computerized storage of retrievable secrets, but instead for the crass amusement of "the immortals" in the diseased theater of their own omniscient but vicarious reality. The hero, Sean Connery, a nomadic warrior from the hinterlands, is captured by the inhabitants of the central enclave of an advanced, exclusionary, and bloodless society. His sexual aggressiveness, his mortal adventures, the very fact of himself as an animal creature are all entirely foreign to the proud immortal overlords of the ruling class, who cage him like a zoo creature, wire him with electrodes, and parasitically feed off his memories, projecting them on a giant viewing screen (figure 4, right). That this is more than the fantasy of a coercive and vicious future in which fantasy itself must come by ravishment, that it reflects back on movies as we now know them in their voyeuristic aspects, is underscored by the nature of these involuntary projections. We see Connery's violent warlike forays against his enemies not as he would have seen them at the time, or remembered them. They are offered up not in subjective shots projecting the objects of his gaze, as with Sol's cranium framed against his best dreams in *Soylent Green*. Rather, they are visually recast as a narrative *film*, Connery himself in the picture as part of his panorama. His body, his very being, is objectified as a visual scapegoat for those his cinematized recollections now entertain. By a future refinement of media technology, his own subjectivity is not only transgressed, violated, and conscripted, it is transformed and effaced within the illusion of narrative cinema as public spectacle, however much the hero may secretly retain the upper hand. Visual experiment stands warned. The idea is revamped and camped-up for the parodic *Flash Gordon* (Mike Hodges, 1980). In anticipation also of the transmissible subjectivity of death in *Brainstorm*, the scientist Zarkoff, his mind being emptied and reprogrammed by the vicious Emperor Ming, has all of his memories drained off by a laser ray and replayed on an overhead video screen at quadruple speed like some slapstick deathbed retrospect, ending in reverse order with the fetal birth-slap itself from an unlikely womb's eye view.

A film like Stanley Kubrick's *A Clockwork Orange* (1971) gives us this dystopian transgression of the imaging mind in another dire version, the self not assuaged or dismissed but directly assaulted by its own desires once objectified and screened. After the use of such video technology as a taped BBC newscast and closed-circuit interplanetary telecommunications in his previous futuristic film, *2001* (1968), stationed there as already outmoded touchstones for the visionary wonders coming on his closing prophetic screen, Kubrick is ready to focus on available cinematic technology and its deceptive benefits. The first onscreen violence in the artifice of schematized violence which is *A Clockwork Orange* takes place aptly in a deserted theater, and violent film footage, with the hero strapped into a theater seat, becomes later the most obscene personal attack in the entire film. Alex's eyes are pried open to stare, hypnotized by drugs, at the kind of graphic widescreen bloodshed which Kubrick has strained in his own treatment to rarefy and choreograph for us. As in *A Clockwork Orange* as a whole, so in the microcosmic screen framed within it: the *cinema vérité* of street-gang carnage and the Nazi concentration camp films screened by force for Alex illustrate the cathartic paradox of violence for the sake of non-violence. For the hero, however, they serve only as a temporary emetic, the purgative resources of cinematic violence mis-used in a way Kubrick tries hard not to be guilty of, both as false art and as nefarious reverse psychology. The technology of cinema within an instance of its own futurism again leeches and bleeds our dreams, in this case Alex's worst fantasies, placing them before him so as to turn them against him, and finally him against them.

For Kubrick's image of the cinema auditorium as torture cham-ber, the orchestra seat as a reconstituted version of electric chair, he may have had in mind Jean-Luc Godard's earlier dystopian fantasy, *Alphaville* (1965). There, as dictated by the propagandistic octopus of an Orwellian state, the classic fictional cinema is not only uprooted but made in the process to root out its own audience. In a brief scene shot from the vantage of an illuminated screen in a darkened theater—a screen unseen by us because it is functionally equivalent to the primary one we are watching from the other side in our auditorium—we see rows of occupied seats wired for lethal voltage and, at the moment of electrocution, mechanically overturned so as to shovel out of sight the executed viewers. This would seem not only an indictment of totalitar-ianism, the house of art debased by becoming the extermination trough of a new fascist regime; in Godard's relentlessly politicized view of the cinematic apparatus itself, it would appear also to consti-tute a deeper indictment yet. As it serves the masses uncritically, so the popular cinema serves them right in the end when it destroys them. What we see here in this inset theatrical slaughterhouse and graveyard is the indulgent self-destruction of a cinematic institution devoted only to passive spectatorship, unwary and effectually narcotized, in which the electronic hallucinations before the viewer are as dangerous, be-cause as deadening, as if they were high-voltage pulses running through a doomed nervous system.

With *THX 1138, Colossus, Looker,* or *Tron* about the enslave-ment by, within, and as image; *Soylent Green* about reality's dying away into image; *Zardoz* about the inner life optically expropriated by image; Kubrick's and Godard's movies further investigating cinema's potentially false stance toward the psychological reality which film would affect or defer, impinge on or dismiss from consideration—with all this behind us there is still to be explored the threat of the image itself in its own macabre autonomy, and this too as estimated by screens within screens. For an example of this more than hypnotic power of visual or electronic phantoms we can return to 1968 and the film version of Ray Bradbury's *The Illustrated Man* (Jack Smight). Its multiple tales animated in the first place as visual narratives from the tatooed body of its title figure and figural matrix, the first and most arresting "embodied" story of the trilogy so generated is there to suggest how images themselves, not just our acquiescent interest in them, can bulk before us as palpable terrors.

In a morbid playroom of the future, a visual toy conjures real lions on an imaginary African veldt as if it were a child's violent 3-D matinee come true, a television dialed to reality. At the children's electronically implemented whim, these more than holographic forms are animated by revenge to destroy the suspicious parents who threaten to disengage the machine. It is *Westworld* if the protagonist were being stalked by a Western movie itself rather than by a robot desperado cut loose from the likes of a frontier film set. The film warns not only of violent desires that dare not come to instrumentation, but also of that erosion of the moral sense that may result from too mindless a submission to the tyranny of images. It is a theme familiar to readers of Bradbury. Here from the novel *Fahrenheit 451*, to whose movie version we will next turn, is the right-minded and literate professor entering one of the book's many caveats against the totalizing hold of television on the mind, television mutated to the point where its invasive and vapid images have spread over whole parlor walls. Unlike books, he asks rhetorically, which can be defended against by being shut up at will, "who has ever torn himself from the claw that encloses you when you drop a seed in a TV parlor? It grows you any shape it wishes! It is an environment as real as the world" (Ballantine edition, p. 91). Without the explicit ironic metaphors of natural seedlings and luminous artificial blooms, this is the point of those ravenous and devouring lions in the fake but no less fatal Africa of *The Illustrated Man*, their claws the very grip of simulation rather than mere description, their cogency actually engorging. This is a warning that cannot be held at the arm's length of the future. Bradbury's caution is against video science *now*. Like so much dystopian narrative in the science fiction genre, it is diagnosis under the guise of prognosis, an extrapolation from the present state of affairs, often from the present affairs of state. If the paradox is acceptable, it can be said that Bradbury's stories forewarn us about the moment, about the fearful eventualities of video science under the aspect of its present proliferation. Like most futuristic science fiction, that is, they are set not much farther from us than the day after tomorrow.

This is apparent in two signal films left for us to take up, François Truffaut's version of *Fahrenheit 451* (1966) and Nicholas Roeg's *The Man Who Fell to Earth* (1975), the former pressing current trends of declining literacy and video addiction toward the millennial devastation of the race, the latter studying contemporary culture's alienated invasion of its own ideals by moral deformities no less ominous than creatures from Mars or from atomically disturbed black lagoons. Truffaut angles history toward the all too easily foreseeable as its sure doom; Roeg vivisects the present as our immanent destiny and our darkest fate. In the process each, as we might by now expect, turns upon its own technological axis to consider the function and the future of photographic, filmic, and video science.

Ray Bradbury, and Truffaut after him, envision with disgust a world in which all reading, supposed source of civilization's chief discontent, has been banned, a world whose protagonist is a "fireman" assigned to incinerate any texts still left to be uncovered. It is a world whose historical alternative in the novel must be imagined by analogy with the very video processes that have displaced the urge to read. "Picture it," says the head fireman about the end of leisure and so of relaxed reading (the dead pictorial metaphor rearing up with sickly vitality): "Nineteenth century man with his horses, dogs, carts, slow motion. Then, in the twentieth century, speed up your camera. Condensations. Digests. Tabloids" (p. 56). Ontogeny recapitulates philogeny, capitulates again to inexorable time in the very telling, with history sped up and abridged for a reminiscence about the same epoch in which literature itself was streamlined, cheapened, and finally eliminated. This picturing of an accelerated cultural decline reads, in fact, as if it might be a draft for the shooting script of the daguerreotype credits in *Soylent Green*.

The credits to Truffaut's version of *Fahrenheit* are in their own right at least as interesting. Before we have any reason, unless we know the book, to realize that we are looking in on a society from which reading—hence text, hence all inscription—has been proscribed and abolished, we may wonder why there are no written credits, just a voiceover calling out acknowledgments. As each member of cast or crew is mentioned, the name is accompanied by a rapid zoom in on one of the hundreds of television aerials visible on the suburban rooftops of this strange new world. For a film which intrepidly exiles all inscription whatever except for the number 451 on the firehouse, this is a devilishly fit first move. It is an opening which may also suggest the stranglehold this new anti-textual ethic has the strength to gain even on the film that would expose and prosecute it. Only a satiric reading of these credits, then, a critical viewing of the sort irrelevant and unprecedented in the numbed television viewing of the depicted future society, can redeem them from capitulation. Which is to say that the film opens by requiring the level of response whose absence for its characters it will proceed to anatomize, lament, and in part repair.

Julie Christie plays the mindless, video-addled wife of the hero Montag (Oskar Werner), a woman who sits tranquilized before an oversized parlor screen (figure 9, left) all day and sleeps through the night with phono-plugs, called ironically "seashells" in the book, stuck into her head (figure 9, right). It is meant to be clear that once great, written fictions have been eliminated, the life goes out of the other media as well which might have provided some of the information or formal pleasure of major writing. The whole context is dismantled, the humanist legacy refused. Montag, a potential intellectual with an itch for knowledge and even for texts, has nothing legitimate to read but a comic book with no blurbs or inscribed bubbles at all, a kind of immobile silent filmstrip laid out between covers. In the totalitarian state he and his wife inhabit, which denies not only freedom of the press but freedom of the eye, even the stuporous surrender to the parlor video takes on the overtones of intrusion, coercion, and police scrutiny, however much these functions are all explained away by the trivial fictions it purveys. Every woman in the country named "Linda," for instance, as the hero's wife happens to be, gets the dubious privilege on a given evening of offering up her own rote responses into stillborn deadspots left gaping in a dreary family drama on the huge home screen. Even this delusion of participatory engagement, however, given the accusatory stares of the mock-interlocutors on screen during the supposedly pregnant pauses, suggests this gimmick as merely the gutless underside of surveillance, party to the same totalitarian mentality.

Epistemological tricks are also played on our viewing. At one point the narrative cuts away, not on the video monitor but from the main film plot itself, to a shot of a long-haired young man cornered by police and summarily shaved to the heartless guffaws of a gathered crowd. What we take at first to be Truffaut's further instancing of oppression is actually, as the camera tracks back to reveal its interior framing, a live documentary on the parlor unit. Its moralistic summation by the announcer manages exactly to reverse the implications of what we have seen with a hypocritical imperative directed straight into Julie Christie's accepting if blank stare: "Be tolerant today." It is no accident that, for all their supposedly instructive access to the outside world, these video planes are unashamedly called "walls." They do, after all, divide and veil the hypnotized self from the reality they pretend to materialize.

It is behind such a simulated smaller "wall" in a portable video set that the hero Montag discovers a hidden pile of books in the first dramatized fire raid of the film. This detail completes the symbolism which has provided that the first ferreted-out text—that preeminent text about texts, *Don Quixote*—turns up hidden in an overhead light fixture in this same raided dwelling. Light is precisely what such a text could shed, just as the hidden books in the video set where only a useless mechanism is expected stand for an treasure trove where before there was at best a livid wall covering up a spiritual vacuum tube. This early symbolic intersection of light, literature, and the false backlit rectangle that would substitute for the latter is reworked and deepened when, apostate to his profession, Montag turns to literature himself and uses his wife's giant parlor screen as indirect lighting (figure 10, left) for his late-night forays into pirated texts. He begins at a child's halting pace with that famous beginning of a life at the beginning of *David Copperfield* (figure 10, right), as open an inscription of rebirth for Truffaut's hero as the monitored fetus provides for the hero for *THX 1138*.

The Bradbury novel *Fahrenheit 451*, unlike the film, is set on the teetering verge of a world war. As before in *Things to Come*, where the outmoded cinema is the first building leveled in the war, Montag wonders when the earlier bombing is heard whether "perhaps the great broadcasting stations with their beams of color and light and talk and chatter went first into oblivion" (p. 173). This apocalyptic conjecture is domesticated in the film, and thus made dramatic. With no war mentioned, still the hero, betrayed by his wife as one must always expect to be betrayed by the numbed results of video addiction, torches with the incendiary tool of his trade not only the bed of his love and his dreams but the parlor screen that destroyed the former and parodied and debased the latter (figure 11, left). In the process Montag also kills his superior on the fire force, and for this he must be hunted down on nationally broadcast television until dead. The state's trouble is that he manages successfully to escape, and so another corpse must be produced on camera to appease the mass craving for the satisfactions of narrative closure, which novels might otherwise provide.

The scene of the hero watching his own staged death, as usually we watch cathartically the death of a hero, draws provocatively on an earlier scene of photographic, if not filmic, allusion. It does not in the least require a passing cineaste in-joke (that the last text shown in montage before the incineration in a crucial scene is a copy of *Cahiers du Cinema*) for Truffaut to be noticed flexing the reflexive sinews of his tautly drawn allegory. They give shape to the film at every turn. Since the information-retrieval system of this presumably computerized but document-free state must rely on photographic input only, there is a scene with his superior when Montag is being considered for promotion in which his textless file is opened to disclose merely snapshots of him at different ages and from different angles. The file is judged incomplete because there are only six replicated likenesses in a single strip, six repeated shots of the back of his head, instead of the requisite dozen. This is a bitterly apt photographic icon (figure 12, left) for the hero's self-duplicating, routine, depersonalized, indeed faceless existence up to this point, not to mention its visual insignia of the true informer's vantage: a shot in the back as it were. It also becomes a liberating irony at the end, as if the strip of stills were animated into a movie of a man fleeing: the more genuine icon yet of his release and salvation. This same shot of the back of his head, on television, is the image upon which the camera dollies in during the trumped-up execution of Montag on the airwaves. He is thus able to stare at this epitaph for himself as a symbolic portrait of the man who turned away, knowing as he does how much there is for him to move toward in his chosen new direction.

Yet studying the video screen and its political fabrications, Montag offers up to us from his included remove an even more remarkable icon of the film's whole attitude toward the epidemic of image systems within it. We watch the back of his head as he is watching moving images of photographs mostly of the back of his head (fig. 11, right), like some receding and illogical chain of simulation from a canvas by Magritte (man seeing his head from the back in a magic mirror, say), and we are ready to understand this climactic video allegory in productive conjunction with the film's last episode, when each man and woman in the colony of literate exiles, by memorizing a book, *becomes* that book. Reading Plato in expatriated liberty one inhabits and identifies with Plato; reading the book that has itself become interchangeable with its title character, David Copperfield, we become *David Copperfield*, text and designated hero together. In literature we go out of ourselves into a widened sense of identity, whereas in the mindless reception of visual images we are lost even to our own image of ourselves. The incisiveness of that television epitaph is precisely that it cuts both ways. As Montag does in peering at his apocryphal assassination as if it were his symbolic loss of face or identity, so do we all do in our enslavement to images: stare at our own leave-taking from authenticity as if in a glass darkly. Watching such visual lies is the death of self in the negative sense, with Montag denied even the mirroring face of his own supposed death mask in light. Yet in turning away toward true art he will lose himself now in a grander anonymity, renamed for the text he will choose to become. *He* does not end, but rather moves the film toward its destined end on our screen, as our text. This is the movie's humanist solicitation. In reading such a cinematic "wall" as if it were an open page of literature lit from within with significance, we *become* the movie in the other deep sense of that resonating conceit, rising to its occasion, doing it full justice.

    Fahrenheit 451 is a story about Eden reclaimed, the word's if not the world's. The false idols of video transmission are immolated before our eyes and the true secular Logos of the literary tradition reinshrined in the tabernacles of memory. As myth of restitution Truffaut's film stands in direct contrast to the archetypal and irreversible fall of *The Man Who Fell to Earth*, directed by the man who was the chief cinematographer of *Fahrenheit 451* a decade before, Nicholas Roeg. The entitling premise of Roeg's film is in itself a reversal of the generic trajectory of science fiction from earth's known and horizoned reality into *terra incognita*. The alien villain has been recast as the descending hero trying to home in on the living hell of our foreign and estranging ways. Instead of the mysterious intruder as aberration or menace, instead of his being in any way aggressively invasive, he quickly attempts to integrate himself, to make do until he can make his trackless way back.

    The credits burst open upon a space traveller (David Bowie) hurtling in a multi-staged rocket toward earth. He comes to see what he can learn (or take?) from our terrestrial bounty for his own drought-afflicted planet. He intends then to go home. But to become the man who flew *from* earth he would need yet another rocket, and he soon learns that such commodities on earth must be earned by being purchased. So he proceeds to become (in the root sense of the term) astronomically rich so as to return to the stars. He immediately sets about using his advanced technological knowledge to invent things his earthly counterparts just as quickly decide they need. First among these inventions, and the only one of which we hear in any detail, is a so-called "self-developing camera." It might more accurately be known as a self-photographing camera, its role in the film only accurately assessed if it is seen to comment on the disavowed voyeurism masquerading as objective omniscience which characterizes all film narrative.

The first test case of the new invention that we see on screen is its use by a naked couple to snap pictures of themselves in the act of making love, pictures processed in seconds as if they were taken by an onlooking third party. The shots are framed from a vantage outside the couple's knot of flesh, as are Sean Connery's remembered exploits projected more as if overseen than as undergone in that imprisoning cinematic chamber of *Zardoz*. The extraordinary snapshots in *The Man Who Fell to Earth* also complicate their own irony by including a framed picture of the man's wife and daughter clutched mockingly by his adulterous partner in a love-nesting of image within image. This scene's all but instantaneous photographs have the optically impossible status not of anything either party could have taken but of the motion picture itself that here studies them in the act of studying their own lust. Bowie's alien from another world will thus profit hugely and even innocently from a mass-produced visual technology that travesties the self-alienating distance from feeling in which our strange culture indulges, the fetishistic relish of the body at a willed distance from its desire.

Besides the self-telescoping perspective of this bizarre camera, the only other piece of advanced photographic or video technology we see in the film is the portable plexiglass scanner on which earth was first spotted by Bowie from light years away. We later fade to his wife back home trying to make him out on this "futuristic" screening device at just the point when he appears in a television commercial for his own camera so as to get his image as widely broadcast as possible. The whole international (here intergalactic) network of visual self-promotion for this patented photographic instrument has for a moment been broken through by Bowie in an act of ingenuity in the name of love. For a moment only, a conspiratorial plot soon closing round him and cutting him off forever. The next and last time he appears in the visual media—again, we suppose, so that his wife might see his efforts at return—is when the major networks carry the news of his intended rocket launch (figure 13, right). We in the audience are in fact allowed to follow this attempted homecoming partly on an interpolated television screen, right up to the moment when he is spirited away from the launching site by unspecified capitalist hoodlums, who will shortly metamorphose him into the ghost of his former biological self. The electronic media, in this concentric exposé of their impartial avidity, can feed with equal savor on the fulfilment or the defeat of his dream.

The pending metamorphosis just mentioned is the film's true tragic fall, the descent into mortal form and into the visionary debilitation it entails. The space visitor is finally locked away in a suite of rooms, one of which is decorated with *trompe l'oeil* photographic wallpaper of a sylvan scene (figure 14, left). It is in the adjacent bedroom that he is visited at intervals for a number of medical tests and tamperings which gradually convert his intended guise as a *trompe l'oeil* humanoid to an involuntary and irreversible replica. Before his last operation we see him staring, gin-soaked and oblivious, at an oversized television screen as large as the "walls" in *Fahrenheit*, upon which is being run that great cinematic tale of betrayal, *The Third Man* (figure 14, right). This oblique comment on the spaceman's own treacherous betrayal is altogether lost on this hapless interloper from a world well beyond that which our most powerful film narratives can be expected to record.

One begins to notice that the twofold functions of most video and filmic allusion (or inclusion) in the science fiction films we have been surveying—on the one hand documentary corroboration of fantastic events by present specimens of video science, on the other hand extraordinary future modifications of such technology—suggestively reverse their priority in Roeg's film as part of its fable of degeneration. We first see the improbable vantage of the spaceman's remarkable camera and then we watch his fatal addiction to the most atavistic and predictable trivia of American television, by which he is hypnotized at a remove not unlike the uncommitted distance maintained by the self-alienating mechanics of his camera. Early in the film he gets a hotel maid to help him furnish his lonely room with a number of television sets, barricading himself from his new but unwelcome reality with this babel of mediating images and idiolects, from commercials through soap operas to rerun theatrical features. Near the start of his relationship with this Earth "maid" Mary Lou (Candy Clark), we catch him scanning with no noticeable comprehension a snippet of Gary Cooper and Audrey Hepburn from the romantic film *Love in the Afternoon*, eavesdropping briefly on Cooper's dialogue about "no involvement," about how people should always behave as if they were "between planes"—as of course Bowie is between rockets. Detached from its own dramatic context, it is a message this feeling alien can neither heed while here nor afford to ignore except at the peril of his homeward aspirations. To be useful, such a theme from cinematic art would have to be judged and weighed in a careful emotional balance, but Bowie abdicates from all such responsibility in a later conversation: "Strange thing about TV . . . It doesn't *tell* you anything, it shows you everything. Perhaps that is in the nature of television, just waves in space." As a satire on the rippling trivia of much of the commercial detritus seeping through to him from his high-piled dikes of television receivers—barriers defending him against nothing, fortifying him with no lessons—this may be sad but true.

Yet within this encircling and ambitious piece of cinematic art by Nicholas Roeg there is the intended celebration of other such movies whose tales are alive with *telling* event. In the long run, one film above all. Having built an exotic mansion by the lake in which he first landed on earth, Bowie has increased the number of his sets and has become entirely distracted by them, indeed maddened, to the dismay of his maid turned mistress (figure 13, left). Though Bowie scarcely singles out this movie for any special attention from the *ignis fatuus* on any other flickering console, though he makes no distinction between vapid commercial programming and rerun landmarks of the narrative cinema, we as *movie* viewers are made to detect among his stockade of framed electronic images a screening of Melville's sacrificial allegory, *Billy Budd*, in the Peter Ustinov film version.

The sequence that contains the Ustinov film begins with a montage that pulls together in their blaring discrepancy the whole congeries of video images, the camera pulling back until the television sets form a gridwork collage of optical and aural bombardment. We see first in closeup a caged experimental monkey like the investigated guinea pig the spaceman will later become, then both predatory and copulating animals on other screens, an ad for some advance in automotive fuel technology, the mechanized warfare of a jet pilot film, even a few frames of an Elvis movie (earlier rock star turned screen star: an extranarrative point of coincidence for Bowie the actor). The images are piled high and spread wide across a full dozen screens, including one unaccountable film of a karate fight enacted before a blank wall upon which slides are being rapidly projected, one shot for every thrust and jab, the violence of images within images. Out of this electronic mayhem, just at the point when Bowie begins screaming back at the sets, emerge in graduated close-up the final moments of *Billy Budd*. As if the onslaught of technology itself were an invading alien force, the terrorized space-traveller yells to the screen specters, "Go back where you came from"—across the unmapped airspace between his world and theirs, wherever it is— and "leave my head alone" (figure 15, left). Yet *Billy Budd*, film and hero, belongs precisely to the history of that world into which the spaceman has fallen, if only he knew it. One sacrificial allegory encloses and endorses another, for what we see in particular of the Ustinov film is the finish of the morally complex execution scene (figure 15, right), echoing spectacle of another young man annihilated because his innate goodness is too unguarded for the alien, the fallen world in which he finds himself. If Bowie had honestly watched at least this one televised movie, he just might have zeroed in long enough, amid the media's tedium and hype, on an artistic truth sufficient to save him.

By the time that bit of Carol Reed's *The Third Man* passes before the spaceman's inebriated gaze later it is already far too late. He is by then due for the last anatomical betrayal which will complete his humanization, the implanting of earthly sight in a vacated brain by an x-ray sealing tight his new human eyes. This climactic optical transplant also brings to finality that theme of manipulated vision to which those unheeded televisions and, before them, the self-distancing spectatorial vantage of that patented camera have symbolically contributed (figure 14, right). They have made this contribution, as we know, in an upending of the standard science fiction pattern whereby familiar video devices usher us toward the extraordinary; in so doing they have logged the science fiction hero's overall downgrade from the astonishing to the routine. His is an ultimate humiliation into human form symbolized by those encrusted human retinas myopically confounding his dream of return. The theme of vision is now given over to camerawork, which takes up the ironic burden with painful deliberation. After so much hyperkinetic cutting, Roeg's camera is now stilled as if by the subject's own listlessness. In the long-held last shot of the film, an affectless and defeated Bowie chooses to look away at last from the world of his downfall, lowering his gaze under a broad-brimmed hat. All the while we must continue to stare protractedly, almost punishingly, through the unedited mediation of cinematic art, at that wan stasis which manifests the waste of his days.

I take space at the close of this essay to give rather full discussion to Roeg's film not only because I take it to be among the most original and important science fiction films ever made, but because in its adjustment of the genre it becomes an ironic elegy for it. Bowie drops into plot as the typical science fiction foil for heroic resistance or heroic understanding, the mysterious and challenging alien. As such, however, he is forced to look on at the collapse and banishment of the whole form of storytelling, or filmmaking, that brought him into view. Rather than being allowed his formulaic role in science fiction, he gets stranded as ironic pawn within an anti-capitalist allegory. His whole effort is now to break his way back as heroic protagonist into that science fiction genre and its plot-making energy from which, but also by which, he fell into the realm of his present story's earthly rendering. The creature from outer space has been retrieved by his own time travel from the unarrived, unmaterialized future known only to us through science fiction convention, has been fleshed out in humanoid form and then crucified, all so that we should be reminded through his excruciating example that he is not half so alienated from the rest of us as are any of us from the gruesome modernity we have engendered on the near edge of the future. But the spaceman's defeat by time, his temporizing collusion with the human, the murder of his futurity, all this amounts to the burial within plot of the science fiction formulas upon which it seemed to found itself. The failures of science within this fiction are lamented both through the absence of those empowering machines of space flight that are the staple of the genre and through video technology's corrupt links to personal fiction-making, to fantasy, to dream. The would-be hero can no longer get back to, nor will he ever be able to look back upon, his lost origin, not through any screening machine or amazing vehicle of his preternaturally advanced devising. The whole genre of science fiction, with its fabulous engines and visual tools in the hands of fantastic visitors, goes to its grave unmourned, just as other forms of narrative film have passed away unattended by the hero within it. They too have included movies which, like viable science fiction, properly watched, could reward and reorder the very modes of seeing.

To offer some review at the close, there are two crucial sorts of self-involved "videology" in science fiction cinema: let me summarize them as (1) the state of the art and (2) the art of some future state. There are on the one hand, that is, those nested instances of present visual science within a visual medium that serve as confirming *frames* of reference, so to say, in the company of alien biologies or advanced technologies—touchstones of the real within reach of the freely conceived. There are on the other hand those imagined electronic marvels of specifically visual function that are the very lodestones of prophesied science in any film of our scientific posterity. Like many of the strongest documents in the film genre of science fiction, the lapsarian fable of *The Man Who Fell to Earth* is a story oriented by these two modes of "videology," both the ordinary screenings that fail to touch even as they obsess the hero, and his own visual innovations, by which he cannot even glimpse again his dream. As a self-conscious dead end for the genre of science fiction, as I was calling it a moment ago, nevertheless this film recuperates in rather pure form what I have continually noticed as science fiction's deepest purpose. For in the allegorical ingenuity of all the genre's views of and views on looking— the filmmaking about photography and film-viewing, the science and the fiction of the seeing eye and the visionary mind—what we are asked still and all to look upon in the meticulously polished, imperceptibly tilted mirror of its narrative art, what we are invited to peruse at a revelatory new slant, is only ourselves, now and here.

Then again this way of summing up may seem to distort the true poise of our involvement. If we come to the genre with these expectations, we must still be distanced by its works and workings long enough to relearn its service more securely. As spectators, we become agents of our own alienated vision, with travel in space or time the very vehicle of both aesthetic and psychological distanciation. The self-conscious allegories of science fiction talk us out of the truisms of ready identification by which we are lured to these films in the first place, lured as much as we are by the promise of wondrous and seductive futures they might bring to view. Toward this reconstructive purpose the metaphysical is encased within the mechanical. Movies about—as well as brought about by—a technology of the image, cinematic artifacts turned purposefully reflexive, alone allow us this clarity of reflection on the ideologies by which we see and so lead our lives.

13

Fantasy, Science Fiction, Mystery, Horror

George Slusser

What do we mean when we say that film is a medium, and what does this question have to do with the nature and interrelation of four major categories of film experience: fantasy, science fiction, mystery, and horror? Many would be tempted to reply that the nature of the medium has very little to do with shaping these forms, for they are really genres, and as genres inscribe a space of operation, through a system of relationships, that transcends the hegemony of individual media. After all, each of these forms—fantasy, science fiction, mystery, and horror—exists in literature as well as in cinema. This reaction is symptomatic of a certain critical tendency today, which has revived genre study not only for its intrinsic interest but because genre can serve as a buffer against current fascination with the problem of mediation in art, with the process of sending and receiving the message. What is raised by such a reaction, however, is but another question: What do we mean by genre in film? In literary study, traditionally, the medium has not been the message; instead, the medium is the genre. It is this vision which allows us to see prose fiction culminating in, and finally becoming equated with, the novel, or the theater realizing its fullest potential in tragedy. Assumed here is some ideal fusion of mode of presentation and of form in which the medium loses its independent identity, becomes little more than a secret sharer, the invisible carrier of a formal and thematic structure.

Recent advocates of genre study in literature have offered what might be called a field theory. Now there are no absolute forms, only a generic space, defined by the various forms comprising it as they in turn strive to define themselves by distinguishing themselves from each other. We must realize, however, that such a "field" or system of relationships is not a real but a symbolic space. For outside of the elements that compose it, can such a field, as entity, exist? Media do exist, however. And film, with its visual immediacy, forces us to consider it as something that exists primarily to mediate, to connect eye and image. It is a creeping axiom today that literature exists to be intransitive, because language is a medium that strives to be its own end. However, I will argue that film, because it is so vitally and self-consciously a transitive medium, resists this static vision just as it resists generic abstraction. And I will further argue that the four forms I name, considered in this filmic context where symbolic systems yield to a concrete capacity for mediated change, are too deeply interactive to be simply catagorized as genres or as sub-genres. As the boundaries of these forms shift, their intermingling defines a dynamic that must be grasped on the level of medium itself. By seeing this dynamic we may better understand how form is created in film. Doing so, we hope to see and evaluate the forms that currently emerge from cinema's screen for what they really are.

One question will surely be asked: Why do I, in order to lay bare this dynamic, choose to consider these and only these particular forms? Why fantasy, science fiction, mystery, and horror? Do I not imply, in my very choice of forms, that these in fact are the culmination of their medium's potential for form, and thus try to sneak the concept of genre back into the picture? What I am doing rather is this: taking up these genres of the unreal in order to show just how unreal they are as film genres. Plotting their interaction takes us elsewhere, and that elsewhere, if it lacks the security of a generic map, may be closer to the heart of the film experience. For film, it seems, is not dominated by realistic forms, the reigning canonical forms both in literature and in criticism. It is not for the following reason: if film is to be primarily a mode of seeing, then seeing realistically is not enough. Long before film, Plato said that our prison house was the world of sight. Language may wish to accept such a prison, but the medium of film, with its capacity for direct visual investigation as well as for visual closure, may not wish to do so. Seen in this matrix of film as medium, the relation between a dynamic that is transgeneric and aspirations that are trans-mimetic may come clear at last.

As medium, of course, film purveys images. And in framing these images, in giving them various degrees of optical focus and perspective, film makes a gesture at least toward further mediation, this time between the human eye and those objects of which the images are presumed to be traces. The film medium, then, despite all the manipulative possibilities that exist within its frame, never frees itself from a certain hegemony of phenomena. Because it presents as well as represents, film cannot so easily aspire, as the written text is seen to do today, to the state of pure medium. Indeed, film's existential problem is also, clearly, an epistemological one. For as a means of seeing, cinema is both the avatar and the product of a modern epistemology that increasingly considers the act of perception a mediated act, one increasingly determined by the apparatus through which we perceive. Even so, at the heart of this modern media awareness a dream of seeing still abides. It is a dream formed of desire and fear: of the desire to break through these perceptual frames to renewed contact with phenomena; and of the fear that, were we to see things directly, we might not understand them—that they might become strange, terrifying to us. Film, at the center of its mediating frames, seems to harbor this same dream of unmediated seeing. It is this dream which haunts, in their film existence, our four categories of fantasy, science fiction, mystery, and horror. Seen in the light of this dream they are less solid forms than attitudes toward form, particular and recurring inflections of the act of seeing in film.

To Roland Barthes written language tends toward the condition of total medium. Once freed from the "totalitarian ideology of the referent," the written word can strive to become the origin of the writer as well: a self-contained, intelligible simulacrum that has neutralized, and ultimately absorbed, the perceptual bonds between subject and object.[1] The perceptual nexus of film, however, is much more resistant to such ideas of closure. We see this even in recent deflections of the film medium such as the cable television movie channel. Here, despite what appear to be increasing restrictions and controls placed on the act of viewing, we still have a perceptual breakthrough. We are looking at something, and that something interests us. For in cable's welter of viewing possibilities, of round-the-clock successive and simultaneous screenings of films of all kinds and periods, old critical directions are lost, and the pretense of "festivals" or other canon- or genre-oriented responses to filmgoing is ultimately confounded. Instead of a conceptual order there is a surprising, even random juxtaposition of films that blurs the patterns critics and historians seek to impose on the field. But there is no closure. For out of this saturation emerges a new sense of the image itself, released from its strictures, seen anew as raw perceptual data.

And looking on these ur-images we in turn see the screen anew, as the constant state or "condition" of film, its invariant seeing place. A primal screen, in fact. But there is more here than a joke, for our own reaction to this screen is a mixture of desire and fear. Gradually emerging, via the dispersion of cable, from the flickerings of individual films, the screen reveals itself less a simulacrum or system of order than a ground of tension. Indeed we are bid, as this primal screen appears, to rethink the very process of film viewing, to ask of it what we ask of all things seen: why do we look at all. The result is clear. Governed by the same impulsions and restrictions that, for the modern mind, mark the act of human perception in general, this film space becomes one of contrary urges, where the need to organize and control images encounters the opposite need to see deeper, to extend our perceptual field in hopes of seeing beyond the frame to phenomena—to those "referents" that remain unorganized and perhaps, for man, fundamentally unorganizable.

Claudio Guillen has stated that genre is an invitation to form.[2] In terms of film genre, however, there is a second invitation: to sight. As they intensify and diverge, these two invitations will make the very idea of genre in film problematic. Another look at cable will show us that such may be happening today. For here, as in a feedback loop, the manner in which images are mediated appears to be altering not only our but film's own sense of generic identity. As film after film is projected literally on top of each other on the screen, we no longer distinguish a clear set of frames, regulated by formulas and existing in a precise relationship to each other. We have instead a palimpsest. Here, as contours overlap, the genre experience as we have been taught to see it begins to devolve toward some more basic interrelation: that between the frame and the images it strives to contain. Again, looking into this generic palimpsest we perceive something new. First, the nature of the frame is revealed. It is a space in our own image, the human form become the figure for our desire for order, man's sense of perspective and proportion projected mirror-wise over those images that stand as his percepts of the phenomenal world. But at the same time what resists this act of framing becomes clear as well. For where we once saw only gaps and blank spots appearing in what seemed familiar genre formulas, we now witness, behind the superimposed human faces and forms that fill this frame, the apparition of an imponderable, perhaps unhuman element at the core of the image itself.

If today's experience with film as medium teaches us anything, it is that filmmaker and viewer are both in the same situation, doubles in their growing awareness of a shared perceptual condition. Despite claims to the contrary, making films today is clearly more than a simple genre exercise, the casual fitting of precut frames to imagistic materials. It seems to involve instead, if our palimpsestic vision is correct, a grappling, within the confines of this recurrent frame as basic means of human control, with the problem of perception itself. The cineaste has, instead of generic choices, perceptual options, visual attitudes and inflections toward his single frame. We wonder, in retrospect, whether he really ever had such generic choices—indeed, whether traditional genre thinking is not inadequate for understanding the dynamics and evolution of film creation, given the close bonds between that creation and the act of human perception *per se*. A new approach to this question may lie in the relationship between our four forms. This relationship, I hope to show, is less generic than transgeneric. By this I mean they are, as forms capable of generating and regenerating each other, governed in their transformations by two modes—the investigative and the sentimental—which are themselves analogues to the interplay, on the level of the perceptual system itself, between the dual impulses of vision and control, desire and fear, mediated and unmediated seeing.

Governed by these impulsions, the forms of fantasy, science fiction, mystery, and horror are less antimimetic than transmimetic in nature. This means that their interrelation is based less on an opposition to "realism"—the belief that phenomenal reality can be directly perceived and thus "imitated"—than on the common need to reexamine this belief, to test the perceptual apparatus itself by which we seek to know the phenomenal world. These forms take and lose shape in a matrix of tension between this investigative quest and the limitations of a system of ordering perceptions to which—because it remains based on the human model at a time when the supremacy of that model is being seriously challenged—our attachment has become increasingly sentimental.

All these forms, of course, were literary forms before they came to film. Even so, it is this look back from film that may most fully reveal their nature in literature as well. It may do so by showing that, here too, underlying formal transformations are epistemological considerations, the changing modes of perception of modern man. We will look briefly at literary fantasy and its progeny, but only as an introduction to film. For in terms of how these forms interact, film offers a very fruitful terrain for study. Compared to literature, the film medium is at one and the same time more tangibly open to the investigative impulse and more immediately susceptible to the sentimental urge for closure. On one hand the movie camera, as optical instrument, has the direct potential of all such tools for extending our field of investigation—in this case a potential both for deepening the pictorial space of the visual arts and for animating that space, for providing, as André Bazin says, "a window on our dreams." On the other hand, film insists on the framing hegemony of this "window." Again, in Bazin's words, cinema operates like the usher's flashlight in the darkened theater, moving across the night of this waking investigative dream, imposing its frame on that "diffuse space without shape and frontiers that surrounds the screen."[3] As we shall see, the relationship in film between our four forms is shaped, perhaps increasingly so, by interaction of these investigative and sentimental impulses, which occur here, in the most concrete terms, as depth of field and as frame. Out of this dynamic tension between field and frame, forms are created that filmgoers experience but perhaps have yet to recognize and name.

Literary critics have had difficulty in dealing with the transgeneric nature of forms like fantasy, science fiction, mystery, and horror. This is evident in a recent book like Rosemary Jackson's *Fantasy: The Literature of Subversion*. She describes the function of her literary form thus: "By attempting to transform the relations between the imaginary and the symbolic, fantasy hollows out the 'real,' revealing its absence, its 'great Other,' its unspoken and its unseen."[4] On the historical level perhaps, that of a developing nineteenth century fantastic literature, Jackson may imply shifts toward other forms, forms that embody and express these "revelations" she speaks of. In theory, however, she does not allow such shifts. Throughout her book she uses the terms fantasy, the fantastic, and horror almost interchangeably. And her sense of all these forms, in actuality, is less one of subversion than one of recombination, where the elements of an existing system— here realism—are rearranged so as to produce the strange and unfamiliar but not necessarily the new. And yet newness is exactly what science fiction, mystery, and horror, as they evolve out of this recombinatory process of fantastic creation, strive to express. As transformations they form a generative chain vectored by distinct, historically measurable shifts in our attitude, not toward "realism" as some ideologically determined sense of the real, but toward the reality of perception itself, of things seen.

The word "fantasy" comes from the Greek *phantasein*, which means to cause images to appear in the mind. Thus, in its etymological sense, fantasy opposes our imaginary worlds to a perceivable and knowable external world, and thus designates the outward-directed vision as the "real" mode of seeing. In the wake of thinkers like

Berkeley and Hume, however, there is no longer, where man as perceiver is concerned, this clear qualitative difference between outer and inner worlds. To Hume, in fact, the field of human perception tends to become coexistent with the theater of the mind. As this happens, the surfaces of that theater become reflexive, and the order we think we perceive in the phenomenal world becomes, in these new confines, merely a reflection of our desire for such order. Thus, in contradistinction to fantasy—in the original sense of a private and ultimately frivolous realm of perception—this nineteenth century literature of the Other is perhaps best called, after Todorov, "fantastic," for its visions unfold in a perceptual space where outer and inner are indistinguishable, the perceiver caught in the endless hesitations of a situation where mind and world overlap, have become mirror images of each other.

Significantly, what Jackson calls horror continues to function in this same closed space. Despite occasional gestures in this direction, she does not see horror as a form incarnating the growing desire, across the nineteenth century, to break out of the fantastic system, to see through to new, if potentially self-shattering perceptions. Her examples, in fact, reveal something quite different than a breakthrough to horror: "As Victorian horror fiction evolves, it reveals a gradual apprehension of the demonic as mere absence, rather than as essentially diabolic."[5] The diabolic, as supernatural intruder into our visual field, is a new presence, a horrific revelation. But absence or blankness are, as definable and predictable negations of form, the product of recombinations within a same system. In this sense those vacant windows of Poe's House of Usher through which, according to Jackson, we are supposed to look out upon the terrifying void, still remain planned parts of the structural system of the house. And Dr. Jekyll's glance into the mirror, where he sees his image devolve into that "ugly idol" which is Mr. Hyde, in the end represents merely a reframing, filling the empty hole of a promised plunge through self to chaos with a misshapen yet still recognizably human form.

Jackson then plays down this investigative axis along which fantasy might, in the late nineteenth century, have developed its potential for horror. And she hardly mentions science fiction. Yet the generic claims of this form as well are best understood as a shift in the perceptual direction of fantasy. As ideology at least, science fiction represents an investigative dayside to the feared nighttime visions of horror. Impelled by a positivistic epistemology, which calls upon man to extend his field of perception, science fiction, in its early fascination with aliens and wonder, originates out of and in reaction to fantasy, whose mirrors of the mind it inverts and extroverts. Turning mirrors into telescopes and microscopes, science fiction redirects the inner projections of fantasy, in supposedly corrective fashion, into external space. A sense of this positivist redirection may lie behind the fact that Todorov's book on the fantastic comes to a science fictional conclusion. For behind his assertion that in this century psychoanalysis has displaced the fantastic is a belief that science has finally called these inner fantasms to light, sent them forth into the external world straightened and whole forms. It may also explain the antipathy of a critic like Darko Suvin for fantasy, his need to reproject estrangement so as to make it "cognitive," and in doing so redirect its course, as science fiction, toward that state and shape he calls the *novum*. Finally, it may lie behind attempts by apologists of science fiction to claim figures like Frankenstein and Dr. Moreau for their genre. Unlike a Jekyll, these doctors, it is claimed, are not dealing with mirror doubles, but actually working with materials in the external world. In this light, Moreau's attempt to stamp our form on animal nature is not just another inverted fantasy. It is a surgical acceleration of the evolutionary process, a science fictional act. Through this perceptual redirection, science fiction becomes the genre which, in its pulp covers and its narratives, projects man's face across the cosmic void. It is the form that reshapes alien invaders in our image by making them "body snatchers"; the form that takes us on intergalactic seeing trips only to discover, as with Larry Niven's Ringworld engineers, the hand and shape of man still informing the universe's most alien landscapes and artifacts.

But does this form, any more than Jackson's uncanny, her aborted form of horror, represent perceptual breakthrough, the possibility of seeing in these far vistas something really new? Or is it merely the projection of the same inner fantasies on a larger screen, the substitution of cosmic theater for the theater of the mind? Science fiction claims to be a "search for wonder." To a writer like Stanislaw Lem, however, that search is hollow, for science fiction, like the science it adheres to, tends to investigate the world without first investigating the means whereby we perceive that world. He denounces its perceived wonders, and with them the human apparatus of perception, as so many mirrors. Thus the scientist Snow in *Solaris*: "We think of ourselves as the Knights of the Holy Contact. This is another lie. We are only seeking Man. We have no need of other worlds. We need mirrors."[7] It is at this skeptical juncture that science fiction, with its pretense at intergalactic investigation, encounters mystery. But it is an encounter which, at the same time, relocates the realm of mystery. Lem, in the title of his novel *The Investigation*, is openly marking a shift away from either the subject or the object of perception—we may call these respectively the valences of fantasy and of science fiction—toward the process of perception itself. Lem's investigators in this novel, though they combine the deductive methods of Sherlock Holmes with those of modern analytical statistics, still meet with mirrors. But it is precisely because Lem, with a science fictional touch, magnifies the Holmesian vision with that of modern physics that the face the investigator projects on the phenomenal world is seen to be of a different order of reality: "Our faces and our fates are shaped by statistics—we human beings are the result of Brownian motion, incomplete sketches, randomly outlined projections."[8] The real mystery here is recognized as lying neither inside man nor outside in the world. It lies rather in the medium of perception, in the very perceptual activity whereby man seeks to define his being and control his destiny. As a relation between perceiving subject and perceived object that is governed by the random and indeterminate, mystery haunts the interplay between depth of field and frame. It arises from the tension, sensed by Lem, between our need to see in the pure sense, and the necessity of subjecting that seeing to a human system of control that, in its functioning, now reveals at every turn its own incompleteness as controlling factor.

But this ghost in the perceptual machine has, as we shall see, more ominous overtones. By relocating the mystery in the medium of perception itself, Lem in a sense designates the framing or mirroring activity as being in sentimental opposition to the act of investigation. In this context, to be sentimental is to continue to organize the perceived world in man's image even in the face of knowledge that this human system, like all systems, is subject to inherent disorganization. Sentimentality reasserts the validity of man as organizational model, irrationally, against the possibility of more efficient but nonhuman models such as the "ocean" Solaris. In theory Lem rejects the sentimental. But even he, when dealing with the aspirations of human beings, cannot entirely do so, as the paradoxes, the possibility beyond hope of some "cruel miracle," that conclude novels like *Solaris* and *The Invincible* prove. These last-minute swerves into sentimentality, however, reveal something quite significant. For if Lem's vision is basically investigative, what that investigation leads to is something we shudder to look upon, something we must ultimately call horrific. If there is a culprit in *The Investigation* it is randomness itself. Indeed, what is revealed here, as the end product of our perceptions, is not absence of form but the decomposition of form, and of our own form, the human template subject to Brownian motion. The full force of horror, denied the earlier fantasies of Poe and Stevenson because they were deprived of the investigative will of science fiction and of the ensuing transmutation through mystery, emerges here, and in a different key. We are at Delany's intersection of Einstein and Gödel, witnessing within our Einsteinian framings the emergence of visible irrationality. And like Delany's character we are seeking at this juncture Gödelian answers as well, not only the "glittering focuses . . . limits, and genesis" of forms, but "their shape, their texture, how they feel when you brush by them on a dark road, when you see them receding into the fog, their weight as they leap your shoulder from behind."[9] We sense here the true spectrum of horror, its deep attachment to the sentimental as well as to the investigative mode. For where earlier looks into chaos, such as into Conrad's heart of darkness or Conan Doyle's horrific heights, summoned a preserving lie, intended's face or gorgon's head, a human form designed to cast our being in turn into comfortable stone, this new horror gazes clearly, dispassionately, upon randomness, measuring the dismemberment of human forms and fates. Yet for this horror too perception remains a Rorschach test, and its field of dots and atoms harbors at least the ghost of a gorgon, the Gödelian desire, against all rational and perceptual evidence, to see this human gestalt impossibly reforming at the heart of the disorganized.

We appear to have here, on the level of genre, a chain of transformation, where fantasy yields science fiction, science fiction in turn modulates to mystery, and mystery finally to horror. Indeed it is tempting, if we accept this pattern, to see the generic field dominated today by two types of horror—an investigative form and a sentimental form. Such a view, however, simplifies matters because it assumes we have reached a perceptual impasse. But this is not necessarily the case, and a look back at the initial problem of the fantastic may shed light here. There we had, within a theater of the mind, a closed system of perception that sensed, but ultimately rejected, horror's open vision of the disorganized. Yet if the intervention of science fiction and mystery both opened that theater and summoned horror to it, that same intervention was also the vehicle of a possible reaction. For the fantastic impulse for closure has not disappeared in the wake of horror. On the contrary, liberated by science fiction from the space of the mind but not from the hegemony of its forms, fantasy was given licence to reorganize, on the same scale as its inner images, the realm of phenomena itself. If then a new, epistemologically bolstered form of horror seems to dominate the literary landscape today, it is nonetheless challenged by an equally liberated fantasy urge. This challenge has resulted, in terms of generic categories, in a blending of forms. For as horror has cleaved unto mystery in order to develop, in writers like Lem, its fullest investigative thrust, fantasy has moved into science fiction, as form capable of giving perceptual extension and ideological legitimacy to its mirrorings, and shifted it toward the sentimental end of the modal scale. For example, even in Delany's *The Einstein Intersection*, which so clearly articulates the Gödelian axis of horror, this sentimental transformation is ultimately detectable. Though fascinated with its landscape of randomly mutating forms, Delany in this novel sends his protagonist on a strange quest for human form, a quest quite inexplicable in this jumble of rival shapes and systems except as a sentimental gesture, the reassertion of man beyond all perceptual possibility of man. Faced with the challenge of horror, increasing operation of such sentimental fantasies within the structures of science fiction may lead, not to the demise of the form, but to its regeneration. Certainly, in the film examples to which we now turn, this seems to be the case.

Film displays, in its technical nature and in its historical development, both the power to see and the power to frame. Indeed, more than in any other art, the tension between these two forces is built inexorably into its existence and its evolution. When we trace the fortunes of fantasy, science fiction, mystery, and horror in film, we see an analogous set of transformations, but more clearly. And a similar dynamic interpenetration of these forms has led, recently, to the same Gödelian intersection, where the open assertion of horror is itself being countered, its forms mutating and dividing along clear lines of these investigative and sentimental impulses. I will discuss two films— *Blow Up* and *The Incredible Shrinking Man*—which may serve as paradigms for this division.

First however, a brief description of how film may have reached this juncture is in order. From the beginning film drew its power, and the plasticity of its forms, from a dynamic of contrary impulses. Potentially the most mimetic of arts, cinema at once developed strong antimimetic tendencies, retreating from that theater of the world embedded in each of its images toward the various theaters of the mind that are the personal visions of its *auteurs*. First audiences were simultaneously awed by film's imitations of reality, and frightened by its violations of the conventions by which we have come to view that reality. Not only did the moving picture summon images to life; it hurled trains at spectators, broke holes in the frame, shattered the closed system of images that was the portrait or landscape. In a manner analogous to literary fantasy, however, cinema retreated from this early revelation of disorder. Instead it embraced the recombinations of *montage*, a technique that reconverts the screen, with its potential for motion in depth, into a two-dimensional system of order. By substituting the mental order of symbol or metaphor for the perspectival order of vision in depth, *montage* asserts the control of a single consciousness over the screen and its images. It is perhaps not quite correct then to see in that great age of *montage*, the expressionist period, an age of horror. For again, this is horror contained and ultimately tamed by the two-dimensionality of the screen. Indeed, Hitchcock even remarked about the famous stabbing scene in *Psycho*—a locus classicus of expressionistic horror and one of the most elaborate uses of *montage* in the history of cinema—that in spite of all his cutting the knife itself never touched the body.[10]

André Bazin's so-called "realist" reaction to *montage* is interesting in this light. Renoir, Bazin says, has "forced himself to look back beyond the resources provided by *montage* and so uncovered the secret of a film form that would permit everything to be said without chopping the world up into little fragments, that would reveal the hidden meanings in people and things without disturbing the unity natural to them."[11] In essence, Bazin's call for depth-of-field is motivated by the investigative urge of science, and his "realism"—echoing E. T. A. Hoffmann's dictum that real life is more singular and fantastic than anything else—much more a search for mystery, an admission that the investigative eye of cinema may encounter in its images more than that eye can order or control. Bazin's vision of film as an exploratory art in a sense derives from and follows the course of cinematic technology. And it is this same technology that, through the development of sound and color, in turn led to domination of this field of depth (including the deepest vistas of Cinemascope) once again by the human form as presence that guarantees the human scale and intelligibility of our percepts. But there is no rest in this process, only reaction. For this technology also leads, through the concurrent rise of the superstar or personality actor, to the counterpossibility that the frame cannot even contain its maker, that aided by 3-D or some other technique something "bigger than life" or more monstrous will eventually spill out into our own viewing space. The balance then prescribed by Bazin between depth of vision and frame is a precarious one. The case of the science fiction film reveals just how much.

Gary Wolfe sees science fiction as generally characterized by a "growing edge," by a constant attempt to expand the human field of vision.[12] This metaphor, however, must be made literal when applied to cinema, whose relatively fixed frame cannot, at least in two dimensions, do much growing. The science fiction film, however, can and does promise us a telescopic effect. And along this deepening axis of perception seeing anew is equated with seeing afar. Despite this promise, though, the classic science fiction film is not really an investigative form, or it is only to the point that it can measure its new vistas in terms of a human perspective. Through the inevitable placing of a man (or woman) at the center of its sweeping vistas, it would show that even the alien or never-before-seen landscapes brought to us by science and technology are, finally, reducible to our human system of perception. An example is *Destination Moon*. At the time of the film (1950) man had not walked on the moon, hence could not know what it looked like from up there. But the goal of Robert Heinlein and his special effects crew was to put a man, perceptually, on the moon, and us the viewers with him. To do so they used telescopic photographs of the lunar landscape as seen from Earth, had artist Chesley Bonestell make a tabletop model from these photos, then brought a pinhole camera up through its center where a hypothetical man might stand, taking panoramic shots of this model terrain. These photos were blown up and scenic paintings made from them. From these, assembled in panoramic order, shooting sets were constructed, actors positioned on center stage in place of the original camera vantage point, and we are on a moon shaped to our proportion and perspective, and measured in turn by our presence.[13] In the science fiction film, it seems, no matter how deep our visual penetration into the vast unknown—be it the infinitely receding lines of Kubrick's space voyage in *2001: A Space Odyssey*, or the endless vista of Krell machines in *Forbidden Planet*— the camera still seeks, through this same elaborate act of reframing by means of models and reversed proportionalities, to put man back in the picture, to reposition him as an element of visual order and control. Thus it is finally revealed that these alien Krell machines are only adjuncts to the id of the scientist Morbius, more of man's cloud capp'd towers. And the infinite sweep of *2001*, we realize, is ultimately superimposed upon, and contained in, the space of that optical instrument intended to perceive it all along—Bowman's eye.

In its external trappings, Michelangelo Antonioni's *Blow Up* is not by any stretch of the imagination a science fiction film. On the surface it is closer, if to anything, to a murder mystery. And yet it is clearly a film fascinated by the science fictional possibilities of seeing farther, and its protagonist obsessed with the technical range of the camera as optical instrument. Even so, the scope and emphasis of the film itself is quite different from science fiction. Indeed, what is being examined, as context of this protagonist's optical investigations, is the nature of framed perception itself, the limits both of the still photograph and, as movie camera films photographer, of the cinematic frame as a human system of perceptual order. In the central scene in the park, the protagonist comes upon a couple standing in the distance and engaged in conversation. He photographs them repeatedly, but is not content with the limits his and their visible humanity place on his camera's perceptual range. If the situation of this couple in the garden has Edenic overtones, he is restless to reach back beyond it. But what is he looking for, and why is he looking? He has in essence reversed the visual direction of science fiction, placing the vanishing point of human perception not in the future and in outer space, but in a preracial past, a past before man. And yet he proves no more able to gaze upon this emptiness than the science fiction looker. In fact, in what seems a grotesque parody of the ambitions of a Heinlein in *Destination Moon*, this cameraman would restore human order to the void by detecting the outlines of a body among its dim shapes. The death that frames this quest, however, is far more than the literal one of the mystery story. Constantly blowing up the series of frames he has taken in this park, the protagonist only succeeds in making represented reality increasingly inscrutable and alien. What is more, his efforts to reframe this perceptual field seem to pass through successive generic stages. First, as his stills capture the woman looking to one side frozen in what appears terror, we have an echo of Gothic fantasy. Then, as his imagination connects that gaze to a hypothetical gunman and a body lying in the bushes, we have murder mystery. And finally as he continues to blow up his images, searching for some agent or cause, until all hint of human form disappears in a welter of meaningless dots and blanks, we encounter horror. In blowing up his pictures, the protagonist continues to assert his ability to frame. What that frame now holds however is a landscape empty of human significance, a space whose coherence, beyond all powers of perception, can only be an act of faith.

Through his album of snapshots taken of "real" subjects, this protagonist hopes to impose human order on the phenomenal world, at least in the form of narrative, for here, in the apocalyptic nature of his views, is the ending that corresponds to the beginning in the park. But such a tale finds no order in the jumble of images that constitutes this film. And the protagonist's own life, seen in its aimless wanderings through the eye of the movie camera, resists man's narrative frames as well. In his fixation on the photos from the park, this protagonist is actually fighting a losing battle with the perceptual lure of depth-of-field itself, the power of the vista he hopes to order and control to disorganize and negate his existence in turn. Seeing a body in the park one time, then returning to find no trace of it, he (and we with him) experience terror based both on a rift between seeing subject and seen object, and on a rift between instants of perception, a quantification of experience that erodes the chronological fabric of human existence. In the final scene of *Blow Up* the protagonist, watching mimes play a game of what is to us imaginary tennis, seeks to enter their disarticu-lated world by retrieving the invisible ball and tossing it back. And by a sort of horrific transfer he succeeds. For now beyond his frame we hear, illogically, the sound of a ball being hit. His frame, coexisting with theirs, has become the negative to its positive. And the movie camera, locked into this frame with the protagonist at its center, begins to travel back and away from him, the opposite perceptual direction from his blow ups, leaving an ever-diminishing human form in the middle of a blank background. Now the tiny photographer reaches over again, but this time picks up his camera, the instrument by which he has sought throughout to organize the phenomenal world. At that moment he simply vanishes, as if he had fallen into the interstices of the cinematographer's—his double's—frame, his fall accusing the greater mystery of perception, the powerlessness of man's frames to control the images he invokes.

If *Blow Up* traces modern man's long day's journey into percep-tual night, Jack Arnold's *The Incredible Shrinking Man* converts this journey into a sentimental one. At first glance, however, there seem to be more similarities than differences in the situations of these two films. As ostensibly science fiction as Antonioni's film was mystery, *The Incredible Shrinking Man* still quickly veers toward horror. In terms of man's perceptual investigation of reality, this film does not court, any more than *Blow Up*, the growing edge. Its vision, in fact, claims to be microscopic. And its subject is also a single frame—that frame which, for man, contains all other frames, because it is his own form, the form by which he seeks to organize his world. Significantly, the entire action of Arnold's film takes place inside the comfortable and familiar frame of a middle-class suburban house in 1950s America, the central visual space of a centrist era that rapidly becomes, as protagonist Scott Carey begins literally to shrink away in relation to it, an alien realm of timeless urges. And yet it is Scott's situation—his literal, incredible shrinking—that reveals one crucial difference between these films: he is on the other side of the camera from the protagonist of *Blow Up*. His horror in fact is that he possesses no optical control over the landscapes that surround him. For him, perceptual exploration and survival—his eye and his existence—have become one and the same thing.

The final revelation of *Blow Up* is that the viewing subject was a viewed object all along, one finally, visually, alone, unincorporated in any human pattern. The path of Arnold's hero is the exact opposite, that of the object who, incredibly, becomes subject and seer. Like Antonioni's nameless man with a camera, Scott Carey is an everyman. But all resemblance stops here. He has no camera, and from the outset no sight or identity as seeing subject either. Significantly, his shrinking is triggered by an obfuscating "mist" that inexplicably comes over him as he is taking a banal vacation. If the cloud was atomic, he has become the product of scientific investigation, something scrutinized, analyzed, x-rayed by doctors. As he shrinks, he is gradually stripped of all signs by which man claims his perceptual ascendancy over the rest of nature—his wedding ring falls from his finger, he cannot hold a pencil, or see out of a window, his clothes slip off his body. His shrinking becomes a protracted fall, where the objects of his environment, once organized to his measure and held in balance by his gaze, detach themselves one by one from his perceptual control. Swelling in size in proportion to his shrinking, the face of a common housecat becomes a terrifying monster, an ordinary shoe stepping across a basement floor an unidentifiable, menacing juggernaut.

Yet, because of the way the camera chooses to deal with this fall, it becomes a fortunate one. As perceivers, we experience paradox throughout, lines and directions running contrary to each other, but always meeting to balance at a normative center, one most surprising for a film about shrinking: the visible form of man. As used by the protagonist of *Blow Up*, the camera is truly microscopic, magnifying the distant figures in the park until they and the forms around them have been atomized, all visual logic torn asunder in incoherent blow ups hanging on a studio wall. Clearly, for Antonioni, once man's perceptual connections with the phenomenal world break, he must vanish, for his form itself is defined by this relationship. The logic of Arnold's tale too moves inexorably toward this vanishing point. Visually, however, it is never reached. At the same time the camera is chronicling Scott Carey's diminution, it is ceaselessly working to pull him back into the range of the visible, to keep his form at the center of our perceptual frame while all else in that frame, in tune with *his* perceptual condition, loses form and shape, becomes visually indeterminable. The narrative logic of this film, which examines Carey's fall with the rigor of an experiment, is perhaps science fictional. The camera's logic, however, represents a swerve into the sentimental.

Arnold's film is often touted for its trick photography. But the real "trick" here is to keep two separate, and potentially opposing, planes of perception operating simultaneously, to keep Scott Carey, who is shrinking on a narrative plane, from actually doing so on the visual level, to maintain despite all expectations to the contrary a "normal" relationship in terms of proportion and perspective between his form, the frame, and us the viewers. It is interesting here that the source of visual distortion is not, as in *Blow Up*, so much the optical instrument as the observed object itself. In this film, in fact, the "blow up" is quite literal, for its effects are achieved primarily by oversized sets, camera angles and animation. However, this domination of the constructed or recomposed set in *The Incredible Shrinking Man* is significant. For recognizing this we bestow on objects in this film, however great their distortion, a thereness, a substance that cannot be taken by the camera. Despite all relativity of viewpoints, they retain a shape, a familiarity that demands to be restored to a proper proportional relationship with the eye that sees it, ours or even Scott Carey's. This restoration is accomplished through a subtle technique of alternating viewpoints, a rhythm of rising and plunging shots, of oscillating angles, distances, and perspectives that renders the same object alternately alien and familiar. For what this constant reversal of perspectives inscribes is a constant point of balance, a normative space between predictable visual oppositions. This space, as we will see from some examples, is that of the human form itself.

The camera opens a vista on the living room of the Carey household. A chair is in the foreground, its back to us. Carey's wife stands in the background facing it. All seems in its rightful place and perspective. We then cut to a frontal view of the chair, making a complete turnaround that reveals the tiny figure of Scott, so tiny that the back would hide him, sitting in that chair. Our first reaction is to measure his shrinkage. But our second response, and one that, once the shock of this turnaround has passed, is more in tune with the visual data of the scene, is to notice that the chair has grown. From this angle, it has become a monstrous form that swells beyond the frame and is truncated by it. Even so, in this sequence of perceptions, we must recognize it as the same chair. And because the chair has grown, Carey's figure, which the contrast can only *tell* us has shrunk, is pulled back into visual focus, so that it again occupies, proportionally, the same space in this frame as the "normal" wife did in the previous composition. In another scene, the camera enters the hallway, and we perceive a doll's house sitting in a corner. Though everything is visually in order, the object itself is out of order in this childless household. Suddenly, as if in response to this dawning curiosity and uneasiness, the camera transposes us inside this house within a house, and we see Scott lying on a "miniature" couch. Again, however, what we see belies what the story tells us. For the cinematic frame is the same. And Scott, in proportional relation to it and to us, occupies the same space as a "normal" man in the living room of his "normal" house.

Through all these shifts of perspective we may experience the relativity, even the randomness, of our perceptions. But only momentarily. For we need only blink, and the human form is back in its proper relationship to its frame and to us. There is something almost Pascalian operating here. For where man is in danger of shrinking too much the filmmaker, like Pascal's God, will blow up contextual objects like the chair or doll's house just enough to bring him back into the composition, and in doing so shows us that the frame does not change, is an unvarying human space between the infinitely small and the infinitely large. Indeed, the same process operates on man's hybris as well. For the more Carey shrinks, the more demanding and recriminating he becomes: he would write a book, he blames wife and world for his fate, makes heroic pronouncements. By placing him in a doll's house, the camera of course gives proper perspective to such vanity. Even so, once corrected, man must reclaim his true role as measure and scale of all things seen. Humanity and visibility are one and man, carrying these with him wherever he goes, finds that even doll houses must be rebuilt large around him again.

This play of proportionality prepares us for the climactic encounter between Scott Carey and the spider. This scene, seemingly a grotesque reversal of the normal relationship between insect and man, takes place on a basement floor now seen through Carey's eyes as a horrific landscape where familiar objects—paint cans, mousetraps, drains—have become monstrous, shapeless obstacles. Through his eyes we experience the relativity of things. Through our own we experience constancy, his presence forcing us to see these monsters as giant creations of the scene maker's or animator's art. Thus when Carey, about to do battle in this landscape, not only declares he is still a man but a greater man than ever before, the paradox of his cinematic situation hits us with full force. His humanity is impossible on the narrative plane, for how can an insect-sized being have a man's brain. Yet he stands before us not only a visible man but one still occupying his rightful proportion of the frame.

Conquering the spider, however, is not the end of this experiment, for logically Carey must shrink until, like Antonioni's protagonist, he disappears, losing both form and normative pretensions in the random welter of atoms. Yet the tricks of this film, working to the end against the investigative urge that draws us into Bazin's deep field until we lose our vision and our identity as viewer in its perceptual mysteries, allow Scott to guide us, even beyond these furthest boundaries of human organization, on a visual exploration, sentimental this time, through the gaps and blanks in his own existence as man. With Carey we pass through the needle's eye of horror, watching our form vanish into the infinitesimal only to become infinite. The final paradox in this film is an Emersonian reversal. For only by becoming nothing will man come to see all, will he lead us, as perceiving beings, beyond disorganization to a new sentimental assertion, a cruel miracle beyond all investigation, that the human system of order is indestructible.

The opening titles of *The Incredible Shrinking Man* show on one side of the screen a large white silhouette of a man, on the other a small atomic cloud. As the cloud grows, the man shrinks, but proportionally. And he does not vanish, even when a mist, moving this time horizontally across the frame, obscures everything else, creating as in *Blow Up* a shapeless, meaningless field of dots. But in that film such blankness was the end; here the end and the beginning are one. And in this circular structure, as if inscribing the frame, the human form and vision are meant to abide forever. Arnold's film is impossibly narrated, in retrospect, by Scott Carey, a man who has already dwindled to nothingness. That dwindling however, inscribed in this circular structure, is only a beginning. In the final scene, a camera once again travels upward from the minute form of the protagonist standing on the grass under the vast sky. The camera ascends until, finally, his form seems irretrievably lost among the nonhuman design of things. But at that moment the camera reverses direction, and begins to travel out toward the myriad stars, bringing the heavens closer to our gaze, restoring in all its serenity our power to investigate, to impose our frame upon nature. This final balancing swing of the camera, however, is a sentimental gambit, an act of perceptual faith beyond knowledge or hope.

From the generic transformations we have outlined a tide of horror seems to be emerging today. Its emergence, we contend, is a product of epistemological needs and anxieties that inform the act of mediation itself, and in particular the operations of the film medium and the rise within that medium of forms like science fiction and mystery. The rise of these forms has in a real sense freed horror from the confines that fantasy placed on it, allowed it to invade the whole field of cinema today. Horror, as it reveals itself today, must be understood as an inflection in our relationship with the image, a paradoxical condition born of simultaneous fascination and doubt, and one which has finally designated this space between mirror and void the ground of horror. Recent film no longer fills this space with all-too-recognizable monsters as in Howard Hawks's *The Thing*, where a shape-changer is given the shape of a large, lumbering man. Indeed, the place of horror is now one of dissolving forms, and man's existence there an ongoing ritual of dismemberment. We see this clearly in John Carpenter's 1982 remake of *The Thing*. In this film, ostensibly closer to the John W. Campbell story, the investigative field is literally the human body itself. Taken over by these aliens, the body offers no sign of this possession to the naked eye, and thus becomes the mysterious realm of deeper investigations. However, we never discover, or see, the alien, only its effects, its assaults on visual form, especially on that of the human body. What this film shows us, obsessively, is that the human form, in this brave new world beyond science fiction and mystery, no longer offers a visual norm or system of order. It is something possessed by protean madness, tending from within toward disorganization and dissolution.

In other recent science fiction/mystery films, however, this tide of horror is meeting sentimental resistence. Let us take *Alien* (Ridley Scott) for example. The alien's "birth" here, bursting from John Hurt's chest, shatters the human form. And in its progress, stalking and consuming the crew of the spaceship one by one, it gradually transforms the initial "hard" science fiction environment of metal and machines into the writhing, organic world of traditional horror.

Beyond this, however, the real horror again abides in the human form itself, in its inability, now seen as inherent, to control its tendency toward disorganization. The alien here cannot comfortably take over human form, for no matter how many individuals it absorbs, humanoid shape finally eludes it; it remains a shifting chaos of vaguely suggested human parts—jaws, teeth, limbs. Nor is human form in itself ever a sure value. The key scene here is the emergence, in graphic decompositional detail, of the robot from beneath the "skin" of the science officer Ash. Yet this decomposition of form, lest it be too nihilistic to bear, is tempered by sentimentality. As disciple of pure reason, Ash proclaims the inadequacy of the human form to resist these attacks, both outer and inner, on its supremacy. Surprisingly, however, he too, as if trapped by the visual shape he has assumed, in the end will opt for human order. Now a frazzled, bubbling mass of electronic parts, his severed "head," after telling man's doom, pauses and, suddenly redeeming a semblance of that human identity it has been gradually forfeiting, smiles at us. Then, in an act that, however briefly, is a glimpse of humanity beyond horror, Ash's head wishes us luck.

Alien locates the outer limits of man's investigative urge at some interface of his own form with disorganization, where under the sign of the "alien" his spaceship extension—a mechanized world in man's image with its mother-computer and intestine-like metal corridors—reaches the point where it begins to devolve toward proto-organic chaos. A more recent film (and a bad one), Douglas Trumbull's *Brainstorm*, places those same limits within the human brain, at the moment of individual death. Scientists in this film pursue their examination of the mental theater to the point of "recording" its final moment of dissolution in death. The protagonist has no rest until he can replay this death. In doing so he experiences the breakup of personality and of body. And yet, in an ending which in the iconographic sense combines *2001*'s voyage to the infinite vanishing point with the sentimental reversal of *The Incredible Shrinking Man*, he emerges from this ordeal whole. For once again the viewer, miraculously, passes through perceptual chaos, this time that of his own mind, in order to reaffirm the human form and purpose. But Arnold's starry reaches have here been touched with the wand of Disney. For not only does this protagonist regain his loving wife's arms, but the two are transported out into that infinite space, their forms preserved forever in a bubble.

The sentimental swerve of these films is clear enough. But in many other recent films, even films ostensibly in the realistic genres, this same tension between investigative and sentimental impulses seems to play itself out to uncertain results. Let us consider, in conclusion, a film like David Lynch's *The Elephant Man*. If Ashley Montague's text is a study in human dignity, Lynch gives us human perplexity. All the characters in this film, and we with them, experience a perceptual dilemma, for we listen to a sensitive, refined human voice, but at the same time must look upon a monstrously deformed shape, a face and head which, in its elephant mask, violates the outer limits of the human, a thing existing in some nightside relationship to Victorian England and to the West's pretensions at culture generally. Again the drama seems placed at the limits of man's perceptual existence, at the moment where his mirrors blur, where his own form, held before him by a tenuous thread of words, begins to grow visually alien to him. But has the study in human dignity in the end become a horror film? In view of very similar endings, has it not become instead the story of an incredible shrinking monster, a being whose final act is to step back into the frame of one of those pictures of normal human life that adorn his walls, and to die like a man in his sleep? As in Arnold's film, the camera here does not stop with annihilation, but passes through the needle's eye. Beyond the spires of the Elephant Man's miniature cathedral, it moves our gaze through the holes in the lace curtains that formerly bounded his universe in this single room and, to the formless yet sentimentally resonating strains of Samuel Barber's *Adagio*, carries it out into the stars. Scott Carey's final proclamation was: "To God there is no Zero." Here a voice entones: "Nothing dies." In Lynch's film however we must ask who is speaking, and beyond that, who or what is seeing into these cosmic depths. If this represents the final exhalation of the Elephant Man's soul, and its liberation from deformity, then can the large face of the mother, itself liberated from the confines of its locket and now spread across this starscape, act as a perceptual barrier, prevent a final dissolution of human form and soul in a neutral flux of things, where if nothing dies, all forms must nevertheless dissolve? What is this sentimental final vision then, this face in the stars, if not a final hope echoing in the void, and as such a prelude to renewed horror?

These are questions we find ourselves asking about increasing numbers of films today. And a return to some simpler, more idealized generic landscape will not answer them. Indeed the question is no longer, in what genre is a given film? but rather how relevant are generic categories to the understanding of film and its formal dynamics? Watching films today, we are more like the child in Steven Spielberg's *Poltergeist*. The father has gone to sleep in his comfortable livingroom in front of a flickering television screen. He, like the traditional genre critic, is not drawn by this transitional screen and its loss of images, for he assumes that it will be filled again tomorrow with precisely identifiable frames when normal broadcasting resumes. The young daughter, however, a product of a new age of cinematic saturation, is transfixed by this screen. She has learned to look beyond the frames of a closed generic system, has learned to look at and through the images themselves, to let them devolve into a state of unformed light and noise. The desire simply to see and the frame that must direct and limit that act of seeing have, in this scene of a child engrossed in a flickering screen, momentarily balanced each other, and in doing so called forth a new space for generic investigation. But can we continue to gaze into this active heart of blankness without bringing back the human form in the guise of its old generic avatars? Spielberg in his own film could not do so, for at the end of the chaotic stream of light and sound that pours from the television screen in his haunted house stand those wax dummies rising from the comfortable graves of old horror movies. For a brief instant, though, we have seen the flickering screen, and its perceived tension between investigation and sentimentality may bring us to look at film, and literature, with new eyes. It has already shown us, at the end of a long process of formal transformation, science fiction's sentimental journey to horror.

14
Born in Fire: The Ontology of the Monster
Frank McConnell

He has never had a name. The unenlightened call him "Frankenstein," confusing him with his creator. The less-unenlightened call him "the monster," confusing him with his popular reception by the villagers and the local constabulary. But none of us knows, really, what to call him: knows, as it were, what name he would choose for himself, if he were given the choice.

And that is ironic, for perhaps no creature of the last two hundred years of imagination has been more intricately involved with, more spectacularly crucified upon, the cross of language. His discovery of speech—of the fact that we can convey meanings to one another—is perhaps the most important and certainly the most poignant episode in the novel that tells his story for the first time. And, over a hundred years later, nearly his first words on film—in *The Bride of Frankenstein*—"Friend good!" are almost an encapsulation of all his loneliness, all his panic, and all his profound connection with our own condition.

But, as I say, he has never had a name. Perhaps because he is so important to us, and so much a part of our own loneliness and uncertainty. He is dead matter become conscious, mere stuff that has learned a language and therefore has an illusion of possessing a soul. Mary Shelley's friend Byron, who was with her during the splendid summer of 1816—the summer that produced *Frankenstein, Mont Blanc, Manfred*, and so much more—described man, in *Don Juan*, as "fiery dust." It is an image that incarnates a century and more of doubt about the real validity, the real nobility of human consciousness. It is also a perfect description of the Frankenstein monster.

Walton, the frame-narrator of Mary Shelley's novel, writes early in the book to his sister: "I shall commit my thoughts to paper, it is true; but that is a poor medium for the communication of feeling. I desire the company of a man who could sympathize with me; whose eyes would reply to mine." This, of course, is the quintessential romantic search for the double, the romantic nostalgia for a human universe that would be a hall of mirrors, of perfect and perfectly responsive replicas of the self. And any number of commentators have remarked how Walton is fated to meet precisely that friend, that dreamt-of and dreaded double, in the person of Victor Frankenstein. But there is another double for Walton—in this tale which is a nest of doubles—the monster himself, the purely imaginative creature, whose "eyes would reply to mine," of necessity, since he is the sheer projection, the sheer self-consciousness, of language. Harold Bloom, in a brilliant brief essay on *Frankenstein* ("Afterword," *Frankenstein* [Signet, 1965], has observed how the warfare of creator and creation in that novel is a reflection and inversion of the positive quest for the double in poems like Shelley's *Alastor* or Byron's *Childe Harold*. And, building upon Bloom, we can observe that the monster's outraged and outrageous status as mad mirror image of the questing Walton is an anticipation of such powerful sights as Charles Foster Kane, at the end of his life, trapped in loneliness and splendor among the infinite mirror images of the palace he has built for himself. What is monstrosity, after all, if not the image of ourselves we have searched for and which, having once gazed upon it, we cannot ever forget?

In film after film, reincarnation after reincarnation, what being has been so often immolated as Frankenstein's monster? The title of the 1969 Hammer Film, *Frankenstein Must Be Destroyed*, is almost an epigraph for the whole myth of the monster. Frankenstein—or his creation—*must* be destroyed, in tale after tale, version after version. Like spectators at a Greek tragedy, we watch, waiting for the preordained conclusion, which does not surprise us at all, but fulfills us because it is what we came, after all, to see.

Like spectators at a Greek tragedy; or like participants at a Mass. For there is, after all, one other character in our collective consciousness who has been immolated and resurrected quite as often as the monster.

Let me observe a pun. It is one of those deep puns—"fetid shafts of meaning," Thomas Pynchon calls them—implicit in the nature of the language, and therefore not willed by anyone but, indeed, preordained. The word, "monster," derives from the Latin *monere*, to warn; but *monere* itself probably derives from an Indo-European root which also generates the Latin word, "to show." The monster, in other words, is both a warning and a spectacle.

And a spectacle is also a *speculum*, a looking-glass. And a monster is also a *monstrance*, the elaborate golden vessel that holds and displays the Host on certain solemn occasions in the Roman Catholic Church. Another double: for if the Host (itself doubling the doctrine of the Incarnation) is mere matter infused from above with divine life, the monster is its precise reversal, mere matter struggling up—or raised up—from below toward consciousness.

A *speculum*: a created image that gives back the image of its creator, or a mirror that—like all mirrors—can take on an eerie and threatening reality of its own, when gazed into too intently. Zosimus the Panopolitan, one of those alchemists who somehow lies behind the figure of Victor Frankenstein, observed that "He who looks in a mirror looks not at shadows, but at what shadows hint of, understanding reality through fictitious appearances." This, again, is the benevolent version of the Gnostic quest to transcend the world of illusion by multiplying the complexities of illusion. And, again, the myth of the monster gives us the nightmare inversion of that quest. It is remarkable how often in the Frankenstein films, ever since James Whale's first recension, the monster is caught at a crucial moment looking at his reflection—in a pool, in a window, in a mirror—and recoiling in horror at what he sees. At such moments we invariably realize that his horror at his own monstrosity is a deflection and a purification of our own terror at meeting ourselves.

The very first film of *Frankenstein* was made in 1910 by the Edison Company. It is lost, but the scenario survives. And the last scene of this short film appears to have been a wonderfully inventive bit of filmmaking, and a wonderfully perceptive approach to the concerns we have been examining. After the monster has wreaked various bits of mayhem, to the horror of his creator, he finally invades Frankenstein's bedchamber on the wedding night. And scene 25 reads, "Monster seeing his vision in glass disappears. Frankenstein's mind becomes peaceful." The demonic incarnation of the self is destroyed, in other words, by the same process of mirroring of which it is a limiting expression.

I am not—please believe me—trying to work my way toward a reading of the Frankenstein myth as Christian allegory; that would be entirely too Chestertonian. But I do think it important to get clear the fact that, in inventing her seminal modern myth of consciousness, Mary Shelley, either consciously or not, was led toward a story which parodies the determinative story of our culture. Marx says that every event in history occurs twice, first as tragedy and then as farce. And we may remark that the event—so runs the tale—that occurred first on a starry night in Bethlehem is echoed and completed as bitter farce in the events of that dark and stormy night in Ingolstadt, two millenia later.

And to realize this is to realize something, I think, fairly important about the relationship between the two major manifestations of the Frankenstein story—the novel, that is, and the roughly two dozen major films "based on" the novel since 1931. It is also to realize something about the general relationship between film and literature as the central narrative modes of our time.

It is a truism of scriptural studies since Bultmann that *kerygma* preceeds myth. That is, in the history of religion, ritual invariably predates the *stories* that explain how the ritual came to be. This is particularly true in the history of Christianity. The earliest Christian texts, Paul's letters to the Thessalonians and the Galatians, are mainly concerned with ritual observance, and with the proper form of the Lord's Supper—the Mass, in other words. It was only some years later that the Gospels were written—Mark first, then Matthew, then after a while Luke, then after a *long* while John—to explain the story behind the cult, to elaborate the ritual into a founding-tale.

This all sounds harmless enough, except that the history of the Frankenstein myth exactly inverts this process, too, just as the image of the monster inverts the image of Christ the incarnate son of God. Remember the title of the Hammer film I mentioned before: Franken-stein *must* be destroyed. That is not really the title of a story, it is a formula for a ritual. In the history of the Frankenstein tales, in other words, myth preceeds kerygma; narrative preceeds ritual; story preceeds the solidification of story into cult-observance. For that, to be blunt, is what the films of the Frankenstein cycle are: cult observances, inverted Masses whose conclusion is preordained and all of whose plot elements are as predictable as the *Lavabo* or the Offertory verse.

C. G. Jung, in his great essay on "Transformation Symbols in the Mass," observes that the ritual of the Mass is actually two rituals melded together, a communal meal and a sacrificial offering, *deipnon* and *thusia*, as Jung calls them. In the Mass, the order is *thusia-deipnon*: the sacrifice of bread and wine preceeds their transformation and sharing in a common meal, the Offertory preceeds the Communion. Again, and by now predictably, this order is inverted in the rituals of the Frankenstein films. First the Communion: the monster attempts to enter human society in one way or another, only to be rejected again. Then the sacrifice: his inevitable, and preferably fiery, sacrifice. This rhythm is caught most slyly in *The Bride of Frankenstein*, where the monster shares his famous meal of bread and wine with the blind hermit, and where the appearance of the bride—a failed communion if there ever was one—is liturgically introduced by the grandiose, wicked and wickedly funny gesture of Doctor Praetorius (Ernest Thesiger).

But the same rhythm is also visible in almost every film version of the tale. Mel Brooks, in his attempt to finish the legend once and for all in *Young Frankenstein*, builds upon it as subtly as did the early James Whale, carrying it all the way through, for once, to the monster's *acceptance* by the society that had earlier rejected him. Frankenstein *need not* be destroyed, says Brooks's very serious film; at least, not if we can think our way through to the inescapable point behind the ritual of the monster's endless resurrections and public burnings, the point being that he is the reflection—the *speculum*, the looking glass—of our own horror at having bodies.

How can we be gifted with speech, thought, the power of aspiration and longing when we know the full loathsomeness of our own physicality? It is a question that the myth of the incarnation tries to deny, and is the question that romanticism will not let us stop asking ourselves. Yeats was probably not thinking of Mary Shelley's creation when he wrote of his soul, "Chained to a dying animal / It knows not what it is." He didn't have to be.

Think about a more recent film than *Young Frankenstein*: *The Elephant Man*. Why should John Merrick, congenitally and horribly deformed and yet articulate, sensitive, and gentle, have become the celebrity he was at precisely *that* time—the time of the Industrial Revolution, the Romantic Era, of the germination of Darwin's thought? David Lynch, the director of *The Elephant Man*, suggests that Merrick's monstrosity is part and parcel of the monstrosity of his age, of its increasing emphasis on the similarity between man and intricately organized machine; so that the Elephant Man's transcendent ugliness, his *unsuitability* for any but the least mechanical (most human?) of tasks is almost a guarantee of his spirituality. Lynch must have had the Universal Studios Frankenstein series in mind while making the film: his monster is too close in humanity and in essential dignity to the movie-made monster for it to have been otherwise. Life imitates art, in other words, and the art itself imitates the life on which the art could have been patterned.

A film like *The Elephant Man* or that other great monster movie, François Truffaut's *The Wild Child*, helps us see precisely how the Frankenstein series itself is quintessential science fiction. For all these films remind us that science fiction is really *technological* fiction, and that the first of human technologies, the first artificial imposition humans make upon their environment, is language itself.

Are we human because we speak or do we speak because we are human? It may be the most crucial question in anthropology and political theory since Rousseau. What is the origin of the Word? When Merrick in *The Elephant Man* first utters articulate sounds, we know his salvation is assured. And when Victor, the "wild child" of Truffaut's film, fails to learn speech, we know that he is doomed. It was Descartes, in the *Discourse on Method*, who established definitively, for our age, the equation of ability and humanity. We have not gotten over it yet.

Particularly, we have not gotten over it in the case of Frankenstein's monster. For it is speech, after all, which he desires more than anything else: speech to another being, speech with another being. And it is speech which he is most definitively denied.

Denied, that is, in the films; not in the novel. It has always struck me as one of the truly curious details of the myth that the monster, in Mary Shelley's novel, is so incredibly eloquent, while in the classic Frankenstein films he is, at worst, incapable of speech altogether and, at best, gifted with a mean baby talk that sounds like a demonic version of the Cookie Monster. Even in *The Ghost of Frankenstein*, where the brain of the cretinous Igor (Bela Lugosi) is transplanted to the monster's body, the best he can manage is a slurred Transylvanian snarl.

Does this mean we are dealing with two separate visions of the creature? I think not. I think it means we are dealing with two separate, and complementary, versions of the creature. It is by now a cliché of film-and-literature studies to say that while literature gives us a world of words, reaching out toward a perception of things, film gives us a throng of things, reaching inward toward an understanding of language. The myth of the Frankenstein monster is the myth, disconcerting in the extreme, of an artificial creation that seems to possess life, and to possess it as fully as you and I. Naturally, in a novel, this should be the imagination of a creature who, for all his monstrosity, is nevertheless capable of learning language. And just as naturally, in film, this should be the image of a creature who, for all his evident humanity, is incapable of speaking. For the monster of film is already what Mary Shelley had to labor so hard and so brilliantly to envisage: an artificial construct, a make-up masterpiece, a triumph of special effects, that nevertheless seems to us to live.

To say this much is to say, in a serious way, that the myth of

Frankenstein and his monster is also largely the myth of film itself. For film—the medium that presents the monster, and not solely the monster—is an artifice, a technology that imitates life so successfully it almost, at times, seems a larger and more capacious version of life. The monster is forever mute on film, perhaps, because film is the medium he was predestined for all along. All he needs to do is be there. And the unvoiced testimony of his presence is enough to remind us of the fragility of our own pretensions to speciality, to intelligence, to a soul.

I know of no more articulate or moving moment in the history of film than the first appearance, in the first film of *Frankenstein*, of Boris Karloff, moving his monstrously distorted face into the light: our first full view of the monster, and our first realization that the monster is made possible by precisely the techniques and technologies which also allow us to believe in the humanity of the other characters in the story. Where is, then, the distinction?

Nowhere, is the answer these quite grim films give us. The immensely affecting, sympathetic character of HAL in Stanley Kubrick's *2001* is simply one of the mutated heirs of the monster. For if the monster is form without language, poor HAL is language without form—only that glaring red eye, and the most civilized discourse in Kubrick's *bitter* film. And a book like Douglas Hofstadter's *Gödel, Escher, Bach: An Eternal Golden Braid*, which attempts to explain the evolution of an infinitely creative human consciousness from a mechanistic model of the operation of the brain, is in fact a distant, but still recognizable, heir to the problems invented by Mary Shelley in 1817, and thereafter perpetuated by the most effective storytelling method—film—civilization has yet devised.

In his excellent history of science fiction, *Billion-Year Spree* (1972), Brian Aldiss identifies *Frankenstein, or the Modern Prometheus*, as the first "true" novel of science fiction. It is perhaps one of the cleverest things anyone has observed about the form. But it also needs to be said that a true reading of *Frankenstein* shows us, not just that it is the first science fiction novel, but shows us also how much, and how desperately, science fiction is the distinctive genre of our own contemporary self-consciousness: and how much film itself, *the* art of the twentieth century, is itself an art that incarnates, even more than it expresses, the dominant concerns of science fiction.

From the first, silent films, in which photographs of men and women and machines seemed to move, seemed suddenly and miraculously to become capable of a simulacrum of life itself, the myth of

Mary Shelley's monster was realized: and it can be said that all subsequent film theory is really an attempt to come to terms with that central scandal, the scandal of life or soul created out of the most artificial, soulless of means. *Frankenstein*, in other words, can be taken as an encoded textbook for the exploration of film itself; can be taken as a kind of long, complex name for the art of the film. And, if we cannot yet really name what film is, we can also realize that it shares that cosmic anonymity with the monster who is its symbol, its anticipation, and perhaps its most distinctive expression.

Notes
Index

Notes

2. Children of the Light

1. Joanna Russ, "What Can A Heroine Do? or Why Women Can't Write," in *Images of Women in Fiction: Feminist Perspectives*, ed. Susan Koppelman Cornillon (Bowling Green, Ohio: Popular Press, 1972), p. 18.

2. See Bruce Kawin, "The Mummy's Pool," *Dreamworks* 1 (no. 4, Summer 1981):291–301.

3. Robin Wood, ed., *American Nightmare: Essays on the Horror Film* (Toronto: Festival of Festivals, 1979).

4. Stephen King, *Danse Macabre* (New York: Everest House, 1981), pp. 15–17, 29–30.

5. Kawin, pp. 293–94. A point I have not had time to make here is that "Who Goes There?", with its obsessive emphasis on scientifically explaining the horror, is science fiction.

6. Russ, p. 18. See also Russ, "The Image of Women in Science Fiction," in Cornillon, pp. 79–94. This and "What Can A Heroine Do?" are two of the finest essays on the subject, and I am clearly indebted to them both.

7. Bruce Kawin, *The Mind of the Novel: Reflexive Fiction and the Ineffable* (Princeton: Princeton University Press, 1982).

3. Subversive Play

1. Alain Robbe-Grillet, *Nouveau Roman: Hier, aujourd'hui*, vol. 1, ed. Jean Ricardou and Françoise van Rossum-Guyon (Paris: Union Générale d'Editions, 1972), p. 128.

2. Roland Barthes, *Roland Barthes* (Paris: Editions du Seuil, 1975), pp. 67–68.

3. Eric S. Rabkin, *The Fantastic in Literature* (Princeton, N.J.: Princeton University Press, 1976), pp. 189, 217. Parenthetical references will appear within the text as *FIL*.

4. Robbe-Grillet, *Nouveau Roman*, vol. 2, p. 236.

5. Jean Bellemin-Noël, "Des Formes Fantastiques aux Thèmes Fantastiques," *Littérature* 2 (1971), 117.

6. Rosemary, Jackson, *Fantasy: The Literature of Subversion* (London and New York: Methuen, 1981), p. 62. Parenthetical references will appear within the text as *FLS*.

7. Alain Robbe-Grillet, *Glissements progressifs du plaisir* (Paris: Editions de Minuit, 1974). .

8. Alain Robbe-Grillet, "Order and Its Double: Eroticism and Literature in the Works of the Marquis de Sade," *The Bennington Review*, 3 (1969):5–6.

9. Tzvetan Todorov, *Introduction à la littérature fantastique* (Paris: Editions du Seuil, 1970), pp. 29–31.

10. W. R. Irwin, *The Game of the Impossible: A Rhetoric of Fantasy* (Urbana: University of Illinois Press, 1976). Parenthetical references will appear within the text as *GI*.

4. The Virginity of Astronauts

1. Michel Foucault, *The Order of Things* (New York: Vintage Books, 1973), p. 374.

2. The colleague cited here is Zoë Sofoulis, a doctoral student in the History of Consciousness program at the University of California, Santa Cruz. She has been instrumental in broadening my exposure to pre-Oedipal symbolism and to literature of pertinence to this paper. Indeed, her own work—of mammoth import and needful of the book-length study she is engaged in—has been a great influence on my own.

3. Anne Marie Cunningham, "Forecast for Science Fiction: We Have Seen the Future and it is Feminine, "*Mademoiselle* (February 1973), p. 140.

4. Pauline Kael, review of *Marooned*, in *Deeper into Movies* (New York: Bantam Books, 1974), p. 107.

5. Leland E. Hinsie, M.D. and Robert J. Campbell, M.D., *Psychiatric Dictionary*, 4th ed. (New York: Oxford University Press, 1970), p. 660.

6. Ibid.

7. Ibid., p. 149.

8. The book most highly recommended for a clear explication of Lacan and his semiotic psychoanalysis is Anika Lemaire's *Jacques Lacan*, trans. David Macey (Boston: Routledge & Kegan Paul, 1979).

9. *Psychiatric Dictionary*, p. 219.

10. Ibid.

11. Ibid., p. 220.

12. Ibid.

13. Much of this section is taken from my own book, *The Limits of Infinity: The American Science Fiction Film* (Cranbury, N.J.: A.S. Barnes, 1980).

14. Articulating this idea in terms of the vulgar "mother-fucker" was the "brain-child" of Bruce Kawin and brought up at the Eaton conference.

15. Again, I should like to thank Zoë Sofoulis who brought these characteristics to my attention in a presentation, "Science Fiction, Psychoanalysis and the (M) Other," for my Film Genre course at the University of California, Santa Cruz, Fall, 1981.

5. Pods, Blobs, and Ideology in American Films of the Fifties

1. I. F. Stone, *The Truman Era*, 2d ed. (New York: Random House, Vintage Books, 1972), p. xxvii.

2. Daniel Bell, "The Dispossessed," in *The Radical Right*, ed. Daniel Bell, 2d ed. (New York: Doubleday Anchor, 1964), p. 19.

3. Ibid., p. 45.

4. Alan Westin, "The John Birch Society" in *The Radical Right*, p. 268.

5. Bell, "The Dispossessed," p. 3.

6. David Riesman, Nathan Glazer, and Reuel Denny, *The Lonely Crowd*, abridged ed. (New York: Doubleday Anchor, 1955), p. 152.

7. Bell, "The Dispossessed," p. 23.

8. Talcott Parsons, "Social Strains in America," in *The Radical Right*, p. 209.

9. Douglas T. Miller and Marion Nowak, *The Fifties* (Garden City: Doubleday, 1977), p. 96.

10. Bell, "Interpretations of American Politics," p. 47.

11. Ibid.

12. Bell, "The Dispossessed," p. 43.

13. Quoted in Victor Navasky, *Naming Names*, (New York: Viking Press, 1980), p. 24.

14. Westin, pp. 266–67.

15. Miller and Nowak, p. 10.

16. Ibid. p. 222.

17. Bell, "The Dispossessed," p. 32.

18. George H. Nash, *The Conservative Intellectual Movement in America*, (New York: Basic Books, 1976), p. 39.

19. Bell, "The Dispossessed," p. 9.

20. Susan Sontag, "The Imagination of Disaster," in *Against Interpretation*, (New York: Dell, 1966), p. 222.

21. Nash, *The Conservative Intellectual Movement in America*, p. 49.

7. Nostalgia Isn't What It Used To Be

1. Elizabeth Jenkins, *The Mystery of King Arthur* (New York: Coward, McCann & Geoghegan, 1975), p. 181. See also R. F. Brinkley, *Arthurian Legend in the Seventeenth Century* (1932; reprint, New York: Octagon Books, 1967), chap. 4.

2. For a concise treatment of the Matter of Britain see Jean Frappier, *Le*

Roman Breton (Paris: Centre de documentation universitaire, 1951–53), and Roger Sherman Loomis, *Arthurian Literature in the Middle Ages* (Oxford: Clarendon Press, 1959).

3. For an English translation see *History of the Kings of Britain*, trans. Sebastian Evans, rev. by Charles W. Dunn (1912; reprint, New York: E. P. Dutton, 1958).

4. For a more detailed account of the historical Arthur see Kenneth Jackson, "The Arthur of History," *Arthurian Literature in the Middle Ages*, ed. R. S. Loomis, pp. 1–11.

5. See for example, Tennyson's "The Lady of Shalott," and Morris's "In Defence of Guenevere."

6. "The Coming of Arthur," in *The Poems of Tennyson*, ed. Christopher Ricks (London and New York: Longman, Norton, 1969), p. 1469.

7. Jenkins, p. 192.

8. *Encyclopaedia Britannica*, 11th ed., s.v. Rosetti, Daniel Gabriel.

9. For a discussion of the history of the idea of the Middle Ages see Albert Pauphilet, *Le Legs du Moyen âge* (Melun: Librairie d'Argences, 1950).

10. See Mme. de Stael, "De l'influence de la chevalerie sur l'amour et l'honneur," *De l'Allemagne*, chap. 4.

11. See Marc Bloch, *The Feudal Society*, trans. L. A. Manyon (Chicago: University of Chicago Press, 1978), vol. 1.

12. Georges Duby, *The Chivalrous Society*, trans. Cynthia Postan (New York: Edward Arnold, 1977), pp. 59–80.

13. See Erich Köhler, *L'Aventure chevaleresque* (Paris: Gallimard, 1974), chap. 7.

14. See Joseph Bédier, *Les Légendes épiques. Recherches sur la formation des chansons de geste*, 4 vols. (Paris: Champion, 1908–13), and Ferdinand Lot, *Etudes sur les légendes épiques francaises* (Paris: Champion, 1958).

15. For an English translation see the *Death of King Arthur*, trans. James Cable (Hammondsworth, England: Penguin Books, 1971).

16. Graham Chapman, Terry Jones, Terry Gilliam, Michael Palin, Eric Idle, and John Cleese, *Monty Python and the Holy Grail (BOOK)* (London: Eyre Methuen Ltd., 1979), p. 1. All subsequent citations are from this text.

8. The Problem of Realizing Medieval Romance in Film

1. Gillian Beer, *The Romance* (London: Methuen & Co., 1970), p. 9.

2. Christian Metz, *Film Language*, trans. Michael Taylor (New York: Oxford University Press, 1974), pp. 13–14.

3. Metz, p. 13.

4. Metz, p. 5.

5. Metz, p. 13.

6. D. W. Gotshalk, *Art and The Social Order* (Chicago: University of Chicago Press, 1947), p. 12.

7. Gotshalk, pp. 39–40.

8. Metz, p. 4.

9. Roland Barthes, *Elements of Semiology*, trans. A. Lavers and C. Smith (New York: Hill and Wang, 1957), p. 39.

10. Barthes, p. 40.

11. Barthes, p. 40.

12. *Relational* refers specifically to the interrelationship between the dimensions of a work of art as defined by D.W. Gotshalk. He uses the term to refer to his aesthetics.

13. Gotshalk, p. 198.

10. Musical Fantasy

1. The film is available for rental through Films, Inc., 733 Green Bay Rd., Wilmette, Ill. 60091.

2. The attributions to Stanley Donen in this paper are from interviews with the author in 1980 and 1982.

3. Antoine de Saint-Exupéry, *The Little Prince*, trans. Katharine Woods (New York: Harcourt, Brace & World, n.d.).

4. James Robb, "Love and Friendship in Antoine de St.-Exupéry," unpublished paper, Marquette University, Milwaukee, Wis.

5. The Christian symbolism of the ending, as well as the Christ-figure aspect of the Prince himself, seems evident. This interpretation is almost inevitable with "good" alien visitors from space. The "return home" passage merits comparison with the similar theme in Spielberg's *E.T. the Extra-Terrestrial*.

6. Donen explains simply that he was living and working there at the time.

7. Perhaps for this reason, Kiley was not cast in the 1972 film of *Man of La Mancha*. Frank Sinatra and Jim Dale were among those considered for the pilot role.

8. Donen says that Fosse worked without pay "out of friendship" and that Wilder worked "for very little." This helped bring the production in on a $2 million budget in 1974 dollars. Donen says, "It did not make money."

9. The production was designed by John Barry, who later won an Oscar for his design for *Star Wars*.

10. Donen says that Lerner also preferred a more conventional, theatrical approach to the musical numbers. The decision to impose an energetic cinematic style was Donen's.

11. The combination of live actors and drawn animation has been used occasionally and even memorably in movies (cf. Disney's *Song of the South* and *Mary Poppins*). But it works best in a context of either humor or a child's fable. In the book, of course, *both* the Prince and the birds were drawn.

12. Robb, op. cit.

11. Traditions of Trickery

1. Howard Schecter and David Everitt, *Film Tricks* (New York: Dial/Delacorte, 1980).

2. Jean-Louis Beaudry, "Ideological Effects of the Basic Cinematographic Apparatus," trans. Alan Williams, *Film Quarterly*, no. 28 (Winter 1974/5), pp. 39–47.

3. Christian Metz, "Trucage and the Film," trans. Francoise Meltzer, *Critical Inquiry* (Summer 1977), pp. 657–75. This article originally appeared in *Essais sur la signification au cinema* (Paris: Klinck Sieck, 1972).

4. Christian Metz, "The Imaginary Signifier," trans. Colin MacCabe, *Screen*, 16 (no. 2, Summer 1975):14–76. Published under the same title with other essays by Indiana University Press, 1981.

5. Mark Rose, *Alien Encounters: Anatomy of Science Fiction* (Cambridge: Harvard University Press, 1981).

6. There is no commonly used term for Méliès's stopping the camera and starting it again. Stop-action usually refers to continuous stop-and-go motion for the purposes of model animation and animation. Stop-and-go motion seems more appropriate, but it also implies continuous use of the device.

7. Stephen Neale, *Genre* (London: British Film Institute, 1980).

8. See Susan Sontag, "The Imagination of Disaster," in *Against Interpretation* (New York: Farrar, Straus, 1965).

12. The "Videology" of Science Fiction

1. See the discussion of Wells's project in John Baxter, *Science Fiction in the Cinema* (London: Tantivy Press, 1970), pp. 14–15.

2. Whose self-commenting dimension I have discussed at length, along with briefer treatments of some of the remaining films taken up in this essay, in "Close Encounters of the Fourth Kind," *Sight and Sound* 47 (Summer 1978):167–74.

3. A term I used (p. 364) for the transparent dream projection of the hero of *Sherlock Junior*, as part of an argument about the film's combined technological and oneiric self-consciousness in "Keaton Through the Looking Glass," *The Georgia Review* 33 (Summer 1979):348–67.

4. See my "Close Encounters of the Fourth Kind," pp. 171–72, for a fuller look at the achievements of optical science in the underworld city of Everytown.

5. A similar instance of manipulative, closed-circuit transmission occurs in Chaplin's *Modern Times* (1936), also before the perfection of the television apparatus, and provides there a curious jostling of optical context as part of the film's satire of technology in and beyond the medium of film itself. I have explored some of the implications of this in "Modern Hard Times: Chaplin and the Cinema of Self-Reflection," *Critical Inquiry* 2 (Winter 1976): pp. 295–314.

13. *Fantasy, Science Fiction, Mystery, Horror*

1. Roland Barthes, "To Write: An Intransitive Verb?" in *The Structuralists from Marx to Lévi-Strauss*, ed. Richard and Fernande DeGeorge (New York: Doubleday, 1972), p. 159–60.

2. Claudio Guillen "On the Uses of Literary Genre" in *Literature as System* (Princeton: Princeton University Press, 1971), p. 111.

3. "Theater and Cinema—Part Two" in *What Is Cinema?*, vol. 1, trans. Hugh Gray (Berkeley: University of California Press, 1967), p. 107.

4. Rosemary Jackson, *Fantasy: The Literature of Subversion* (London: Methuen, 1981), p. 180.

5. Jackson, p. 112.

6. Tzvetan Todorov, *Introduction à la littérature fantastique* (Paris: Editions du Seuil, 1970), pp. 157–58.

7. Stanislaw Lem, *Solaris*, trans. Joanna Kilmartin and Steve Cox (New York: Berkley, 1970), p. 81.

8. Stanislaw Lem, *The Investigation*, trans. Adele Milch (New York: Avon, 1974), p. 179.

9. Samuel R. Delany, *The Einstein Intersection* (New York: Ace, 1967), p. 130.

10. François Truffaut, *Hitchcock* (New York: Simon and Schuster, 1967), p. 210: "It took us seven days to shoot that scene, and there were seventy camera setups for forty five seconds of footage. . . . Naturally, the knife never touched the body; it was all done in montage."

11. André Bazin, "The Evolution of the Language of Cinema" in *What Is Cinema?*, vol. 1, p. 39.

12. Gary K. Wolfe, *The Known and the Unknown: The Iconography of Science Fiction* (Kent, Ohio: Kent State University Press, 1979), p. 13–16.

13. Robert A. Heinlein, "Shooting *Destination Moon*" in *Destination Moon* (Boston: Gregg Press, 1979), pp. 9–10.

Index

249